FIREBOMBERS INCORPORATED

by Michael Archer

Firebomber Publications

This is a work of fiction. All the characters and events portrayed in this book are either products of the author's imagination or are used fictitiously.

Firebombers Incorporated

Published by Firebomber Publications

www.firebombersincorporated.com

Firebombers Incorporated is a registered trademark.

ISBN 0-9707980-1-6

Second Printing: June 2002

Printed in Hong Kong by Elite Printing International

This book is dedicated to all those who risk their lives to save the lives of others.

"Greater love hath no man
than this, that a man lay
down his life for his friends"
- John 15:13

Acknowledgements.

I wish to thank the following people for their invaluable assistance in the preparation of this novel:

Connie Cejmar - Dispatcher, CDF - Grass Valley Air Attack Base, Grass Valley, California

Arlen Cravens - Smokejumper Base Commander - USFS, North Ops, Redding, California

Alice Forbes -   Assistant Director - USFS, North Ops, Redding, California

Bryan MacCormack - Manger, Marketing Services Bombardier Incorporated, Montreal, Canada

Vern Schendele - Pilot, CDF - Hollister Air Attack Base, Hollister, California

Ken Schleintz - Captain, CDF - Ukiah Air Attack Base, Ukiah, California

James Taylor -   Manager - Lockheed C-130 Service Center, Ontario, California

Ira Townsend -   CDF Base Commander, Grass Valley Air Attack Base, Grass Valley, California

Many thanks to Tom Cheng, Anthony Honore, Sue Matovich, and the folks at Elite Printing International for the excellent printing job on this second edition.

And a special thanks to Bob and Melody King for their help in the preparation of this second printing.

Chapter 1

"Green curtains? You know I hate green!", said Joe in exasperation.

"But Joe, you know that they would look great in your study", answered Martha soothingly.

"Look, I don't mind you 'dolling up' the rest of the house, but would you mind leaving the study for me to decorate? I had wanted blue curtains for that room!", shot back Joe. He wasn't about to back down on an issue as important as this. After all, if his home couldn't be his castle, he thought Martha would at least leave him the study for a refuge. Green anywhere in sight would be unacceptable in his opinion and he was prepared to fight to keep the colors that he had set his heart on. That was before he saw the glint of steel in his wife's eyes.

"Joseph Talon, you may be a financial genius, but you know nothing of interior decoration. You may run your little empire as you see fit, but when it comes to household matters, I will not have you bringing a bunch of yucky looking blue curtains into this study. That is final!". Martha decided that the sweet approach had not worked, so she would try bluster instead. It seemed to be working, she noted with satisfaction.

"Yucky curtains? What did they teach you in that secretarial school about the English language?", he asked more calmly. He had seen her this way before and the word 'stubborn' didn't begin to describe her mood now.

"They taught us how to type, file, and handle office operations. They never bothered with all that adverb, adjective, and noun stuff. We have dictionaries and spellcheckers to help us spell it right. The words we use are up to us. How does your secretary at work talk? With a proper Vasser vocabulary I suppose!". Martha decided she might be able to resolve this by changing the subject while throwing Joe on the defensive.

"And a very nice vocabulary it is, too", replied Joe evenly. Now he knew what that cartoon meant that showed the charicature of a rooster strutting through the house saying 'I rule the roost', followed by the charicature of a hen wearing an apron and carrying a rolling pin saying 'And I rule the rooster'. Best to cut my losses and run, Joe figured. "All right, all right, you can put up those blasted green curtains, but it just won't be the same!"

Martha fairly beamed. "You wait and see. It will look just fine in here, and you won't even give a second thought to the color of the curtains."

Joe grimaced and replied, "I think I hear my office calling. It's already almost 9 A.M., so I'd better get going. We're closing the deal on Davis Aircraft today and I don't want to miss any of the proceedings."

That hit a nerve. "My husband, the corporate raider", said Martha as she shook her head. "I thought your wild days of raping and pillaging other peoples' companies were over when we got married. You *are* going to stop doing this aren't you?"

Martha had been raised in a Christian household and believed in helping people, not hurting them. Many people had lost their jobs due to these takeovers and she didn't like Joe continuing the practice.

"This is the last one, I promise. The owner is about as sleazy as they come. In landing the contract for the C-35 military transport plane a couple of years back, he was caught doing some, shall we say, creative lobbying. The Senate subcommittee which investigated the deal exonerated him of any wrongdoing under some suspicious circumstances. Once we close this deal, he'll be stripped of his power base and should have a good deal of trouble getting back into the industry for a long time". At least, I hope so, thought Joe.

"Well, try to be home by six tonight. The Johnsons are coming over for dinner and I have Marie fixing up something special: roast duck", Martha said as she began to leave the room.

"Cooked goose might be more in line with the way I feel now".

"Now don't sulk, dear. I'm right and you know it", cooed Martha as she turned the corner and vanished from sight.

"Yes, dear", Joe called after her. No use in bemoaning the point, she had won fair and square. Besides, she might be persuaded to change her mind given the right circumstances. The trip to the mountains this coming weekend might put her in a receptive mood. She always enjoyed visiting the cabin in Kingfisher Creek. Maybe, just maybe she would be willing to compromise. Blue-green curtains? Time would tell. Speaking of time, it was getting later and he wasn't getting any closer to work. Time to go.

On the way to work, Joe looked back on the past few years. Things had certainly changed. He had gone from a swinging 50-year-old jet-setter who made money at other people's expense, to a homebody. Well, a multi-billionaire homebody. And now he had embarked on something completely different: Building an empire instead of dismembering someone else's. He now controlled a chemical company, Bergway Chemical, which worked on military and commercial products; Talon Electronics, the family electronics firm which his dad had started; Caprock Drill, a heavy equipment and oil-drilling equipment plant; and, with today's acquisition, an aircraft manufacturing facility. Along with his financial and consulting firms, this gave Talon Industries a pretty well-rounded business portfolio.

More importantly, he now had a family. That had been a real surprise. Joseph Talon, toast of the town. Every political bigwig was his pal, the media loved him (well, most of them), and he was on everybody's 'A' list for parties and benefits. Granted, he had gotten his hands dirty in raiding other people's companies, but the takeovers had been more benign than most. He didn't rob the companies blind, and most were absorbed to some degree or another into his growing empire, so maybe 'raider' was incorrect. He was a corporate 'enhancer', deep-sixing unprofitable companies and acquiring those which were good performers.

Of course, his rationalizations were supported by his staff. That is, until his executive secretary went and got herself pregnant. Then he had to get a new one. Several from within the corporation interviewed for the position, but none really had what it took. Then the personnel agency sent over someone new. She was relatively young for an executive secretary, being only 27 years old. She was not particularly attractive, though it didn't matter. Owlish-looking behind those oversized glasses, with a trim but not overly curvaceous figure, and relatively small, barely topping 5' 2" tall. Her qualifications, though, were impeccable. She had started work as a secretary for her father at 17. With 10 years of experience behind her, she was already a pro. She was given a 90-day trial period, with the understanding that if she was not found to be satisfactory during this time, she would be replaced at once. Joe just hoped she could type.

The days and weeks that followed were most enjoyable. Not only could she type, but she was witty, sharp as a tack, and had enough sense to know when it was wisest to say nothing (Joe could have a fierce temper at times). She had started out rather shy, but that didn't last long. Having been her father's secretary, Martha was used to expressing her opinion from time to time. Joe had not been attracted to her at first. The rather plain way she dressed was in sharp contrast to the flashy debutantes who had tried to win his heart. He had always seen them coming and been out the door before they could get him to commit to anything serious. Martha, on the other hand, turned on the heat more slowly, and ended up getting the gold ring. Not only did she pass her 90-day trial, but less than a year later Joe and Martha were married.

Society was in quite a stir about that. 'Commoner marries royalty', as Martha had put it succinctly. It took some time before Martha accepted High Society, and vice versa. As with Joe, however, her charm and wit won the day. They were both soon on the 'A' list again and Martha, though never completely enthralled with jet-setting, put on a good face and actually enjoyed herself at the doings (sometimes). Certainly the children at the shindigs enjoyed Martha's presence. Everyone said that she was a natural at understanding and catering to children. It was only a matter of time, therefore, before Martha announced plans for a family of her own. Joe had been a bit resistant at first. What would a family do to his highly mobile lifestyle? Besides, he was no spring chicken, being as he was already well into middle-age. Martha's reply was simple and straight-forward. 'Fiddlesticks, Joe, you won't have to do anything. In having kids, it's only the mother's age which is important, not the father's. When they get to be too much trouble, you just leave them to me. It will be no problem at all, you'll see'.

Desiree had been born about a year later, and now another was on the way. By early next year, they would have a son. Then they could wrangle with the issue of whether two was enough. Martha's argument was that finances usually limited family size. Since she had come from a large one (six kids), she wanted a large one herself. Joe had no opinion - yet. True, Desiree had been a gem, but having a whole house full could prove to be a bit much to control, even for a workhorse like Martha. It would be over a year before he had to confront that issue, so Joe was not tremendously worried. Martha was about four months pregnant now as the end of summer approached. She and Joe were still haggling over their son's name. Joe wanted Nicholas, but Martha was leaning towards Joe Jr. Joe protested this on the basis that one Joe in the family was enough.

The issue was not nearly resolved yet, but it was one of the less important items on the agenda for the day ahead.

Joe arrived at Talon Industries just before ten. His staff had been there since 7 A.M. working out the last details of the buyout before the losers got there. Joe was not sorry to be participating in this last buyout. Ethan Davis was a crook, no two ways about it. He had cheated and bought his way to the top in Collier Aircraft, changed the name to Davis Aircraft, then embarked on a campaign to secure a big government contract by buying everybody he could. Only one government official had stood in his way, Jason Gottlieb. Jason had been an acquaintance of Joe's from previous contract dealings when Bergway Chemical was getting its first government contracts with the Department of Defense several years before. When Davis couldn't get past Jason, he paid somebody off to drug Jason and take some compromising photos of him in bed with a prostitute. By blackmailing Jason with the photos, Davis got the contract for the C-35 military transport. Then the photos were leaked to all of the right people and Jason's credibility was ruined. Jason committed suicide shortly thereafter, leaving a wife and son behind. Only after pressure from Joe and several other prominent businessmen did any kind of investigation get underway. Unfortunately, a pair of key witnesses to the orgy 'disappeared' at an inconvenient time, and the investigation bogged down. Davis was let off for lack of evidence. He was not going to get off today, though.

Shortly after the investigation had stalled, Joe started looking into an attempted buyout of Davis Aircraft by some stockholders. It seemed that some of the major shareholders didn't much like Mr. Davis either, and were attempting to get control of the company from him. The problem was that they didn't have enough shares, nor did they have sufficient funds to purchase more. Enter Joseph Talon. He put up enough cash to enable the renegades to gain control and force Davis out of the picture. Today was the official changing of the guard. Joe would add Davis Aircraft to his collection of prizes. With the consent of those majority shareholders, Joe would take over as CEO of what would now be Talon Aerospace. Davis must be livid.

Davis was also late. It was nearly noon before he finally showed up. He had made one last attempt to wrest control of the company from the rebels through its most influential shareholder, one Mathias Flick. Even as slick an operator as Davis couldn't hoodwink the staid New Englander. Davis did not realize it at the time, but Flick had been the one who led to his overthrow. At all of the stormy meetings leading up to the revolt, Flick let the others do the shouting while he remained passive and appeared not to care one way or the other who prevailed. Davis thought him the weak link in his chain of enemies, not realizing all the time that Mathias was in reality the padlock. Davis was a defeated man, though he did not yet know it.

"Jerry, lay out the final proposal", ordered Joe. Jerry Porter was Joe's executive aide and privy to all the documents for this buyout. He quickly organized the documents and began the proceedings.

"Mr. Davis, we are prepared to offer you a $2 million severance package along with an offer of $120 million for your shares in Davis Aircraft. I don't believe you will find a better offer anywhere, but it will only be offered once. Take it or leave it".

Ethan Davis, a man in his mid-60's and more than just a little overweight, flushed visibly. "Listen here, boy. I'm not interested in anythin' less than $200 million for mah shares. Y'all can take that and stuff it in your pipe! Ah don't intend to be tossed onto the scrap heap like some wore out wheelbarrow, and ah surely don't mean to settle for no measly $120 million".

"Mr. Davis", Jerry continued, "you know as well as I that your stock is worth about $100 million under the best of circumstances. Our offer is very generous and your counter of $200 million is outrageous. We will not move above the originally stated sum. If you do not accept it, we will simply have to pass on buying your stock and you will be left with a non-controlling interest. As for being 'tossed on the scrap heap' as you put it, you are already out of a job. We are here simply to discuss the conditions of your departure. This is no longer Davis Aircraft, but rather Talon Aerospace henceforth".

"Yew talk a good fight, boy, but yew don't know everythin'. Ah haven't put all of mah cards on the table yet. Ah'm still negotiatin' with Mathias Flick to get control back. Ah believe we have what could be called an understandin'".

At this point in the conversation, Joe pressed a button on the intercom which sounded a buzzer outside the conference room. On cue, Mathias Flick entered the room.

"Greetings gentlemen", he said as he walked in. "And a good day to you too Mr. Davis".

Ethan Davis looked warily at Mathias as the latter took his place at Joe's left side. Jerry spoke up at this point. "You see, Mr. Davis, your estimate of which side Mr. Flick is on is somewhat incorrect. He has been supporting us from the beginning. You, I am afraid, are counting on support where there is none. Are you now ready to settle on this issue of your selling price?"

Ethan Davis' face became beet red and he began clenching and unclenching his fists. Finally he blurted out: "So that's the way it is, is it? OK by me. I never cared much for that Boston weasel even when I thought he might be of some use. Here's mah answer to yer offer!" He picked up the contract Jerry had handed him and ripped it to shreds. "That's mah answer for now. But it ain't the last yew'll hear from me. That yew can count on!" Davis rose abruptly and stormed out of the room, cursing up a blue streak as he went.

"I believe we can interpret that as a 'no' from Mr. Davis", said Jerry softly.

"You always did have a neat way of understating the facts, Jerry", replied Joe. "Well, I guess we can consider this to be a done deal and good riddance to Ethan Davis. Although I wish we had videotaped the proceedings. It might have made for some interesting entertainment at the next shareholders' meeting".

"I think I would be careful about tweaking his nose too much", said Mathias quietly. "He still has some loyal employees here who might pass along details of our conversations and he does have an unsavory reputation for exacting revenge on those who cross him. Personally, I hope that this is the last we ever see of the gentleman".

"I doubt it", replied Joe. "Grease like him always floats to the top sooner or later. Let's just hope that his threats are as empty as his head". He couldn't help but think of those two witnesses who had disappeared during the investigations. Just coincidence? Maybe. Maybe not.

Firebombers Incorporated

Chapter 2

It never failed to amuse Joe whenever they were getting ready for a trip to the cabin. This must have been the eighth time he and Martha had gotten ready for such a journey, yet the drill was always the same. Joe and Martha would meticulously plan what to take. They would get everything packed to go. Then Martha would need something she had packed, but not remember where she had put it. They would unpack nearly everything they had for the trip, only to discover the necessary item in the last piece of luggage unpacked. Martha would vow never to do this again and Joe would just placate her with a simple 'Yes, dear'. He often thought of that old saying about those who forget history are doomed to repeat it. Needless to say, he never brought this saying to Martha's attention. It was nearly midnight Friday when they reached the cabin at Kingfisher Creek. They were both too tired to unpack much at that time, so they simply went to bed, figuring that they would tackle the luggage in the morning.

Joe awoke to the smell of fresh coffee, bacon, and toast. It was well after 8 A.M. when he got up and he was starved. He looked out the window of the bedroom and marveled at the view. The cabin was up on a high ridge overlooking miles of pine forests below. California might have its share of glitter and power, but he found the simple vista of the mountains to be much more fulfilling. He dressed quickly and went to the kitchen. Martha was still in her bathrobe and slippers. She was cooking up a storm with the provisions they had brought from home.

"By golly, you do still remember how to cook", teased Joe as he pulled a chair up to the kitchen table.

"I suppose it's like learning to ride a bicycle", chuckled Martha, "you never forget".

She had learned early how to cook, since, with so many brothers and sisters to cook for, her mother had taught her all she knew about it. Being the third child and the first girl, she was her mother's principal aide in domestic affairs. As a result, Martha was able to do wonders with almost nothing in the kitchen. Omelets were her specialty and Joe could easily have made a meal just off of those. This morning's fare was cheese and jalapeno omelets along with toast, bacon, grapefruit, and coffee. Everything was delicious, as always, and Joe wondered that Marie, their cook at home, had ever gotten the job considering Martha's culinary talents. Martha, as always, had a healthy appetite, made the more so by her eating for about one-and-a-half people.

"Hey, leave some of the omelet for me!", protested Joe. "I know you're hungry, but let me at least try a little!"

"Oh Joe, you are such a baby! There are more fixings in the bowl. I'm just especially hungry this morning".

"Nicholas must be growing again, huh?"

"Yes, I think Joe Jr. *is* growing again".

"My, testy today aren't we?", said Joe with a conspiratorial look in his eye. "Did we get up on the wrong side of the bed this morning?"

"No we did not! I'm in a perfectly good mood today, thank you very much".

"Yes sir, whatever you say sir!"

"I am *not* a sir, Joseph Talon!"

"No, of course not. You just act like it sometimes". Hormones were a wonderful thing, thought Joe ruefully. Martha had had wide mood swings when she was pregnant with Desiree. It looked as though this would be the case with their son. Ah well, he thought. Another five months and she would be back to her old self again. "Where's the youngster today?", asked Joe.

"She was up about seven, so I gave her something to eat and packed her off to bed again. With luck, she will sleep until nine", Martha answered with a yawn.

"Well, I think I'll go do a little fishing on the lake this morning. Want to come along sweetie?"

"Are you going to use lures or worms?", Martha asked guardedly.

"I thought I would use worms. Those lake trout bite best on nightcrawlers up here. I might go bass fishing along the shore tonight. That's when I use lures".

"I am not really interested in cutting up those poor worms, then sticking them on a hook", said Martha with disgust. "I think I'll wait until this evening to join you. I need to get things unpacked today anyway. Want to help?", she asked with a glint in her eye. She knew Joe disliked unpacking, knowing that everything would have to be repacked in a couple of days.

"Is that a trick question?", Joe asked sheepishly. He had tried to conveniently forget the luggage. But in her condition, Martha had no business doing it all herself. "I suppose the fishing can be delayed for an hour or so, anyway".

"After all, you should not be getting any important phone calls up here this weekend to spoil your playtime, should you?", she asked sweetly. Taking the office on vacation had never been one of Joe's faults. He always devoted his time to Martha on the vacation trips they took.

A little more than an hour later, everything was unpacked and Joe was collecting his fishing gear. As he headed out the door, he heard soft crying from Desiree's room. It looked like Martha would have a busy morning at that.

The fishing was not particularly good that morning, but improved that night as they fished from shore. Martha hooked a two-pound bass (the largest either of them got that night) on her first cast. She needled Joe about it several times that evening, jibing him in a good-natured manner. Finally, about 9 P.M., she was beginning to get tired (Desiree had long since passed out on the blanket next to them) and they decided to call it a night.

Once they got back to the cabin, Desiree was put to bed and Joe went in to change for bed. He hadn't realized how tired he was, and dropped off to sleep almost immediately, much to the disgust of Martha who had planned a more romantic evening.

The next morning was Sunday. Joe had never been a very religious man, but Martha always insisted on going to church on Sunday morning, even if they were on vacation. Joe went along reluctantly, dreaming more about the future and not paying much attention to the sermon that morning. Once they got back to the cabin, he quickly changed and went out on the lake for a short 90-minute excursion. By that time, Martha had lunch ready and Joe was called back to the cabin. Desiree was fussy throughout the lunch and Martha was not in the best of moods either. A nap for both after lunch would do them good, Joe decided. He thought that it would probably do everybody good to stay up there an extra day, so he planned to go into town after lunch to call Jerry Porter about extending his vacation through Monday. Nothing major had been scheduled for Monday, now that the Davis Aircraft deal was sewed up, so it shouldn't be a problem.

Kingfisher Creek was a pretty little town. Nestled in the valley between two mountains, it was about a mile above sea level. The town was almost as appealing as the cabin, being sprinkled with houses topped by steep aluminum roofs. The residents said that the roofs were designed to keep the snow from building up on them in the winter time, but, along with the gingerbread trim on most buildings, they gave the town an almost fairy-tale-like effect. Joe half-expected to see elves popping out of the doors at any moment.

The general store had the only pay-phone in town and was a fairly busy place in the summer months. Today it was relatively quiet, though. A couple of old geezers were having a vicious game of checkers (taking at least five minutes to make a move) and the wife of the owner was sweeping the front porch off. She gave Joe a cheery 'Good morning' as he approached and ushered him inside to sample some of the cookies she had baked that morning. Joe made his call down to Los Angeles and managed to reach Jerry on the second ring.

"Well, how is the fishing?", Jerry asked.

"Martha caught the biggest so far, a two-pound bass", replied Joe. "We had a hard time getting her through the door Saturday night, her head had swelled so much. It'll be a pain putting up with her for the rest of the trip, as proud as she is of that fish!"

"A little-bitty bass like that?", chuckled Jerry. "You folks have to go deep-sea fishing with me if you want to see a *real* fish".

"Did I detect a slip in that Harvard accent, Jerry? I do believe I heard a little bayou sneaking into your speech. First thing you know, you'll be sounding like Ethan Davis!"

"Perish the thought!", replied Jerry coldly. "That redneck and I have nothing in common, including the accent. You would have thought I was a plantation slave, the way he talked to me at that meeting last Thursday!"

"He seems to act that way to everyone", said Joe. "But never mind about that, how about you and Diane coming up here tonight. You could hear Martha's fish stories and stick around Monday to get some sun. Do you good to get away from the smog for awhile".

"I am afraid that I have too much yardwork to do today, and Diane has some dinner engagement planned tonight. Besides, I am the last person who needs any sun. If I get any blacker, Diane will not be able to find me in the dark".

"Well, you can't say that I didn't try, Jerry. As to going out on your boat, though, you can forget it. You know how seasick I get. I can watch boats bobbing around at Marina Del Rey and get green around the gills! Lakes are about my speed. They don't get many waves!"

"Yes, I had forgotten about that. Sorry Joe. Well, have a good time up there and we shall see you back here bright and early Tuesday".

"Yep, bright and early around 10 A.M. Tuesday", Joe replied with a chuckle. "I want to go over plans for restructuring Davis... er, Talon Aerospace. We'll need to switch some of the military production over to commercial products, if I read the market right. After all, the Cold War is over".

"And thank God for it, too", exclaimed Jerry. "We have enough problems in this world without having to point nuclear missiles at each other".

"That's for sure. See you Tuesday, Jerry, and give my best to Diane".

Joe hung up the phone and grabbed a couple more cookies on his way out. So what if he had a tiny weight problem? He'd been good and gone to church that morning, so he could bend the rules a little that afternoon. As long as Martha didn't find out. Well, only one way to prevent that. Destroy the evidence. He waved to the owner's wife on his way out and headed back to the cabin.

When he got back, both Martha and Desiree were sleeping, which sounded like a good idea to him, so he went out on the back porch and settled into the hammock. The birds were chirping in the trees, a couple of squirrels were cavorting in the back yard, and everything was generally peaceful - the perfect conditions for a nap.

About an hour later, Joe awakened to the sound of Martha talking to Desiree. He decided to spring his surprise now.

"Hey there cutie, how would you like to spend another day up here in the mountains?", Joe asked, feeling very pleased with himself.

"Really Joe? Why that sounds wonderful!" She gave him a big hug, followed by a kiss. "I was really dreading getting all of that luggage together today. I guess this pregnancy is taking the wind out of my sails. I really have felt tired. But now I feel great!" Then she gave him a sidelong glance. "This isn't going to end like the last time you extended the trip, is it. You remember, the sudden call back to the office with me getting stuck with the packing?"

"I promise, no interruptions. There are no foreseeable problems on the horizon, and I'm sure Jerry is more than equal to the task of running the shop for one more day".

"We'll see. Personally, I think you arranged that early departure last time just so you could get out of the packing".

"Nothing of the sort!", Joe proclaimed. "That was strictly an accident. How did I know that we were going to have a plant fire at Talon Electronics? I'd say that's a bit extreme as an excuse for getting out of packing!"

"Just kidding, just kidding", said Martha with a gleam in her eye. "Although", she mused, "I have known you to go to extremes to get out of something before. Remember the charity ball at the Amundson's last year?"

"Yes, well, that was a nice interruption, you must admit", said Joe wistfully. "Who would have guessed that so many dogs could have been able to get in through the garden gate and chase her Siamese cats clear across the yard? Strictly an act of nature, and it couldn't have happened to a nicer socialite. She always did say that her cats were well ahead of any others in breeding and carriage. They certainly got a chance to show off their carriage that night. I've never seen two cats move so fast, not to mention the people in the path of that pack of dogs!"

"Yes, and you sent poor Mrs. Amundson up to her bed in hysteria once the cats were treed and the dogs removed!", Martha accused. "Not to mention the dozen people knocked into the pool in the fracas. Really, Joe!"

"But we did get out of there early and didn't have to listen to her carry on about charitable causes for two hours like the previous year", Joe stated firmly. "I'd call that a rather neat bit of plan... er, a happy coincidence, wouldn't you?"

"Coincidence my foot!", Martha practically shouted. "I saw that entry in the checkbook for $100 to the dogcatcher, dated the day of the party. You paid to have those dogs brought there, didn't you Joe?"

"Strictly happenstance, my dear. I had picked up a pet for a friend's daughter that day, that's all".

"A $100 dog from the pound? I find that very hard to believe. You never could lie convincingly to me, especially in money matters. Dogs are never that expensive at the pound. And besides, why was the dogcatcher there so promptly to round up those 'strays'?"

"Me? Lie to you? Moi? I suppose the dogcatcher had received a report of a pack of strays in the neighborhood and was out looking for them".

"At nine o'clock at night? I hardly think so , Joe. They go home by six".

"Oh", said Joe, sensing defeat once again. "Well, maybe I did have just a teensy bit to do with it, but it was all for a good cause. I'm sure everyone was just as pleased as I was to get out of there early".

"Maybe you could have talked to Mrs. Amundson privately sometime before the party about not speaking at such length. Did that ever occur to you?"

"I thought this would be a lot more fun, myself", answered Joe sheepishly. "And the look on the faces of those two cats, not to mention Mrs. Amundson, was priceless, you must admit".

"It was pretty funny at that", said Martha, a smile beginning to spread across her face. Then she caught the grin of triumph on Joe's face and realized what he was doing. "Oh no you don't, Joseph Talon. It was wrong, and that's the important point. I want your promise that you won't do anything like it again".

"Oh, you're no fun", said Joe, the grin slipping off his face. "All right, I promise".

"Good", replied Martha, beaming. "There might be hope for you yet, Joe".

Yeah, thought Joe bleakly, but a lot less fun.

They spent the rest of the day on the cabin's back porch watching the antics of the animals in the back yard. That evening, Martha cooked her bass and the fish Joe had caught. After dinner, they all went on a moonlit cruise on the lake in the little rowboat. Desiree was soon fast asleep in her mother's lap. They got back to the cabin about ten and, this time, Martha got the romantic evening she had wanted. They didn't know that it would be their last together.

Chapter 3

High clouds along with a few thunderheads were scattered as far as the eye could see, Monday morning. Joe crept out early to get some fishing in before breakfast. When Martha finally called him in two hours later, he had bagged five lake trout. Not bad for a start, Joe thought. Martha had prepared another award-winning breakfast and she and Joe smiled at each other across the table, still warmed by the glow of the previous evening.

"So, the fishing looks like it was pretty good this morning", Martha remarked.

"Yep. I seemed to have found a hole the fish liked to hide in", Joe replied. "I figure I should be able to catch enough for dinner tonight before I'm through".

"I doubt that any of them will beat my bass, though", needled Martha.

"True, true, but don't count me out yet. I've still got a few hours left to try and salvage my dignity".

"And I won't have a chance to better my score on this trip", lamented Martha. "Life's unfair".

"Not to worry", said Joe with a smile on his face. "There will be plenty of opportunities in future trips. Who knows, next time we might have Nicholas along".

"Well, I doubt that I'm going to feel much like coming up here before that time", said Martha. "And I still want to name him Joe Jr."

"Yes, dear", replied Joe, trying unsuccessfully to hide a smirk. "Look at the time, will you? I'd better get out there and fish heavily if I want to get us enough for dinner".

As they were cleaning up the breakfast dishes, a rickety old truck pulled up outside. An older man got out and ambled up to the cabin.

"Hello in the house", he shouted. "Is this the Talon cabin?"

"Joe stepped out onto the porch and answered, "Yes, it is. What's up?"

"I'm the postman", answered the stranger, "and I got an urgent phone call from L.A. Somebody named Jerry Porter called and asked me to get you to a phone as soon as possible. You are Joe Talon, I 'spect?"

"That's me", answered Joe glumly. He caught a glimpse of Martha glaring at him. If Jerry was calling it must be important. Joe could see his pleasant day of fishing go down the tubes very quickly. "I think I'll drive my own car back into town".

"Probably not a bad idea", answered the postman. "My jalopy may not make it back that quick. Just go to the general store. You can use the pay phone there".

"All right", said Joe dejectedly. "I'll be back as soon as I can, honey". He gave Martha a peck on the cheek and went out to the car.

The drive into town didn't take long (Joe was glad they didn't have any speed traps up here). He went into the general store, pretty much ignoring everyone as he went, and dialed up Talon Industries. Jerry was on the phone almost instantly.

"What's up, Jerry?", Joe asked guardedly.

"We seem to have a major problem over at Davis Aircraft", Jerry answered. "The whole computer network has gone off line. It appears that a virus is invading their mainframe. I am afraid that it may show up in our computers, too, since we started linking them this morning. I am doing what I can in the way of damage control, but we need a better crisis coordinator here. I am simply swamped".

"Sounds like Mr. Davis has left us a going-away present", Joe said with a groan. "All right, send the plane up to Big Bear Airport. I'll drive over there and have someone bring the car back for Martha. I should see you in a couple of hours".

"All right, Joe. Sorry about the vacation".

"Yeah. I'm really going to catch it from Martha. Funny thing is, we were just talking about this sort of thing last night".

"You can hide over at my place for a few days if it really gets too tough at home", said Jerry cheerily. "Have a safe trip down".

Joe didn't exactly speed back to the cabin. How to break this to Martha, he thought. Well, she already knew something bad had happened. Jerry wouldn't have called unless it was urgent. He might as well just lay it all out for her and be done with it.

"So, did your new secretary break a fingernail?", Martha asked sarcastically.

"Careful dear", Joe answered evenly. "Your claws are showing. No, it seems that our friend Ethan Davis left a virus in his company's computer. It's going hog-wild now, and Jerry is afraid that it will spread into ours. I have to get back and give some direction to the damage-control effort. Jerry's being overwhelmed".

"Fine thing", replied Martha. "I was really looking forward to a pleasant day together. Is that too much to ask?"

"I know. I was looking forward to a quiet day too. Just you, me, Desiree, and lots of hungry trout. Such is life".

I'm sure the trout will be very disappointed", said Martha with a scowl. "As for me, I guess I get stuck with all the packing - again!"

Sorry, it wasn't my choice. I'm afraid I won't have time to help. In fact, I had better get moving. The plane is probably already on the way to Big Bear."

"You *are* going to send the car back, aren't you? Or do you want me to call a cab?"

"I suppose I should have arranged to have a driver sent up. Sorry, hon. It didn't occur to me. I'll have someone from Big Bear drive the car back out here so you have a way home. Is that going to be a problem? I can call Jerry back and have him send a driver up".

"Not to worry, Joe. I am perfectly capable of driving Desiree and myself back down the mountain. I'm not quite an invalid yet".

"Just trying to be helpful", answered Joe defensively.

"I'm sorry. I guess I'm just a bit frustrated, that's all".

"That's OK. I don't imagine either of us is going to have a very pleasant day today".

"Well, just be careful, honey", said Martha quietly. She gave him a big hug.

A sudden wave of anxiety washed across Joe and he hugged her fiercely.

"Easy, dear, easy!", protested Martha. "You just about squeezed the breath out of me".

"Sorry. You sure you'll be OK? It's not too late for me to call up Jerry for a driver", said Joe anxiously.

"Stop worrying, Joe", answered Martha, a touch of exasperation in her voice. "We'll both be fine here! Just go get the worms out of your computers".

"That's bugs, dear". Joe pushed his concern off to the side and gave her a crooked smile.

"Whatever", said Martha absently. "Have a good trip and drive carefully".

"Yes, mother", chided Joe. "See you tonight. Love you".

"Bye, Joe", said Martha as he headed out the door. "I love you too". She still couldn't quite understand that bearhug from Joe, but she had more important things to do now, such as packing.

On the way to Big Bear, Joe noticed the darkening sky. Summer thunderstorms in the mountains could be pretty sudden. He hoped Martha got down the mountain before this one hit. He arrived at the airport without any problems. Once inside, he called up a local taxi service and asked them to drive his car back out to the cabin. They would get paid a double fare, since two cabbies were required, one to drive the car out and the other to follow him, then take him back. A tidy profit for the cab company, plus a generous tip. Joe still wished he had told Jerry to send up a driver for Martha. She was right, though. She had been a can-do type of person all her life. A minor crisis like this wouldn't even slow her down. Joe had noted that the plane was already there when he had parked. The trip down would take no time at all.

Once back at Talon Industries Joe could see the panic on the faces of his staff. If this virus got into his system, it could wreak havoc on lots of irreplaceable files.

"Well Jerry, what have we got?"

"Trouble, Joe. This thing is smashing files like a paper shredder. It seems to be a tapeworm of some sort, but just when we think we eliminated it, it appears somewhere else in the system. The good news is that it does not seem to be in any Talon systems yet".

"Well, at least that's good news. How much have we lost so far?"

"Most of the financial records have been destroyed. It appears that Mr. Davis was trying to cover his tracks there first. I have a suspicion that the rest of this is just window dressing to cover the main assault on the pay vouchers. I would not think he would be stupid enough to keep sensitive data like payoffs on the main computer, but he is so arrogant that perhaps he did not care about it - until now".

"Is it possible that we're not fighting just one virus, but several?", asked Joe. "If there were several little time-bombs dropped into the system, then you might actually be nailing the viruses which are on at the time, but more sprout up later".

"That is something I will have to ask our computer experts about", answered Jerry. "You might just have something there".

"What I'll have is hot tongue and cold shoulder for dinner tonight, I think".

"Left her with all of the packing again, did we?", asked Jerry, a hint of merriment in his eyes.

"Yeah, and I don't think I'll hear the end of this for many a long night", said Joe with a groan. "She had her heart set on one more day up there as a family".

"Do not concern yourself", assured Jerry. "All will be forgiven in time. Diane has given me a great deal of heat about worse things, and it all blew over in a few days".

"Sure, sure", said Joe mockingly. "And then she'll really let me have it. Ain't marriage wonderful?"

"Just one of those little bumps along the blissful road of matrimony", said Jerry, waxing philosophically.

"Yeah, but what about that Mack truck coming the other direction?"

"You simply must learn to be fast on your feet, my friend. Mack trucks cannot maneuver that quickly".

"I suppose", said Joe with a chuckle. "Anyway, lets handle one problem at a time. Back to tapeworms".

"Now that you mention it, it *is* getting rather close to lunchtime".

"Sorry, pal", said Joe pointedly, "No rest for the weary. First we get a handle on this problem, then we eat".

"As you wish", replied Jerry. Too bad, too, he thought. The pot roast scheduled for lunch today was always delicious. Ah, well. This was why he got the big bucks, or so Joe always informed him during crises.

Three hours later the pot roast was cold and the crisis was nearly over. No new viruses had popped up in the system and no contamination of the Talon systems had occurred. The computer aces were taking no chances. They put all the Talon computers through an extensive series of diagnostic tests and ran similar tests on the Davis Aircraft systems. The damage to the financial records had been done, however. Almost nothing of those files remained intact. Whatever Ethan Davis had been attempting to cover up, he seemed to have done a thorough job of it.

"What is the status of tape backups on Davis Aircraft financial records?", asked Jerry hopefully.

"No good", answered Dave Albrecht, the chief engineer and primary virus killer. "I imagine that Davis spirited them away before we took over. The systems operators claimed to have made regular backups, as per standard operating procedure, but they found nothing in the storage locker. It had been picked clean fairly recently. No records of the shipment of those tapes out the gate, either. I'd say we've been had".

"Maybe we can press criminal charges", said Joe without conviction.

"Computer viruses are not that uncommon, even in operations like this", replied Dave. "There is no agreement about Davis leaving the tape backups behind, is there Jerry?"

"No, I do not believe Allen Sims had such an agreement filled out", said Jerry glumly. "It appears that Mr. Davis tweaked our collective noses good and proper".

"Well, I suppose the good news is that the Talon computers were not touched", said Joe. "That is a fair assumption, isn't it Dave?"

"Yes, I suppose so. I think we have enough safeguards in place now to sterilize any little bugs that happen to poke their ugly little noses into our computers. We've scanned for anything suspicious and come up clean. I doubt that Davis was counting on taking down our system. This tapeworm was tailor-made to blow-out his financial records, and that's about all. Those other viruses were just diversions, as you suspected at first".

"Good. We don't need any more bad news today", said Joe with a sigh. "I'm going to get enough of a pounding when I get home this evening. I imagine Martha is getting close to home by now. If you guys think you have this situation under control, I'll head home. If I help her unload all of that stuff, I might only be in the doghouse for a couple of days instead of a week".

"You go ahead Joe", said Jerry. "We can finish cleaning up here. Sorry to have truncated your vacation. Who knows, perhaps if you act nice to her she will let you off the hook. Why not pick up something for her on the way home. Diane always likes getting flowers or candy. If you bribe her, she might grant you clemency, perhaps even commute the sentence".

"Say, that's not a bad idea", said Joe. "But this is going to take a *major* bribe. Ah, I think I know. She had her eye on an emerald necklace at Canton Gems. I might have just enough time to swing by to pick it up and make it home before she does. Excellent suggestion, Jerry. Remind me to give you a raise on your next review!"

"You can be sure of that", said Dave with a laugh.

"Now, now", said Jerry in his best school-master voice. "Do not be so disparaging about other people being rewarded for good ideas".

"I wasn't", chuckled Dave. "I was merely stating a fact. Congress never forgets to give themselves a raise, so why should you?"

"Yes, but do they deserve them?", asked Jerry pointedly.

"Probably not", answered Dave. "But that doesn't stop them from doing it".

"Well, I'll leave the political debates to you gentlemen", said Joe as he started walking out the door. "Let me know if anything more pops up. But if it isn't anything major, don't call! I'm in enough hot water over office problems as it is. OK?"

"OK, boss", said Dave.

As Joe headed down the corridor from the computer room, he could hear the debate between Dave and Jerry picking up again. Those two were always debating about something. They had been Joe's companions for better than 15 years, now, and each of them was still finding out things about the other that he never knew before. Well, Joe decided, that's what keeps things lively.

Joe managed to make good time heading over to the jewelry store. The cute Asian girl working the counter had been there when Joe and Martha had stopped by two weeks ago. Martha obviously like the necklace, but, still being a thrifty one, had decided not to take it. Joe had explained to her before that he could certainly afford any jewelry she wanted. But she still refused to be spoiled by all of Joe's wealth. He didn't forget the look in her eye when she saw that piece, though. Obviously the girl remembered him, too.

"Good afternoon, Mr. Talon", she said graciously. "Is there something I may interest you in?"

"I would like to see that necklace you were showing my wife the other night, if you still have it".

"Certainly, sir. I will bring that item out immediately. Please, have a seat".

It seemed like Joe had just sat down when the girl reappeared with the necklace.

"An exquisite piece, wouldn't you say, Mr. Talon?", asked the salesgirl. She made sure to rotate it slowly in the light so that the sun's rays broke into thousands of dancing lights. The emerald in the center shone brightly, and the salesgirl could see that she had made a sale.

"You have a good memory, miss", said Joe, still admiring the necklace. "Yes, that's the one. I'll take it. Could you gift-wrap it for me, please?"

"Of course, Mr. Talon. It will only take a moment", she replied as she disappeared into the back room.

A short while later Joe was speeding home. Perhaps creeping home would be more correct, as the traffic during rush-hour slowed him considerably. An hour later he arrived home. He didn't see the car in the driveway and thanked his lucky stars that he had beaten Martha home. He found Marie and set her to work making dinner. Then he changed into his work clothes and sat down to watch the Five O'clock News.

Joe was hardly paying attention to the news for the first ten minutes or so. It was the usual mix of murder and mayhem which made up news headlines. Then a huge column of smoke appeared on the screen. Widely forested land below the helicopter cameraman was burning fiercely. Then Joe saw the location identified on a map which was displayed next: Kingfisher Creek!

"Shortly before noon today a fire broke out in the vicinity of Kingfisher Creek, California", he heard the announcer say. "The fire has spread quickly through tinder-dry brush until it has covered over a thousand acres. Several companies of U.S. Forest Service personnel and contingents from the surrounding communities have been rushed in to fight the blaze. As of yet, the town itself has not been directly threatened, but residents have been advised that they may have to evacuate on a moment's notice. Most residents we interviewed said they were ready to leave, but hoped the fire would be contained before this was necessary. A few outlying cabins and vacation homes have been destroyed, but the firefighters hope to have the fire under control by early Tuesday".

Joe was numb. Martha had still not arrived home. The car she was driving didn't have a car-phone (one of the ground rules for a vacation: no cellular phones anywhere in sight), and, even with heavy traffic, she should have been home by now. Joe called up Tim Bathas, Talon Industries' chief pilot, and asked him to be ready for an immediate trip back up to Big Bear Airport. He then summoned his driver and asked him to bring the car around front. Joe had to get up to Kingfisher Creek quickly and didn't feel he could keep his concentration on driving. Marie was instructed that if Martha got home while Joe was gone, she was to call Joe as soon as possible on his private line. This would link her to his portable cellular phone wherever he was at the time. The driver sped away to the airport and Marie was left wondering what was happening. The gift-wrapped package remained forlornly on the table by Joe's chair.

Bill Thompson had been the family chauffeur for thirty years. He had driven both Joe's parents and, later, Joe's family around. He had seen Joe happy, angry, reflective, and roaring drunk. He had never seen him as pensive as he was today, though.

The drive to the airport and the flight up to Big Bear were unique in that Joe was so silent. Both Bill and Tim were used to at least some conversation along the way. Joe had not told anyone what he was worried about, so they assumed that there was something wrong, just not how bad. Once the plane approached Big Bear Airport, they began to get an idea of why Joe was so worried. The sky to the north was filled with smoke. Planes were buzzing around the smoke plume like angry hornets and occasionally a tongue of flame could be seen to lick skyward. Tim set down at Big Bear just as a CDF OV-10 spotter plane was taxiing for take-off. "Busy day for the Forestry Service", he commented. Joe headed out the door without a word. Tim and Bill exchanged worried glances as Joe walked briskly across the tarmac towards the car rental office.

Joe finally spoke when Bill got into the rental. "Kingfisher Creek as fast as you can", he said forcefully. Bill nodded and raced out of the airport parking lot. The drive up to Kingfisher Creek was as quiet as the plane ride had been. Once they got into town, though, Joe began to perk up. The normally sleepy little town was full of activity. People were loading up possessions on trucks and cars in haste. Some cars were already heading out of town, back the way Joe and Bill had just come, fully laden with family belongings. At the other end of town, the road was blocked by Forestry Service signs. An old ranger walked up to the car.

"Afternoon, folks", he said amiably. "I'm afraid this road is closed until further notice. Seems the fire is heading this way and the authorities don't want anyone blocking the emergency equipment from getting up there".

"My wife and daughter may be up there!", said Joe excitedly. "I've got to find out if they're all right!"

"I'm sorry, sir", said the old ranger calmly. "But I've been given strict orders: no civilian vehicles go up this road for now. If you would like to give me a phone number I can reach you at, I'll be glad to pass it on to those in charge. They can call you as soon as they have any information".

"But I've got to get up there!", pleaded Joe. "They may need me!"

"No sir", the ranger answered back. "No one passes this point without permission. Sorry, but that's the way it is".

"OK, how much is it worth to you to let me past", Joe asked as he pulled out his wallet.

The ranger began to get angry at this. "Look, I've been very patient, but if you don't move along, I'm going to call the police down from the fire line and have you arrested", the ranger said evenly. "You won't do your family much good sitting in a jail cell, now will you?"

"Very well", said Joe sullenly. "Here's my number. It's a cellular, so the authorities can reach me anytime, anywhere. Ask them to please hurry".

"Yes sir", the ranger replied with a nod. "As soon as there's word we'll call you. Sorry about the inconvenience".

Bill thanked the ranger and backed away. "Back to Big Bear, sir?", he asked gently.

"No", said Joe slowly. "Pull over to the general store. Let's see what news they have".

The store was open, as Joe had hoped. Seeing so many leaving town, he hadn't been sure the owners were still there. Both looked concerned, although the owner's wife greeted Joe cordially.

"What news do you have?", asked Joe.

"We've seen more than forty firetrucks and busses go up that road so far", the wife answered. "The word we have from the few who have come back is that they guess it was a lightning strike which started the fires. It seemed like it was no time at all from clear air to billowing smoke. We've had a drought up here for the past couple of years, so I guess the forest went up pretty quickly".

"Has there been any news of a woman and child being seen up there?", asked Joe, a look of concern on his face.

"None that I've heard", the woman answered. "We haven't seen any of the ambulances come back down yet, so I would guess there's been no injuries or burn victims".

"Bill", Joe said quietly, "bring the car around back. I want to see if there's a way we can get around that barricade. I must get up to the fire. Maybe the people in charge can tell me more".

"But sir", Bill protested, "the ranger told us that no one was allowed up there without permission. We could get arrested if we try to drive up there!"

Joe shot the chauffeur a venomous look, then fairly shouted "Do it!"

Reluctantly, Bill went out the door and started the car. Joe waited for him to drive around the corner of the building, then asked if he could use the bathroom. The woman smiled politely and motioned him into the back room. Once Joe was sure she had gone back to the counter, he slipped out the back door and got into the car. "Drive", he said quietly.

Half an hour later, they were well past the roadblock and heading towards the cabin. They reached the fire line about three miles short of the cabin. Over two hundred firefighters were clearing brush and digging up plants to make a firebreak. Ten firetrucks were deployed behind the line. The fire looked to be about a mile off and was apparently getting closer. Just as Joe was about to get out of the car, a burly policeman walked up to it.

"What do you think you're doing here?", he boomed at them. "No civilians are allowed in this area, only fire personnel!"

"My family may be out there!", Joe shouted, gesturing at the fire. "I've got to know if they've been found yet! I've got to know if they're safe!"

"Didn't they tell you in town to stay out of here?", the officer asked more calmly. "We can't be nursemaiding a bunch of people who've got no business here".

"Like my boss said", answered Bill, "his family is missing and they were last seen up here. His cabin is about three miles in that direction. He needs to know if they are safe. Is there someone in charge here who he can talk to?"

"Go see that fellow in the red jacket", growled the officer. "The one standing on the roof of that firetruck over there".

"Thanks", said Bill. He parked the car out of the way and let Joe out. Joe practically ran over to the firetruck.

"Hey you!", Joe shouted when he was still 100 feet away. "I need to talk to you!"

"What do you want?", the man said without turning around, intent on the approaching fire.

"My family may be out there somewhere!", shouted Joe. "Have you gotten any reports of a woman and a little girl driving a blue Mercedes 500SEL, license 2FJL305?"

The fireman suddenly turned around and shouted, "What in blue blazes are you people doing up here? Didn't you see that roadblock? We've got a major fire on our hands here! No, I haven't received any reports of people out in that fire, but if I had they would be moved back into Kingfisher Creek. If they aren't there, then we haven't seen them. Now get out of here and let us do our jobs! Rudy, get these people out of here!", he called over to the officer.

"All right folks, you heard the man. Back to Kingfisher Creek before I run you both in!", the officer shouted.

"We're going", said Joe, "but if anything happens to my family, I'll hold you personally responsible!", he shot back at the fireman. "Take us back to town, Bill", Joe said angrily.

The drive back to Kingfisher Creek was uneventful (and uncomfortable for Bill) until they reached the roadblock at the edge of town.

"What the...?", the old ranger exclaimed when the car came down the road. "How did you get out there?", he shouted, his face turning red with anger. "I thought I told you that the road was closed? I've got half a mind to have you arrested right now!"

Neither Bill nor Joe said anything. Bill just drove the car slowly around the roadblock and left the ranger to fume. Back at the general store, they both collapsed into chairs and waited for word.

It was after dark when the first ambulance rolled through town. It hardly slowed down, continuing on towards Big Bear. Several more firetrucks from outlying areas moved through town heading up to the fire an hour after that. Finally, Joe heard on the radio that the fire was now considered contained. Shortly after midnight, the first vehicles began rolling into town from the fire line. About forty-five filthy and exhausted firefighters shuffled out of several busses which had pulled up to the general store. The store owners brought out sandwiches and drinks for the firefighters and set up cots and sleeping bags on the floor and porch for some to catch a little sleep. Joe saw the battalion chief who had been standing on the top of the firetruck several hours before and moved over to talk with him. The man was obviously exhausted, but pleased.

"Hello again", said Joe cautiously, pulling up a chair. "Tough day, huh?"

"Yeah, but I've had worse".

"My name's Joe Talon", said Joe, extending his hand.

"I'm Zack Dobson", said the fireman, returning Joe's handshake. Joe winced at the man's grip. "Sorry about shouting at you up there at the fire, but I had a little crisis to deal with. We almost didn't stop that fire in time. Lucked out again, though".

"That's OK", said Joe, relaxing somewhat. "I'm afraid I was getting a little unruly myself. So tell me, any word on rescued people?"

"Nope, not yet", answered Zack. "'Course we probably won't have a clear picture till tomorrow anyway. We had people fighting this thing from four sides. If your family went toward Potterburg, we never would have seen them. The good news is that we've had no reports of any fatalities. Like I said, wait till tomorrow. We should know for sure by then. Now if you'll excuse me, I think I'll get some shuteye. If this thing brews up again I'll need whatever sleep I can get now".

"Sure. Thanks for the information. I don't think I'll be able to sleep for awhile, myself".

The two of them parted company and Zack was quickly asleep on the front porch. Joe, however, found that he couldn't sleep. His thoughts kept going round in his head. He still thought of that farewell at the cabin, about his odd behavior. Had he had a premonition? No, he decided, it was nothing. Martha was probably just lost in the woods and would turn up in the morning. Joe finally nodded off about 4 A.M.

It seemed like Joe had just closed his eyes when someone was shaking him awake.

"Mr. Talon", said Bill deferentially. "This officer would like to speak with you", he said pointing to a policeman.

"Are you Mr. Joseph Talon?", the officer asked.

Joe tried to shake off sleep and answered, "Yes I am".

"You own a blue Mercedes 500SEL, license number 2FJL305?"

"Yes, that's right", answered Joe more anxiously. "Have you found my family?"

"No sir, not yet. We have located the remains of the car, though. It was about five miles north of here, stuck in a ravine. It appeared to have been driven cross-country. The occupants have not been located as of yet".

"My wife and daughter were in that car!", shouted Joe. "Do you need a description? Can I help you in the search?"

"A description would be helpful, Mr. Talon. We have several hundred people conducting organized searches now. I think it would be best if you stayed put here until we find them. You might get lost out there yourself, and there are still some spot fires to put out".

"It's just that I feel so helpless sitting here doing nothing", said Joe despondently. "I have an aircraft at Big Bear Airport. Could we use that to search from?"

"Yes, that could be useful at that. I'll have some people contact you here in about fifteen minutes about joining the search. In the meantime, can I get that description from you?"

Joe obliged him with a full description, then waited for the fire personnel to come get him. It was the battalion chief, along with two younger men.

"Hello again, Zack", Joe greeted wearily. "It seems I can help a bit after all".

"Hello, Joe. Yes, we can use all the eyes in the sky we can get. Search and rescue is a tricky business. The more planes in the air, the greater the chance of spotting someone. It won't be easy as finding a boy scout troop, but it should help. From what I'm told, we should have about twenty-three aircraft to help in the search".

"Well, let's get going!', said Joe. "I've been useless long enough".

On the drive to the airport, Joe asked a few questions about where this fire had started and what the probable cause was. Zack said that they expected it had been a lightning strike, but that no actual strikes had been seen in the vicinity. There had been several thunderheads rolling through which could have caused it, however, so this remained the chief suspect. When they arrived at the airport they found the aircraft already tanked up. Bill had taken the liberty of calling ahead for Jim to be ready when they got there. Zack said he had some things to take care of, and parted from their company. In a few minutes, they were off the ground and starting their search. The search pattern took them over Joe's cabin. It had been completely gutted by the fire. All the timber around the lake had been torched as well. There was still a small plume of smoke off to the northwest which seemed to be attracting a number of aircraft. Joe supposed they were air-tankers.

For two-and-a-half hours they searched the woods, but found nothing. Then Jim received a call from Big Bear Airport to return at once. When Joe asked why they were being called back, Jim said that no specific reason was given. Joe felt his stomach begin to tighten and asked one of the firefighters to call in on his radio to see if any word had been received yet. The voice on the radio replied that he had no information on this matter, but that he would check with someone else and call back. In the meantime, Joe continued to fret.

On landing, Joe popped the hatch and ran into the airport. Two policemen were waiting just inside the door, one of them the officer who had shouted at him up by the fire the day before.

"Mr. Joseph Talon?", the older officer asked.

"That's right", said Joe quickly. "Do you have word about my wife and daughter?"

"Yes sir, we do", said the older officer slowly. "Mr. Talon, I regret to inform you that your wife and daughter are both dead. They apparently died due to the fire".

Joe was stunned. "Are you sure it's them?", he asked anxiously.

"They exactly match the description you gave us, sir", replied the officer.

"It can't be", Joe exclaimed. "It just can't be!" He began to tremble violently, then his knees started to buckle.

Bill had lagged behind Joe when he left the plane. Jim was still talking with the firefighters as they filed out onto the tarmac. As Bill neared Joe and the two policemen, he saw Joe begin to sway to one side, then settle uneasily into a chair. He quickened his pace and was practically running by the time he reached the little group.

"What's the matter?", he asked, a concerned look on his face. Joe's face was gray in color, his eyes lifeless. Bill turned his attention to the two policemen.

"What has happened?", he asked them.

"We found Mr. Talon's family out in the woods", replied the older officer. "I'm afraid they were already dead. It looked as though they were trapped in a pocket of trees. The smoke and heat must have gotten to them. Their clothes were hardly even singed. Mrs. Talon had her purse along, and her description matched the one Mr. Talon had provided. We didn't want to broadcast the news until we had a chance to verify it with Mr. Talon first. We will need him to come into town with us and make a positive ID of the bodies".

Bill could not believe it. He had hoped that Martha and Desiree were all right, but that hope was now as shattered as Joe appeared to be. Joe simply sat and stared at the floor. No tears appeared in his eyes, no sound left his lips. He simply sat there, unmoving.

"Sir", Bill said gently. "These officers need you to go with them, now. Do you wish me to drive you?"

Joe looked up blankly at Bill, seeming not to have heard what Bill had said. Bill repeated his question. Joe looked at the two officers, then back to Bill. He nodded sluggishly. Bill helped him to his feet, then they slowly walked out to the rental car, Joe leaning heavily on Bill's shoulder.

Chapter 4

The flight back down to L.A. had been even quieter than the flight up. Neither Bill nor Jim talked, and Joe stared out the window, hardly even blinking in the sunlight which poured through the window. Once back in L.A., Bill helped Joe over to the car, then drove him home. He helped Joe inside the house, then pulled the car around back. Marie had met them at the door and couldn't seem to stop crying. She had finally gone into the kitchen to compose herself. Bill had come around and talked to Hodgekins, the butler, explaining in detail what he had related to Marie over the phone. Hodgekins listened silently, then thanked Bill, dismissing him for the night. Bill was reluctant to go, but he was exhausted and didn't protest too much. Hodgekins went into the study where Joe was sitting and asked him if there was anything Joe wanted. Joe simply shook his head and motioned for Hodgekins to leave. A short while later, Joe trudged upstairs to try to get some sleep.

Joe couldn't remember all of the nightmares he had that first night, fortunately. Marie never told him how much he had cried out that night. She had had difficulty sleeping and decided to get something from the kitchen to help put her to sleep. It had been shortly after midnight when she got up. She had been warming milk when she thought she heard shouting from upstairs. She hurried out into the foyer, then rushed upstairs to see what the commotion was. The shouting was coming from the master bedroom. As she approached, she could hear Joe's voice crying out.

"Get away from there!", he shouted. "Stay back! Don't go near that fire! Martha, Desiree, come here! No, not that way! Watch out! That tree is falling! Get out of there...!"

On and on Joe shouted, first pleading with his family, then angrily yelling at them to come to him. The outcome always seemed to be the same, though. They would drift into the flames and be lost. Joe would cry out in anguish, then the cycle would start over again. Marie thought of going in and awakening Joe, but she knew that he would simply drift back into these nightmares again. Better to let him think he remained undiscovered, rather than embarrass him by waking him. She walked quietly back down to the kitchen to her now-scalded milk. She poured it into the sink, then washed out the pan. As she crept back to bed, she noticed that her hands were trembling slightly. It appeared that neither she nor Joe would get a very good night's sleep.

Wednesday dawned bright and cheery. When Joe finally woke up for the last time (having awakened frequently in a cold sweat the night before), he wearily crawled out of bed and went into the bathroom to clean up. Marie had heard the shower running upstairs and began to prepare Joe's breakfast. Joe ate hardly anything that morning, despite not having eaten much the day before. Breakfast was a quiet time, neither Joe nor Marie having much energy left for conversation after the previous night.

Joe made arrangements to bring the bodies of Martha and Desiree down from Big Bear, then spent the rest of the day making arrangements for the funeral. Hodgekins had offered to help, but Joe had just waved him off. Joe explained that this gave him something to do. Hodgekins couldn't help but think that this was the wrong thing for Joe to be doing with his time. Marie agreed with him and tried to talk to Joe about it, but to no avail. Joe had thrown himself into the job with a vengeance.

The funeral was four days later. It looked like a who's who of L.A.'s upper crust. Joe was fairly silent throughout the service, speaking only briefly with a few of his closest friends. Joe didn't attend the reception after the funeral and Bill drove him straight home. It was another nightmare-filled night for Joe. In his dreams, he would reach out to his family, almost touching them, only to see them drift away into the flames. he finally went downstairs to the small wet bar to get a drink. After he had finished most of a bottle of whiskey, he found that he could finally drift off to sleep with no more nightmares.

The next day, Monday, Joe was up shortly after 10 A.M. Once he had showered and shaved, he went downstairs for breakfast. His head felt like it would split open at any minute, but Marie prepared him some sort of a tomato-juice concoction which tasted awful but seemed to help his hangover. Once Joe began to feel better he asked Marie to have Bill bring the car around. Joe was going to work. Marie regarded him skeptically, thinking that Joe was not up to work today, but complied with his wishes. Bill brought the car around front and drove Joe to Talon Industries. Bill decided it would be best if he hung around for awhile, so he drove over to the parking lot and pulled out a book to read. It was going to be a long day, he figured.

"Good morning, Mr. Talon", Joe's secretary, Nancy Westmore, said, a look of sadness on her face. "We all heard about your wife and daughter. If there is anything I can do to help, please let me know".

"Thank you, Nancy", Joe said as he walked into his office. "Would you please set up a meeting between myself and the department heads for this afternoon, then call Jerry Porter into my office?"

"Of course, sir", Nancy answered.

Jerry arrived a few minutes later, along with Dave Albrecht, Allen Sims, the head of the Legal Department, and Horace Melton, the office manager.

"Morning boss", said Horace. "I was really sorry to hear about Martha and the kid...", he began. Joe waved his hand for silence.

"What's gone is gone!", Joe said forcefully. "Let's get on with the business at hand. What's our situation with Talon Aerospace? Have all the software problems been resolved?"

Dave flashed a concerned look at Jerry and Allen, then said, "Yeah, I think we've killed the last bugs. The system has been pretty well sterilized. We're still keeping a close eye on everything, but I think we're out of the woods now".

"Of course, we lost all of the financial records for Davis Aircraft", added Jerry.

"There isn't enough left of the files to reconstruct anything meaningful", said Dave. "Looks like Davis had a top-notch programmer put together that package of viruses".

"What damage does this do to our long-term plant operations?", Joe asked Jerry.

"We will have to reconstruct what we can from the paper records still on file", Jerry replied. "That will be a difficult and time-consuming job. I would estimate a time-frame of three to four weeks of sifting before we have a completed picture of what our obligations are. Until that time, our customers are going to be severely inconvenienced by our ignorance of their relationship to us. To put it succinctly, we will not know what we owe them, nor what they owe us. This could provide a great many headaches in and of itself. Add to that the day-to-day operation needs for payroll and expenses, and you have a most difficult situation".

"I believe that we can handle any legal problems which develop from this situation", said Allen hopefully. "The customers will probably not expect a smooth transition, and delays of a month due to this transition will probably by acceptable to most of them. We could extend credit to those who need it for the short-term until the financial records are put in order. I can have my people draw up the necessary contracts to cover this contingency at once. Do you wish me to begin collecting data on Mr. Davis and his computer prank so that we can prosecute him?"

"Absolutely!", said Joe. "I want to nail him for this one. Nobody does this to me without getting pasted!"

Although this response pleased Joe's advisors, they couldn't help but notice the overly vindictive tone in his voice.

The meeting that afternoon was very stormy. Joe was on the offensive from the moment he entered the room.

"All right everybody", Joe began. "Let's get started. What's our status in the neural network research at Talon Electronics?"

"We are still having difficulty getting our contaminants in the silicon matrix down to an acceptable level", the head of the division responded. "We will need another month, maybe two before we can begin serious development".

"You're already over a month behind now!", shouted Joe. "I want to see this problem resolved by next week, no later!"

"But that's impossible!", cried the division head. "We can't possibly be done in time!"

"Then work harder!", raged Joe. "I've already taken a beating on this Davis Aircraft deal! I can't afford any more delays! Get it done, or I'll find someone who can!" He turned to the head of Bergway Chemical, his chemical division, "What about that new defoliate for the Army?"

"Production is coming up to speed on the new batch, sir", answered the chemical head warily. "We expect to be turning out two thousand gallons a week by the end of this month".

"I'd like to see you increase that to a target of three thousand gallons a week before the end of next month", said Joe. "Using the existing equipment and without hiring additional personnel".

"I don't know if we can meet that target under those conditions", said the division head. "We have barely enough men and equipment to meet the present goal. In order to fulfill your new requirement I would need to work all of my people 60 hours a week year round. Even then, if anything breaks down our schedule would slip badly. I don't believe I can do it under these new conditions".

"Then you're fired!", barked Joe. "Give the pertinent documents to your assistant, along with my new orders, and clean out your desk".

Jerry spoke up at this point: "Joe, you cannot just arbitrarily fire this man for pointing out the difficulty of the task you have assigned him. Give him a chance to at least talk it over with his staff to see if they can come up with a workable plan".

Joe glared at Jerry, then back at the head of Bergway. "All right!", he growled. "You have one week to prepare a workable plan for implementing my instructions. If it is acceptable to me at that time, then you can keep your job. Otherwise...", he trailed off menacingly.

"Thank you", said the division head sullenly.

The remainder of the meeting was equally stormy. No one in the room had ever seen Joe this combative. One other thing that they noticed: Joe had started using the bar in the back of the conference room. Several times during the meeting he walked across the room to refill his glass with whiskey. His speech was beginning to slur a bit by the end of the meeting. No one was smiling when they left. Several had considered expressing their condolences over the death of Joe's family, but thought better of it and filed quietly out of the room.

Back in his office, Joe settled unsteadily into his chair. His head felt better now, but he was still not feeling very good. Jerry walked into the office with a scowl on his face.

"What was that meeting all about?", Jerry asked pointedly. "Those people are all giving you the best efforts they can provide! You have no cause to go jumping down their throats like that!"

"Maybe I've been too soft on them for too long!", said Joe with a glare. "And if I wanted your opinion, I would have asked for it!"

"Look, we are all sorry about what happened up in the mountains, but that is no reason to take it out on your staff!"

"I'll thank you not to bring the incident in the mountains up again! That's none of your business!"

Jerry could see that Joe's face was reddening dangerously and decided to back off. "Sorry sir", he said quietly. "I suppose that it is none of my business at that".

"You got that right!", shouted Joe angrily. He started to settle down at this point and asked more calmly "How is the restructuring of Talon Aerospace coming along?"

"I think we should have a clearer picture in a few more days", replied Jerry, a bit of relief entering his voice as he realized that the situation was defusing. "The senior staff replacements are being drawn up now, and I would expect that the rest of the changes could be started as early as November. Their staff seems to be willing to work with us. I don't think Mr. Davis made too many friends there".

"Good. I expect we will be back up to full-scale production by the first of the year. The end of the year is always a slow time in the defense industry anyway. That would be the best time to make any changes".

"I believe so. That should all fit together nicely for a timetable".

"Well, don't let me keep you from your work", Joe said. His throat had begun to dry out and he decided a drink would go well about now. "I think I'll head home. It's been a tiring day".

"Yes, I suppose that it has been at that", said Jerry. For all of us, he thought.

Joe was completely drunk by seven that evening. Hodgekins had to get help from Bill in carrying Joe up to bed that night. Joe slept soundly, not being disturbed by the nightmares all night. He was not up until almost eleven the next morning. When he finally dragged out of bed, it was all he could do to get into the shower. The hot water helped to revive him a little, but he didn't bother to shave that morning. Marie had her hangover tonic prepared and Joe forced himself to drink it. It was not quite as effective this morning though. Bill brought the car around when Joe was finished with breakfast. Joe walked slowly out and got in.

Joe decided that a small shot of whiskey from the car's wet bar would do him good. By the time he got to Talon Industries, he had convinced himself to have two more. By the end of the day, he had finished off half a fifth of whiskey and asked Nancy to send out for a refill. She made sure that it took until quitting time for the bottle to get there, but it didn't really matter. Joe was barely able to walk out to the car at the end of the workday. He had accomplished virtually nothing all day, signing a few unimportant papers while nursing his bottle along.

Joe never even made it through dinner that night. He passed out before Marie even brought out the main course. She had thought of hiding the remaining bottle of Scotch, but decided against it, since Joe had already become violent once when he couldn't find the bottle, smashing a priceless Ming vase. Joe was carried upstairs again and spent another dreamless night in bed.

Marie checked on him at noon the next day. He was still snoring loudly at that time. She called Jerry and told him that she didn't think Joe would be in today.

"It would probably do him good to take a few days off", said Jerry amiably. "At least he is getting a good night's sleep now".

"I don't much like the way that he's getting it", said Marie. "Sooner or later, he will have to sober up. My father was an alcoholic, and it was extremely painful for all of us, including him, when he finally started to dry out. I hope that isn't the direction Mr. Talon is headed".

"Oh, I would not worry if I were you, Miss DeLautier", said Jerry soothingly. "I imagine that he will snap out of this in another week. Until then, just see to it that he is comfortable. We can run the corporation from this end until then".

"I hope you're right. I don't relish going through life with another alcoholic".

"Everything will be fine in two weeks, three at the worst".

That's what my mother kept saying about my father, thought Marie. It took five years with him.

Chapter 5

Jerry called over the next morning to see how Joe was feeling. Marie answered the phone.

"Good morning Marie. How is Mr. Talon today?"

"Good morning Mr. Porter. I'm afraid that Mr. Talon is not up yet".

"But it is nearly noon", said Jerry with a note of concern in his voice. "When do you think he will be up?"

"I do not know Mr. Porter. He seems to be sleeping quite deeply and I don't wish to disturb him just yet. He has suffered a good deal since... since the mountains, sir".

"Yes, I know", said Jerry quietly. "Very well. When he does finally wake up, have him give me a call. I should be here at work until late. Tell him that it is nothing urgent".

"I will, Mr. Porter. As soon as he is up I will have him call you".

"Thank you Marie", said Jerry. As he hung up the phone, several worrisome thoughts crossed his mind, but he dismissed them.

Jerry finally left work at nine that night. Jerry had never heard back from Joe and was a bit concerned about him. He tried several more times to speak with him, but Joe was always indisposed, according to Marie. One time he would be in the shower and couldn't come to the phone. Another time he would supposedly be out strolling in the gardens and Marie didn't know exactly where he was. In every case, Joe failed to return Jerry's calls. Jerry was always swamped at work, staying until late at night. By Friday night, Jerry had had enough and determined to stop by and see Joe on Saturday.

As he drove up to the house, Jerry noticed how peaceful and orderly everything looked outside. He rang the doorbell and Hodgekins came to the door.

"I was surprised to hear you call in from the gate, sir", Hodgekins said formally. "I expected you to call before coming over. The house is not exactly in order for visitors at the moment. Would it be possible for you to come back later on this evening?"

"No Hodgekins", said Jerry firmly. "I have been trying to get through to Mr. Talon for several days, now. Since he will not return my calls, I decided to come and see him myself. Friends and business associates of his have been calling me asking about his health and voicing concern over his lack of response to their calls and letters. I have come to assess the situation for myself".

"His, er, condition has not improved substantially", said Hodgekins evasively. "I'm afraid that he is indisposed at the moment. As I say, if you could come back later, it would be of enormous help to all of us".

"No Hodgekins. I have been put off long enough. Show me to Mr. Talon immediately." Jerry forced his way past the butler and waited in the entry hall until Hodgekins led him hesitantly across the foyer into the study. There he found Joe, sprawled out on the couch, still wearing his pajamas. In his right hand, Joe clutched a nearly-empty bottle of Scotch. Scattered around him were several other bottles of Scotch, some empty, some still unopened. Hodgekins came rushing in and began picking up bottles from the floor, a look of anxiety on his face. At this point, Joe stirred and looked drunkenly around the room

"Whash going on, Hodgekins?", he asked as he looked at the butler cleaning up the mess. "Don' take any of thosh full ones away. I'm not done wish them yet!"

Hodgekins froze at his task, then looked pleadingly at Jerry. Joe followed his gaze, then brightened into a drunken smile.

"Jerry, old buddy!", Joe exclaimed happily. "Come on over here and shet yourself down! Here, have a drink, complementsh of the housh!"

Joe attempted to sit up, then slumped back down into a reclining position on the sofa. he brought the bottle he was holding up and offered it to Jerry, who declined. Joe shrugged with an air of disappointment, then took a long drink from the bottle. Hodgekins exited the room at this point with his collection of bottles.

"How are you feeling, Joe?", Jerry asked, a look of concern on his face.

"Me?", asked Joe with a leer. "Why I'm doin' fine, Jerry, jush fine!"

Jerry was at a loss for words. On the one hand, he thought about wrenching the bottle from Joe's hand, then thought better of it. Joe was a pitiful sight. It didn't appear that he had been showering lately and he was in need of a shave as well.

"So, howsh tingsh at the office?", Joe asked smiling. "Everythin' runnin' OK?"

"Fine", said Jerry, trying unsuccessfully to return Joe's smile. "We will conclude the restructuring at Talon Aerospace in another two weeks. No sign of any more viruses in the system. I believe we should be able to make most of the changes you proposed at the last department meeting without too much trouble".

"Changesh?", asked Joe with a puzzled look on his face. "What changesh? Oh yeah, all that stuff I shaid at the lasht meeting. Don' worry your head about that shtuff, Jer. I was jush blowing off shteam".

"Well, some of the things did make sense. We could increase production of the defol ..."

Joe's concentration began to wander at this point. he slowly glanced around the room until he got to the bare windows.

"Green curtainsh!", he protested. "She knowsh how much I hate green!"

"Who are you talking about?", asked Jerry, confused by the sudden turn of the conversation.

Joe looked as though someone had stabbed him. Even through the fog of the liquor, the pain of his loss seeped in.

"Nobody", Joe answered with a grimace. "Jush talking to myshelf, thash all".

Joe took another swig from the bottle, then threw it across the room at the wall. The crash caused both Hodgekins and Marie to rush into the room. They looked at Jerry with concern, then back to Joe, who was still frowning.

"Bring me another bottle!", Joe shouted at them. Marie remained standing, the color draining from her face. Hodgekins left the doorway, then returned quickly with a full bottle of Scotch. Joe grabbed it greedily from this hand, Jerry put his hand on Joe's.

"Joe, this is not the answer", he said softly. "You must pull out of this depression".

"Get you hand off me!", Joe shouted. "I know what I'm doin'. Jush leave me alone!"

Joe opened the bottle and began to guzzle noisily from it. When the bottle was almost a quarter of the way empty, Joe came up for air. The look of anger began to leave his face at that point, then he slid down a little farther on the couch and smiled drunkenly at Jerry. Jerry couldn't stand it anymore. he stood up without a word and stormed out of the room, practically bowling over the two servants as he went.

Marie hurried after him and put her hand gently on his shoulder. Jerry turned around and looked at her for a moment. He could see the fear and sorrow etched deep in her face. Her eyes had dark circles under them and looked dull and lifeless.

"You don't know the pain he was going through, sir", she said quietly. "I heard him crying out those first few terrible nights after. . . after the accident".

"Marie, he is drunk!", Jerry shouted. "He hardly even recognized me! I have seen him drink some before, but for almost two weeks now? I would say that it is time for professional help!"

"Please, sir, not yet!", pleaded Marie. "The strain might be too much for him to stand. He must overcome his grief first. Once he has done that, then we can get him some help".

"I do not agree!", shouted Jerry. "I think he should be institutionalized now! What happened to Doctor Jacobs? Has he been notified about this?"

"Yes sir, he has. I'm afraid that he was very insistent about Mr. Talon 'drying out' in a hospital. Mr. Talon fired him on the spot. We tried to convince Mr. Talon of the need for him to follow the doctor's request, even going so far as to let Dr. Jacobs in unannounced. There was a terrible fight and the doctor was knocked unconscious. When we finally brought him around he swore that he would never set foot in this house again. Mr. Talon has not returned any of the doctor's calls since then".

"Weren't the police called in by the doctor?"

"No sir, they were not. The doctor apparently never filed a police report."

"Perhaps I should try to convince him myself, then".

"He will not go, sir. We have already tried to convince him of the need. He will not agree to it. Until he accepts the need himself, I think it would be best just to let him continue drinking. At least he can sleep at night. Think of what it would do to his reputation if we had him hospitalized? It could ruin him!"

"Well, I am still not convinced", said Jerry, who was beginning to cool down now. "But we will wait another week and see what happens".

"Believe me, I have seen this before. My own father was an alcoholic for many years. He was seldom this bad for such a long time, but he never suffered such a loss, either. Given time, I believe Mr. Talon will begin to bottom out. Then he will be ready for help. He must grieve for awhile. I only hope that it is not too long. If we try to snap him out of it too soon, he could be emotionally scarred for life. Just let him go for a short time more, then we can truly help him".

"I only hope that you are correct", said Jerry dejectedly. "In the meantime, I will try to keep the company afloat. It would seem that we all have a difficult time ahead. Let me know if you need anything, Marie".

"I will, Mr. Porter", she said with a weak smile. "Have a pleasant evening".

"Doubtful", said Jerry with a tired look on his face. "Very seriously doubtful".

On his way home, Jerry thought about the company and Joe. He couldn't help thinking about the company and his own situation in the midst of all this. It just wasn't fair. He was being asked to do too much. He wasn't cut out to run the whole corporation by himself. He would need help. Joe had always had a knack for knowing the right thing to do at exactly the right time. Although Jerry prided himself on being highly educated, he didn't have the gift of genius in financial matters that Joe had. He had seen Joe pull victory out of defeat more than once in their long years together. "Nevertheless", Jerry said aloud, "it is up to you now to run the company until Joe is able to again, so run it you must!"

As Jerry thought about this situation, he remembered a story from the late nineteenth century. The British, in trying to colonize South Africa, had brought disaster down on themselves. An entire regiment of over 1500 British troops had been wiped out by Zulu warriors. The Zulus then sent 4000 warriors against a small detachment of British holding a place called Roarke's Drift. About 100 British against four thousand Zulus. When one soldier asked why they were being asked to fight against such impossible odds, his sergeant replied, 'Because we're all there is. Just us, and nobody else'. Against all odds, the British held Roarke's Drift. Jerry would have to hold the company together himself. he was all there was. Just him, and nobody else.

When Jerry came through the door at home, Diane greeted him with a big kiss. He thought of what Joe had lost, and decided that, given the two situations, Joe's and his, his was infinitely preferable.

In the days and weeks that followed, Jerry was swamped, but never overwhelmed. Dave Albrecht helped out by doing several jobs outside of computer operations, and by lending personnel out to Jerry where they were needed. Allen Sims made sure that all the legal angles were covered and effectively gave Jerry the power-of-attorney necessary to oversee daily operations. He also provided legal advice and wisdom on the matters which gave Jerry the most trouble. All told, the weeks slipped by quickly and the three friends forged a stronger friendship in the face of adversity. By this time, the situation began to take a turn for the better. The company was running almost as smoothly as when Joe had been at the helm. But something was still missing. They still needed Joe for that creative spark necessary to turn a good company into a world-class performer. It was time, thought Jerry.

Chapter 6

Once again, Jerry arrived unannounced at the front gate of Joe's mansion. Hodgekins answered the gate summons and reluctantly let Jerry through. Marie met Jerry at the front steps. She looked better than when Jerry had last seen her, but she still had more worry-lines on her face than Jerry had remembered. This was probably not going to be pleasant, Jerry thought, but it had to be done.

"Good afternoon Marie", said Jerry cheerfully. "You look a bit better than the last time I saw you. Is Joe at home?"

"Yes, sir, he is here", Marie answered warily. "But he is sleeping right now, and I don't really wish to disturb him. Could you come back later when I've had a chance to clean up?"

"Is that time to clean up Joe or the house?", asked Jerry pointedly.

"He isn't ready yet, sir", she protested. "Just give him a little more time. He has gotten less angry in the past week or so. If you would just let him be for a few more days, a week perhaps, I think he might be better able to pull out of his depression".

"I do not agree with you", said Jerry firmly. "I think that the time to act is now. It has been too long already, Marie. He has had time enough to finish his grieving. It is time for him to rejoin the living. I have made arrangements for him to stay at the Chartwell Institute. They have an excellent program for recovering alcoholics".

"But sir! If news of Mr. Talon's true condition reaches the press, they will have a field day with it. He will be ruined!"

"Chartwell has agreed to keep the entire matter confidential. He will be registered under an assumed name and their records will be kept confidential. No one will ever find out, under threat of lawsuit".

"Secrecy of that level can hardly be kept with someone of Mr. Talon's notoriety. Someone will surely recognize him and alert the press".

"He will be kept sequestered from the rest of the patients. That, along with the Institute's policy about privacy, will prevent any leaks. If something should come of the episode after he is released, we will deal with it at that time. By then he will be recovered and, no longer being an invalid, he will be able to prove to everyone that he is fit once again"

"Please, sir!", Marie pleaded. "Don't do this to him! It could destroy him! Just give him a little more time!"

"I am sorry, Marie", said Jerry as he walked past her to the front door. "But the arrangements are already made. We need Joe back. It is time for him to wake from the nightmare".

Marie continued to protest as Jerry walked into the study. Joe was sprawled on the couch, much as Jerry had seen him several weeks before. He was relatively clean, though not clean-shaven. There were fewer bottles surrounding him, but he still stank of liquor. Jerry lifted him to his feet. Joe staggered as he tried to walk.

"Ish it bedtime already, Hodgekinsh?", Joe asked sleepily. "I shtill haven't had my nightcap, yet".

"No, Joe, it is not bedtime yet", answered Jerry, still struggling to keep Joe upright as they headed for the front door. Hodgekins was standing off to the side with a concerned look on his face.

"We will be going for a little ride, Joe. That sounds good, does it not?"

"Shure, shure. That shounds fine to me. Where're we goin', anyway?"

"Oh, just out for a drive", answered Jerry innocently.

"Will we be back in time for my nightcap?", asked Joe as they reached the car.

"Well, I cannot say for sure", answered Jerry as he struggled to keep Joe upright while opening the car door.

"I can't mish my nightcap. Thash the besh part of the day, jush before I go to shleep. Ish so nish to go to shleep. Thash my favorite time of the day".

"I'm sure Mr. Porter will have you home in time for bed", said Marie. She shot Jerry a withering look, which was ignored. Jerry continued to strap Joe in and made sure he locked the door on Joe's side so that Marie couldn't have him pulled out of the car.

"I will give you the address and phone number where you can reach Joe in a few days", said Jerry, as he started the car. "In the meantime, you can reach him through me. you have both my home and work numbers, do you not?"

"Yes sir, we do", answered Hodgekins. By this time, Marie was fit to be tied. Jerry drove away without a wave, deciding he had pressed his luck enough for one day.

The drive to the hospital was fairly pleasant. Joe sat quietly, looking out the window like a two-year-old seeing the world for the first time. Occasionally, his head would loll to one side, then he would pull it upright again and resume looking. He didn't speak much, and what he did say was incoherent and disjointed. Jerry hoped that this hospital knew what it was doing. He missed the old Joe.

Jerry drove up to the hospital receiving entrance. He had phoned ahead to let them know he was coming, and two burly orderlies were waiting with a wheelchair at the entrance. Jerry unlocked Joe's door, then got out as one of the orderlies unstrapped Joe and lifted him into the wheelchair. They all proceeded into the lobby where Jerry met Dr. Wilkens, the head of the clinic.

"Hello, Mr. Porter. So, this is Mr. Nolat?"

"Yes", answered Jerry, with a sly look in his eye, "this is Mr. Nolat".

Jerry turned to Joe and said, "Joe, this is Dr. Wilkens. He will be taking care of you for a little while".

Joe looked up at the doctor and gave him a drunken smile. "Hiya doc!", he said enthusiastically. "Got any Scotch? I'm gettin' real thirsty!"

Dr. Wilkens turned back to Jerry and said, "We'll take it from here, Mr. Porter. Check back with us tomorrow. We should be able to give you a better appraisal of the situation by then".

"Very well, doctor. I think you have your work cut out for you".

"We know what we're doing", the doctor answered confidently.

"I hope so", said Jerry, an anxious look crossing his face. "I hate to do this to a friend".

"Believe me, Mr. Porter, he will thank you for it when he is well again. Just give us a little time with him and let the results speak for themselves".

"Joe, I will be leaving now", said Jerry slowly. "I will come by to see you again tomorrow. All right?"

"Shure, ol' buddy! I jush hope they give me a drink shoon. My moush ish gettin' pretty dry. Hey, doc, how about that drink now?"

"I have something for you in the back. Why don't you come with us and see what we can find?"

"Shoundsh good to me!", answered Joe eagerly. "Shee you later, Jer!"

Jerry looked after the little group as they moved away from him. He hoped he was doing the right thing. he decided that he was. Joe couldn't go on like this and this was the best place to dry him out. Jerry was anxious to see what they could do with Joe here. he wanted his friend back.

When Jerry came to visit a few days later, Joe was not in a very friendly mood. he had decided to bring along Dave Albrecht and Allen Sims for support. They had been as anxious about Joe's condition as Jerry was. They were pleased to see Joe sitting up in bed when they got there.

"Well, if it isn't the Three Stooges", said Joe sarcastically. "I thought you guys would pop up sooner or later".

They each greeted him timidly. They had hoped he would be a little less angry about this, but it looked like that had been wishful thinking.

"How do you feel?", asked Jerry. "You look better than I have seen you for many a day".

"How do I feel?", asked Joe angrily. "I feel awful, that's how I feel. It's bad enough to go cold turkey on this drinking, but they gave me a shot of something, then offered me a drink a little while later. I've never been so sick in all my life! As soon as that whiskey hit my stomach, it came right back up! They told me that if I try to take a drink of anything with alcohol in it, I'd do the same again. Pretty drastic treatment if you ask me!"

"Well, you were in very bad shape when I brought you in here", said Jerry. "I would suppose that radical treatment was necessary to bring you out of it. This hospital is supposed to be the best in California for recovering alcoholics".

"So they tell me", said Joe, his anger beginning to subside a bit. "What I'd like to know is why they keep calling me 'Mr. Nolat'? The first couple of times they called me that I thought they were talking to someone else".

"The doctor, Dr. Wilkens, and I came up with that", answered Jerry. "We felt that it was best to keep your true identity a secret until you got out of here. Who knows what it would have done to the corporation if it was discovered that you were institutionalized here".

Sudden realization crossed Joe's face. "I see", he said more thoughtfully. "A smoke screen so jittery shareholders don't start dumping stock. That would drive down the value of the company in a hurry. We might need a few years to recover from the loss. Yes, that was a wise move on your part, Jerry".

"Thank you, sir", said Jerry, a slight smile on his face. "By the time anyone finds out who you are, you should be back at Talon Industries running the show. There might be a minor hiccup in our stock, but nothing like the disaster we would have had if we were found out while you were still institutionalized".

"I suppose you're right", said Joe. "I just wish there were an easier way to do this. My head feels like someone's taken a hammer to it. I think it's in competition with the stomach to see which can make me feel the worst. Right now I'd say they're dead even on that score".

"I talked to Dr. Wilkens a few days ago, when I was arranging for this visit", said Jerry. "He was rather upset with me about having let you deteriorate this much before bringing you in. We did nothing about getting you help right away, in order for you to vent your grief. He said that we should have brought you in immediately so that they could begin treatment for you drinking and your depression. I guess I was wrong in waiting".

"I don't suppose any real harm has been done", said Joe comfortingly. "I've lost some time, but I don't think it will make much difference in the long run. You guys have kept the company running while I've been gone. That's the important thing".

"I think we all have a good deal more respect for you, after trying to fill your shoes for the past few weeks", said Jerry. "It has not been easy for any of the staff", he said as he looked at Dave and Allen. They both nodded in agreement. Looking back at Joe he said, "We will certainly be glad to have you back Joe".

"Well, then", said Joe with a twinkle in his eye, "see what you can do about getting me un-institutionalized".

"The doctor says you will still need to stay here for a few more days, just for observation", said Jerry. "Then they have some sort of outpatient program to enroll you in. He called it the Recovering Alcoholics program, or RA for short. Apparently, they will also be teaming you up with a partner, another recovering alcoholic. My understanding is that you are supposed to keep each other from going back to drinking. I am sure Dr. Wilkens will fill you in on the details in time. For now, you are supposed to rest and relax. When you are healthy again, they will send you home".

"Home", said Joe, a hint of sorrow creeping into his voice. "Yes, I guess that's inevitable. Home to face the ghosts".

Jerry felt himself beginning to choke up. "I think we should probably be going", he said finally.

"Yeah, I've still got a couple of diagnostics to run on Talon Aerospace's computers", said Dave hastily.

"And the folks I have preparing some documents for Bergway Chemical needed my decision on some briefs", added Allen.

"I will see you tomorrow, Joe", said Jerry as the three friends walked through the door. "Give me a call if there is anything you need".

"Thanks for stopping by, guys", Joe called after them. Home, he thought after they had left. What an empty place that would be now. What an empty place, indeed.

Several more days passed. Jerry came to the clinic to see Joe each day, usually with Dave or Allen (or both) in tow. Joe improved steadily and became more jovial. Finally, it was time to leave.

"Mr. Nolat, I have one last form which needs your signature", said Dr. Wilkens. "This is in regards to our outpatient program at Recovering Alcoholics. We strongly recommend this program to all of our patients when they leave. I also have the name of a psychologist who is quite good. Both of these are optional, but, as I say, they are highly recommended".

"Thanks, Dr. Wilkens. I expect that I will take you up on both suggestions. I can't afford to lose any more time and I certainly don't intend to go through another period like I've just had. I'll enroll in both. Well Jerry, I guess it's time to go".

"Thank you, Dr. Wilkens", said Jerry as he shook the doctor's hand. "You have done us all a great service, and I appreciate it".

"Just doing my job", said Dr. Wilkens. "It does me good to see people walk out of here healthy again. That's one of the rewards of this job. It helps to counter the negatives involved in my work. I'm just glad to see you whole again, Mr. Tal... rather, Mr. Nolat", he said with a conspiratorial look in his eye.

As they were driving home, Joe was very quiet. Jerry felt a little uneasy, but decided that it would pass. The gates opened as soon as they approached the mansion. He guessed that the household was keeping an eye out for Joe. He pulled up to the front steps and the front door opened. The whole staff came rushing out the door. It was all Joe could do to get out of the car, with the small mob trying to greet him.

"We are so glad to see you back, sir!", said Hodgekins enthusiastically.

"How do you feel, Mr. Talon?", asked Marie.

"Fine, Marie, just fine", answered Joe. "How are you all doing?"

"I don't know about the rest of them", answered Bill, "but I'm bored stiff. I haven't had anything to do for weeks, except driving Marie around when she's shopping. Where do we go first, boss?"

"Well", said Joe thoughtfully, "I had considered a quick trip to the liquor store".

The smiles disappeared from everyone's face and a stunned silence settled over them. Jerry coughed a little. Hodgekins shuffled his feet. Marie was aghast. Suddenly, Joe's face broke out in a big smile.

"Just kidding, just kidding!", he laughed. "I just wanted to see if you were all paying attention".

The little group laughed somewhat nervously, then more easily when they saw that he was just joking.

"I think that the first place to go would be to work, don't you Jerry?"

"It has been a long time since you have been there", answered Jerry. "I imagine that it would give morale a boost if you were to tour the building. People have been fairly curious as to why you have not been present for so long. We managed to keep the true reason quiet, but rumors fly in the absence of the owner".

"I'll bet they did", said Joe. "All right, let's get going. Well, Bill, what are you waiting for?"

"Nothing boss", answered Bill as he hurried toward the garage. "Nothing at all!"

Shortly after Joe arrived at Talon Industries, the whole place was buzzing. Several people did double-takes as he walked by. One office worker ran right into the mail cart. Once they got the mess cleaned up, the office worker and the mailroom clerk looked at each other in amazement.

Nancy was busily typing up a document for Jerry Porter when Joe walked by.

"Any calls, Nancy?", Joe asked nonchalantly.

Nancy's finger froze on the 'y' key long enough to type the letter about ten times. Her mouth opened in surprise, then closed again as she recovered herself.

"Mr. Talon?", she shouted gleefully. "Mr. Talon, it is you!" She rushed over and gave him a warm hug, then remembered herself and stepped back. "No sir", she answered formally. "No calls for you today".

"OK, thanks", said Joe breezily. "I should be here for awhile if any come in

"Welcome back, sir", Nancy called after him.

"Thanks, it's good to be back", said Joe as he went into his office. "Oh, and would you arrange a meeting of the department heads for this afternoon, please?"

"Right away, Mr. Talon", she answered.

Several phone calls came in for Joe as word of his return spread around the company. By the time the department meeting commenced, the entire office seemed to be charged with electricity. When Joe walked through the door of the meeting room, a great hush fell across the assembly.

"Hello, everybody", Joe said with a smile. "It's been a long time. Let's get down to business".

Jerry Porter led off. "Talon stock has shown a minor slump since the last quarter.", he said. "We can probably attribute that to the disappearance of our CEO and the fallout from the Davis Aircraft fiasco. Now that we have the finances straightened out over there and our CEO is back", he turned and smiled at Joe, "we can expect a much better showing in the next quarter".

"As far as legal matters are concerned", Allen Sims began, "I am afraid that we ran into some problems trying to prosecute Ethan Davis. He covered his tracks quite well on the Davis Aircraft virus. We have not been able to find any evidence which conclusively links him to any of the problems there. Insofar as the missing records are concerned, we have not been able to turn up anything on who took them or where they are. I am afraid we have hit a dead end".

"And as far as that virus in the Davis Aircraft computer is concerned", Dave Albrecht chimed in, "I have a few ideas on who could have put it together, but I haven't been able to locate a couple of suspects. If I could get some help from your investigators, Allen, I might be able to find them".

"My resources are at your disposal", said Allen. "I will send a few of my people over to see you tomorrow in regards to 'missing persons' research".

"Thanks, we sure need them", said Dave.

The remainder of the meeting was division reports given by each division head. Joe listened quietly, occasionally asking a question. After two hours, the meeting adjourned. Unlike the previous meeting Joe had presided over, this one ended with almost everyone smiling and talking excitedly. The boss was back and was once again himself.

Joe met with Dave, Jerry, and Allen at his office after the meeting. They were all a bit tired after the meeting, and Joe was exhausted from his first day back at work. It had been an emotional day for him.

"Well, they seemed to be happy to see you back, boss", said Dave with a smile.

"Yeah, it went a little better than the last one, didn't it?", Joe mused.

"I should imagine our stock will go up appreciably within the next few days", said Jerry. "Even though we were able to keep the true situation under wraps, the media was still having a field day with speculation about what had happened to you. Everything from a stroke to kidnapping was posited by them".

"I had one lady ask me if you had committed suicide", chuckled Allen.

"Not far off the mark", said Joe sadly. "There were times I considered it, even when I was plastered".

The mood in the room became more somber after this. Finally Joe said that he thought it was time to go home. He said goodbye to his friends and snuck out the back way. Bill met him around the back, then drove him home. Joe had no trouble sleeping that night. No nightmares disturbed him all night, since the doctor had given him a sleeping pill.

<u>Chapter 7</u>

On the following Monday, Joe went to his first Recovering Alcoholics meeting. It was an upbeat meeting and the people there represented a fairly complete cross-section of the population: the rich, the poor, and everything in between. Joe was introduced to his RA 'buddy', as the organizers called him.

"Hi, I'm Pieter Van Vrees".

"Pleased to meet you, Pieter. I'm Joe Talon".

"I remember reading about a Joseph Talon in the papers. That wouldn't be you would it?"

"The same".

Pieter's mouth just about hit the floor. "I don't believe it! What are you doing here?"

"The same as you, I expect. Drying out".

"But the papers said you went into seclusion or something. It had to do with losing you family in that forest fire up by Big Bear, didn't it?"

"Yeah", said Joe, looking away for a moment. "And I *was* in seclusion. More precisely, I was dead drunk for several weeks. That's what I'm doing here now. I'd appreciate it if you kept my true identity under your hat for a little while, though".

"Well I'll be a son of a gun! I figured someone with your kind of money would just buy a cure or get a shrink from a fancy clinic to treat you, not hook you up with some broken-down old pilot like me!"

"There are some things that money can't buy", said Dr. Wilkens, as he ambled up to the men. "Hello again Joe".

"Hello Dr. Wilkens", said Joe, extending his hand. "What brings you here tonight? Checking up on your old patients?".

"Let's just say I have a vested interest in some of them", Dr. Wilkens said with a smile. "How are you feeling, Joe?"

"Much better, thanks. But I wouldn't want to repeat the last few days again. Not for any amount of money".

"Yes, it has been a rough road, hasn't it?"

"Rough is the word, all right. I haven't been to see that shrink yet. Any words of wisdom before I go?"

" Just be yourself", answered Dr. Wilkens. "Honesty is the best policy when it comes to analysis. If you give the counselor straightforward answers, he or she will be able to solve your problems that much more easily".

"They've been able to help me a bunch in the short time I've been going", said Pieter. "I found out all sorts of things that were wrong with my attitude. Turns out that I was a perfectionist and that was making me kick myself every time I made a mistake. I'm a little easier on myself now, and I feel a lot better because of it".

"Well, lets hope that they can help me. I need all the help I can get. That sleeping pill you prescribed is letting me sleep at night, doc, but I still think about my family sometimes when I'm awake. I'll see something that reminds me of Martha and then I get depressed again. I hope they can snap me out of this vicious circle of hope and depression".

"It may not happen overnight, but they have had considerable experience with grieving patients. You're not alone, Joe. Many people have lost someone they loved. They go through a bad time, but then they pull out of it, often without any counseling. You will just have to be patient and not lose your confidence".

"I hope you're right, doc", Joe said quietly.

As the meeting was breaking up, Pieter and Joe exchanged addresses and phone numbers. While Joe was driving home, he thought about what the doctor had said and decided he would call for an appointment at the psychologist's tomorrow. He was still running tired. After no exercise for so long a time, he felt his heart pound after emotional or physical activity. He had gotten plenty of both for the past few days, but he was beginning to get back in shape. Patience, he told himself. You have to learn to crawl before you can run again. He just hoped it wouldn't take too long. He had already lost so much time.

Joe had Pieter over two nights later. Pieter was astounded at Joe's home. He had grown up in a lower middle-class household where his dad had rented the house they lived in. He had only seen mansions at a distance, never up close like this.

"The only thing this place doesn't have", Pieter said after they finished the tour, "is a bowling alley!"

"Well, my dad and I were never into bowling much", said Joe, trying hard to suppress a smile. "But if I ever take up the sport, I'll have you over for a game".

"Thanks. That might save me a few bucks now and then".

Joe motioned Pieter into the study. Pieter slowly scanned the room, taking everything in. He noticed the shelves of books, the old mahogany desk, the pictures on the walls, then he stopped at the windows.

"Redecorating?"

Joe followed his gaze to the windows, then understood the question. He sat down heavily in his desk chair. "My wife was in the process of picking out the curtains when she...", Joe broke off suddenly.

Pieter saw Joe's discomfort and sat down opposite the desk. "Sorry", he said, looking away from the windows. "You must miss her a lot, huh?"

"Every day", said Joe sadly. "I thought the pain would ease with time, but it hasn't. The psychologist says that grief takes time to overcome, especially for people who have lost a spouse".

"Yeah, I remember what it was like. My wife died about five years ago. Took me almost a year to get past the pain. That's what started me drinking, but it took the loss of my business to finally make me get help".

"What did your wife die of? That is, if you don't mind talking about it".

"Nah, it doesn't bother me anymore. She had cancer. Took her about two-and-a-half years to die. It wasn't so sudden as yours, so I had time to brace myself. I don't know which is worse: having your wife die suddenly without suffering for a long time, or having her wither on the vine with cancer. Oh, you can see the end coming, but it's very unsettling watching them go through all of that pain. There was absolutely nothing I could do for her to stop the cancer, and, close to the end, the pain-killers didn't seem to work too well. I guess you could say that I had my nightmares before my wife died, while you had yours afterwards. I still have nightmares from time to time now, but they aren't as bad as seeing her suffer in real life".

"I'm sorry. I probably shouldn't have asked".

"Don't worry about it", answered Pieter. "She's out of pain now. That's what is important".

"I guess we've all suffered our losses over the years. You said something about losing your business, too. What business were you in?"

"I was a commercial pilot. I had a small air-tanker business during the fire season, and I would do short-hauls of cargo the rest of the year. It was a pretty good business, too. Only problem was that I started to drink the profits. Then I started drinking while I was flying. I came in too hard on a landing one day and cracked-up my plane. That was the end of my business, since I didn't have enough money left to repair or replace my plane".

"What kind of plane did you fly?"

"An old C-119, a Flying Boxcar", answered Pieter wistfully. "She was old and a little cantankerous, but she got me from here to there in one piece. Even when I wrecked her, I walked away from it. That was a good old plane".

"What was this about operating during fire season?

"That was the best part of the business. During fire season, I contracted with the U.S. Forestry Service to fight forest fires. I would fly up to a small airbase near a forest fire when the Feds or California Division of Forestry gave me a call. I used to carry retardant over the fires and help to put them out. Waterbombing, some called it. I preferred to call it firebombing. After all, we were bombing fires, not water."

"How effective could one plane be against a forest fire, though?"

"By myself, I wasn't much good, usually because by the time they called on me, they were already fighting a major fire. The CDF planes usually snuffed the fires out when they were just getting started. For the major fires, though, they couldn't always handle it by themselves. Get a few contractors together with the Forestry Service planes, though, and we could really slow down a fire. We liked to think that we put out the fires, but looking back on it, it was a team effort. The boys on the ground did more work than we did, but it wasn't as glamorous. I remember fighting a fire up in Northern California one season a few years back. They had some smokejumpers brought up to that one. Now there were some impressive ground personnel. About a twenty of these guys parachuted into an area in the path of the fire and built a firebreak to stop it. The bombers narrowed the fire down by dropping retardant on the flanks. By the time it reached that firebreak, it was down to only about a mile wide. We stopped it cold and most of the credit goes to those smokejumpers. Nobody could have gotten in there any faster, or done so much in such a short time. Although, they could sure have used some heavy equipment to help. A bulldozer is always worth its weight in gold for making firebreaks".

"How expensive was it to operate your plane?", asked Joe curiously.

"Not bad. Only a few thousand a year for upkeep, and the purchase price was real low, since it was Air Force surplus. They have a lot of aircraft that get sold dirt cheap as surplus. If I hadn't drunk the profits, I planned to get another plane to help with the business. I could have expanded my operations with just a bit more money. It probably would have been an S-2 this time. The Forestry guys offered a deal where contractors could turn in their old planes for newer S-2 torpedo bombers. I guess they got worried about our old bombers crashing or something".

"What could you do with a few million dollars?", asked Joe pointedly.

"Who knows? Done a whole lot more hauling, that's for sure!"

"Or fought a lot more fires", said Joe, a thoughtful expression coming across his face.

Pieter suddenly fixed his gaze on Joe. "What are you thinking?"

"I'm thinking of a new hobby. Everybody should have a hobby, don't you think?"

"I suppose. What kind of hobby did you have in mind?"

"A firefighting organization".

Pieter's face showed his surprise, then understanding.

"The perfect way to get revenge for that fire that killed your family, huh?"

"Exactly! Imagine an organization which could send fifty firebombers out to fight forest fires. That would take the punch out of just about any blaze, don't you think?"

"It would slow it down. But like I said, it takes more than just planes to kill a fire. If there's any embers left smoldering down there, your planes could pack up and head for home, thinking their job was done, only to have the fire reignite. You would need to work with the Forestry people on the ground. Planes by themselves aren't enough".

"What if we added a ground contingent to the force?", asked Joe, as he looked off into a corner of the ceiling.

"Fine", said Pieter skeptically. "But how do you plan to get them there?"

"Fly them in", replied Joe simply.

"Fly them in?", asked Pieter incredulously. "Do you know how much it would cost to transport a couple of hundred guys around the countryside? And what about heavy equipment?"

"As you said at our first meeting, it's nice to have money. I can afford to fly them around. What's more, I think I could probably buy the transport planes *and* the equipment. We could have a completely self-contained firefighting force at our disposal, any hour of the day or night. All we would need would be the location of the fire. We could do the rest".

"Sounds like pie-in-the-sky to me", snorted Pieter. "You couldn't afford the cost. I used old beat-up surplus aircraft. Even those weren't cheap. If you're thinking of fifty tankers and a bunch of transports, you're talking hundreds of millions of dollar. Plus you would have to hire personnel to operate all of this. I think you should consider a different hobby, Joe".

"You don't mind if I think about it a while, do you?"

"Be my guest. Just don't get too hopeful about all this. I don't think even you can afford it!"

"We'll see", said Joe distantly. Pieter could see he was getting nowhere trying to dissuade Joe, so he decided to call it a night. Joe saw him to the door, then went back to the study. A mobile firefighting force. That had possibilities, he decided. He would definitely have to look into this tomorrow at work. Now he had something more interesting to do. He had no idea, however, just what sort of genie he had let out of the bottle.

Chapter 8

Joe was at work at 7 A.M. the next day. Nancy greeted him when she came in 45 minutes later.

"Good morning Mr. Talon", she said cheerfully. "You are certainly here early today".

"Morning Nancy", Joe replied. "Yes, I had a few things I wanted to get organized first thing. I've put together a short list of people I want to contact today. Would you see if you can reach them for me?"

"Certainly", Nancy answered. She began to examine the list. "I see you are calling some of your friends in the Department of Defense. Are you getting ready to bid on another contract?"

"Not really. I need to talk to them about surplus equipment we might use for an organization I'm thinking about starting".

"I should have no trouble reaching them. It is almost eleven o'clock in Washington. Just right for catching them between breakfast and lunch".

"Fine", said Joe absently. He was already thinking about something else, thought Nancy. She had seen him this way before, when an idea struck him, taking him in a completely different direction. 'LFP' was what Joe's confidants called it. That, coupled with his uncanny sense of future events, had saved the organization more than once. He had managed to turn events to his advantage, to quickly capitalize on changing markets, to increase both his personal fortune and his standing among his peers. She began dialing the first number on the list, still musing about these things.

"Pentagon , how may I direct your call?", answered a male voice.

"Could you connect me to General Walter Budman, please", answered Nancy.

"One moment, please. May I ask who is calling?"

"Mr. Joseph Talon".

"Very good. Please hold on a moment".

Nancy buzzed Joe, who picked up the phone in his office as she hung up.

"This is General Budman", answered a deep voice.

"General? This is Joe Talon".

"Good morning, Mr. Talon. It's been awhile since we spoke last. How may I help you today?"

"I'm interested in purchasing some surplus military aircraft. I'm particularly interested in cargo aircraft. What types do you have for sale at the moment?"

"It depends on who is doing the buying. Would these be used domestically or are you going to sell them to a foreign country?"

"These would be used in the U.S. by my people".

"Very well. Let me turn you over to my aide for the details. We have a number of aircraft available at the moment. He can give you the specifics. I believe the Major is out of the office now. I'll have him call you back as soon as he gets in".

"Thank you General Budman. I appreciate your help".

"Certainly, Mr. Talon. It's always a pleasure doing business with you".

By the time Jerry arrived, Joe had completed several other calls to people all over the U.S. and Canada.

"Good Morning, Joe", Jerry said as he walked in. "Sorry to be late. Traffic accident on the freeway".

"Morning, Jerry", said Joe. "I've got a few things to talk over with you. I think it would probably be a good idea to get Allen and Dave in here, too".

"Sounds important. Are we taking over another company?"

"No, we're starting another company. I'll explain as soon as the others get here".

Ten minutes later, Allen and Dave arrived. Then Joe dropped his bombshell.

"Gentlemen. We are starting a new organization. I want to call it Firebombers Incorporated. The primary purpose of this organization will be to fight fires, mostly in wilderness areas. Most of the aircraft to be used can be purchased as military surplus. I've already made some inquiries about this. I will be handing off assignments to each of you. Jerry, as usual you get the lion's share of the work. You'll be responsible for coordinating the hiring of personnel, purchasing most of the equipment, and interfacing with the various government agencies responsible.

"Allen, I want you to handle all of the legal problems. There are a lot of people who are going to be involved in this effort, either directly or indirectly. Somewhere along the way, we're going to step on somebody's toes. It will be your job to anticipate legal problems to be circumvented and to perform damage control if we make any mistakes.

"Dave, I want you to talk to a friend of mine, Pieter Van Vrees, about useful electronic and computer devices we could employ. He's done wilderness firefighting before and may be able to give you some ideas on things to make our job a lot easier. Being our resident computer and electronics whiz, I want you to work up plans for the on-board systems to be installed in our equipment. Now let me give you the details on what I have in mind".

He walked over to the coffee bar and poured everyone a cup as he talked.

"I met a gentleman several days ago at a Recovering Alcoholics meeting who turned out to be an ex-firebomber pilot. After talking to him for awhile, I became convinced that there was an opportunity here which I had never considered before. Right now, the Cold War has effectively ended. As a result, there are substantial cutbacks-underway in our military. What will happen to all the personnel and equipment which is surplus now? Most of the equipment will be sold for scrap or mothballed. Most of the personnel will be out job-hunting with an economy that is already boasting almost 10%-unemployment. In short, we have a perfect situation here in which to mate up the personnel with the equipment they are familiar with, and do it at a substantial savings".

Joe moved around the room and distributed the coffee to his friends. Then settled into his chair.

"At the moment, there are a few contractors out there who do firefighting in the forests", Joe said as he sipped his coffee. "In addition, the Forestry Services operate their own aircraft. From what Pieter has told me, these guys are very good at their jobs, but there's never enough of them. That's where we come in. We could build up a force of, say, fifty to seventy-five firebombers, along with a small force of tankers to refuel the aircraft and provide air-traffic control".

"That is going to cost a tremendous amount of money!", exclaimed Jerry. "How could we afford it? We are still paying off the debt for Talon Aerospace".

"I'll be kicking in my own money to cover some of the start-up costs", said Joe. "The Forestry Service will pay a fee for firebombers used in actually fighting the fire. The transport costs would probably be on us, unless one of you can figure out a way to get the government to pay for that, too", he added, looking expectantly around the room.

"Nothing occurs to me immediately", replied Allen. "I will make some inquiries and see if there is a legal precedent for it. Perhaps such a thing has happened in the past. If so, we might be able to capitalize on that incident to justify charging the government for the cost of transport. I will see what I can turn up".

"We might be able to defray the costs of the aircraft by using the bulk of them for commercial transport during the off-season", said Joe. "That was how Pieter ran his operation. He said that it was lucrative enough for him to consider expanding his operations. That's something for you to look into, Jerry".

"I would imagine this would be strictly cargo, no passengers?", asked Jerry.

"That's the way I see it", said Joe. "I bet Allen's people would have a fit over the insurance and legal costs of carrying passengers, right Allen?"

"To be certain", Allen replied.

"I plan to talk further with Pieter in order to get a better idea of what I want", said Joe. "I think you guys have enough things to do for now, right?"

They all agreed that they did. The meeting broke up and Joe got to work with the business of the corporation.

Joe's mind kept drifting back to his new endeavor, though. He called Pieter up and asked if they could meet that night for further talks. Pieter came by at six and joined Joe for a splendid dinner. Afterwards, they wandered into the study and began talking.

"I sprung the idea on my staff at work, today", said Joe triumphantly. "I think they were interested. I gave them a few preliminary things to do and told one of them, Dave Albrecht, to get in touch with you. He should call in a day or two".

"He already did. We're meeting over at Talon Industries tomorrow about lunchtime".

"Good. He's not wasting any time, I see".

"Neither are you", said Pieter guardedly. "Are you sure you know what you're doing?"

"We're only into the research phase of this right now", said Joe smoothly. "No money has been committed to anything, as of yet. If we find out that this isn't feasible, or that it's too expensive, we haven't lost anything. If we discover that it is feasible, though", he paused for effect, "then we jump in with both feet!"

"Just make sure there's no potholes where you plan to land", said Pieter quietly.

"So, Pieter", said Joe, using his most charming smile, "tell me more about firefighting".

"I don't know whether I should", said Pieter with a frown. "We talked about it for less than an hour last night, and look at you today. You seem to be the kid in the candy shop, all ready to raid the shelves!"

"Well", said Joe with a hurt tone in his voice, "I guess I could talk to someone else about it". Joe turned his head to the side, then glanced sidelong at Pieter. "But you've already lit the match. I'm afraid this is one fire you won't be able to put out. Best thing to do is give me the right information, otherwise I might go talk to someone else and get the wrong information. Now wouldn't you feel bad if that happened", Joe said teasingly.

"All right, all right, enough already! What do you want to know about?"

"How did they tell you where to go when you had to fight a fire?", Joe asked.

"Forestry Service people would call me up if the weather looked bad in a particular area. Once the fire season was underway, I would keep one ear glued to the National Weather Service radio to find out if any lightning storms were predicted for an area. Once they were, I'd plot out a course to get up there and cancel my freight hauls for that period of time. Four out of five times, the system worked pretty reliably. It was usually busiest in the summer, but there were some isolated incidents in the off-season. Sometimes, I got to pick up a little extra pocket-change from an arson fire".

"You mean people even set fires in wilderness areas?", asked Joe in surprise. "I thought the only places arsonists worked was in the city. What is there of any value in the forest?"

"I wish I knew why they did it", said Pieter, shaking his head. "I guess some people just get their kicks out of setting fires".

"Well, once you got a call, then what happened?"

"I would fly up to the air attack base where Forestry was servicing aircraft. They usually had a strip big enough to handle the Forts and other big planes, along with the gear to fill them up".

"What's a 'Fort'?"

"That's a B-17 Flying Fortress. You know, the big bombers we used in World War II to bomb Germany?"

"You mean, people still fly those things?", asked Joe incredulously.

"Not much anymore. Like I said the other night, Forestry is trying to phase out the older planes. Only one or two outfits still operate Forts. They tell me that they're steady as a rock on the approach to a fire. That's an important feature in a situation where you've got thermals all over the place. Fires can produce some fierce updrafts. My poor old plane would buck like a bronco sometimes when I flew over hotspots".

"What do you drop on the fires?", asked Joe. "Water?"

"Mostly long-term retardant with my plane. Helicopters dumped water a lot. But there are all kinds of retardants out there. Water is the least effective. Some of the long-term retardants will snuff a fire right out. Those that are nitrogen-based, like Phos-Check and Fire-Trol, fertilize the ground after they've stopped the fire. That helps the area to regrow again. Sort of a dual-purpose chemical. In between, there's gels and short-term retardants that will take some of the fight out of the blaze, but may not kill it. Even if you use long-terms, they may not be able to reach the actual fire if they get hung-up in the trees on the way down. Firefighting is an art and, even though I've been doing it for almost twenty-five years, there's still things to learn".

"What about fighting the fire on the ground?".

"Ah, now you've moved into something I know very little about. I'm afraid you would have to ask the ground commanders about that. My bag is flying, not shoveling".

"Hmmm...", Joe said, a thoughtful look on his face. After a moment his face brightened. "I think I know just the guy! There was a battalion commander up at Kingfisher Creek during the fire there. I'll bet he could answer my questions. But what was his name", he said with a frown. "I'll have to think about that. Maybe I can remember it tomorrow. I'm feeling kind of beat, now".

"I think that's my cue to leave", said Pieter with a chuckle. "Boy, I think I ate too much tonight!", he said as he struggled to get up. "That cook of yours really serves a mean dinner".

"Of course", said Joe with a smile. "Why do you think I keep her around? You available tomorrow night to sample her cuisine again?"

"Well, if you insist. After all, I wouldn't want to hurt her feelings by not coming back for more!"

"Of course not!", said Joe with a laugh. "Six o'clock, then?"

"Sounds good to me", said Pieter, as he walked out the door to the study. "I'll let myself out. Good night Joe".

"'Night, Pieter", Joe called after him. He heard Pieter say goodnight to Hodgekins, then Joe started upstairs. This was getting more interesting all the time, he thought. Maybe life was worth living again, after all.

Pieter and Joe met for dinner several more nights. Joe was still having difficulty remembering the name of the firefighter up in the mountains. Finally, he asked his chauffeur, Bill Thompson, if he could remember the man's name. Bill said he couldn't, but that he would think about it for awhile. After racking his brain, Bill remembered the name, Zack Dobson. Joe hurried back to the office and called Allen Sims into his office.

"Allen, I've got a job for one of your investigators to do", said Joe as Allen walked into his office. "I need to find a fireman by the name of Zack Dobson. He was at the fire up at Kingfisher Creek, so I would assume that he works around there somewhere. I need to talk to him about some things in regards to this Firebombers project".

"I will have my people get on it right away", Allen assured him. "And I have also taken the liberty of bringing some preliminary documents over which deal with the Firebombers project. I believe they cover all the areas of risk and liability which such an operation would entail. See if they meet with your approval".

"OK, Allen. I think that covers everything for now. Let me know as soon as you find that fireman".

After Allen had left, Jerry came in.

"Hello, Jerry. What have you got?"

"I have compiled a list of possible transport aircraft for you to peruse, Joe. I am still working on some of the other details. Has Allen brought the legal documents by yet?"

"Yes, he just dropped them off. I still have to check with Dave to see if he's found out anything on the electronics".

"He has had lunch with Mr. Van Vrees two or three times, as far as I know. He seems to be learning a great deal from the gentleman, and has begun to form some ideas of what we will need".

"Yes, Pieter told me about the meetings. It looks like things are progressing nicely. What's your opinion on this project, Jerry?"

Jerry began to shuffle nervously, then looked away from Joe. "The project may not have validity", he said finally. He turned back to face Joe and said, "Of course, that is my personal opinion.

I cannot form a worthwhile opinion until all of the information has been analyzed".

"Pieter said almost the exact same thing when I first proposed it to him", said Joe. "I'll tell you the same thing I told him: If it turns out not to be feasible, I'll drop it. But not until that time".

"Yes, of course", said Jerry evasively. "Is there anything else you need, sir?"

"No, I think that covers everything", said Joe, a hint of exasperation in his voice. Maybe a little more confidence from my friends, he thought.

At dinner that night, Joe read off the list of available surplus aircraft to Pieter. After Joe had finished, Pieter spoke up.

"What exactly are you planning on carrying in this transport?"

"Whatever it takes to fight a fire".

"Well, I've seen all kinds of equipment at fires. I've seen firetrucks, helicopters, bulldozers, and ambulances. Some guys even rent U-Haul trucks to carry water from engine to engine. I don't imagine you're going to bring along any helicopters, at least not on board a transport, so we can scratch that from the list. Your bombers are going to have to be propeller driven, so the transports should probably be the same. You'll be flying into and out of small airports, maybe even fields. And you'll want something that has a pretty good range, in addition to being able to carry a heavy load. I imagine you want it capable of carrying paratroopers? You know, firejumpers?"

"Yes to all of the above. What would you recommend?"

"I'd say the best choice for the job is the C-130 Hercules. I liked my C-119 for a bomber, but for maximum transport versatility, the C-130 is hard to beat. In fact, I've seen Army photos of C-130s dropping cargo by parachute and doing a nifty little maneuver where they drop the rear gate down and just touch the ramp down long enough to push a truck on a pallet out the back. The plane's wheels don't even touch the ground, if the pilot is good enough. 'Course it might be a little hard on the truck's suspension, but if the Army can do it, I don't see why we couldn't. If we could drop the equipment off without the pallet, it could be driven out of the way of the next transport dropping a vehicle off. That would be a good way to use fields or dirt roads or even highways, if they were straight enough and didn't have any wires around them. We could even put JATO packs on the sides to give them extra lift once the truck was dropped off".

"You said we", said Joe quietly.

"I guess I did at that", said Pieter sheepishly. "Well, after all, if you're going to go into this thing, and it looks like you are, you're going to need all the help you can get, even from a broken-down old pilot like me".

"You're right there", said Joe with a smile. "And what the heck is a JATO pack?"

"Oh, it's something they use on planes in short-takeoff situations. Basically, they're rocket packs which are bolted onto the outside of the aircraft's fuselage. When the plane starts down the runway, the co-pilot ignites the JATOs to give his plane more speed. They're usually angled down so they provide more lift for the plane, as well. A handy item for short take-offs. We could probably pick some up with the rest of this surplus stuff. I don't think we could use them around areas with dry grass during the fire season, though, unless your whiz kids could come up with something that didn't throw off any embers".

"I suppose that would be a job for the Bergway Chemical folks", said Joe. He proceeded to pour some more cider into each glass. "What would you recommend for bombers?"

"Well", said Pieter, scratching his head. "I'm afraid my recommendation for a bomber won't show up on this list. It's not a surplus aircraft. In fact, it's not even an American-made aircraft. It's manufactured in Canada. It's called a Canadair CL-415. It's an amphibian, a plane that's built to land in water. They can skim across the surface of a lake and suck the water right into the tanks, then lift off again and bomb the fire. Then, they turn right around and come back to the lake to reload. Those planes can deliver a phenomenal amount of water onto a fire. I heard a story of a CL-215, its predecessor, that the Yugoslavians bought a few years back which dumped over 137,000 gallons on a forest fire in one day!"

"That's incredible! Where can we buy these things?"

"I think they're only made in Canada, so I guess you'd have to talk to the folks at Canadair about it", answered Pieter. "I've only seen a couple at fires in the US, but I think the Canadians will let them be exported".

"But you said that water alone was not enough to put out the fire", Joe protested.

"Unless you can mix the water with a fire-retardant. There is a short-term retardant called Class A Foam, but no long-term mixable retardant. The planes always have to return to an air-attack base to reload with that stuff.

"A few companies have experimented with systems to inject long-term retardant into the tank and mix it with the water. If you could perfect that, then you could have the best of both worlds. You'd have the ability to drop long-term retardant on the fire combined with the ease of reloading your tanks with water. If your people could work it out, you might be able to make a mint rich enough to keep your 'hobby' affordable".

Joe's mind shifted into high-gear at this point. He suddenly realized that if he could make this idea work, some of the other ideas they were kicking around might also work. If they could be marketed worldwide - paydirt!

"Pieter", Joe said excitedly, "I think you just hit the nail on the head. Not only could we fight fires, but some of this technology could be sold to other companies for a handsome profit! It looks like my 'hobby' has the potential to become a first-rate business!"

"I think you may be right. But first, you've got to *make* it work. That's one little hitch that has stopped a whole bunch of people from making money on better ideas than this".

"Well, if we can't do it with the resources I can bring to bear on the problem, then I'm a monkey's uncle!"

"I'll keep a spare bunch of bananas handy just in case we need them", said Pieter with a smile. "You never know when some of the family might drop by".

"Everybody's a comedian", Joe sighed. "I swear, none of my friends has any confidence in me. You wait and see. This project will fly. If I have to throw it off the top of a building, it's going to fly!"

I just don't want to be next to that building when he tries it, though, thought Pieter.

Chapter 9

Monday morning, Allen Sims came by to see Joe again. Joe was on the phone, so Allen sat down and started to read some of the paperwork he was carrying.

"Morning Allen", said Joe, as he put the phone down. "And what may I do for you, this fine day!"

"You certainly seem to be in a good mood for a Monday", observed Allen. "We found your missing fireman. It seems he resides up in Big Bear and works for their fire department. I have his phone number and address here for you", he said as he handed them to Joe.

"Excellent!", said Joe. "I want to set up a meeting between our executive staff, Pieter Van Vrees, and Zack Dobson as soon as possible".

"What do you plan to discuss?"

"Ways and means of implementing this idea of mine", said Joe, stretching luxuriantly. "Now that we have all of the key players accounted for, I'd say it's time for a meeting of the minds".

"On a more disappointing note, my investigators were unable to identify the hacker who developed the Davis Aircraft virus. We located all of the people Dave Albrecht listed, but none of them would claim the virus".

"Not surprising, considering the negative publicity it received. I don't think it will matter much. I would have liked to have been able to tie Ethan Davis to that fiasco, but we'll just have to wait for another opportunity".

Zack Dobson couldn't make it to a meeting any earlier than Friday, so Joe had a few more days to think things through. Pieter came over to Joe's for dinner Wednesday night. Pieter hardly had time to take the first bite before Joe was firing questions at him.

"How do you bomber pilots know where to make a drop? It seems like you might have some collisions with all those planes trying to get at the fire".

"It probably would be more dangerous if we didn't have some coordination", said Pieter around a mouthful of food. "There's a Forestry Service guy who flies around in a light plane, directing the air attack. He makes sure that everybody has a specific orbit and altitude, and directs individual planes onto the fire. He can also give advice on which direction to approach the fire from to get the best results".

"What difference does angle of attack make?"

"It can make a lot of difference. For instance, if the fire is approaching a ridge, the pilot wouldn't be able to get a good shot at it if he approached from the other side of the ridge. The best attack would be from the same side. The spotter would give him the correct direction to approach from so that he could see the fire ahead of him and make any last minute adjustments. After the load has been dropped, the spotter would tell him whether he'd dropped it on target or not. It isn't easy trying to fly straight, open the tanks at just the right time, see through the smoke, and avoid hitting any trees or bluffs that stick up, not to mention power lines. I saw a Canso, another type of amphibian, make a beautiful drop one time, then turn right smack into a high-power line. That poor pilot never knew what hit him. There's more danger in flying these missions than most people realize".

"Couldn't he see the power lines coming?"

"Like I said. There's lots to do up there. If he had flown straight ahead, which is probably what the spotter expected, he would have been OK. I seem to recall the spotter warning him about those power lines, but the pilot must have misunderstood the warning. Maybe he thought the spotter said starboard side instead of port side, making him think it was safe turning the direction he did, who knows. One thing's for certain, he didn't get a second chance. None of us do".

"Have you mentioned this incident to Dave Albrecht? He might be able to come up with some means of detecting obstacles automatically to avoid running into them".

"No, I haven't. I'll try to remember to ask him at lunch tomorrow".

"Another lunchtime get-together, huh?", Joe mused. "Looks like you're making out pretty good on free meals, lately".

"I can't complain", said Pieter with a smile. "Speaking of which, would you pass the rolls. I love sesame rolls like these".

"Sure. I was wondering, though. If we're going to field a hundred planes at one time, along with a bunch of contractors and Forestry planes, how are we going to coordinate them all? One guy in a Cessna can't do it".

"That's true", said Pieter, as he bit into the roll. "We would need some kind of air-traffic control system. Problem is, if you set up a ground radar system, the hills are going to block the signals. We couldn't effectively control planes if the fire was behind a ridge". He thought for a moment as he buttered the other half of the roll. "I've got it! A Hawkeye!"

"What's a Hawkeye?"

"A Grumman E-2 Hawkeye is what the Navy uses for air-traffic control during carrier operations. They can also be used for radar early warning, but I don't think we'll have to worry about that too much. Forest fires don't generally shoot back. Anyway, these babies can control a hundred aircraft easy. They've usually got three radar operators on board, which is plenty for our needs. The question is, will the Navy let us buy a couple? They're pretty possessive about these birds, and it's easy to see why: They're worth their weight in gold for air-combat direction".

"I'll hand that off to Jerry to take care of first thing tomorrow. We're still setting things up for the other aircraft purchases, so this is just one more thing to add to the package. Any other suggestions?"

"Yeah, see if the boys at the Pentagon will sell us some KC-130 tankers. That way, we could swap parts between our transports and our tankers. Keeps the spares inventory to a minimum".

"We're in contact with the folks up in Canada about buying a few of their planes. They seem to be open to our purchasing them, but they may not be able to deliver all of them right away. I'm afraid I just about gave the plant manager a heart attack when I said I wanted to buy around forty CL-415s. I guess they don't usually get orders that large", he chuckled.

"I don't suppose they do. At least not from one source. Bear in mind, though, even the Forestry Service only operates about twenty bombers for all of Northern California. Their bases probably couldn't support all of the aircraft you're talking about. Besides that, only a few fires ever reach a size large enough to need contractors to fight it.

"The way the Forestry guys do this is to send out one or two planes at a time to snuff out small spot fires before they get big. They also only drop a handful of smokejumpers to put out larger fires. You try maintaining a force with fifty planes and a couple of hundred firejumpers and you're liable to find yourself staring at the walls waiting for a phone call that never comes".

"My, aren't we cheery tonight".

"Just trying to inject a little reality into your fantasies".

"Anything else positive you can think of?"

"Like I said before, you need to talk to some ground commanders to find out what your ground personnel are going to need. I don't know much about those things".

"I've taken care of that", said Joe confidently. "There was a battalion commander up at that fire in Kingfisher Creek. He'll be at our meeting on Friday".

"Good. I'd like to hear what he has to say about our plans so far".

"Me too. The more qualified people we get on this project, the better. Amateurs like my staff and me can't cover all the possibilities. That's why you're here".

"Really?", said Pieter in mock surprise. "I thought I was just here to keep you company".

"That, too", said Joe, a look of sadness spreading over his face.

"Still miss them, don't you?", asked Pieter quietly.

"Yeah, sometimes. But I'm getting better. As the shrink says, I just need to reconcile the loss somehow. I haven't been able to come up with a good reason why they had to die. And I still blame myself for not preventing it somehow".

"I know. After my wife died, I was tortured with the thought that there might have been something more I could have done. Maybe there was a specialist out there who could have cured her. Another clinic might have caught the symptoms sooner. All kinds of 'What Ifs'. It all boils down to the fact that there's nothing you can do about it now, so you just have to learn to live with it. Brutal, but that's the way it is".

"I guess so", said Joe dejectedly. "But there's still hope. After all, you've managed to overcome the worst of it yourself, right?"

"For the most part, yes. But it's taken me a few years. I don't think you want to wait that long, do you?"

"Not if I can help it. This analyst seems to think he can help me to snap out of it soon. He hasn't found the key yet, though".

"Well, I guess you'll just have to be patient", said Pieter sympathetically. "So what time is this meeting tomorrow?"

"Zack Dobson, the fireman, needed a couple of hours to drive down here, so we'll probably start right after lunch", said Joe. "Say about one thirty?"

"Fine with me", said Pieter. "I'm surprised you didn't offer to fly him down in the company plane".

"I did, but he didn't want to fly. Seems he's afraid of flying".

"Another one of those, huh?", said Pieter, shaking his head. "I never have been able to figure out fear of flying. You run a bigger risk of being killed in a car crash than you do of crashing in a plane".

"Nevertheless, that was his final word on the subject", said Joe. "Too bad, too. I had considered offering him the job of ground commander for our firefighting organization. I guess I'll have to consider someone else".

"Or only choose fires that are within driving distance", said Pieter with a smile.

They talked a bit longer that evening, then moved to the study. Pieter decided it was time to go when Joe started nodding off in his chair. Joe was still not fully recovered from his ordeal, Pieter thought. Or maybe he was still more depressed than he let on. Certainly, that would tire Joe out more quickly. Time heals all wounds, thought Pieter on the way home. He just hoped it wouldn't take too much time in the case of Joe.

Pieter met with Dave Albrecht at lunch the next day. As usual, Dave had a lot of questions (just like Joe, Pieter thought) but Pieter started the conversation off today.

"Hello Pieter", said Dave, as he carried his tray over to Pieter's table.

"Hi, Dave", greeted Pieter. "The boss wanted me to mention some things to you today."

"OK, shoot", said Dave as he sat down.

"Have you ever heard of an E-2 Hawkeye?"

"Oh, yeah. I used to service them when I was on the 'Kitty Hawk' during the Vietnam War. Nice planes, but a little cramped. There was a piece of waveguide that ran from the radar transmitter up to the radome on the roof. One solid piece of hollow brass a few feet long. Man, was that a pain to get out for servicing. We hated to do that job, but we always managed to get it out of there somehow".

"Joe wants to purchase a couple from the Navy. He told me to mention it to you so that you could think about the extra gear we might need to put in the plane when we get it. That is, if we get it".

"Oh, I think we'll get it", said Dave with a smirk. "Joe usually gets what he's after, one way or another. As far as electronics go, I imagine we would want to add some thermal scanners to help us spot fires. I think some Forward Looking Infrared sensors would work. FLIR pods were real handy for spotting hot targets on the ground. You can't get much hotter than a fire!

"We'd have to be able to talk to everybody at once, so most of the communications gear would be left in. Navy will want all the crypto gear pulled out. I don't think we'll need to send any coded messages, so we won 't need it anyway."

"You'll need more than just FLIR equipment. Forestry planes have experimented with them for some time, but still run into problems seeing terrain that isn't hot. I think you'll need something more. Maybe radar or something".

"How did you spot fires from your plane?"

"Stuck my head out the window most of the time. Used to circle the fire until I got a clear view of it, then dropped".

"I think we can improve on sticking your head out the window", Dave said with a smirk.

"That would be great if you could".

"I could also add in some electronics to connect the individual firebombers to the Hawkeye", said Dave, a thoughtful look on his face. "That would allow the Hawkeye to see what each firebomber was seeing. We could also put transponders on the firebombers to let the Hawkeye know where everybody was down to the square foot".

"Cubic foot", corrected Pieter. "Don't forget, we're talking altitude as well as ground position".

Dave didn't even seem to register Pieter's barb. "How about a readout of aircraft status? We could hook in sensing gear for each of the planes so that the guys in the Hawkeye could see if anything was wrong on the firebombers".

"Hold on, there!", said Pieter in alarm. "There's only three guys in that Hawkeye who handle air-traffic control. You go putting a lot of unnecessary gauges and displays in there and you're going to overload the operators. I think the transponders would be enough to link with the Hawkeye. The controller will have his own FLIR pods to see the fire with, he doesn't need the firebomber's display, too. And as far as the gauges go, I'm sure the firebomber's crew is up to watching them".

"Sorry. I just get carried away with electronics sometimes. When I worked over at Talon Electronics, I used to get accused of finding the most complex way of doing the simplest task. Old habits die hard, I guess".

"Don't worry", said Pieter with a laugh. "I'm sure we'll let you know if you start foaming at the mouth, mad scientist".

After lunch on Friday, Joe gathered his friends together for the long-awaited meeting. Anticipation ran high in the room. When Zack Dobson finally arrived, Joe introduced him to everyone and they got down to business.

"Zack, I need to know from you what we will need in the way of equipment for doing a proper job of fighting a fire like that one at Kingfisher Creek", Joe said.

"Well", said Zack, "you would need a few hundred men on the ground, about ten or fifteen air tankers, probably twenty-five engines minimum, and a few assorted Cats and busses".

"What is a Cat?", asked Jerry.

"A Caterpillar", answered Zack. "A bulldozer. We use them to clear firebreaks to channel and contain the fire. Sometimes we use a ball-and-chain attachment to clear a wide path. This gadget attaches between two Cats, then they drag it through thick brush, ripping it up as they go. It clears an area much wider than two blades could. If we have time, or several Cats, though, the blade is still the most effective means of clearing a break. We can put them shoulder to shoulder and clear off a nice wide area all at once".

"How much area can you clear at a time?", asked Joe.

"Well, it depends on the conditions. In heavy brush with a moderate slope, say 20%, a Cat can clear around 500-700 yards per hour. The rate varies depending on whether it's moving upslope, downslope, through light brush, heavy brush, and so forth. The bottom line is that this is a lot faster than a ground crew with hand tools could do it".

"I'd say we're going to need some Cats, then", said Joe. "How about if we paired them up together. Say, two groups initially, more once we see how they do?"

"That would be good for a start", said Zack. "You might want to consider an idea I had a few years back. I was thinking of having some busses or ambulances work in conjunction with the Cats for extended periods. The Cats could build the firebreaks for the other vehicles, while the busses and the rest followed along to establish a firebase in the vicinity of the fire. It would give the Cats support in case they broke down or needed help from ground personnel, and it would allow the firefighters a chance to set up a camp where they could return when their shift was ended. It's the same idea as the all-arms concept of modern warfare. Keep all of the fighting units together so they can support each other".

"Can the bulldozers drive right into the fire?", asked Allen Sims.

"Not hardly", said Zack. "The driver is out there in the open. He's already equipped with a breather unit which includes a small oxygen tank and air filters, but he'd get fried if he tried to drive too close to the fire. Wouldn't do much for the Cat either".

"How about if we fireproofed the Cats?", asked Joe.

"You have to realize that a fire is sucking in all of the available oxygen", said Zack. "Even if the driver was completely protected from the heat, he could still suffocate from lack of air, or have his lungs scorched from the heat of the air he was trying to breath. Besides that, the Cat needs more air than he does. It would probably stall before the driver passed out. No, you'd have to completely isolate both the driver and the tractor engine from the environment".

"We might just do that", said Joe. "If the Army can seal up their tanks from nuclear, biological, and chemical threats, why can't we fireproof a couple of bulldozers? Make them completely immune to the heat and smoke by carrying their own compressed air on board for both the crew and the diesels, at least enough for short time periods."

"There's been more than once when I would have given my eye-teeth for such a machine", said Zack wistfully. "But is it feasible?", he asked, looking hard at Joe. "Can you really enclose one to be survivable? Remember, we're talking temperatures in the hundreds, maybe thousands of degrees".

"It won't hurt to try", replied Joe. "Jerry, talk to the engineers at Caprock Drill. See if they know of a way to do this. If anybody in the corporation can do it, they can. They've got the best machine shops and engineers money can buy".

"I will see what I can find out", said Jerry.

"You guys are requisitioning surplus military equipment for this organization, right?", asked Zack.

"Yeah, it's the cheapest way to go, for now", replied Pieter.

"I just had another harebrained idea", said Zack. "How about making your ambulances and transports self-contained, too. Then they could follow the Cats anywhere they went, even through the fire!"

"It would be pretty hard to fireproof a bus, though", said Joe. "The tires would probably explode when they caught fire, not to mention the gas tank".

"What if they weren't trucks or busses?", said Zack thoughtfully. "What if they were Armored Personnel Carriers?"

"APCs?", asked Dave incredulously.

"Why not?", replied Zack. "The M-113 is completely enclosed. Even the fuel tank is carried inside. And tank treads don't burn too easy. You could put breather gear inside just like the dozers and have a dandy transport for your money!"

"Why not just buy some tanks and shoot the fire!", said Dave sarcastically.

"I'm serious!", said Zack as he turned toward Dave. "I think it could be done. Look, if you have firefighters cut off behind a fire, you may not be able to get to them. I've seen firefighters cut off by a fast-moving fire. Some were injured, and some were even killed before help could get to them. Fires are dangerous things. People get hurt, even professionals. If we had some means of rescuing them, I think it would be worth the extra expense. Sure, it's not going to be cheap to convert these vehicles, but what's the current price of a human life? I think the idea should at least be explored".

"I agree", said Joe quietly. "Remember, guys, this is a brainstorming session. We are all here to express our ideas, no matter how far-fetched they may seem. As of the moment, nothing has been done to make any of this come about. We're still collecting data, and until that's been completed, we don't spend one thin dime on anything".

"One thing I've been thinking about", said Pieter, "is the possibility of using our refueling tankers on the firebombers themselves. The CL-415 doesn't have an in-flight refueling receptacle. We could probably design a retrofit package for attaching one, though. It would give them increased range and much greater loiter time over the fire. I don't think it would be that expensive to bolt one on, and it would be something else for you to market once it was perfected. Besides that, if you plan to bring a lot of planes to a fire, you're going to overload the ground fueling facilities when they have to land and refuel every couple of hours".

"That's a good possibility", said Joe. "Jerry, see what Talon Aerospace can whip up in that regard. Give it a level three priority, no big rush. Have them interface with Bombardier, Inc. at their Canadair Division, then get back to me as soon as they have something. What about attaching Forward Looking Infrared pods to the Hawkeye and the firebombers?", asked Joe, as he turned to face Dave and Pieter.

"I know the idea is feasible", answered Dave. "But I don't have all the details worked out yet. We'll have to interface it with some sort of look-down shoot-down radar system. I'll have to talk to some friends who work in military aerospace to see what they think of my ideas. As far as bolting the pods onto the aircraft, I don't think that will be any problem. All of these aircraft are subsonic, so there shouldn't be any major problem with excessive drag or structural fatigue. I hope to have an answer for you in another two weeks, three at the latest".

"OK, Dave. Allen, I want you to work with these guys when they talk to vendors. Make sure we observe all the legal proprieties. The last thing I want is a lawsuit from somebody who thinks we infringed on their patents or designs".

"I have already assigned a legal counsel to each of them for advice", said Allen. "If there are any problems, it is best to have someone who is familiar with all the negotiations up to that time handling them".

"Sounds good", said Joe. "All right, then, is there anything else?"

"What about hiring your personnel", asked Zack. "Where are you going to get the people to work the firelines?"

"We plan to hire primarily military personnel at first", said Joe. "They've already trained with much of the equipment we plan to use, and they should be well-disciplined for the sort of operations we have planned. In addition, they will probably be available in large numbers as the military services continues to trim their organizations down to a smaller size. We expect to offer them premium pay, so as to keep them with us for the long-term. Once they have built up the infrastructure, we will hire in non-military along with the military personnel to fill out the ranks. I want a cadre of professionals, though, to train the rest of our organization".

"I'd suggest you also consider hiring some experienced firefighters", said Zack. "After all, you're going out there to fight fires, not enemy troops".

"Can you give me a list of qualified people?", asked Joe.

"I can put one together by tomorrow", said Zack. "I have several friends in the Forestry services, as well as some city firefighters who would jump at the chance for an assignment like this".

"And would you jump at a chance like this too?", asked Joe, staring fixedly at Zack.

Zack looked away for a moment, then looked back at Joe. "I've thought about it. But I'm not too keen on flying. Most of your deployments are going to be by plane, right?"

"I would imagine that *all* of our deployments would be by plane", Joe answered.

"That's what I was afraid of", said Zack dejectedly. "I would really like to join you guys, but I just can't stand flying".

"Why not?", asked Pieter.

"I was flying with a fire spotter, several years ago", said Zack slowly. "We got caught in a downdraft and crashed. Fortunately, the canopy of trees was pretty thick at the crash-site, so I only suffered a broken collarbone and a few cracked ribs. Everybody else survived, but the spotter suffered a broken back. He's confined to a wheelchair for the rest of his life. I couldn't live like that, and I've never been able to face flying again. I'm afraid the same thing would happen to me next time".

"That is a pretty good reason", agreed Pieter. "I've been flying most of my life, though, and I've only crashed once. I walked away from that one. You can't let one incident spook you. If you like, I'll take you up and we can help to get your confidence back. I've helped people to overcome their fear of flying before, and I think I can help you too".

"We'll see", said Zack noncommittally.

"Consider the benefits", said Joe with a smile. "You would be in charge of the entire operation, including the bombers. You could tailor the organization to the form you wanted, add the personnel you wanted, fight fires the way you wanted. That's a pretty nifty package, wouldn't you say, Zack?"

"It sounds pretty good", said Zack as he shifted uncomfortably in his chair. Then he brightened up a bit.

"Say, you don't suppose I could drive to the fire, do you?", he asked hopefully.

Joe looked at Pieter with an I-told-you-so expression on his face, then back to Zack. "In a word, no", he deadpanned. "You would be in charge of the ground personnel, which would be airlifted to the fire, and the bombers, which would be flying to the fire. If everybody had to wait for you to drive from, say, Big Bear to Yosemite, the fire could have spread from a little one into a major fire. No, Zack, I'm afraid you're stuck with flying. One way or the other, you're going to have to get over this phobia of yours. I can recommend a good psychologist", Joe added teasingly.

Zack's face flushed an angry red. "No thanks!", he shouted, much to the amusement of everyone in the room. "I'll take Pieter up on his offer. Maybe together we can lick this problem".

Game, set, and match, thought Joe with satisfaction. Now we have our team. And now comes the hard part, putting the pieces together. It's one thing to spout ideas, it's another thing trying to carry them out. "OK, guys", Joe said finally. "I think that's everything I wanted to cover. Has anybody else got anything to add?"

"Yeah, I've got one question", said Pieter. "Have your people come up with any ideas on mixing the retardant with water in-flight? You know, that technique we talked about a couple of weeks ago where the bomber could scoop up water and automatically mix long-term retardant in with it. It would save us a whole bunch of time and effort. That, along with aerial refueling, would allow us to put out fires much quicker".

"I haven't heard anything back from Bergway Chemical on that", replied Joe. "I'll give them a call after the meeting to see what they've come up with. You might want to stick around, Pieter. You could explain more clearly what it is you want, maybe give them a few suggestions".

"Good idea", said Pieter. "I think you might also want to get the technical people from your machine plant and the aircraft company in here. They could probably suggest some things and point out problems the rest of us might miss".

"OK", said Joe. Everyone else began to get up and head for the door. "I'll let you guys know when our next meeting is in a day or so. Thank you for coming".

They all said their good-byes, then filed out of the room. Joe called up Bergway Chemical and let Pieter talk to them. It took over an hour to finally get the problems resolved over the phone. Joe and Pieter agreed to meet there in a week to look over their plans. Joe also arranged for technical people from Talon Aerospace and Caprock Drill to be present.

After finishing up a few items for the rest of the company, Joe decided to call it a day. He was slowly getting his strength back, but he still tired more easily than he would have liked. Of course, the emotional high of working on this new project drained him more than any other project he could recall having worked on. And it was exciting! Things were finally coming together. He would have given anything to see what this would produce in, say, five years time. It was like looking at a new baby and wondering what they would be when fully grown. Time will tell, Joe thought. Time will tell.

Chapter 10

The weekend was a time of rest for everyone. Joe slept in late both Saturday and Sunday, slumming around the house both days. Monday, though, started off fast and furious. Joe wanted another staff meeting on Tuesday to talk over the plans for Firebombers with the technical staffs from each of the Talon firms involved in the operation. He contacted Zack and Pieter, asking them to bring along any people who they thought could be contributors to the discussion. Everyone agreed on the Tuesday date, but the technical people were reluctant. As is typical with technical people, they wanted more time to work out their ideas before presenting them. Joe, as is typical of executives, wanted the ideas *now*. Both groups compromised on Tuesday late afternoon, instead of the morning meeting Joe had wanted. Joe busied himself with corporate matters for the rest of Monday and the time before the meeting Tuesday, constantly checking the time. Everyone finally got there at 2 P.M. and the meeting commenced.

"Welcome, everyone", Joe greeted. "I'm glad you could all make it today. As you know, I've embarked on a new project, Firebombers Incorporated. The basic idea behind this outfit is that it will provide a highly-mobile, hard-hitting firefighting organization. I plan to use some military surplus equipment, former military personnel, and our own people and material to produce this outfit. In addition, we'll be procuring new equipment from some companies where needed. I would like to keep costs to a minimum, while maintaining a high level of effectiveness, as well as safety. Even though we'll be starting out with military and fire personnel in key positions, aside from the executive staff, we will have the ultimate goal of employing anyone who is qualified later on. In this manner, we'll have experts training those who follow. I hope to keep a high level of professionalism in the ranks by doing this.

"The organization as it stands consists of the following. I will be the CEO of the company, with my executive staff as it now stands. The overall fire commander will be Mr. Zack Dobson, who is presently working for Big Bear Fire Department".

At this point, Joe motioned for Zack to stand. After everyone greeted Zack, he sat down and Joe continued.

"Assisting Zack in the area of air operations will be Mr. Pieter Van Vrees ". Pieter stood up uncomfortably, then quickly sat down again, much to the amusement of Zack, who needled him about 'Boardroom Phobia', which Zack offered to help him overcome. Pieter's only reply was a scowl in Zack's direction, which caused Zack to start chuckling uncontrollably. Joe frowned at both of them, then continued.

"I think we should probably hear first from Dave Albrecht", said Joe.

"Of the tasks I've been assigned", Dave began, "I've come up with the following. As far as using Forward Looking Infrared pods in conjunction with terrain-mapping radar on the firebombers, it would seem to be feasible. I have the structural specs for both the CL-415 and the FLIR pods themselves. We'll mount a radome on the nose and develop a display which combines FLIR, radar, and visual images - the whole thing to be called a TRIDINT or "triple display interface". I'm in consultation with Talon Aerospace as to proper placement of all of these. Not only will these see infra-red, but they will also incorporate a low-light TV system for night-flying operations. We should be ready to fit the aircraft as soon as they are available. I have some firm ideas on customizing the Hawkeye systems for our needs, but I have yet to get some necessary information from the Navy on system specs. It looks like they're still a little close with information of this sort. I think that's your cue, Jerry", he said with a smile.

"We are working on it", said Jerry simply. He looked back at Dave and motioned for him to proceed.

"Once we have the necessary system specs and structural data on the Hawkeye, I can do some planning for attaching the FLIR pods and radome", Dave continued. "We have also contacted several vendors about information on avoidance radar for power lines and other small obstacles which we might encounter in rural and suburban areas. If we can find a workable system, it would probably save a lot of lives which might be lost to aerial collisions. We will need to do further study on this.

"We should be able to use the standard communications gear provided with the aircraft, so no new gear should be needed there. We can use commercially available radio-beacons to identify our aircraft from the Hawkeye. Oh, and we can also use commercial short-wave radios for our vehicles. That should allow the Hawkeye to communicate with everybody".

"Thanks, Dave", said Joe. "Jerry, I think you're up next".

"We are still in negotiations with the Navy on the Hawkeyes", said Jerry. "There have been several obstacles, not the least of which is that there are very few surplus Hawkeyes which are still serviceable. It appears that the Navy uses them until they begin to fall apart. We may have to approach Grumman directly about purchasing a pair of new ones, which could prove quite costly" .

"Maybe so", said Joe. "But they're the best platform for what we want".

"I will continue negotiating and see what develops", said Jerry. "Insofar as the C-130s are concerned, I believe the Pentagon can provide us with all we need at a very reasonable price. We should also have access to substantial spare parts, if we are willing to cannibalize the C-130s already deemed unserviceable".

"The DOD version of 'Pick-A-Part', huh?", said Pieter with a smile.

"Quite", replied Jerry. "The same conditions seem to apply to the acquisition of M-113s and bulldozers. The Army has a plethora of both, and has offered us an attractive price on fairly new equipment. We have put together an order for eight M-113s and five bulldozers. We will need your approval on this, Joe".

"Just send it over to Nancy and I'll sign it", said Joe. "How many C-130s are you planning to requisition, Jerry?"

"We have not settled on a number, as of yet", Jerry answered. "We were waiting for a better idea of how large a force you wish to start out with".

"I guess I'll have to sit down with Pieter and Zack to discuss that some", said Joe. "Anything else, Jerry?"

"No, sir", Jerry replied, "I believe that covers everything for the moment".

"OK, thanks", said Joe. "Allen, do you have anything to add from a legal standpoint?"

"Nothing which anyone other than a lawyer would care to hear", Allen said with a grin. "Of course, if any of you are having trouble sleeping at night, I could send a copy of my findings home with you".

"Thanks, but that won't be necessary", said Zack with a moan.

Everybody laughed a little, then settled down as Joe began to speak again. "Zack, now that I think about it, we haven't discussed what kind of fire trucks we're going to be using for our operations. Suppose you fill us in on that matter".

"Well, I've worked with quite a few in my time", said Zack slowly. "I think the primary factors in picking one are going to be how much water you want to carry, and how much weight one of these C-130s can lift. As far as the water problem goes, we're probably not going to have a source available most of the time. If you're throwing out 1500 gallons a minute, most engines are going to be dry in no time. Water weighs about eight pounds per gallon. If we're flying them in full, then we're going to have to take that extra weight into account.

"If you want a force which is able to deploy quickly, then you should bring them in full. You should plan for the worst case: no water source available at the drop-zone or the fire-line. That way, if you do have water available, you're covered. If there isn't any water available, you're also covered because you've brought some along. What's the average cargo capacity for a C-130?"

After a moment of silence, the technical representative from Talon Aerospace piped up. "I believe it's just a little over eighteen tons, sir", he said.

Zack thought for a moment, then said, "Assuming a maximum load of water of, say, 3000 gallons, which would weigh 12 tons, we could assume a maximum engine capacity of 5 tons, allowing for personnel and equipment. A truck which carried 3000 gallons would be hard to maneuver around winding forest roads, so we had better cut the weight to 1500 gallons. If you plan to carry firejumpers along, then we would have to cut the maximum engine weight somewhat. How many firejumpers per plane?"

"I don't know that we had really settled on a fixed number yet", said Joe. "How many would you recommend?"

"Well, I would like to take in as many as possible", said Zack. "The problem is that they'll each weigh around 250-300 pounds. If we have an engine that weighs close to 11 tons, that leaves 7 tons carrying capacity for jumpers. I think we should consider a custom-built engine, something made out of aluminum or composite materials. I'd recommend putting out a bid to several contractors for a new design for an engine which combines a maximum water capacity with a minimum empty weight. If you are going to carry firejumpers, then you might want to cut down on the water capacity of the engine. It looks like it's going to be a trade-off between number of jumpers and size of the tank on the engines".

"Is there anyone you would recommend as a technical source on this?", asked Joe.

"Probably FMC, for two reasons", answered Zack. "The first is that they acquired an outfit called Van Pelt, a few years back, which is known for good custom work, which is what you are going to be shopping for. The second is that they also make the M-113, which you are getting for the Cat Teams. If you can establish a rapport with them, you might be able to get some advice on fireproofing your APCS".

"That's an excellent suggestion, Zack!", said Joe. "Jerry, see what you can do on this matter. See if FMC will loan us some of their design people on a consultation basis. If we build the equipment under their direction everybody wins. They get nice, fat consultation fees, along with the rights to manufacture these themselves after we've spent the time and effort for research. And we get a special purpose engine which fits our needs, along with the capability of doing in-house manufacturing and modifications. Caprock Drill will handle the production of the firetrucks, OK?"

"Understood, sir", answered Jerry, writing furiously in his notebook. "And in regards to modifications of the bulldozers and APCS, do you wish to also do those in-house?"

"Yep, in consultation with both Caterpillar and FMC representatives", answered Joe.

"I'd recommend talking to the folks from Caterpillar about the M-9 armored bulldozer they produce for the Army. It's completely enclosed, such as what you want for fireproofing reasons".

"I shall add that to my list", replied Jerry.

"We still have the issue of firejumpers to resolve", said Zack.

"Let's put that question off until we find out more on the fire engines, Zack", said Joe.

"OK. I've put together a list of about 35 people who would qualify for your fire-line commanders. I think they'll all do a fine job, and they've all expressed an interest in what you have to offer them".

"Good", said Joe. "Give the list to me after the meeting and I'll have Personnel call them in for interviews. Anything else, Zack?"

"Nope, I think that covers everything for the moment", said Zack.

"By the way, Dave", Joe said. "What have you found out about aerial refueling of our aircraft?"

"The C-130 is capable of refueling in the air. I think Jerry has already contacted Department of Defense about getting some KC-130 tankers".

"Yes, seven to be precise", said Jerry.

"In the case of the E-2s, I haven't received any information as of yet", Dave continued, with a glance over at Jerry, who pointedly ignored him. "The CL-415s should be able to take a bolted-on receptacle, I think, but we're still working out the details over at Talon Aerospace. You did, after all, make this only a level three priority, I believe".

"Yes, I guess I did at that", said Joe as he squirmed in his seat. "Maybe we should upgrade it somewhat, say to a level two priority?"

"I don't really think there's a rush, since we don't even have a plane to fit a mock-up to, yet", replied Dave.

"You're probably right", said Joe. "OK, leave it as a level three priority for now", said Joe, at which point an audible sigh of relief could be heard from the Talon Aerospace staff. "Any input from Bergway Chemical on that retardant for in-transit mixing?", Joe asked.

A man at the far end of the conference table answered, "We are working on a formula at the moment, sir. It will be some time, however, before we can offer you any conclusive answers. This is a technical problem which companies with a background in firefighting have been pursuing for some time. I would estimate that we will have something concrete to present within nine months".

"Not until then?", said Joe anxiously. "I was hoping for something a lot sooner that that!"

"Sorry, sir", answered the representative, "but these things take time. We must first research what is already out there. For obvious reasons, competitors do not identify all the ingredients in existing fire retardants. If we are to develop something new, we need to know what has already been produced - in detail. Our chemists will do the best that they can, but without an accurate chemical breakdown of existing retardants, it is not an easy task. The nine-month date may even be optimistic".

"Oh", said Joe quietly. After he thought for a moment, he brightened up visibly. "Since we plan to market this retardant if - correction, when - we develop it, why not steal the help we need from other companies? Jerry, find out who the best chemists in the business are and see if we can, shall we say, persuade them to join us.   Explain the situation to them and offer them whatever incentives they need to hire on. You know the procedure".

"Perfectly", said Jerry dryly.

"Would that help you to get the job done quicker?", Joe asked the Bergway spokesman.

"Yes, quite a bit", he answered with a smile.

"And what about a mixing system for injecting the chemical into the water storage tanks on the bombers themselves?", Joe asked. "Do we have any thoughts on that yet?"

"The actual mechanism will depend on the chemical we develop", answered Bergway's chief chemist. "We can't design the mechanism until we know what pressure we need, the kinematic viscosity of the chemical, the Reynold's number which optimizes mixing, the..."

"I get the picture", said Joe quickly. "All right, see what you can find out and get back to me on it. Jerry, the chemist hiring has top priority.   It looks like this will be the slowest item to be acquired, and therefore the pacing item for the whole project. We'll need speed here, so don't waste any time diddling around. Whatever it takes to get the talent we need, see to it!"

"Very well", answered Jerry.   He turned to an assistant and began speaking quickly to him. Joe looked around the room for a moment, then settled back into his chair. "Well, I guess that covers about everything for the moment. Does anyone have any suggestions or questions, before we break up?"

"Just one", said Zack. "When do you plan to start hiring your ground personnel?"

"We'll probably start hiring the aircrews and maintenance crews in the next month or so. But I'd like to get the fire engine issue resolved before we start hiring anyone else".

"OK, but just remember, fire season will be starting in another few months. I'd like to have some sort of organization established at least two to three months before that time. We'll need to train as a team if we're expected to fight as a team. And you're going to need those military personnel to operate some of the equipment that my commanders work with. Just don't wait till the last minute to hire people, then expect us to go fight a fire".

"Understood", said Joe. "I'll try to give you a firm timetable by the end of this month, say, ten days?"

"That would be sufficient", Zack replied.

"Anything else?", Joe asked, as he scanned the room. "No? Then we'll call this meeting a wrap. Thank you all for coming".

Bill Thompson drove Joe home that night. He noticed how pleased Joe seemed. "You look like the cat that just ate the canary, boss".

"Let's just say I'm the cat who's thinking about eating a very large canary", said Joe with satisfaction. "We had a great meeting today on my new project".

"That firefighting outfit?"

"That's the one. Everything seems to be coming together. We've got the talent and the resources to pull off something big here. I can hardly wait to begin operations".

"When do you think you will?"

"Sometime next year. Probably at the beginning of the fire season, say, by May or June".

"Sounds like this is going to be an expensive proposition".

"I think we can cover the costs", said Joe confidently. "My staff is checking everything out thoroughly beforehand, just to make sure we don't stub our toes along the way".

"Well, it's sure good to see you happy again, boss".

"It's good to *be* happy again". I only hope it lasts, he thought to himself.

Chapter 11

As Christmas approached, Joe immersed himself in the details of running the corporation, as well as the day-to-day details of building Firebombers Incorporated into a fully-functional company. The first new-hires were brought into the company. Some of them were fire personnel who Zack had picked. The rest were former military personnel who were linked up with the military-surplus equipment as it arrived.

Joe set aside a 500 acre parcel at the Talon Aerospace site, out in San Bernardino County, for a practice area. The location was ideal, as it was away from any other structures, and had the airstrip used by the aircraft company for bringing in planes, as well as testing out aircraft designs.

Zack quickly converted the 500 acres into a first-class training facility. The fire-line commanders began training the arriving personnel in the finer details of fighting fires. As Zack put it, though, it would take an actual fire to complete their training. There was nothing to substitute for the real thing, with the desperate circumstances of actually trying to control a wildfire. He felt confident, however, that they would be ready when the time came.

Joe was invited over to Jerry and Diane's house for Christmas, since he had no family to spend it with. Joe put on a cheery face, but the pain inside was noticeable to him throughout Christmas Eve dinner.

Since Christmas fell on a Sunday, Jerry and Diane invited Joe to go to church with them on Christmas Day. Joe was reluctant, but finally agreed. As with the service he had attended in the mountains just before the fire, Joe paid little attention to the sermon. As they filed out of the church, Jerry pulled Joe over to meet the pastor.

"Pastor Walters, this is my friend Joe Talon", Jerry said, as the pastor and Joe shook hands.

"Good morning, Mr. Talon", greeted the pastor warmly. "Or should I say 'Merry Christmas'? Jerry has told me a fair amount about you".

"Merry Christmas", Joe said. "A good service today, Pastor Walters. Do you usually have this large a turnout?"

"At Christmastime, yes. We don't have quite as large a service on an average Sunday, though.   But attendance is steadily improving. Hopefully, we will continue to grow".

"Well, let's hope so", said Joe.

"How are you feeling now, Mr. Talon?", Pastor Walters asked quietly, so as not to be overheard by the cluster of people nearby. "Jerry told me about the tragedy up in the mountains last summer".

Joe's smile vanished, replaced by a more somber look. "OK. I'm past most of the nightmares, but I still feel an emptiness inside. I miss them".

"Yes, I imagine you do", said Pastor Walters sympathetically. "God works in mysterious ways, as the old saying goes. Sometimes, we suffer a loss ourselves in order to provide either ourselves, or mankind in general, with a gain.   There are many instances in the Bible where an individual suffered what appeared to be a crippling loss, only to discover God's hand in it all and a spectacular outcome.

One example which springs to mind is the one of Joseph. I won't bore you with all the details, but the gist of the story was that Joseph was sold into slavery by his jealous brothers. After several years and a number of adventures, Joseph became the Egyptian Pharaoh's right-hand man in Egypt and saved his own family, including his brothers, from starvation. As a result, the people who founded Israel were saved. You can read about it yourself in your Bible. It's in Genesis, Chapters 37 through 50. Perhaps this could relate to your situation. God never does anything without a reason, although we may not understand the reason at the time. I hope you figure out His plan for your life".

"Thank you", said Joe. "I appreciate your concern".

"Certainly", said Pastor Walters.   "And I appreciate your humoring an old preacher".

Joe's frown disappeared and he looked up to see a good-natured twinkle in the pastor's eye.

"Perhaps we could talk about this some more later?", asked Joe.

"I'm available any time you like", replied Pastor Walters. "Just stop by or give me a call whenever you're ready".

"Thanks, I'll let you know", said Joe, once again shaking hands with the Pastor, then walking with Jerry and Diane to the car.

Joe went home after dinner at Jerry's that night. The staff had been given the weekend off, so the place was dark and quiet. Joe went into the bedroom and rummaged around for Martha's old

Bible, then went down to the study to read about Joseph. After he finished, he thought about it awhile. Maybe the preacher was right. It could be that some good would come from his family's death in the form of his new project. Perhaps he could do for others what he hadn't been able to do for his family: save their lives. He thought about this and other things for awhile, then trudged up to bed. He forgot to take his sleeping pill, but fell off to sleep and was untroubled by nightmares that night.

Talon Industries was closed through the holiday season. Joe spent New Year's Eve with the executive staff and their wives, along with Pieter and Zack. They had all gathered over at Joe's mansion and then retired to the guest rooms once the celebration was over. As Joe pointed out, there was no point in everyone driving home snockered, so why not spend the night. After all, he certainly had the room. Joe, of course, didn't have a drink, nor did Pieter. They toasted everyone with non-alcoholic sparkling cider.

New Year's Day, everyone gathered around the big-screen TV in the family room to watch the Rose Parade. There was a bit of a debate over how high the volume should be, due to an epidemic of hangovers, but Marie came to the rescue with her patented tomato-juice concoction. By the time the bowl games started, everyone was at least civil, if not downright friendly.

The wives beat a hasty retreat into the study when the football games began. The guys all crowded around the TV and cheered on their favorite teams. There was another debate over which game to watch, but it was finally resolved by taking a poll of favorite games (several later teased that Joe had stuffed the ballot box, at which time he protested his innocence). By the time dinner rolled around, everyone was feeling fairly congenial and the wives offered to help Marie with the dinner dishes. The guys, however, hurriedly ate their dinners and rushed back to see the umpteenth bowl game of the day. The party broke up about ten that night. Joe bid his guests farewell and reminded his lieutenants of the staff meeting planned for Friday, then went up to bed.

The next week started out slowly, but Joe's excitement once again peaked on Friday. When the meeting began after lunch, he was eager to see what new developments had come about. Jerry led off this time.

"We have begun negotiations for the following aircraft from Department of Defense. We will be purchasing seven KC-130 tankers, two E-2C Hawkeyes, and forty-two C-130 transports. We have access to more if we should need them, but this should be sufficient for our present needs. We are already in possession of eight M-113s and five Caterpillars, all of which are presently at Caprock Drill being fireproofed. Representatives from FMC and Caterpillar are working with our people there to convert the existing vehicles.

FMC has also loaned us several of their top people for consultation on our fire engine project. Mr. Dobson recommended a Van Pelt body type which we will probably use, but constructed of composites instead of steel, thereby lowering the weight of the final product. I am sure he can give you a more detailed account of the features than I can".

"More details than they probably care to hear, you mean", said Zack with some amusement.

"Insofar as the actual bombers are concerned", Jerry continued, "we are in contact with Canadair about requisitioning approximately thirty CL-415 aircraft immediately, with a follow-on buy of several more spares, once the first lot is delivered. They have given us a tentative agreement to modify the existing design, but no permission to manufacture any ourselves, as of yet. We will continue to pursue a manufacturing agreement".

"Keep after them", said Joe. "I want to be able to make that plane under license ourselves, just in case we needed replacements quicker than they could deliver them".

"That is my feeling on the matter as well", said Jerry. "Personnel hiring is continuing apace, and I believe Mr. Dobson will have more to say on the present training program later".

"How soon will the aircraft be arriving?", Joe asked Jerry.

"We can have the surplus aircraft within 60 days of purchase", replied Jerry. "The Navy wants to strip the two Hawkeyes of everything, then let us install the new electronics we need, including communications gear".

"Will that be a problem, Dave?", Joe asked.

"I don't think so", said Dave. "We plan to customize both planes to our needs, anyway. Most of the equipment in there is no longer state of the art, and this will give us a chance to design the electronics from the ground up.

"It doesn't look like it'll be any trouble at all installing the TRIDINT pods on the fuselage. I'll check out the radar systems as well, while I'm at it. See if I can make any improvements to the existing design. There have been a lot of changes in radar since 'Nam. As soon as the C-130s and the tankers get here, I'll have the communications gear ready to install in them. The CL-415s will be a little more tricky. I'm going to have to keep the TRIDINT gear out of the water as much as possible. In addition, I want to link the drop-tank mechanisms so that we can computerize the operation. Maybe even have the lead bomber synchronize the drop of an entire squadron".

"Just don't get carried away, Dave", Joe cautioned. "We want these available ASAP, not three years from now. If you can't get your super whiz-bang gadgets to work, we'll simply do it the old-fashioned way: by eye".

"But we can get better coverage this way", Dave argued. "If we use a ballistic computer along with the TRIDINT gear, I think we could guarantee a hit every time. If several planes could be linked, you could have coordinated drops to cover a much larger fire. Think of the possibilities!"

Think of the time delays due to teething problems, thought Joe. "We'll see", was all he said. "By the way, when are we expecting the first CL-415s to arrive?"

"Canadair has promised us as rapid a delivery date as possible", said Jerry. "In light of the enormity of our order, we should receive a priority on shipment".

"Good, then I'll be able to get to work on fitting them with their electronics, too", said Dave, as he rubbed his hands together in anticipation.

"And I can begin training aircrews", said Pieter. "The first crews should be ready for this year's fire season. I would suggest that we send them out individually. Let them get their feet wet with the pros before you confuse them with all of this electronic stuff", he cast a sly look over at Dave, then continued, "and then you can link them up with the new equipment. They should learn how to operate on their own under a veteran pilot before you actually put them into the hot-seat.

"I've already talked to some friends who are contractors, and several outfits have agreed to take them on as trainees. We, of course, will pay their way. This will also establish a rapport with the contractors that could pay off when we come into a fire as our own organization. The worst thing that can happen is to get friction between pilots. No telling what might happen. If our guys have worked with these guys already, then we'll all have an understanding of what we're capable of doing".

"I was hoping we could at least field a small demonstration group this season", said Joe dejectedly. "But I suppose you know what you're talking about, Pieter. Of course you realize that this will give Dave more time to equip our planes with every gadget he can think of", Joe told Pieter with a twinkle in this eye. "After all, if our crews are piloting someone else's planes, that means that our planes will just be sitting here doing nothing".

Dave brightened considerably at this. Pieter simply rolled his eyes and replied, "I still think this is the way to go".

"OK, then, that's the way we'll go!", said Joe. "Zack, how do the ground personnel look. Do you think they will do?"

"My people are putting them through their paces out at the training ground now. They appear to be well-disciplined, but they still lack some of the basics in firefighting. We really need to get them into an actual wildfire before I'd consider them to be ready. I plan to loan them to California Division of Forestry this summer. Let them get the feel of sweating on the fire-line. We don't have to use them as firejumpers this season, but I think we should have practice jumps regularly just to keep them in shape. Not being a parachutist myself, we have recruited a few trainers who were with the 82nd Airborne Division. They'll recommend a training program to keep the men and women sharp".

"Sounds good to me", said Joe. "How about your aircraft ground crews, Pieter? When will you have them ready to go?"

"We've already got more than enough candidates for the available slots", said Pieter. "We'll have a competition among the candidates to see who the best are, then select our actual crews based on the results. I expect we'll have a fully operational organization by late summer. The first people should arrive shortly before the planes begin arriving, say in about three weeks".

"They should also be helpful in the modifications to the C-130s, I would imagine", said Joe.

"I think so", said Pieter. "We've hired a few retired master sergeants from the Air Force to coordinate all the ground crews. I've met them and they seem to be good people".

"It appears that everything is proceeding well", said Joe with a look of satisfaction. "1994 promises to be a Happy New Year indeed! Thank you gentlemen, if there are no further questions, the meeting is adjourned".

Chapter 12

Over the next few weeks, the pace of operations began to increase. Joe had meetings every week to report on the Firebombers situation. Several minor hitches developed, but they were quickly solved. The personnel began pouring into the training center and the planes began arriving at Talon Aerospace. Most of the aircraft were in fairly good shape, but all needed at least some minor maintenance. Dave Albrecht began assigning work crews to fit and test the electronics on the various aircraft. He personally took charge of retrofitting the Hawkeyes.

The design of the *Zephyr*-class fire engines proceeded with some difficulty at Caprock Drill. Making a composite which could mimic steel at less than half the weight was no easy task, but scientists from the consulting companies and Bergway Chemical began to make progress as fire season approached. The heavy equipment would not be ready for this fire season, but had a good chance of making it by the next.

As fire season approached, Zack deemed his crews ready to try their hands at real firefighting. Pieter had already begun to parcel out his aircrews to the contractor air-tanker companies. It was going to be a confusing year, thought Joe, with people scattered all over the state. If they learned their trade, though, it was worth it.

Pieter dropped off the first two pairs of aircrews at a small firm called Humboldt Air. He had known the owner, Charlie O'Shaunessey, for most of the years he had been flying for the Forestry Service.

"Welcome back, Pieter!", said Charlie. He gave Pieter a slap on the back that nearly knocked his teeth out. "So, these are your young pups, huh?", he said as he eyed the four pilots carefully. "Any of you children ever flown through a forest fire before?"

Everyone remained silent, a couple looked indignantly at Charlie. Pieter broke the silence. "All of these fellows have flown several hundred hours each. They're experienced pilots".

One of the pilots, Bob Mitchell, spoke up. "I can't say that I have, Charlie", he replied. "Have you ever flown through any SAM belts?"

"Aha!", said Charlie with a laugh, "this pup has teeth! No, lad, I've never flown through any SAM belts. When I flew in the Air Force, that's the Army Air Force by the way, they didn't even know what a Surface-to-Air Missile was. The only thing we had to dodge were Messerschmitts and Focke-Wulfs, along with a little flack. Funny thing is, I'm still flying B-17s".

"We've all had to fly through hostile airspace ourselves", continued Bob, "either real or simulated. We may not have fought any fires, but we're not wet behind the ears, either!"

"So I see", said Charlie, a devilish glint in his eye. "They might cut it at that, Pieter. But not without smoothing down some of the rough edges. How long do I have?"

"The whole season", replied Pieter. "We have more available if you finish with these. The Talon lawyers talked to you about liability and payment for your help, didn't they?"

"Yep. Well, at least I think that's what they were talking about. I have a hard time understanding most lawyers. I'm doing this because you wanted the help, not because of what some lawyer said".

"I figured as much", said Pieter. "Well boys, I guess you're on your own now. I'm sure Charlie will take good care of you. Just keep your hands on your wallets! See you, Charlie!"

"Take it easy, Pieter. All right, children, let's go over some of the basics inside. Before you get behind the stick on one of *my* planes, you complete a little basic ground instruction".

Charlie led the pilots inside, then pulled out some maps and instruments. "First, you pull out the sectional maps for the area you are going to be working in. You may have to tape a couple of these together to cover the whole area you plan to fly in. You want to make sure you cover a wide enough area, just in case you get diverted by the air boss.

"Once you've made your sectional map, draw circles at ten-mile intervals radiating out from your tanker base. That will make it easier for you to gauge how far away the target is. I usually put a compass rose on the map, just to make it easier to get bearings".

"From what they've told us at Talon, the bombers we fly will have computerized navigational equipment inside", said Dick Morrison, another Talon pilot. "Why do we have to learn all of these archaic methods? Why can't we just wait until the new bombers are ready for us, then learn how to fly them?"

Charlie got a stern look on his face, then replied, "Because we don't have your fancy new planes here, just my old crates. I guess Pieter wants you to learn how to fly the tried-and-true way before you get soft relying on too many gadgets".

The pilots made no further comments on Charlie's lessons that day. They all sat quietly taking in what he had to say, then followed him out behind the building to the airstrip. Two old B-17G Flying Fortresses stood at the end of the airstrip. Charlie walked up to the nearer one and patted the fuselage affectionately.

"This is 'Gertie's Garters'." said Charlie reverently. "I've flown this plane for close to a quarter of a century. She flies as solid as a rock through updrafts and turbulence. She's gotten me to a couple of hundred fires, and then brought me home safe again. She and 'Hot Lunch' over there are the last B-17s being used to fight forest fires in the U.S. Next year I plan to retire. These babies get turned over to the Confederate Air Force. They've already got plans for them".

The Talon pilots just shook their heads in disbelief. It was hard for them to imagine this old piece of junk being able to even get off the ground, let alone fight fires. No one said anything, though. They could see that this was Charlie's pride and joy.

Charlie took Bob and Dick up into the cockpit with him. He showed them all of the instruments and explained each one's function, then brought the other two pilots, Ralph Gautier and Chet Farley, up for the next tour. Once everyone had been introduced to the plane, Charlie offered to take them up, two at a time. When no one volunteered immediately, he grew a bit angry.

"What's the matter with you guys?", Charlie demanded. "I know she doesn't look like much, but this baby is solid. I'd like to see what kind of shape your planes will be in after fifty years of service. Now c'mon, who goes up first?"

Finally, Bob and Dick volunteered. Ralph whispered something in Dick's ear as he started for the plane. Dick's response was a grimace. Charlie called out something to the hanger behind the two planes. When they had climbed aboard, Charlie directed Bob to the co-pilot's seat and Dick to the flight engineer's seat. In a moment, an older man in coveralls appeared at the hanger door. He was looking at his hands as he wiped oil off of them with a rag. He ambled over to the plane and pulled the wheel chocks out. Charlie began flipping switches and the first engine coughed, then roared to life, followed by the second. When all of the engines were up to full power, the plane began rolling slowly down the runway. As the plane moved away from them, the older man came up and introduced himself to Ralph and Chet.

"Good day to you, gentlemen", he greeted with a thick brogue. "And who might you be?"

"Hi, I'm Chet Farley and this is Ralph Gautier", answered Chet. "We're from Talon Industries. We're supposed to get some experience in fighting fires up here this season. Who are you?"

"Patrick O'Toole, at your service", he said with a flourish.

Both pilots looked at each other with amusement at Patrick's posturing, then back at the unperturbed mechanic, who had pulled out a pipe and was proceeding to fill and light it as he continued talking.

"So, you've come up here for training, is it?", Patrick said thoughtfully. "Well, you've surely come to the right place. There's not a better pilot for fightin' forest fires than old Charlie. He's a grand lad, and a good teacher too. We've known each other since he was flyin' Forts over in England durin' the war. 'Twas him who got me into this wonderful country in the first place".

"Are you from England?", asked Chet.

"Good Lord, no lad", said Patrick as he relit his pipe. "I'm from Ireland. From Londonderry, to be precise. I just happened to be in England durin' the war. We met at the air base where Charlie was stationed. I was fixin' the planes that the RAF flew there and Charlie was flyin' Forts. Before you know it, we were carryin' on like long-lost friends.

"When Charlie finished his second tour, he asked me if I wanted to come to the States to see what it was like. So I said to meself, 'Patrick, you've never traveled outside of the U.K. This would be the perfect opportunity to see someplace new'. So, I says to himself, 'I'd be right pleased to visit your country, Charlie'. He pulled some strings and got me permission to visit for awhile, I believe it was a three-month pass, or some such thing. Anyway, while I was stayin' with Charlie in Portland, Oregon, I meets the most beautiful girl I'd ever laid me eyes on, Lorraine Scott. Well, when she found out that I was goin' back to Ireland in another few weeks, she was heartbroke. We decided the only thing to do was to get hitched good and proper, so's I could stay here. Well, it's been fifty-one years ago this year, and we're still married. I would say that that was the luckiest trip I've ever taken!"

"And now you work here?", asked Ralph.

"Since Charlie started the business over thirty years ago", said Patrick proudly. "I'm never happier than when I can get me hands oily. Engines and airplanes are me life, besides me Lorrie, of course. And how long have you lads been flying?"

"Well, I've been flying about seven years", said Ralph.

"I've flown about eight", said Chet. "Mostly military transports, although there was a short stint where I flew two-seater trainers to and from airbases. I never qualified to be an instructor, though".

"Is that what you wanted?", asked Patrick.

"I wasn't really sure what I wanted", answered Chet. "I knew I wanted to fly. I could never make up my mind as to what I wanted to do in flying. I had wanted to be a fighter jock, but I couldn't qualify for that, either. Flying transports was OK, but I still wanted something more.

"I thought I could make more money flying civilian aircraft, so I processed out of the military about six months ago. Then this opportunity came up. You can't beat the pay, and the benefits are pretty good, too. I figure I'll try it for awhile, see how I like it. There's always airlines out there to work for if this doesn't work out".

"I was a tactical fighter pilot with the 81st Tactical Fighter Wing", said Ralph. "We flew Warthogs, the Fairchild A-10. I enjoyed having something where I could pound the other guys on the ground. I never saw real combat, but it felt good to blast something on the ground even if it was only practice. When I heard about this job, I jumped at it. This is even better than bombing opposing armies. We get to pound a target that doesn't shoot back. What a piece of cake!"

"I know", said Patrick. "Nothing makes Charlie feel better than to come back from a successful Forestry tour. He truly enjoys puttin' out fires. And the people who do this sort of thing are usually pretty good lads. Oh, we've got a few rotten apples, but then you always will have. I think you lads have made the right choice for a career".

As the conversation was finishing, the B-17 returned to the airstrip. Charlie taxied the big plane up close to the waiting pilots, then killed the engines. After a moment, Bob and Dick emerged from the belly hatch and walked over to the gathering. Both of them were smiling and Dick slid over to stand beside Ralph. He whispered something in Ralph's ear, then pointed to the plane. Ralph grimaced a bit, then motioned to Chet to follow him. Reluctantly, both walked toward the plane, looking as though it was going to fall apart if they touched it. Once again the engines roared to life and the plane taxied back down the runway. When they could hear each other talk, Pat introduced himself to the two pilots.

"What sort of planes have you lads flown?", asked Pat.

"Intruders", replied Bob. "We were with VMA-242, 'the Bats'. We flew tactical bombing missions in the A-6 in the Marine Corps".

"Flying Leathernecks, were you now", said Pat with a smile. "Aye, we had a Marine pilot flew with us for a few years here. That is, until he picked one fight too many. A few of the local loggers decided to teach him a lesson about barfights, only it got a wee bit out of hand and they fractured the pur fellow's backbone. He never did like sitting in the pilot's seat after that, so he quit. You young fellows don't like to start quarrels, now do ye?", Pat asked slyly.

"Us?", said Dick with an innocent look on his face. "No, we don't start any barfights".

"We just finish them", said Bob, an evil smile spreading across his face.

"Saints preserve us!", said Pat. "We'll have no peace in this town for the rest of the summer, I'm thinkin'".

"I don't suppose *you* ever got into any barfights when you were younger, did you Patrick?", asked Bob.

"Well, I might have at that", said Pat thoughtfully. "It seems to me as though there were a few impolite lads who persisted in calling me a Scot. It took a couple of visits to the local doctor, generally in a deplorable state, to break them of this habit. After that, though, all the fun went out o' the local taverns at the RAF base. Then Charlie and me came over here and these folks were positively genteel. Why, I've never been so bored in all me life. It's a good thing I married me a fiery lass, otherwise I would have died of boredom long ago".

"She's a little opinionated, huh?", asked Dick.

"Opinionated!", Pat snorted. "Laddie, she is the most obstinate, cantankerous, hot-tempered woman I've ever known. She can take a tiny little disagreement and blow it up into somethin' the like of which would try the patience of a saint. If I didna' know better, I would say she had been raised in Ireland. And I love her dearly for it, though maybe not at that exact moment!", he said with a bit of a laugh.

"She sounds like a handful", said Dick.

"Too spicy for me", agreed Bob.

"Well, you lads just don't appreciate the finer things in life", said Pat with a chuckle. "So, tell me now, what did you think of your flight with Charlie?"

Dick looked inquiringly at Bob, who shrugged his shoulders, then turned toward Pat. "It was all right", said Bob noncommittally. "I guess I've flown in planes that were in worse shape, but not much".

"I was afraid one of the wings was going to fall off, the way they were vibrating", chuckled Dick.

"Don't worry, lads", said Pat, who was relighting his pipe. "I keep a close eye on every bolt and rivet on these beasties. They're both in good runnin' order, though not as good as I'd like. But as far as wings fallin' off, you needn't worry. You might catch your deaths in them during the wintertime, but other than that, they're both perfectly safe".

"Of course", Bob replied blandly.

The B-17 once again landed and taxied over to the hanger. As soon as the engines stopped, the pilots climbed out. Charlie came out last and secured the belly hatch, then walked over to the group.

"See what I mean?", Charlie asked cheerily, "fit as a fiddle!"

"What's next?", asked Dick.

"Next we discuss strategy and tactics for bombing fires", replied Charlie. "Then we practice flying a bit. Once you boys are confident of your birds, we'll practice dropping water, then retardant out in the woods. Then, hopefully, you children will be ready for the real thing. Fire season is just about here, so we don't have much time to practice. With two birds, though, you shouldn't have too much trouble logging enough hours each. Why don't we meet back here at, say, six-thirty tomorrow morning".

"OK, Charlie", said Bob. "We've already got our rooms in town. Uh Pat, can you recommend any good bars?"

Dick gave Bob a sidelong look, as Pat answered, "You might want to try the 'Lone Pine', lad. I believe you'll find what you're lookin' for there".

"Thanks, Pat", Bob replied with a grin. "See you guys in the morning".

"What was that all about?", Charlie asked Pat, after the Talon pilots had left.

"Marines", Pat said simply.

"Oh, I see. Well, I hope they can still see straight tomorrow".

Everyone was on time the next day, although Dick was sporting a black eye.

"I just ran into a door, that's all", he said in embarrassment.

"Yeah, with a little help from a lumberjack!", said Bob with a laugh.

"All right, children", said Charlie. "Let's get started. Today, we learn something about what to look for when approaching a fire. Let's begin with a couple of terms. The starting point for a fire is called the base. The sides of a fire are called the flanks. The front edge of the fire, the part which is moving into the forest, is called the head. There are two basic types of attack: ground attack and air attack.

"Ground attack is carried out by men and equipment on the ground. It usually will start at the base of the fire and move towards the head. Air attack is carried out by planes and is generally done at the head, moving back towards the base. There are several different methods for attacking a fire, which are loosely grouped under the headings of direct, indirect, and parallel".

Charlie moved to a chalkboard at the front of the room, then continued, "Direct means that the main attack is carried out against the head, usually with the fire line anchored on a natural fire barrier, like a road or a river. This is the most effective type of attack, but it's also the most dangerous. If the wind whips up, firefighters can be cut off by the fire. This is also the most dangerous for the ground crews when we bomb the fire.

"I know of several times where ground personnel and equipment have been accidentally bombed. In all cases, some injuries occurred. In a couple of cases, deaths occurred. You have to remember, when we drop a load of retardant, it doesn't just vaporize; it hits the target like a tidal wave. Even if no injuries occur, it's a mess to clean up the equipment. Make sure of your target before you release. Make another pass, maybe two passes before you release".

He began drawing a diagram on the board. "Suppose this is your fire. With an indirect attack, you do what's called 'fireproofing'. Basically, you drop retardant well ahead of the fire so that you can have the firebreak ready when the fire gets there. This is more effective for fires where you don't have enough personnel or planes to fight it head-on. It's also safer for personnel. They can start a back fire out in front of the retardant and do a controlled burn back in the direction of the oncoming fire. If they can keep that backfire under control, they deny the incoming fire of it's fuel and, effectively, make an even bigger firebreak. Using the Indirect method, the fire crews can avoid the heat and smoke of a particularly intense fire and the planes can avoid the thermals thrown off by the hot spots in the fire".

Charlie erased the diagram, then began a new one. "The last method is called the Parallel method. This is where the fire line is made about forty feet back from the flanks of the fire. It has the advantages of the Direct approach, where a minimum of excess fire line has to be constructed, and the advantages of the Indirect method, since the line is constructed back away from the fire. The disadvantage is that, if the fire is fast-moving, the ground personnel are endangered by sudden wind changes and the planes are subjected to thermals".

"So which method is the best?", asked Chet.

"They all have their advantages and disadvantages", replied Charlie. "It's up to the commanders on the scene as to how they want to prosecute the fire. Usually, the Direct or Indirect methods are used. Since fires are unpredictable, the Fire Boss, the guy in charge, will want to keep the retardant drops as close to the predicted path of the fire as possible. He will have to trade off between the safety of the aircrews and the need to stop the fire. If the retardant drifts into the fire, it's pretty-much wasted. If the fire changes direction from the predicted path, an entire fire line may be wasted".

"Is there any variation on these methods that works better?", asked Bob.

"My favorite approach is to pinch off the head", Charlie answered. "The bombers make a series of drops on the flanks of the fire, moving from the base towards the head. Once the head is reached, the drops continue past it and slowly close the gap between the flanks. By the time the fire reaches the main firebreak, the head may have shrunk from several miles wide to only a mile wide. The only problem with this method is that it wastes space. You have to project your retardant drops out beyond the head, instead of attacking the head directly. But if you're limited on ground personnel, it's the best method I've found for consistent containment".

"How do you know which direction the fire is heading?", asked Ralph. "By the wind direction?"

"Usually", said Charlie. "The smoke will drift in the direction the fire is heading, so you assume that your drops will be along that axis. But like I said, fires are unpredictable. They may change direction real quick. When we fight fires in Southern California, there's a wind down there called a Santa Ana. It can whip the direction of the fire around so fast you can't respond quickly enough to contain it. I've seen fires that were 95% contained get out of control again if one of those Santa Anas picks up. It's not much fun to fly through either".

"I think that's enough about fires for today", said Charlie as he erased the board. "Let's talk about the B-17s you're going to be flying. I'll start it off with a little story we used to tell at my base in England. The two main types of planes we flew were the B-17 and the B-24. The B-17 was a sturdy old war-horse. The B-24, though, was a prima-donna. The story goes that a B-17 was returning from a mission with the pilot and co-pilot dead, two engines out, the tip of one wing shot-off, and a lot of damage to most of the control cables. The navigator was flying her in when the tower told him to do a go-around. Seems there was a B-24 with some trouble in one engine which needed to make an emergency landing. In short, these babies could take a lot of punishment and still keep on flying. That's probably why those two crates out by the hanger are still running. I've seen a number of B-17s fighting forest fires, but I can't recall seeing more than one B-24 in recent years".

Charlie spent the rest of the morning explaining the systems on the B-17, then took his class out to familiarize them with the controls on the planes themselves. When he took each pair up for a flight that day, the pilots began to get more comfortable with the planes. Over the next few weeks, each pilot was given a chance to fly the bombers. Once they had mastered the basics, they were taken to a remote area and practiced doing retardant drops empty. After Charlie felt they were ready, he had Pat fill up the planes with water, then repeated the dummy drops. The first time out, Chet nearly lost control of the plane when he released his load too fast and the plane pitched up. After several more tries, all of the pilots became more confident of their ability to carry out water drops. As Charlie reminded them, though, this was just practice. The real test was yet to come: dropping on a fire. Their opportunity was not long in coming.

Chapter 13

Dick was sound asleep when the phone rang. "What is it?", he said drowsily.

"This is Charlie", said the voice on the phone. "Get your buddies and meet me at the hanger. We've got a fire to go fight!"

"At two in the morning?", said Dick as he looked at the clock.

"Fires don't just burn from nine to five, Dickie boy", said Charlie. "See you in fifteen minutes".

Dick dressed, then went down the hall and awakened the rest of the Talon pilots. They all plodded downstairs and piled into their car. They were at the hanger ten minutes later. Pat already had the place lit up and Charlie was checking over each bomber.

"Top o' the mornin' to you lads!", said Pat cheerily. The pilots just mumbled their greetings, then went over to see Charlie.

"Well boys, this is it, your first fire. Bob, I want you and Dick to take 'Hot Lunch' up to Ukiah. I've already marked up your flight plan on the map in the pilot's seat. Take Pat along with you. Chet and Ralph will fly up with me in 'Gertie's Garters'

"The fire appears to be in Indian Valley just east of there. Looks like lightning started it. I think we're going to have our hands full for the next couple of days so I hope you guys have rested up. You probably aren't going to get much sleep for awhile".

The pilots helped Pat load up what tools and parts they could carry, then taxied the planes out to the end of the runway. 'Gertie's Garters' took off first, followed by 'Hot Lunch'. Charlie made one circle of the field, then headed off in a northwesterly direction. The flight up was uneventful until they approached Ukiah. Even in the darkness, the plume of smoke could be seen, the quarter moon throwing enough light on it to make it visible for miles.

"Looks like this one's got a head-start on us", said Charlie grimly. "This won't be a one-dump job, that's for sure"

"I see a couple of planes circling the smoke", said Chet. "Do you think they're trying to bomb it already?"

"More likely they're spotting for ground crews", replied Charlie. "This sucker looks like it already covers almost four hundred acres. I'm surprised we didn't get a call until now. Well, let's see where Forestry wants us to park these crates".

Charlie received his directions and landed at Ukiah Air Attack Base. A CDF S-2 was preparing to load retardant. Another was just topping off. Charlie pulled up beside them, closely followed by

'Hot Lunch'. Once they had shut off the engines, everybody got out and chocked the wheels, then walked over to the ready room where the Forestry people were talking to the bomber pilots.

"Hello Charlie", said a short, squat little man.

"Hello Abner", Charlie replied. "What's new? I see you have a little problem out there".

"Little!", grunted Abner. "This one's already chewed up 500 acres, and it looks like that number will double by dawn!"

"From what I saw on the way in, I think it already has", said Charlie. "But I'm forgetting my manners. Let me introduce you to my crew. This is Abner Hollis, California Division of Forestry spotter. He's the one who will probably eat you for lunch if you miss a drop" .

"Oh, come now", said Abner. "I'm not really that bad. Not if I've had my coffee in the morning, that is. Did I mention that we'd run out of coffee Charlie?", he said with a predatory grin.

The pilots all introduced themselves, then Abner noticed Pat hanging back behind the group.

"Patrick, you Irish devil, what are you hiding back there for?", Abner roared. "You aren't still sore about that poker game last season, are you?"

"Never you mind, about that poker game!", said Pat with a scowl. "I still say you had an ace up your sleeve, and that's the truth of the matter!"

"Don't pay any attention to him, gentlemen", said Abner with a laugh. "He just can't stand to lose, that's all".

"To blazes with ya!", said Pat in a fury. "I don't mind losin' fair and square. But to have a full house come out of nowhere, now that takes the cake!"

"It was all done fair and square, Pat", said Abner. "It looks like the Irish aren't the only ones who have all the luck".

"Bah, a pox on you and yours", said Pat as he stalked off to sulk. Abner chuckled a bit, then returned to the rest of the group.

"Well my friends, we have a major fire on our hands", Abner began. "It appears to have been several lightning strikes up in Indian Valley over an area of about five miles. The ranger station first spotted the smoke at sunset. We had expected something would develop sooner than that, but we couldn't get enough planes on it before we lost the light. We've kept several spotters up there directing ground ops, but none of the bombers have been able to work it. so far. It'll be another hour until we get enough light to see clearly. We'll wait until half an hour before sunrise, then hit it with everything we've got. Why don't you guys check out your aircraft in the meantime, then I'll fly up there and see what we can do".

Charlie introduced his crews to the CDF pilots and ground crew, then showed them around the ready room. Photos of old World War II aircraft dropping on fires were mounted on the walls. After they had finished their tour, he took them out and had them give the bombers a thorough going-over. Once everyone was sure of their mounts, they taxied over to the retardant tanks and began to load up. Abner took off in an OV-10 while they were filling up, then the two S-2s took off as well. Charlie had Bob taxi 'Hot Lunch' to the end of the runway and wait to take off. Twenty minutes later, Charlie's two planes lumbered down the runway. Once they were airborne, Abner directed them into an orbit to the east of Ukiah, slightly above the S-2s they had seen before. Then they waited.

"When do we start our run?", asked Chet anxiously.

"When Abner gives us a target", replied Charlie. "Nervous son?"

"Excited", said Chet. "I've been waiting to try this ever since I hired on".

"Yeah, that first live drop is the one you remember the rest of your life", mused Charlie. "Although, I have a hard time remembering back that far, myself".

Their conversation was interrupted by a call from Abner telling one of the S-2s where to drop, and instructing the other to follow the first in and drop behind him. The two planes moved off east, leaving the two B-17s doing lazy circles.

"When do you suppose we get to go?", Dick asked Bob in 'Hot Lunch'.

"When the man gives the signal", replied Bob calmly. "It gives me a chance to look over this fire some. See the dark smoke over towards the center?"

"Yeah, I see a couple of plumes of it".

"Charlie says those are hot spots. He said to never drop on one of those unless it's a spot fire. If the fire is hot enough, it will vaporize the retardant before it ever hits the fire. Best to drop around the edges and box it in. Then it will burn itself out".

"You've been doing a little extra studying, I see", said Dick with a smirk. "Trying to score points with the teacher?"

"Just trying to learn the tricks of the trade".

Their conversation was interrupted by another call from Abner. "Charlie, take your planes on a heading of zero-nine-zero to a distance 30 miles from your present position", Abner said. "You'll see a small ridgeline to the south of the fire. Drop two salvoes on that location just to the right of the fire linking with the previous drops, understood?"

"Two successive salvoes, understood", replied Charlie. "Bob, did you get all that?", Charlie asked over the radio.

"I heard him", replied Bob.

"OK, here's the drill", said Charlie. "I'll make my drop while you follow me in. See how my drop lands, then make any adjustments for your own drop. My first run will be just a dummy run to gauge the wind. My second run will probably be the real thing. Follow me out of the smoke, then make your own run, understood?"

"Roger that", replied Bob.

"Keep the chatter to a minimum when we get over the fire", said Charlie. "Too much talk is distracting".

"Whatever you say, Charlie", Bob said. Bob lined up behind Charlie, keeping enough distance so as not to get caught in his prop wash, then the pair proceeded to the fire. As they approached, Bob saw that there was a great deal of smoke blowing across the ridgeline they were using for their reference point. It would be a little tricky to navigate safely along the ridge in so much smoke. Charlie led them into it without a moment's hesitation, though. After they had followed the ridge for over a mile, several patches of black smoke appeared to their left.

"Hotspots!", said Dick excitedly. "We must be getting close to the head".

"Looks that way", said Bob, a hint of apprehension in his voice. The thermals would get worse as they flew near more hot spots.

"We're coming up on our drop-point", Charlie called over the radio. "Mark the terrain carefully, Bob. See where the last guys dropped their load. I'll link mine to theirs, you can link your drop to mine".

"Will do, Charlie", replied Bob. "Look for anything prominent in the landscape, Dick".

"It looks like there's a little knoll up here ahead", said Dick. "Yeah, I think that will be a good reference point for the drop".

"We're going to bank right, then come around for another pass", Charlie called over the radio.

"We're right behind you, Charlie", Bob called back.

Charlie banked off to the right just past a splotch of red retardant, evidence of a previous drop. As they turned slowly back toward Ukiah, Dick looked out his window. The whole horizon was filled with smoke, and flames could be seen shooting up along the front edge of the fire to the north of them.

"The flank must be three or four miles long".

"And that's just what's burning now", replied Bob. "It looks like it's already burned up five or six miles from where it started".

"I wonder who's dropping on the head of this thing?", asked Dick.

"Probably somebody who has a lot more experience than we do. I have a hunch that Abner wants to see what we're made of in a less critical area before he turns us loose on a critical one".

"We'll be turning to starboard and commencing an attack run, now", said Charlie over the radio.

"Roger that", replied Bob. He banked the B-17 right, following behind Charlie. Once they had lined up on the ridge again, Charlie straightened up and reduced his altitude to barely above the tree-tops. Bob followed at a higher altitude, slightly above and well behind Charlie. In this way, he could see how Charlie's load landed and make corrections accordingly.

"Abner, Humboldt Air making first drop now", Charlie called over the radio.

"Understood, Charlie", replied Abner. "Be advised, we have a shift in the wind from 5 knots east-southeast to 10 knots east-southeast".

"Copy that, Abner", said Charlie.

The radio remained silent for a moment as Charlie approached the release point. Suddenly, a bright red stream appeared from underneath his B-17. It fell quickly into the trees, about 25 yards to the south of the fire. It overlapped the previous drop slightly, almost arrow-straight in line with the other retardant.

"Bullseye!", crackled the radio, as Abner assessed the drop. "Nice drop Charlie".

"Thanks, Abner", Charlie replied as the big plane began to climb. Once he was several hundred feet off the ground, he began to bank off to the right. "All right, Junior", he said over the radio. "See if you can top that!"

"Roger that", replied Bob noncommittally. He followed Charlie around until they had moved a few miles east of the smoke.

He then began to drop in altitude as he banked right and lined up on the ridgeline. Charlie moved behind and above him. Bob began to sweat a bit as he approached the target.

"We'll want to undershoot Charlie's drop", Bob said nervously. "Let me know when you see that knoll, Dick".

"OK", replied Dick as he scanned the ridgeline. After what seemed like an eternity to Bob, they both saw the knoll.

"I see the knoll!", said Dick.

"Me too. All right, here we go". Bob keyed the mike and said, "Abner, Humboldt Air making second drop now".

"Understood, Humboldt Air", replied Abner. "Wind conditions have not changed since first drop".

"Roger that", replied Bob. The thermals from a pair of hot-spots near the drop-zone began to buffet the plane slightly as Dick prepared to drop the retardant. The previous drops were off slightly to the right of the plane as they approached them.

"Don't you think you should be a little to the right?", asked Dick.

"I'm trying to get us over there, but this thing is handling like a cow. Let's try another go-around".

"Sounds good to me", said Dick as he removed his hand from the release lever.

"Abner, we're going to try this again", Bob called on the radio.

"Understood, Humboldt Air", Abner replied.

"That was a good call, Bob", said Charlie over the radio. "You never would have made that drop successfully from that position".

"Yeah, I know", replied Bob as his plane gained altitude. "I'll try to line her up better next pass".

"I think you'll probably have to drop this time", said Charlie. "The fire is already beginning to reach the projected line here and other planes are lining up waiting for their drops next".

"Roger that", replied Bob. Nothing like a little pressure, he thought as he banked the plane around for his next pass.

A few minutes later, he once again reduced altitude and lined up on the ridgeline. The smoke was making visibility even worse as the fire approached the ridgeline. They passed the knoll and closed distance on the target.

"It's hard to see in here", said Dick as the smoke began to block his view. "This is almost as bad as trying to fly in fog".

"I wish we had all-weather systems on this thing like the Intruders had", replied Bob. "Can you see any sign of the retardant yet?"

"I thought I caught a glimpse of it for a second", replied Dick. "Just a second... Yeah, I see it up ahead. Better sound off".

"Abner, Humboldt Air making second drop now", Bob said into the mike.

"Copy that, Humboldt Air. Be advised, wind has increased to 10 knots, east northeast.

"Roger that", said Bob as he concentrated on flying. "I hope we're far enough to the right this time".

"Looks good from here", said Dick. "We're a good 10-15 yards to the right of the retardant line. Here goes!"

Dick released the retardant while Bob kept the plane straight. The stream of red liquid drifted into the oncoming flames, landing in the midst of a hot-spot near the edge.

"Inside", pronounced Abner over the radio. "Better luck next time, boys".

"Blast it all!", Bob cried out. "That blasted wind carried it right into the fire!"

"Tough break, Bob", said Dick. "Well, I guess it's time to go back and reload".

"Nice try", Charlie called over the radio. "Let's head back to base. I need another cup of coffee".

Charlie didn't get his cup of coffee once they returned to Ukiah. Abner wanted as many planes in the air as he could get. Another series of fires had been started over close to the Sacramento National Wildlife Refuge, hereagain by lightning. This fire was being given priority and Abner was being forced to give up many of his planes. Charlie was directed to reload and return immediately. His crews didn't even get out of the planes. They simply taxied over to the retardant tanks and reloaded, then took off again. Abner assigned them an orbit to the west of the fire again.

Bob found out that the shift in wind direction which had spoiled his shot had also changed the direction of the fire enough that the other bombers had been able to completely fireproof the right flank of the fire. Parallel operations on the left flank had also been successful. Unfortunately, the head of the fire had passed the incomplete line of retardant and was proceeding east faster than anticipated. The Ground Boss was hard-pressed to close up the gap between the unfinished frontal fire line and the existing left flank. He wanted air drops on the widening gap pronto.

With fewer aircraft to work with, Abner decided he would have to trust the pilots in Humboldt Air to carry out the more difficult drops on the head of the fire. Chet had changed places with Charlie in 'Gertie's Garters', so there were now two relatively green pilots flying. Charlie was in the co-pilot's seat, though, so he could take over if necessary. Bob, however, was on his own.

After orbiting for ten minutes, Chet received a call from Abner directing him to a new orbit northeast of the fire. Bob followed him over, then began orbiting again. Five minutes later, they all saw a succession of drops by several CDF S-2 bombers on the advancing edges of the fire. The incomplete line of retardant was clearly visible to the south of them, as was the left-flank line to the west. The other planes were attempting to link the two lines up, but it would take at least two more drops to do the job. As the other planes cleared the area, Abner called up.

"Humboldt Air, I need two drops linking the previous drops just made", Abner said. "Do you see the target zone?"

"We do", replied Chet. "Are we cleared to begin attack run now?"

"You are cleared to begin your approach now", replied Abner. Be advised that winds are now blowing north by northeast at fifteen knots".

"OK, Abner", replied Chet. "Beginning attack run".

Charlie called up over the radio, "Bob, follow us in and line up on the fire. There's no time for a practice run this time, so you'll have to drop right after we do, understood?"

"Copy that", replied Bob tautly. Let's hope I don't blow it this time, he thought.

'Gertie's Garters' began dropping down in altitude while banking right to line up on the previous retardant drops. As the plane approached the end of the line, the bombay doors opened and the retardant streamed out over the trees. The drop lined up slightly off to the left of the existing line.

"Bullseye! , called Abner over the radio.

Bob was now down to treetop level with 'Hot Lunch'. He was fast approaching the target and Dick was a little edgy waiting to release. The smoke was obscuring the view again, since the fire was only fifty yards to the right and the wind was blowing towards them. Knowing that the wind was going to carry the load to the northeast, Bob lined up to the left of the previous drops. Some turbulence still bucked the aircraft, but he kept her on course. As they approached the end of the line of retardant, Dick eased his hand over to the release lever. When they were opposite the middle of Chet's drop, Dick pulled the release. The big plane lurched upwards as the cargo fell to the ground. Bob continued flying straight and level for another thousand yards, then began to climb away from the forest and bank right.

"Bullseye!", shouted Abner over the headset. "Well done, Humboldt Air!"

"Nice drop, Bob!", called Charlie. "Perfectly lined up. Couldn't have done it better myself".

As they orbited right, Bob and Dick took a look at their drop. It was aligned perfectly with the existing line and corrected the slight indentation Chet's drop had made. The fire was now roped in.

"Return to base", called Abner. "Reload and return when you're ready, this bugger's not dead yet".

"Roger that", replied Bob. He turned back towards Ukiah, then glanced at Dick and smiled. Dick returned his smile, then Bob looked proudly out the window at his first successful drop.

That day, Humboldt Air dropped many tons of retardant on the fires around Ukiah. The fire in Indian Valley was contained by noon, and the one over in the Refuge was 90% contained by nightfall. When dark finally came, a tired group of pilots gathered in the Ready Room to eat some grub, some going to their hotel afterward to get some sleep.

"I hear you lads did a fine job today", said Pat as he joined them for dinner. "Abner said he'd seldom seen such good results from beginners".

"My first attempt wasn't too good", said Bob as he wolfed down some pork and beans. "But they got better as the day went on".

"There's always room for improvement", said Charlie. "But you shouldn't kick yourself too hard when you fail to get a bullseye. The wind can change fairly fast out there. I've seen drops that should have been right on the money fall uselessly inside the fire because of a wind change only a couple of seconds before release. Add to that the problems caused by shadows close to sunup or sundown, and you can get a lot of error in your drops".

"They've told us the bombers we fly will have computerized bomb-sights", said Ralph. "If they're anything like I've seen on Air Force bombers, we should be able to get some good accuracy with all of our drops. There was a training film at Nellis when I was going through orientation that showed the difference between dropping iron bombs with an optical bombsight and smart bombs with a laser. The difference was like day and night. Iron bombs didn't do much damage to a bridge, but smart bombs smashed it!"

"I wouldn't mind having something better for my rigs", said Charlie. "But I'm used to the gear we've got. I can get by. Look at the advantages of learning how to bomb by eye. If your computer ever goes belly-up, you've got the option of switching to optical to do the job".

While Ralph sipped his coffee, he said, "I guess that's one of the reasons Pieter sent us up here. He probably wanted us to get our feet wet the hard way, just in case we had to fight fires that way again".

"I 'spect", said Charlie. "Well guys, I don't know about you, but I'm ready for a little shuteye. Give me a call about 5 A.M. so I can prep my bird. 'Night, all".

"I think Charlie's got the right idea", said Chet. He had just finished his third plate of food and was beginning to feel drowsy. "See you guys in the morning

When 4 A.M. rolled around, Pat begin his inspection of the planes for the new day.

Charlie wasn't up much behind Pat. He grabbed a quick cup of coffee in the Ready Room, then walked out to inspect the planes himself.

"Well Charlie, what do you think of the lads now?", Pat asked Charlie as he approached.

"I think they'll make it. Bob is tenacious. He just won't quit until he has the right angle on a drop. I saw him make three passes on a spot fire before he finally dropped on it. He still has to improve on speed. We almost lost the fire once because he was taking too long to drop. If he can improve his eye so he drops on the first pass most times, I think he would rank right up there with the best in the business".

"What about Chet, your co-pilot?"

"He shows promise", said Charlie while he checked a tire. "He needs more time to develop, but I think a few more fires will smooth off his rough edges. Same for Ralph and Dick. Given a few more drops, I think they'll all be fine".

"How has this beastie been running lately?", Pat asked after he checked the cowling on engine number 3 on 'Gertie's Garters'.

"Fine. Why do you ask?"

"It just looks like this engine has been overheating a wee bit, that's all. You might want to keep an eye on this one next time you're up there".

"OK, worrywart", chided Charlie. "I'm sure we'll get there and back just fine!"

"It never hurts to be a wee bit cautious", said Pat defensively. "After all, we Irish have to look out for each other".

"Ah, is that what it is. Well, I think you've got enough Irish for the both of us. My grandparents never talked much about Ireland when I was growing up. I think they were just glad to get out of there. My grandmother refused to speak Gaelic around the house because she said we were Americans now and should speak English".

"I remember you telling me that before. Why do ya suppose she was that way?"

"She never said. Dad mentioned one time that they had lost everything in that famine that hit Ireland in the 1880's, but wouldn't say more. I guess it was too painful a subject".

"Sure and it would be", said Pat thoughtfully. "Leavin' Ireland behind must have been mighty hard for your family. If it hadn't been for me Lorrie wantin' to live here, I think I would have moved back there long ago. But I can't complain. I've had good friends here. This is a fine country, after all" .

"Yep. Well it's going to be a fine country minus a few thousand acres of trees if we don't get these birds tanked up. Sun's going to be coming up in another half hour and I want to be ready to get out there".

"Right you are, Charlie", said Pat. He rolled a ladder over and climbed up onto the wing. Charlie finished his inspection of 'Gertie's Garters', then moved over to check out 'Hot Lunch'. Fifteen minutes later, Bob brought the Talon pilots over to the planes.

"You two get any breakfast yet?", he called over to the planes.

"I had a cup of coffee", replied Pat. "That's enough for now. I'll get somethin' more once you lads are airborne".

"How about you, Charlie", Chet asked.

"Well, if you boys want to taxi these babies over and tank them up, I'll grab something to eat", Charlie answered.

"Fair enough", said Chet. He and Ralph climbed into 'Gertie's Garters' while Bob and Dick began to fire up 'Hot Lunch'. Both planes were soon being tanked up over at the side of the airstrip while Pat and Charlie got some breakfast. Once the planes were tanked up , Charlie and Pat were outside waiting. Abner came on the radio and announced the routes to the first targets of the day. A few minutes later, both B-17s were heading east.

Chapter 14

While Humboldt Air was grappling with the fires up north, Talon Aerospace was completing the electronic retrofit on the first CL-415. Pieter had asked to be the first to take the plane up at night and was immediately impressed. Dave flew along to provide instruction and technical assistance.

"Wow, look at that picture!", Pieter exclaimed. "It's like looking at the hills in broad daylight!"

"Ain't TRIDINT a wonderful thing?", asked Dave with a smile.

"There's a lot of times I would have killed to get this clear a view of a fire. Will it be this clear through smoke, too?"

"You'll be able to see the flames through the smoke with the infrared sensors. The Army uses these to see through smoke-screens on the battlefield. The radar will give you a good feel for the terrain, and the low-light TV will let you see in the dark. We'll just have to wait till a fire shows up and try it!"

"This bird really handles nice. I had never flown one of these before. I'd seen a few around, but never got a chance to get behind the wheel".

"Have you tried scooping up water yet?", asked Dave.

"As a matter of fact, I haven't. You got time?"

"I've got the time. Where do we go?"

"How about Big Bear Lake?"

"Let's go!", said Dave enthusiastically.

A short while later, Pieter slowed the plane and dropped altitude until he was skimming across Big Bear Lake. Ten seconds later, the indicators showed a full load. Pieter applied power and pulled back on the yoke. The plane, now almost 5 tons heavier, slowly climbed out of the lake and banked left. Pieter increased power until the plane reached 140 knots.

"That was easy enough", said Dave. "How did she handle?"

"Like a dream", said Pieter. "That sure beats reloading a C-119. I had to land the plane and taxi over to the retardant tanks, then wait for the ground crew to pipe the retardant into the belly tanks. What a pain compared to this. If that refueling receptacle on this bird works, we wouldn't have to land all day. How's that retardant mixer coming along?"

"They haven't even gotten that far yet", replied Dave as the plane leveled out. "They're still working on the formula for the retardant concentrate. The chemists at Bergway Chemical are evidently burning the midnight oil trying to puzzle it out. They say they should have a workable formula by the end of the year".

"When do you expect to have the other aircraft fitted with their electronics?"

"The Hawkeyes will probably be the last. We've run into a couple of snags with the TRIDINT displays on them. Other than that, everything is ahead of schedule. I'd say we could put a demonstration force together by the end of September. That is, if Caprock can get those new *Zephyr*-class fire engines built by then".

"Good. That will give me plenty of time to finish training my crews. Most of the ground crews are already fully trained. Once the pilots come back from up north, we can get them acquainted with their new charges and start training them as squadrons".

"From what Zack said, it sounds like our firefighters are doing well on the ground up north, too", said Dave. "I just hope the new ground equipment works out OK. We're trying a lot of new stuff at once. We could get into problems if several key items fail to work as advertised".

"It's our job to make sure they do work right", said Pieter matter-of-factly. "We have enough bright minds on this project to at least give us a fighting chance".

"I hope you're right. Sometimes I have my doubts. It's not just a game. People's lives depend on this stuff working right first time, every time".

"Hey, don't go getting melancholy on me, mad scientist!", said Pieter with a grin. "Everything will work out fine. Cheer up! We'll be famous!"

"Yeah, why worry?", said Dave. He brightened up a bit after a moment's pause. "After all", he continued, "we'll triple-check every system before any of it is used. I'd say we're covered".

"Right! "Now, let's see how this baby does in making a bullseye. You can be the bombardier. I'll tell you when to release the load. OK?"

"Sure. Say when!"

Pieter flew in low over the trees, scanning the forest ahead with his TRIDINT gear. "Looks like a few hikers on the trail tonight".

"I can't see anything but trees. Ah yes, I see something on the display."

"Yeah, something", answered Pieter. "I guess they're people, but I can't be sure".

"I don't suppose people would like it too much if we dropped this on them, would they?", Dave observed.

"It would be pretty uncomfortable for them. I think I'm going to take us up a bit higher. That way, the stream will disperse by the time it reaches the ground. If there is anybody there, they'll just get a shower".

"You want me to set the release for 'salvo' or 'trail'?"

"Better play it safe", said Pieter. "Set it for 'trail'. That will stream it out slowly, instead of dumping the whole load at once".

"You got it!", said Dave. He entered the setting in the control panel. "You know, with this thing being computerized now, we can link several planes to drop simultaneously. That means you can create a continuous line of drops".

"I know", said Pieter. "I think that's the fourth or fifth time you've mentioned it".

"Sorry", said Dave shyly. "I sometimes forget who I've talked to about things".

"That's OK, Dave. I guess you have a lot on your mind these days, so it's understandable. I think we're high enough now. Get ready with the release. *Now!*"

The plane climbed slightly as the water streamed out of the tanks. Pieter compensated for the change and returned the plane to level flight. When the tanks were empty, he banked left to see how the drop went.

"Hard to tell how it hit without any color to it", he told Dave.

"Look at the TRIDINT display. There should be some drop in temperature where the water hit".

"By golly, you're right!", said Pieter excitedly. "This is pretty neat equipment you've added, Dave".

"I thought it might be helpful", said Dave proudly. "You can see some variation off to the left, can't you?"

"Yes, it's slightly cooler there. It's not as noticeable now, though. It must be warming up".

"I doubt that there was more than a ten degree drop in temperature from that shower", said Dave. "If you dropped a salvo at lower altitude, I think you would probably see a greater variation".

"I'm satisfied with the results. I'm impressed that we can see even so slight a variation in temperature. Fires should show up real good on this display".

"We should probably set a few burn-barrels on fire on the training ground and see how they show up. I think you'd really notice the difference - especially at night".

"It looks like we'll have no problems doing night ops", said Pieter. "That right there will gain us a whole bunch of notoriety with the Forestry Service. Nobody's bombers fly at night, especially in hilly country. With this gear, we can fill a need that has been around since firebombing first began".

"How about making a few more runs?"

"We could do a couple of salvoes over the lake itself. That way, we'd be sure not to hit any people".

Pieter and Dave made several more practice runs up at Big Bear, then headed for home. Several hundred miles to the north, Charlie and the Talon pilots were also calling it a day. They had successfully eliminated a number of spot fires started by lightning close to Ukiah, all of them before they became anything more major. Abner congratulated everyone on a job well done. The storms had rolled on east and the hazard in the Ukiah area was steadily reducing.

The ground crews at the Ukiah Air Attack base prepped most of the planes for their journeys home, then bedded down in town for the night. By all projections, they would be heading home the next day. The Talon pilots had just successfully fought their first campaign and, although they were tired, they were satisfied with their progress. Charlie praised all of the Talon pilots as the best beginners he had ever worked with. He looked forward to more successes in the new fire season. There were still several more months and many more fires to fight before the pilots would go back to Talon Industries, however.

Back at Talon Industries, all was not well. Jerry walked rapidly down the hall and entered Joe's office, then shut the door.

"Hi Jerry", said Joe. "What's up?"

"I have a friend down at police headquarters who just called. It seems that Mathias Flick died last night".

Joe was stunned. "What did he die of?"

"It was made to look like a gas explosion in his water heater. The police found the remains of an explosive device in the wreckage. They are certain that an arsonist did the job".

"Have they got any leads on just who's behind it?"

"Not yet. They are still working on it. They said that there are only a handful of people who do this caliber of work. He appears to have been quite professional. It was apparently a major stroke of luck that the police found any evidence of the incendiary device".

"OK, keep me informed. How's everything else going?"

"Pieter and Dave took one of the new firebombers up to the mountains for a shake-down of the new equipment they have added. I have not talked to them yet to see what they thought of it. Progress is still slow on the other firebomber-related projects. We hope to hear some news soon on the heavy equipment conversions. Those are apparently proceeding quite well".

"Fine", said Joe absently. "Let me know if you hear anything more on Mathias Flick's murder".

"Very well", said Jerry. Once he had left the room, Joe's thoughts turned to what Jerry had just said. An arsonist had been used by someone to kill a friend. Why would someone want to kill Mathias Flick? Joe called up Allen Sims.

"Allen, could you spare me a few minutes please"

"I will be right over", replied Allen.

Allen walked through the office door a few moments later. Joe directed him to a chair.

"Has Jerry told you about Mathias Flick?", Joe asked as Allen sat down.

"No, what about him?", Allen replied.

"He died in a fire at home last night", said Joe. "It appears that an arsonist set an incendiary device of some sort in his water heater. The police haven't released a general statement on this yet. I want you to assign a couple of your investigators to find out what they can. Check with the police, any witnesses, and any arson experts you know of. I want this thing thoroughly researched. Let me know if you find anything the police are not disclosing in the papers. I want top priority on this, Allen. Put your best people on it".

"I will get them started immediately", said Allen. "Is that all?"

"One more thing. Ask Jerry for the name of his source down at police headquarters. That source will probably be your best starting point".

"Consider it done", said Allen. A bell had gone off somewhere in the back of Joe's head. As he watched Allen leave the room, he realized that he was overreacting to this situation. People were murdered all the time. He had only known Mathias Flick briefly, and powerful men generally accumulated powerful enemies. There was something more to this case, though. He couldn't put his finger on it, but that sixth sense of his had seldom been wrong in the past. He was most interested to see what Allen and Jerry could turn up on this affair. He had no idea just how close to home their findings would eventually come.

Chapter 15

Pat was not a happy man. He frowned as he looked over engine number 3 on 'Gertie's Garters'.

"This engine is in need of an overhaul, Charlie", he shouted, as Charlie walked into the hanger. "I wouldna' recommend takin' the beastie up again till I've done a proper job of fixin' it".

"We can't wait", replied Charlie. "There's a fire that was just spotted outside of Whispering Pines. We'll be heading up to Ukiah again".

"Ah don't like the looks of this engine!", Pat said heatedly. "It's going to give out soon if you aren't careful!"

"Pat, how many times do I have to tell you. I've flown Forts with only three engines in the past. Even if the engine cuts out, I've still got three others to keep me aloft. Even with a full load, that's plenty of lift".

"These planes are not as young as they used to be, and neither are you!", said Pat angrily. "You are goin' to ask too much of them one of these days an' it will be the end of ya!"

"We'll be fine", said Charlie with a smile. "Trust me!"

"You're too bloody cocky for your own good, if you ask me!", said Pat, as he returned to his work.

Charlie just shook his head in amusement and continued on over to the office. The Talon pilots were all waiting anxiously to see what the story was this time. They had already fought over a dozen fires that summer and were looking forward to this one. They had crisscrossed the state all season and would now be returning to where they had started out so many weeks ago.

"Another lightning bust?", asked Dick.

"Looks like it", replied Charlie. "There are at least seven small fires all around the area east of Whispering Pines. We'll want to get up there before they link up. They could produce a major headache if they do combine".

"When do we leave?", asked Chet.

"As soon as that mutinous mechanic of mine gets 'Gertie's Garters' back together", Charlie said with a smirk. "I think he's getting just a little too cautious in his old age

"We had better go get our gear then", said Chet. "We'll be back in an hour, Charlie".

"Don't take too long, boys", Charlie said. "I might give up waiting and leave before you get back!"

"Not from what I saw of your plane", chided Bob. "It's going to take a good two hours for Pat to have everything back together and checked out".

"Not if I get after him, it won't", replied Charlie. "I'll beat him over the head with his shillelagh if he isn't done in an hour!"

When the Talon pilots returned an hour later, both B-17s were sitting in front of the hanger. Pat and Charlie were having an animated conversation about something as the pilots approached. They abruptly fell silent when the pilots came within earshot.

"Are we ready to go?", asked Ralph.

"No!", replied Pat with an angry glance at Charlie.

"I think we are", said Charlie, who pointedly ignored Pat's glare. "Load up, everybody".

Pat stomped off to the hanger grumbling under his breath, then returned a few moments later with his tools and gear. He was the last one to board 'Hot Lunch', still grumbling to himself. As the planes circled the field, Charlie looked fondly down on his little empire, then set his course northwestward and began climbing. 'Hot Lunch' followed and the woods around Humboldt Air were soon peaceful again.

The sky was once again blanketed with smoke as the two planes approached Ukiah Air Attack Base. As soon as they had landed, Abner told them to hurry up and load their tanks. He wanted to get a handle on this fire before it got dark. Charlie led them up to the retardant tanks.

"Hi there", said a CDF pilot who walked up to Charlie's plane. "You suppose I could borrow one of your guys to act as spotter for me?"

"Why, do you need one right now, Paul?", asked Charlie.

"Yeah. My copilot had to leave because of a family emergency. I noticed you guys had doubled up and I was wondering if you could spare a guy to spot for me today?"

"Fine by me", replied Charlie. "I'll ask the guys and see if I get any takers".

After talking it over, Ralph volunteered to spot for the CDF. "You've still got Chet to help you, and Bob and Dick make a good team in 'Gertie's Garters'", Ralph said. "I'd just be a fifth wheel anyway".

"That's the way I figure it, too", said Charlie. "OK, Paul, he's all yours".

"Thanks Charlie", said Paul. "I'll try not to break him".

"You'd better not!", said Charlie with a laugh. "I've only got him on loan myself!"

Charlie started up the engines. "Well, Junior, what do you say we go kill us a couple of fires?"

"OK, but can I drive dad?", asked Chet.

"Later. The first run of the day is mine. You get your turn next".

The CDF ground crew had 'Hot Lunch' tanked up and ready to go a few minutes later. The plane was soon taxiing down the runway. She joined up with 'Gertie's Garters' in an orbit 20 miles southeast of Ukiah. As Abner had hoped, these fires were still just spot fires. With three more hours of daylight, there was a good chance of killing them before they got any larger.

"Humboldt Air", called Abner, "I need two drops on a spot ten miles due east of your present location, please acknowledge",

"That's a roj", said Charlie. "Dick, you copy that?"

"Affirmative", replied Dick. "We'll follow you over Charlie".

"OK Dick, out", Charlie said. He banked his plane to the left and began heading east. The spot fire was plainly visible ahead of them.

"Dick, I think this one can be snuffed with two drops", Charlie said over the radio. "Do you agree?"

"I'd say so, Charlie", Dick replied. "You want me to follow you in?"

"No, stay here and monitor my drop. The wind is a little tricky today and I may drop wide".

"Understood Charlie. Good Luck".

"OK, out", said Charlie. His plane began to descend. He was five miles out from the target and closing on it at 120 knots. He reached treetop level three miles out. "Humboldt Air making first drop", he said into the mike.

"Understood Charlie", said Abner. "Winds are steady at 10 knots, due east".

"Piece of cake", said Charlie. "No smoke in our faces, no crosswinds, no hurry. Life is good".

At that moment, the number three engine began to heat up. The temperature was steadily climbing and finally showed up on the console.

"Engine three is running hot", said Chet suddenly. He looked out the right-side window at the wing. "I see a little smoke coming from the cowling. We had better pull up, Charlie".

"Nah! She'll hold together long enough for me to make this drop, then we can shut down number three and coast back to base. Looks like Pat was right, that engine did cause me some trouble after all".

Charlie was less than two miles from the fire when a muffled explosion shook the aircraft and the number three prop froze. Flames began spurting out of the cowling.

"Fire in number three!", Chet yelled.

"Shut down number three and bring up power on number four!", shouted Charlie, who fought to keep the plane level. They were practically on top of the fire now, but their altitude was beginning to drop. Chet did as Charlie said and the plane began to gain altitude slightly. The flames were still coming out of number three.

A few hundred feet above the trees, Bob and Dick looked on apprehensively as they saw the smoke trailing out behind Charlie's plane.

"Should I call them up about it?", asked Dick anxiously.

"I'm sure they know the situation", replied Bob, fighting to stay calm. "Abner, this is Humboldt Air, we have an emergency. One of Charlie's engines appears to be on fire".

"Understood, Humboldt Air", Abner answered. "I will advise other aircraft to stay clear until he's out of there".

"Copy that", said Bob. Let's hope he can *get* it out of there, he thought.

"Number three is still on fire!", Chet yelled excitedly. "Number four is overheating! You've got to get us out of these trees, Charlie!"

"Hit the extinguisher for number three again", said Charlie. "Hang on, I'll get us out of here Junior".

As Charlie began to pull back on the yoke, engine number four began to smoke and lose power.

"My God, number four is starting to smoke!", yelled Chet. "We're going to have to bail out! Get us some altitude, Charlie!"

"I'll try!", Charlie replied. He continued to pull back on the yoke as they passed through the smoke from the spot fire. A momentary updraft helped to lift the plane slightly, but not much.

Far above, Bob saw the smoke coming from the number four engine on 'Gertie's Garters', then saw the plane fly into the spot fire. Bob suddenly realized that Charlie hadn't dropped his load yet. He keyed the mike, "Charlie, drop your load!"

"Best do as he says, Chet!", Charlie shouted. He was still fighting to bring the crippled plane up. Chet quickly reached over to pull the release lever. At that moment, a tree which was taller than the rest of the forest canopy brushed against the plane's right wingtip. The wing dipped slowly into the canopy and lodged between several trees. The entire plane flipped upward and cartwheeled across the treetops. 'Gertie's Garters' finally penetrated the trees and crashed to the forest floor below. A huge orange fireball engulfed the trees an instant later.

Bob and Dick were speechless. Their friends were both gone in the blink of an eye. The only thing visible now was the fireball which was turning into smoke as it rose skyward. Abner kept calling frantically on the radio, but neither of the Talon pilots could tear their eyes away from the scene below them. Finally, Bob managed to key the mike.

"Abner", he said woodenly, "They're gone. Charlie and Chet are both gone. No survivors".

"Are you positive they didn't bail out before impact?", Abner called back.

"I'm positive, Abner. Charlie didn't climb high enough for them to safely bail out. The plane exploded when it hit the ground".

"Understood, Humboldt Air", Abner replied sadly. "Return to base. Abner out".

Dick slowly turned the plane back towards Ukiah. Both he and Bob took one last look at the burning wreckage below, then turned their eyes away from it and stared blankly out the windshield.

Pat knew what had happened almost the moment it occurred. There was a radio back at Ukiah which the ground crews used to listen to the action. He simply dropped his head, then walked slowly off to the lounge in back. That's where Bob and Dick found him a short while later.

"Pat, we're sorry about Charlie", said Bob.

"I shouldna' have let him bully me", said Pat between sobs. "I should ha' put my foot down and refused to let him fly it!"

"He knew the dangers", said Dick quietly. "I guess his luck just ran out, that's all".

"It's all me fault!", Pat cried. "I shouldna' have let him fly that bucket o' bolts. Ah, me pur dear Charlie, what ha' I done to ya?"

"He had a chance to pull out", said Bob. "I guess he wanted to get that one last fire before he..."

Everyone grew silent for a few minutes, then Pat looked up. "What about your friend, Chet?"

"He's gone, too", replied Dick sadly.

"That's two I've killed then!", said Pat despondently. He began to sob uncontrollably now. Pat continued sobbing and wringing his hands for several minutes. Bob waited until Pat's sobbing had begun to subside, looked at Dick, then back to Pat.

"Pat", Bob said softly, "you tried to warn him. He was a man full-grown, not a child. You couldn't have done anything more. You didn't kill him, you tried to save him from this very thing. It was his own bullheadedness that caused this tragedy. He could have dumped his load and pulled up the instant that engine began to smoke. He chose not to, and it was the wrong decision. *His* decision, not yours got them killed. You said yourself this is a dangerous business. I don't think Dick and I realized just how dangerous until today. Let's go get the plane ready for another run, huh? There's still work to be done".

Pat perked up a little at that. "So mayhaps I'm not to blame after all?", he said.

"Precisely!", said Dick. "You did all you could short of hog-tying Charlie. There was nothing else you could have done that would have made any difference. Now c'mon, help us get 'Hot Lunch' ready to go".

Pat got unsteadily to his feet. The three of them walked slowly out to the plane.

"*This* beastie doesna' leave the ground until I've given her a thorough check from stem to stern!", said Pat defiantly.

Bob and Dick both put their hands above their heads in mock surrender and stepped back from the crew access hatch. Pat slowly rolled out a ladder, propped it against the wing and proceeded to begin checking the number one engine. Bob turned and winked at

Dick who smiled back. Well, at least Pat's back in order, Bob thought. For the moment at least, he corrected. For the moment.

The second visit to Ukiah closed out the fire season. Once all the fires up there were out, the Talon pilots took Pat back down to Humboldt Air. The flight down was very quiet. Pat had hardly spoken since Charlie's death. Once the B-17's engines stopped, Pat sprang out the hatch and walked quickly over to the hanger. The Talon pilots shut down the plane's systems, went through the crew hatch, and filed over to the hanger. Pat was digging out equipment and tools from various cabinets in the shop. The Talon pilots stood there looking on in confusion, then Bob spoke up.

"What are you doing, Pat?", he asked.

"Gettin' me belongins together", he panted. "You lads are goin' back to your company now, isn't that so?"

"I guess so", said Bob. "Why do you ask?"

"Because I've made up me mind to go along", said Pat, stopping for a moment to catch his breath. "I've been thinkin' about it all the time since pur Charlie passed on. You lads need a good mechanic and I needs a job. You suppose that fancy boss of yours will be wantin' an old airplane mechanic like me?"

"I can't say", replied Bob. "I hadn't thought much about it".

"The way I sees it", said Pat, "it wouldna' hurt to ask his lordship, now would it?"

"All's we can do is try", said Dick. "What harm can it do?"

Dick looked at Bob who merely shook his head, then walked towards the office. "Best thing to do is to find out now before Pat gets all of his gear out for nothing".

Bob called up Pieter, who was by his desk at Talon Industries, for a change. He had just returned from a particularly long and nasty staff meeting and was planning to take his CL-415 up for another flight to unwind. When the phone rang, he was more than a little annoyed.

"What is it?", he asked testily.

"Pieter, this is Bob Mitchell up at Humboldt Air".

"Oh, hi Bob. How's business up there. You guys giving Charlie a run for his money on drops?"

"Not anymore. Charlie's dead, Pieter".

Pieter sagged into his desk chair. "Dead?", he said in disbelief. "What happened?"

"He and Chet Farley augered in up near Ukiah".

"I don't believe it. I never would have thought he would crash. He'd been flying those things for almost fifty years. What was the cause?"

"Mechanical trouble", Bob replied. "Two of the engines on Charlie's plane caught fire before he had a chance to drop his load. The plane hit a tree before he could pull up".

"Incredible", Pieter said quietly. "Chet too?"

"Yeah, Chet too", Bob replied. "I imagine you'll be getting notification on it soon yourself. Oh, the other reason I called was to ask you if you have room in your ground crews for another mechanic? Pat O'Toole was Charlie's mechanic up here. He's more or less out of a job now and wants to join us down there. Do you think there's any chance of his landing a job with Firebombers?"

"I don't see why not", said Pieter, as the shock of Bob's statements wore off. "I've known Pat for a number of years. I know Charlie thought highly of him. Bring him along and I'll see what I can do about a job for him".

"Will do. I guess we'll see you in a day or so. You got any planes there we can fly?"

"Have I ever! Wait till you get a look at what you have to fly now. You won't believe the difference".

"Must be a pretty nifty plane at that", replied Bob. "I think Pat will be selling off the business up here, so it will probably take him a few weeks to get everything in order. I'll have him let you know what his schedule is later".

"Tell him not to worry, we'll have plenty of work for him to do when he gets here. Talk to you when you guys get back. I've got some important business to attend to now".

"What's her name?", asked Bob teasingly.

"I haven't thought of one yet", said Pieter. "But I'll let you know when I do. See ya!"

Bob hung up the phone and walked back out into the hanger. "He says fine", Bob told Pat. "I told him it would be a couple of days before you could set a starting date".

"Thank ye, lad. Well, then, it appears that I've a wee bit o' work ahead of me. The Confederate Air Force showed some interest in 'Hot Lunch'. I do believe it may be high time I was givin' them a call".

"We're going to pack our gear while you two draw up your plans", said Dick. He and Bob walked over to 'Hot Lunch' and began unloading their duffel bags from the plane.

Chapter 16

When the Talon pilots left Humboldt Air the next day, Pat was already deep into negotiations with the Confederate Air Force. The way Pat was negotiating you would have thought he was selling his own children, Bob thought. In a way, he probably was, he decided. Pieter called Dick, Bob, and Ralph into his office as soon as they checked in.

"Hi guys!", Pieter greeted enthusiastically. "How was the trip down?"

"Nothing exciting, which is fine with me", said Bob. "I've had enough excitement for awhile".

"I guess you have at that", said Pieter, some restraint entering into his voice. Then he brightened up again, "Wait till I show you your new mounts! You won't believe what they can do!"

"Can they make coffee?", asked Ralph with a grin.

"Everything but that", said Pieter. "If you boys have the time, I've got a tour for you!"

"So, what are we waiting for?", asked Dick.

Pieter drove the three friends over to the Talon Aerospace hangers and conducted them inside. Sitting in neat rows were seven royal-blue twin-engined amphibious planes. A colorful picture had been painted on each fuselage near the tail. The picture consisted of a blazing fire in the middle over which flew the blue silhouettes of a C-130 four-engine transport plane on the left and a twin-engined CL-415 amphibious plane on the right. Slightly below and to the right of the fire was the silhouette of a *Zephyr*-class fire engine, and on the left was one of a CAT Team bulldozer. Above and below the picture in gold lettering were the words "FIREBOMBERS INCORPORATED". On the closest plane, a large golden number "100" was visible on the fuselage just forward of the tail and behind the company logo.

"So, what do you think?", asked Pieter expectantly.

"Do they fly as good as they look?", asked Ralph.

"No, they fly *better* than they look", replied Pieter with a chuckle. "The electronics Dave's people have installed give you the ability to bullseye a lit match in the middle of a firestorm with a 50-knot crosswind on a moonless night".

"A slight exaggeration Pieter?", asked Bob skeptically.

"Not by much", Pieter answered. "I've already taken this bird up about thirty times. She flies like a dream, reloads in ten seconds, and can bullseye a burn barrel better than 98% of the time. A *burn barrel* for pity's sake! Imagine what a machine like this could do at a fire! And there's going to be upwards of twenty-five to thirty more!"

"We're liable to put all the contractors out of business", said Dick with a grin.

"Not quite, Dick", said Pieter more calmly. "But these babies will take down fires a lot quicker. We'll be able to give the Forestry firefighters a *big* assist".

"Mind if we take one up to try it out?", asked Bob hopefully.

"Be my guest", said Pieter. "That one over there is yours, Bob - Number 101. The rest of you guys can pick any one you want".

"I'll copilot with Bob", said Dick.

"How about if I copilot with you Pieter?", asked Ralph.

"Fine by me. Well, what are you bozos waiting for? Rev 'em up and move 'em out!"

Thirty minutes later, Pieter led the pair up to Big Bear Lake. After scooping up a load of lake water, he led Bob around the lake, then climbed to start a bombing run on the lake itself.

"Take a look at that TRIDINT display, Bob", Pieter called over the radio. "Can you see the heat from my engines?"

"Not only that, I can see the heat trailing *behind* your engines!", said Bob excitedly. "This display is fantastic! I wish we had had one of these up north this season. We could have really cleaned up on some fires!"

"Plus the fact that you can see right through the smoke, according to Dave", said Pieter. "We haven't tried them out over a fire yet, but I think he's probably right".

"I can hardly wait for a chance to fly this plane through a real brushfire", said Dick. "We can probably snuff 'em as fast as they start!"

"One question, Pieter", said Bob over the radio. "What about using water on the fires? Charlie said that water is the least effective fire-stopper. We always used long-term retardant for that reason".

"By the time we start operations, we'll have a long-term retardant in our loads", said Pieter. "They're working on a chemical right now that will be mixed with the water when it's loaded. The chemical will turn our loads into long-term retardant. Pretty keen, huh?"

"Yeah, if it works", said Bob.

"If those chemists are as good as the rest of the people Joe Talon has hired on, I don't think there's any doubt about the chemical working", said Pieter confidently. "Besides, I parceled you guys out to the best outfits in the business. Even if we do have to use water, we can mix a little Class A Foam with it and get short-term retardant. That's almost as good as long-term and that chemical has been used by waterbombers for years. With the accuracy of these planes and the training you guys got, we can get the effect of using long-term in direct-action drops. We just won't be able to fireproof a line like we could with long-term".

"I'd say we're on our way, then", said Dick. "Those wildfires don't have a chance!"

"We'll see", said Bob more evenly. "Never underestimate nature, or luck for that matter. Look what happened to Charlie when he did".

"Yeah", said Dick more thoughtfully. They were both quiet for a time. The planes made several more water drops. Finally, Pieter called up again. "OK, boys, let's head for home. I think we've scared enough fish for one day".

"Roger that", replied Bob. The two planes climbed, then banked west and headed into the setting sun.

"We have traced the arsonist to the airport, Joe", said Allen as he settled into a chair in front of Joe's desk.

"Left the country, huh?", asked Joe.

"Yes, it would appear he was heading to South America, Rio to be precise".

"You're sure this is the one who killed Flick?"

"We will not know for certain until we have questioned him, of course. He does appear to be our best candidate, though. We have done thorough checks on everyone capable of this level of skill, those we know of, and this fellow is the only candidate who fits".

"Doe this 'candidate' have a name?", asked Joe.

"Henry Holmstead. His previous residence was in Cincinnati, I believe. That was only a temporary address, as were the ones previous to that one. It appears that he seldom stays in one place for very long".

"Can't imagine why", said Joe dryly. "What about the authorities?"

"They are working on the necessary paperwork to send some people down there now. Do you wish us to continue to pursue him?"

"By all means. Just keep a low profile down there. I have some business interests in Rio who I don't want to upset. We don't want the authorities jumping down our throats either".

"Very well".

"Anything else?"

"No, I believe that covers everything for now".

"OK. Let me know when you find out more".

"I shall", said Allen as he walked through the door.

After he had left, Joe thought about Mathias Flick. Granted, he hadn't known the man very well. Still, this murder unsettled Joe for some reason. He wondered if this had anything to do with Ethan Davis. The man hadn't been seen or heard from since his stormy exit from Talon Industries the day the deal was closed on Davis Aircraft. That had been over a year ago, thought Joe. And a long year it had been, too.

Well, there were other matters to attend to now. The chemists at Bergway Chemical were getting very close on the elusive retardant formula. They estimated another three months tops before they had the problem resolved. Then they could begin work on the mixer in another two to three months time. The heavy equipment was coming along well, too. Van Pelt had submitted a structural design for an engine which would begin construction at Caprock Drill in another month. Joe hoped the composites worked as well as everyone said they would.

The fireproofing of the Cats and APCs was done. They were being run through their final checks at Caprock. They should ship in another month. Zack would put them through their trials at the Talon Aerospace Training Center once they arrived.

Everything was coming together, Joe thought. Soon, he would have to schedule a demonstration for the local fire authorities, something to show them how effective his firefighting force was. After all, what better way to drum up business? If the equipment was as effective as it should be, contracts would begin flooding in for Talon Industries' assistance in equipping other firefighting outfits. Who could say? Foreign countries might even be interested. And even if no one was interested, Joe was satisfied that he had done something important. If even one life was saved by his organization, then he felt that the price had been worth it.

Quite a turnabout for a dedicated corporate pirate, Joe mused. But he would have to be cautious. How many robber barons of the past had set out with noble ideals, only to rape and pillage humanity in order to achieve their purpose? He would have to trust in himself and his friends that such a thing didn't happen this time.

Yes, and even, perhaps, in God. Joe had started to read the Bible some in his quiet moments. He wasn't going to church, but his thoughts were turning more towards religion as his organization took shape. Perhaps that old preacher had been right. Maybe God had brought tragedy on Joe in order to bring about something which otherwise might never have existed. All that mattered to Joe, at the moment, was that he felt good about what he was doing.

"Well Pat, you old scalawag, how are you doing?", asked Pieter as Patrick
O'Toole walked through the door.

"Fine, your lordship, and how's about you?", replied Pat as he sat down.

"I'm just peachy! I'm having more fun than a bear at a honey contest! Have you seen those beauties parked outside?"

"I have indeed. I'm almost afraid to touch 'em for fear they'll disappear like a mirage!"

"Go ahead and touch them, you old coot, they're solid enough! I know. I've been flying one of them for the past few weeks. They ain't no Forts, that's for sure. They turn on a dime and handle like a dream. The way we'll conduct operations, the pilots won't even have to land them when they need to reload or refuel. The only limitation will be pilot endurance".

"Well I do hope you have somethin' for me to do", said Pat. "I don't fancy sittin' around with nothin' to do all the day long!"

"Oh, we'll have plenty for you to do. There's a list of maintenance checks a mile long for these birds, and more planes than even *you* can shake a stick at!"

"An' how many planes might that be?", asked Pat skeptically.

"How does three dozen strike you?", asked Pieter with a smirk.

"Glory be!", exclaimed Pat. "'Tis a fair number of planes at that!"

"They're even talking about expanding overseas", continued Pieter. "Who knows, they might even open up a base in Ireland!"

"Now that does give a body somethin' to think about, that it does", said Pat thoughtfully. "Ah, but I wouldn't want to be separated from me lads, now would I?"

"What lads are those?"

"Why the lads I worked with up there at Humboldt Air, of course! Those are mighty fine pilots, and don't get me wrong, but they don't know much about plane mechanics. Why, without me, there's no tellin' what trouble they might get themselves intah. No, I'll stay wit' them for now. I might like to visit Ireland sometime later on, but there'll be plenty o' time for that".

"Whatever you say, Pat. I've put together a list of things that need checking on some of the birds first. We need an injector test on number 103, a 100-hour check on both engines for number 104, a..."

"Which ones are the lads flying?", Pat cut in.

"Numbers 100 and 101, why?", asked Pieter.

"I'll be checkin' those two first, then", said Pat resolutely. "If I have time left, I'll do the others as well".

"Well... OK Pat", said Pieter warily. "You really are going to stick to those guys, aren't you?"

"Like glue", said Pat, his eyes flaring up. "One o' them died because I was derelict in me duties up north. Never again. These birds don't fly until *I* say they can fly!"

"I see...", said Pieter thoughtfully. "Take your time and do it right, just don't neglect your other charges".

"You have me word on that", said Pat. He spit on the palm of his hand and extended it to Pieter, who looked at it suspiciously, then took it gingerly and shook it. "That seals the bargain", said Pat, a look of quiet satisfaction crossing his face. "Now, show me to me charges!".

Chapter 17

While the Talon pilots were beginning training on the bombers and transports, Zack's ground troops began returning from their summer assignments. All had fought in most of the campaigns that the Talon pilots had flown in. New recruits were also being brought in and joining up with their equipment. The heavy equipment operators had been the last to arrive, since their machines were not yet ready for them to train on. Zack wanted to indoctrinate them in firefighting tactics while the equipment was still absent.

After another month had gone by, the bulldozers and Armored Personnel Carriers (APCs) arrived by train. The drivers, who had just finished the first phase of their training, rolled the equipment off the flatcars onto truck transports for the trip to the Training Center. Once there, they were rolled off onto the practice field. Zack wanted to put them through their paces before they did a demonstration for Joe and the rest of his staff.

"OK, gentlemen, this is what we're going to do", Zack began. "As discussed in class, we're going to break up into two teams of five vehicles each, two Cats and three APCs. I'm going to start a practice fire over there and I want you to drive slowly through it. Keep an eye on your instruments. At the first sign of any trouble, I want you to give a holler. We've got fire equipment standing by to douse the flames if anything goes wrong, understood?"

"Understood, sir", said the lead Cat driver for the first group, George Ostermann. "OK Panthers, let's load up!" The crews moved quickly to their royal blue vehicles. On the side of each vehicle was the picture of a panther leaping on some burning grass, with the name "FIREBOMBERS INCORPORATED" in block letters below it.

The engines on each vehicle roared to life, and the lead Cat began to move toward the fire, followed in single file by another Cat, then the three APCs. All vehicles were completely enclosed. As they approached the flames, each driver switched from outside air to recirculated air inside each vehicle, while compressed air supplies provided the oxygen needed by the engines. Air conditioners kicked in as the hull temperatures rose. The vehicles disappeared into the flames one-by-one as six airbase fire engines sat off to the side.

The engine crews stood nervously by their water cannons and hoses, ready to douse the fire at a moment's notice. A few seconds passed with no problems. Each vehicle was churning through the inferno without difficulty. Finally, after what seemed like an eternity to the onlookers, the first Cat emerged from the fire. A rousing cheer went up from the crowd as each vehicle in turn emerged until all were outside of the fire. As soon as they had come to a halt, the hatches opened and the crews emerged.'

"Nothin' to it!", shouted the lead APC driver, Jose Gomez, as he clambered out the driver's hatch. "Just like a Sunday drive in the Cav!"

"Pipe down Jose!", growled the APC commander as he climbed out the commander's hatch.

"What's the matter, Sarge?", asked Jose innocently, "you mad 'cause you don't got no fifty on top to shoot anymore?"

"Not only are you ugly, you're stupid, too!", the commander shouted as he came up face-to-face with the driver, who just kept smiling. "I'm mad because you did a sloppy job of keeping up with that 'dozer!"

"What seems to be the problem here?", asked George as he walked over by the APC.

"No problem, sir", answered Jose. "The sarge and me always do this. Keeps the juices goin', know what I mean?"

"Who are you guys?", asked Zack as he walked up.

"First-serg .... uh, I mean Manuel Hermosa, sir", said the commander sheepishly.

"Hi, I'm Jose Gomez!", said Jose, extending his hand to Zack.

"You say you always act like this?", Zack asked.

"Ever since we first teamed up in the 11th Armored Cavalry, yeah", Jose answered. "He was the commander and I was the driver there, too".

"Well, try to keep it to a minimum here, OK?", said Zack. "We're here to fight fires, not each other".

"Yes sir", Jose and Manuel answered in unison. Manuel had to stifle a salute. Zack continued down the line along with George, the team commander. They both inspected the vehicles closely for any signs of damage. When they were satisfied that none had occurred, Zack called over to the other group, Team Tiger. "OK, boys, it's your turn, now. Remember, if you have *any* problem, call out over the radio and we'll douse the fire, understood?"

The men all shouted their acknowledgement, then climbed into their vehicles. Team Panther moved their vehicles off to the side, and the exercise was repeated. Once again, the vehicles came through with flying colors. The only apparent sign of having passed through the heat being a small amount of ash on the hulls or a bit of discoloration on the paint from the heat. Zack conferred with the Team commanders and it was decided to repeat the demonstration the next day for Joe's approval.

At 10 A.M. the next morning, Joe and his staff sat down in folding chairs assembled along the training ground. Off in the distance, two rows of royal blue vehicles could be seen. Zack gave the signal over the radio and the first line of vehicles, those sporting a picture on the side of each hull of the face of a tiger with flaming eyes, moved out.

At his word, airbase firemen along the test track lit several pools of oil, each six inches deep. Team Tiger moved onto the track and plunged into the first fire, emerging unscathed seconds later. They then climbed a steep earthen rise. Once they scaled the top, they each plunged down a steep gradient on the other side into a trench, also filled with burning oil. The first Cat climbed out, followed shortly by the remaining vehicles.

Once they had scaled several other obstacles, each vehicle pulled off to the side and Zack called for Team Panther to begin its run. When the first APC reached the first earthen wall, a hidden loudspeaker burst forth in a rousing charge similar to the one played by an organ at sporting events.

"What the heck was that?", shouted Zack into the radio.

"Sorry, sir, it won't happen again", came the reply. A considerable amount of swearing in Spanish could be heard in the background.

Joe nearly fell off of his chair laughing after the APC had cleared the first wall. "Does the music help the M-113 climb better?", he asked Zack, once he had stopped laughing.

"Not that I know of", replied Zack angrily. "It may make a certain APC crew wish they hadn't installed it, though!"

"I wouldn't be too hard on them Zack", said Joe soothingly. "They were just having a little fun, that's all. This isn't the military, you know".

"No, but I do expect a little more discipline from these guys. They're supposed to be professionals!"

"They appear to drive like professionals", said Joe. "That, I think is more important than strict regimentation. We don't want to stifle them".

"No", said Zack more calmly, "just strangle a few".

Once Team Panther had cleared the track, Zack walked over to the lead APC. Manuel was dragging Jose out of the vehicle. Jose was talking rapidly in Spanish, so Zack could only understand a few words. As he walked up, he could see both men go rigid.

"OK, what was that all about?", he demanded.

"Sorry, sir", answered Manuel. "Jose rigged up a public address system on the vehicle last night after I left the shop. I didn't even notice it today when I was checking the APC out before the demonstration. It's history now, though", he finished with an angry look at Jose.

"Why'd you have to smash it, man?", Jose demanded angrily. "You could have just told me to knock it off. I paid fifty bucks for that thing!"

"I wanted you to understand how I felt, buddy!", Manuel shouted back. "Maybe if I hit you in the wallet, you'll remember next time, comprende?"

"Si, comprende", replied Jose sullenly. "Oh man, the speaker melted too! That's another twenty bucks!"

"Maybe the fire didn't like that any more than I did", said Manuel, a satisfied look spreading across his face.

"OK boys", said Zack, "I'll let you off this time, but don't let it happen again, understood?"

"Yes, sir", they both answered quietly. Once again, Manuel had to stifle a salute.

Zack turned back to the group of onlookers and walked over to where Joe stood. "Well, what do you think".

"Impressive", said Joe. "Why the names, Tiger and Panther?"

"Both are big cats", said Zack. "It's a name that will stick with the crews and it refers to the main reason we organized the teams, the Cats or Caterpillars".

"Makes sense said Joe. He turned to Pieter and asked, "Have you thought of something similar for your squadrons, Pieter?"

"As a matter of fact, I have", said Pieter. "I've already picked out the names for the squadrons themselves, pending your approval of course, but I thought I would also offer the option of naming the individual planes to the crews. Like the nose-art the pilots used in World War II".

"Fine by me", said Joe. "What names did you pick out for our five start-up bomber squadrons?"

"The Pathfinders', that would be mine", Pieter began, "'the Night Hawks', 'the Ridgerunners', 'the Linebackers', and 'the Black Widows'".

"What about your own plane?", Joe asked.

"I was thinking of 'North Star'", Pieter replied. "After all, a good navigator always plots his course by the North Star, just like my squadrons will be directed by me".

"Conceited son-of-a-gun, aren't you?", Joe teased.

"You asked", said Pieter blandly. "Since we're on the subject", he said with an impish grin, "why not come over to the hangers and I'll take you up? You know, show you what these beauties can do?"

"Why not?", said Joe. The two of them walked over to the hanger with Zack and a few others still in tow.

"Are you coming too Zack?", asked Joe slyly.

"I'll pass", Zack replied. "Pieter still hasn't quite cured me of my fear of flying. I'll watch from a safe spot here on the ground, thank you very much".

"Chicken!", replied Joe as he climbed into the 'North Star'.

Pieter revved up the engines and the plane was soon taxiing down the runway. Once Pieter had gotten takeoff clearance from the tower, he put the throttles to the stops. The plane began speeding down the runway, then lifted off. Pieter banked left and circled the field twice, then headed off for a nearby reservoir to tank up.

"Notice the TRIDINT display", he said to Joe as the plane settled into the water. "See how hot the dam is in comparison to the water?"

"Yeah. This going to help you fight fires better?"

"You betcha'", replied Pieter as the tanks finished filling. He lifted slowly off the reservoir, then headed back towards Talon Aerospace. "Watch this!"

Pieter brought the plane in low over the training field just as the last APC was moving off of it. The airbase fire engines were moving in to douse the practice fires.

"Notice how clearly the fires stand out, even with the smoke the burning oil is giving off", said Pieter.

"It does show up pretty well, doesn't it?", agreed Joe as he looked into the display. "It's as though the smoke isn't even there".

"Uh-huh, and it will work just as well at night, what with that low-light TV system Dave included with the TRIDINT gear. Once the range to target is determined, I just punch it into the computer keypad and press the button for what type of drop I want: salvo, trail, or successive. Each plane can drop individually or linked to other planes".

"Linking is what Dave was talking about where several planes can drop in quick succession?"

"Right. The ballistic computer on board each plane figures wind velocity, speed of the aircraft, and all the other parameters which go into making a normal drop. Then it interrogates the Hawkeye's computer to find out what the distance to the next plane is and figures out the time needed to link this drop with that of the plane ahead of it. That way, it drops the load in such a way that each one links together, making an unbroken line of retardant".

"How does the Hawkeye know which plane is in front of this one?"

"Each plane has a transponder in the tail. Each transponder is encoded with that plane's call-number. The incoming request from our bomber tells the computer our call-number. The computer figures out which plane is in front of us, then sends back the necessary speed and distance information to our on-board computer".

"Sounds pretty complicated", said Joe. "How long does all this take?"

"Only a second or two. Computers are fast!"

Pieter watched the display intently, punched something into the keypad next to him, then selected 'salvo' on the drop controls. A moment later, as the plane flew over the fires, the bombay doors opened and water came streaming out onto the fires. All four of the flaming trenches were hit, most of the fires going out immediately, oil and water splashing everywhere. The advancing fire equipment stopped dead in their tracks, then began to hastily reverse as the water and oil oozed their way.

"Wahoo!", yelled Pieter happily.

"You must have been drinking from the same bottle as that APC driver", said Joe, shaking his head.

"Just havin' a little fun, boss", Pieter said enthusiastically. "Wait until you see what we can do with *five* of these babies, all computer linked!"

"Just remind me not to be on the ground when you demonstrate that, OK?"

"Oh, you're no fun!", said Pieter with a laugh.

'North Star' circled the field once more, then landed at the far end and taxied back to the hanger. The airbase fire commander had a few choice words for Pieter when he got there, but Pieter took them all in good humor and the incident quickly blew over.

"As soon as we get our chemical problems straightened out, we can start killing fires!", said Pieter.

"I still need a little more equipment", said Zack. "I don't think they've finished even one engine yet. I guess they're still working on forming the composite bodies for them".

"So I've heard", said Joe. "I guess that zirconium diboride is tricky stuff to work with".

"They tell me it's nearly as strong as steel", said Zack. "I had hoped it would be a lot lighter, though".

"Nothing to worry about", said Pieter confidently. "From what you've told me, they'll be light enough for the Herky-birds to lift. Like I said when I recommended the C-130, they can haul a whole bunch of cargo. And since you guys aren't going to be putting any firejumpers on board at the same time as the trucks, we can use the full capacity to lift the engines and their crews. Eighteen-and-a-half tons of carrying capacity adds up to a fair amount of equipment, don't you agree Zack?"

"It'll be enough for what we've got in mind, that's for sure".

"How much heat can those fancy new toys of yours take, Zack", asked Joe.

"Enough to waltz through a medium-sized spot fire, from what the whiz kids at Caprock tell me. I haven't tested them at maximum heat yet, but I've seen the results from the tests at Caprock. If that data is right, we can pull people out of just about any fire we're likely to encounter, excluding a firestorm".

"And do a little firebreak construction while we're at it!", said one of the bulldozer drivers. "That retractable ball-and-chain clearing gear is pretty neat, Zack. We can clear a swath three times our blade size with that thing."

"We'll see when we get out there", Zack said guardedly. "I'll reserve judgment until I see all of this gear work. If it does as well as the designers say, then I'd say we've got something special. Otherwise..., well, we'll see".

"Skeptic", said Joe with a smirk.

"Cautious", Zack corrected him. "I'd rather be a little too cautious and lose a few acres of timber, than be too aggressive and lose a few firemen".

"Well put", said Jerry.

"I guess so", said Joe. "After all, we're here to save lives, not to waste them".

"If you don't mind, I'd like to get my aircrews going practicing take-offs and landings with full loads", Pieter cut in. "Since we've got the Cat Teams now, we can at least get the Heavy Lift squadrons in shape".

"Have you guys tried air-dropping any of this equipment yet?", Joe asked.

"Not yet", replied Pieter. "We've got the parachutes and pallets, but the drivers haven't been practicing any airdropping. I figured Zack was going to turn them over to the tender mercies of his firejumper trainers".

"I'm sure the instructors will be delighted to have more victims, er, customers", said Zack with a devilish grin. The Cat Team crews moaned at this news.

"I never did like jumpin' out of airplanes", Jose whispered to Manuel. "Maybe I could get an excuse, huh?"

"You *are* an excuse, peabrain", Manuel whispered back. Jose ignored the rebuke.

"We've just received the specs from the Army about airdropping APCs and Cats", said Pieter. "The engineers at Caprock said that the fireproofing shouldn't suffer any from drops below about 50 G's, so I think we're safe".

"Why don't you drop a few before you get too cocky", said Zack. "As I recall, the Army wrecked quite a bit of equipment before they finally got the optimum conditions figured out".

"True, very true", said Pieter. "All right, then. Let's go see what kind of trouble we can get ourselves into. Zack, suppose you could lend me a couple of drivers to load this stuff onto my planes? I only need two, one Cat driver and one APC driver. You could excuse them from parachuting for a couple of hours couldn't you".

"Can do", replied Zack. "Do I have any volunteers to load equipment on planes? I need one Cat driver and one APC driver".

Jose rushed to the front of the crowd and began jumping up and down with his hand in the air shouting, "Take me! Take me!"

Zack looked over at him with a grimace and said, "OK, Mr. PA System, I'll take you for the APCs and Mr. Ostermann for the Cats. Mr. Ostermann, I want you to keep an eye on this rascal!"

"Yes sir", said George. He gave Jose a hard look. Jose replied with an innocent smile.

There's a handful of trouble, Zack thought as he walked away. "The rest of you people come with me. You have a little jumping practice to look forward to. Another collective moan went up from the ranks as the Cat Team members fell in behind Zack.

On the walk over to the hangers, Jose reflected on how quickly his fortunes had changed. He trailed along behind Pieter and Joe as they walked toward the transport hanger. Once they got inside, his eyes widened in awe. Lined up in two neat rows sat about a dozen of the big four-engined C-130 Hercules transports. Each plane was painted royal blue and had a Firebombers symbol and a gold-colored number printed on the fuselage just in front of the tail, similar to the arrangement he had seen on the twin-engined bombers in the other hanger. On the tails of the first line of planes was emblazoned the picture of an alley-cat leaning against a trashcan picking its teeth. The second row had a picture of a smiling tomcat about to stomp a burning bush.

"Sharp, very sharp", Jose said quietly. George Ostermann turned around and smiled slightly. The other two men were still walking ahead, talking privately, the remainder of the executive staff following at a discrete distance.

"You have done simulated drops with dead weights, haven't you Pieter?", Joe asked anxiously.

"Yep, just finished the last drop two days ago. Haven't lost a sack of concrete yet", Pieter said with a grin.

"OK, but just be careful with these vehicles. It's not the money I'm worried about so much as the time element. It will take Caprock at least three to four months to modify more Cats and APCs as replacements".

"I thought we were ordering more of these for the follow-on Cat Teams?"

"We will once we see how these work out. We've got the equipment at Caprock, or on the way, for four more complete teams, plus spares. The problem is that they all have to be fireproofed and tested before we get them. The testing alone takes almost a month right now".

"I didn't realize that. I could run some more simulations if it would make you feel better".

"As long as you're satisfied that we have enough margin of safety, you can go ahead. I just wanted you to be clear on the strategic picture, that's all".

"I guess Caprock is a pretty busy place right now, huh?"

"Oh yeah. I keep getting these calls from the plant staff asking for more manpower, more machinery, more time, more of everything! General Motors it ain't".

"Are you thinking of opening an assembly plant for the heavy equipment?"

"We've considered it", Joe answered. "We've got constraints due to the agreements with Caterpillar and FMC over manufacture of the equipment ourselves. I guess Allen Sims and Jerry Porter are living on Pepto-Bismol at the moment. I keep after them about getting us licenses to manufacture and the manufacturers keep putting him off. I suppose it will be resolved in the near future, but I don't know when".

"As my father used to say, never open a can of worms unless you plan to go fishing", mused Pieter as they reached the lead C-130. He called over to the pilot and motioned for the ground crew to stand clear as the pilot climbed into the plane.

Following a quick pre-flight check the powerful Allison turboprops sprang to life. When the pilot was satisfied that everything was in order, he slowly taxied the plane out onto the tarmac.

"We'll load up a Cat first, I think", Pieter told the two drivers. George walked over to his bulldozer and revved up the engine, then drove it over to the back of the idling plane. The loadmaster motioned for George to go up the ramp onto a pallet inside the plane. He carefully inched up the ramp and onto the pallet. George killed the engine and left the cab, then the plane's crew secured the Cat to the pallet. Once the Cat was tied down, the parachute package for the pallet was hooked up and the ramp closed. The C-130 taxied down the tarmac a few hundred feet and parked. The pilot killed the engines and walked into the hanger. He climbed into the next C-130 and began his pre-flight checks. This loading procedure was repeated until all of the equipment for both Cat Teams was loaded onto their respective transports.

"OK guys, thanks for your help", Pieter said to the two drivers. "You can go catch up with your buddies over at the parachute training center".

"You sure you won't need some more help driving those things around after you drop them?", asked Jose hopefully.

"I'm sure. This will take the rest of the afternoon to do", replied Pieter with a grin. "By then, you and your buddies will be done with your training. Everybody can help put their toys away. After all, you don't want to miss the fun part of your jobs: jumping out of airplanes".

Jose winced at that statement and sullenly fell in behind George, who was already heading for the training room. Pieter waited until they were out of earshot, then began laughing. "If ever there was a reluctant paratrooper, that guy's got to be it!", he said.

"Maybe we should put him together with Zack", offered Joe. "You could take them both up at the same time. That would be a sight".

"Like watching two cats slipping down a steep roof into a water barrel!", Pieter shouted out in glee. "If I did it I'd want pictures for my album".

"Maybe we could get in touch with Candid Camera and make a little money in the process"

"Something to think about. But in the meantime, what say we drop a few Cats ourselves?"

"Gently, please", said Joe pleadingly. "Remember, you break 'em, you buy 'em".

"All right, all right! We'll be careful, I promise. You can dock my paycheck if my boys do any damage".

"You don't earn enough!", Joe snorted derisively.

"Yeah, I've been meaning to talk to you about that", said Pieter with a sly look on his face.

"Try earning your money first before you go asking for a raise. *if* you pull this off, then we can talk".

"Hard sell all the way, aren't you?"

"How do you think I got this far in the world? It wasn't by being free with my money, I can tell you!"

Pieter chuckled, then turned to the lead plane in the line and spun his hand in the air. The pilot fired up the engines as the co-pilot made his last-minute checks. The pilot taxied his plane down the runway, followed by nine others. Once he had received clearance from the tower, he brought his engines up to full power and the plane slowly began rolling down the field. The roar from the engines was deafening by the time it drew opposite Joe and Pieter. The nose came up and the lead transport lifted off. Joe was filled with pride and awe as he stood by the edge of the runway watching the squadrons take off. Each plane followed in quick succession until all ten were airborne. He and Pieter walked over to the control tower and sat down to watch what would happen.

Up in the lead C-130, the pilot, Steve Guzman, banked slightly to the east in order to come back across the landing area of the practice field.

"Five miles and closing", called off his co-pilot, Glenn Washington. "Looking good Steve".

"Loadmaster, lower ramp", Steve called into the headset.

"Ramp down, sir", came back the reply.

"Prepare to drop", Steve called back. "Range to target?"

"Two point four and closing", Glenn replied.

"Call it off", said Steve.

"Two miles", Glenn intoned. "One point five ... one mile .... point five .... zero".

"Drop load!", Steve called out.

The drogue chutes began to open in the slip-stream and yanked the pallet out the back of the transport.

"Cargo clear!", called the loadmaster.

"Secure cargo door!", Steve called back.

The ramp slowly lifted back up into the rear of the transport. "Ramp secured, sir!", the loadmaster called into the headset.

"Once around the block, then we head for home", said Steve with a grin at Glenn.

Glenn returned Steve's grin, then said, "Just like downtown!"

The transports were flying in echelon formation, the planes sweeping back in a half "V" formation. When the lead plane disgorged its cargo, each of the other transports dispatched their loads as well. Soon the sky was filled with pallets drifting to the earth, half-a-dozen parachutes billowing above each.

"Here they come!", said Pieter as Zack sat down beside him.

"Pieter said he'd pay for any that broke", Joe told Zack playfully.

"He doesn't make enough!", said Zack.

"Hey, how do you know how much I make?", said Pieter in surprise.

"Ve haf our veys", said Zack with a sinister grin.

"Keep your fingers crossed, gentlemen", said Joe anxiously. The first pallet came drifting rapidly down towards the earth below. Joe held his breath as it neared the ground. It finally hit with a thud and a dust cloud blew up around it. It was followed in quick succession by more pallets landing to the southwest of it. Each one came down hard, but the equipment stayed on the pallets. When the last one touched down, Joe was out of his seat and racing down the stairs, closely followed by Zack and Pieter. The three ran across the tarmac to the nearest pallet. Zack began climbing around on the pallet, carefully inspecting the bulldozer attached to it.

"Sound as a dollar!", he exclaimed after finishing his inspection.

"Let's go see how the rest are before we begin celebrating", said Joe.

"*Now* who's the skeptic!", said Pieter with a grin. "They all came down the same way. I think we've done it, by golly!"

"Is the parachute class just about finished?", Joe asked.

"They should be any minute", replied Zack as they all walked to the next pallet.

"I'd like to get these things off of the pallets as soon as possible", said Joe. "Give them another thorough series of tests to see if they're still in good shape".

"Whatever you say, Joe", replied Zack.

By the time they had checked the fourth pallet, the C-130s were landing. Each plane taxied over to park in front of the hangers. The cargo crews emerged from each plane and began moving towards the landing area.

Parachutes were being gathered in and vehicles unfastened as the first people emerged from the training hall. Jose came rushing over and began checking his APC, quickly followed by the rest of the crews from both teams.

"Gomez, drive that APC off the pallet and see how it feels!", shouted Zack.

Jose waved and climbed in the driver's hatch. Manuel was just mounting the vehicle when the engine kicked to life. The APC began to ease off of the pallet, nearly toppling Manuel off before he made it in the commander's hatch. He swore vehemently at Jose in Spanish as he squeezed in the hatch. Jose could be heard to reply indecipherably. The APC teetered on the edge of the pallet, then eased down onto the ground and roared down the field a few hundred feet, pivoted, and came back up the field. When it was opposite Zack, it lurched to a halt and Jose popped his head out of the driver's hatch. "Seems OK to me, sir!", he sang out.

The field was soon covered with a confusion of Cats, APCS, forklifts recovering pallets, and people gathering up parachutes. Zack, Pieter, and Joe stood off to the side watching the activity.

"We seem to have jumped this hurdle successfully", said Zack.

"See? I told you guys! No problems!", said Pieter triumphantly.

"I admit, I had my doubts", said Joe. "But you guys have made a believer out of me. It looks like we might just be able to pull this off after all. Of course, we haven't tried doing this under actual field conditions yet".

"There's not much difference", said Pieter confidently. "The only thing to worry about there is that we don't try to be too hasty or do anything fancy, like landing these too close to a fire. Remember, the bombers can see through smoke; my transports can't", he said looking sideways at Zack.

"Yeah, I know", said Zack without turning his head. "I've seen that happen a couple of times before, usually with a fast moving fire where the wind changed. The entire landing zone was blanketed in smoke. The transports had to drop their firejumpers several miles away in rougher country. Took them over an hour to get up to the fire, which was too late to be of any use. What a waste".

"When will your crews and technicians be done checking over the vehicles?", asked Joe.

"How thorough a set of diagnostics do you want run?", asked Zack.

"As thorough as possible", Joe answered.

"Day after tomorrow", said Zack.

"Pieter, I want you to check with all the transport crews and see if they noticed any problems or have any suggestions for improving our drops", said Joe.

"Will do, boss. All in all, I think this came off pretty much as planned. Wouldn't you say that this calls for at least a minor celebration, Joe? I promise, we'll invite you".

"Mighty nice of you!", said Joe indignantly. "Here I was thinking of giving you guys a raise, and all I get is wisecracks! Why it's enough to drive a body to drink!"

"I didn't say anything!", said Zack in a hurt voice.

"Sorry, Zack", said Joe. "I'll give you a bigger raise to make it up to you".

"Hey!", yelled Pieter. "I didn't say anything that bad!"

"Gotcha!", said Joe with a merry look in his eyes.

The vehicles were all lining up in their holding area while the three friends walked back to the hanger. The crews headed for the cafeteria as Jerry met Joe inside the hanger.

"Satisfactory progress, Joe?", Jerry asked.

"Splendid progress!", replied Joe. "If the Zephyrs unload this well, I'd say we're in business".

"Good", said Jerry. "One of my aides brought over some papers for you to sign in regards to additional personnel. We have the last of the refueling tankers acquired and it would appear to be time to hire on the crews for each".

"Fine", said Joe. "What about the crews for the fire engines?"

"We will begin to screen candidates soon", said Jerry. "Mr. Dobson's associates are interviewing the applicants beginning Monday, I believe".

"Any of your people going to be in those crews, Zack?", Joe asked.

"Yep. After all, they aren't going to walk to the fires!"

"Why not, it might be good exercise for you?", chided Pieter.

"Sure beats flying", groused Zack.

"Speaking of which, I believe we have an appointment for that very thing tomorrow morning!", said Pieter cheerily.

"I'm sure I have something scheduled", said Zack.

"Un-schedule it", commanded Joe. "Remember, Zack. The deal is you *have* to fly to the fires. Understood?"

"Understood", said Zack with a sigh. "What time tomorrow, flyboy?"

"Eight o'clock, sharp", replied Pieter. "Right after breakfast".

"I think I'll wait to eat until we get back", said Zack sullenly.

"We won't be back until after lunch", said Pieter. "We're flying up the coast. Take in some pretty scenery, smell the salt air, and all that".

"Wonderful", said Zack despondently. "OK, I'll see you then. I have to go make funeral arrangements now".

"Funeral arrangements?", said Joe. "You didn't tell me anyone had died in your family, Zack".

"They haven't", said Zack. "The arrangements are for me in case I don't survive tomorrow's flight".

"*What* a worrywart!", said Pieter as he shook his head. "I'll take good care of you, old buddy. I'll tiptoe through the clouds. No barrel-rolls or loops, I promise!"

"Would you mind putting that in writing?", said Zack. "I know a notary service that stays open late. I think I could just get there before they close".

Joe just shook his head as he and Jerry parted company with Pieter and Zack. Jerry and Joe said their goodbyes out in the parking lot. Bill Thompson was waiting with the limousine. Joe reflected on the day's events on his way home. Most of the major pieces were now in play. By the end of next month, we might be able to put on a demonstration of air-delivery and water bombing, Joe thought. Once the new retardant gear was installed in the bombers, say by the beginning of next year, they could be ready. The force wouldn't be full-size yet, but would give he and his staff a better idea of how to refine the organization for optimum performance. It was all just a matter of time, he thought as he dozed off in the back seat.

As the sun set in the west a few moments later, Bill looked through the rear-view mirror at Joe and smiled. It had been a busy day for some of us, he thought.

Chapter 18

An airborne army of both paratroopers and equipment was once again descending on the Talon Aerospace Training Center landing zone. Firejumpers were landing at the extreme southern end of the field while C-130s did touch-and-go landings on the runway at the other end of the base. Everything proceeded like clockwork, aside from an occasional sprained ankle or streaming chute. One APC had to be repaired when one of the chutes on its pallet failed to open, causing the pallet to land harder than usual. An overnight visit to the shop was all that was required to put the vehicle back in order.

Bergway chemists had finally managed to synthesize the desired retardant formula and extensive testing of the compound was underway at their labs. The first of the *Zephyr*-class fire engines would be arriving the next week, to be followed by two per week thereafter (too slowly for Zack, who wanted to get his crews up to speed as quickly as possible for the pending full-scale demonstration slated for the end of April).

Joe sat back with a satisfied look on his face. The prospects for his organization (his hobby, as he still referred to it) were quite good. If the retardant worked as well as Bergway was saying it had in preliminary tests, and if the new Zephyrs could be successfully air-landed, then his doubts would be completely dispelled. Even with the force as it stood, he could offer a substantial amount of assistance to the Forestry Services in time of need. It appeared that his dream was about to come true at last.

"Well Allen, what do you have for me today?", Joe asked as he walked through the doorway of Allen Sims' office.

"Nothing firm yet, I am afraid", replied Allen. Joe sat down across from him. "My investigators traced our elusive arsonist to Sao Paulo in Brazil, then lost him for a short time. By the time they picked up the lead again, he had disappeared. It appears that he left South America entirely. His new address is as yet unknown".

"This guy is a pro, isn't he?"

"Decidedly. I am sure our paths will cross again, though. We have extended our network to cover all possible destinations from Sao Paulo for the period of time we lost contact with him. We shall find evidence of him in one of those destinations, then trace him from there. Believe me, this is not the first time we have been led on a merry chase. My operatives are also professionals. They will not give up until you tell them to. Do you wish me to cease the operation?"

"Absolutely not! Keep after him. I still get a funny feeling we'll find Ethan Davis at the end of this puppet's strings. If that's the case, then I want him picked up. Several unsavory things happened to enemies of his before. Those 'accidents' are looking less and less accidental the more I think about it. This arsonist could be our key to finding out a great many things. Just don't lose him".

"Rest assured, we will not", said Allen firmly. "On a lighter note, how is your new organization coming along?"

"Quite well. I think we'll be ready by next fire season".

"With Thanksgiving only a few days away, I am sure that the time will pass more quickly than you think".

"Yeah, I hope so. I wish we were up and running now, but I guess I'll just have to be patient".

"I understand that you have scheduled a full dress rehearsal for April. Are you planning to invite any dignitaries to look on?"

"I haven't decided yet. There's a lot on the line. If we muff it, we could lose a lot of income which I was counting on to offset the costs of this organization. We may just wait until fire season and get our publicity by actually fighting fires, instead of showing off ahead of time. It would give the crews a few more weeks to practice before being put under public scrutiny. I'm still considering, I guess".

"It would seem to be wiser to wait", said Allen. "As you say, a great deal is riding on your making a good showing. Certainly the costs have been greater than you expected".

"That's for sure!", Joe snorted. "Those chemists and consultants have been eating me alive. The overtime on the fire engine bodies alone is going to put the corporation into the red for a couple of quarters if we don't get some contracts to offset the research and development costs".

"When do you plan to begin marketing the merchandise?"

"That's tied to what I decide on the demonstration. If the demonstration goes off as planned, and if the VIPs are suitably impressed, I may begin marketing the stuff immediately, which would be the middle of April. If we wait until it's been proved under actual firefighting conditions, then we're talking the middle of summer. So many choices!"

"As you often tell me, that is why you make the big bucks!", said Allen with a smile.

"No respect even from my legal counsel", said Joe dejectedly. "Well, at least I've still got time in which to make my decision. It's four months until the deadline. We'll see what the future has in store. Who knows? Maybe those slick new fire engines will fall apart on the first landing".

"I do not believe I would want to be in the designer's shoes if such a thing did occur".

"Oh, I'm sure the designer could find another job right away", said Joe with a devilish grin. "Someplace nice, like Antarctica, for instance.

"Perhaps you should consider sending a photograph of Antarctica over to Caprock Drill. It might, shall we say, stimulate the sort of results you seek".

"You might have something there", said Joe thoughtfully. "I'll get Nancy on it right away".

As Thanksgiving week approached, tension began to run at a higher level at the Training Center. Everyone knew that the last major piece of equipment was due any day. When it finally did arrive, the excitement was overwhelming.

"Zack, we need your advice on something over at the garage", said one of Zack's lieutenants, Jack Bazranian.

"*Now* what?", Zack said irritably. "Did somebody get a paper-cut or something? Do they want me to kiss it and make it all better?"

"No sir", replied Jack seriously. "This is an important matter. We need your input right away".

"Oh, all right", said Zack glumly. He grabbed his coat and headed for the door. The days were beginning to get chilly, now that it was approaching winter. As Jack led him over, several people were seen to be peering expectantly after Zack from his training school. Jack opened the man-door at the garage and Zack stepped through into utter darkness. Jack closed the door behind them.

"What happened, you guys forget to pay the light bill again?", Zack yelled at Jack. At that moment, the garage lights flared to life. As Zack turned towards the center of the garage, his eyes opened wide and his jaw fell open. There, standing before him, was the most beautiful fire engine he had ever seen. The lines were more aerodynamic than the usual blocky engines he had worked with. As with the aircraft, the color scheme was royal blue with gold lettering. On the body was the standard Firebomber's logo, two planes, a bulldozer, and a fire engine surrounding a fire. Zack was speechless.

"Ain't she a beauty, boss?", asked Jack. "Notice the front suction capability. We can get water from hydrants in tight streets, and the special filtration system means we can pull in water directly from streams. They tell me she can stop on a dime, take a hill with a full 1500 gallon load like she was empty, and accelerate like a Ferrari on the open road. Add to that the best electrical system in the business, and I'd say we've got ourselves one hot engine!"

"Look at those lines!", said Zack, when he finally recovered his voice. "I'll bet this baby gets good gas mileage, too!"

Jack and Zack looked at each other, then broke out laughing. "I suppose she does at that!", said Jack.

"So! You guys pulled a fast one on me, huh? I wondered why all that paperwork showed up on my desk this morning!"

"We had to find some way to make sure you were inside when we brought this in. We were terrified that you would look outside when we snuck it around the garage. Then Herb forgot the combination to the door! What a lame-brain!"

"Excitement was too much for him, huh?", said Zack with a chuckle.

"I guess so", said Jack, shaking his head. "But it worked! You never caught on, did you?"

"Nope, you guys got me good", said Zack with a grin. "So, what are we standing here for? Let's ring this sucker out!"

"No driving over 50 mph for the first thousand miles. The engineer told me if we do, he's not guaranteeing the engine".

"Same as a new car, I guess", said Zack opening the driver's side door. "Well, don't just stand there. Open the garage door!"

"OK, boss!", said Jack, rushing to comply.

A moment later, Zack rolled the new truck out onto the tarmac and floored the accelerator. Both he and Jack were pushed back into their seats.

"Wow! Now that's what I call git-up-and-go!", yelled Zack.

"Don't push her too hard, yet. Remember, not for the first thousand miles".

"She's running empty, right now", said Zack as they passed 50 mph. "I don't think we'll cause any problems at no load".

"You've exceeded fifty, Zack. Slow down some!"

"You take all the fun out of this, you know that Jack?", Zack said, easing off the accelerator.

"I just don't want to see you break it before I get my turn!", said Jack excitedly.

"Well, that ought to be about next June, the way I figure it", said Zack happily. "So, what other specs does this thing come with?"

"I haven't read all the specs yet, but I recall that the pumps are twin dual-stage series-parallel types. We've got a maximum output capability of 1750 gallons-per-minute, using hydrants, and about a thousand gpm using the filtering systems".

"The pumps are rotaries, right?", asked Zack.

"Nope. They're centrifugal", replied Jack. "I understand that the rotaries weren't as effective in the configuration we needed".

"I don't really care as long as the things throw enough water far enough", said Zack. He stepped on the brakes as he reached the end of the tarmac and left a smoking trail of rubber behind him. "Man, this honey *can* stop on a dime! Sonny boy, I think we got ourselves a mighty nice ride here!".

"Just let me know the next time you decide to slam on the brakes, OK? I just about lost my false teeth on that one!"

"Sorry kiddo", replied Zack with a grin. "Want a lift back to the garage? Or would you prefer to walk?"

"I *had* planned to drive, remember. How about it?"

"Oh, I suppose!", said Zack with a frown. "I get cooped up all day in an office and then I don't even get to enjoy my new truck. What's the world coming to?"

"Hey, you got your turn", said Jack as they traded places. "Now it's mine!"

"Ah, so they did decide to enclose the cab for the back-seaters, too", Zack observed as he climbed in the rider's side.

"Oh yeah, I forgot to mention that", said Jack. "We all have air-conditioning and air-filtration, plus double roll bars in the roof".

"I'd say we're ready for anything. Where's the cooler with the beer?"

Jack turned the truck around and headed back to the garage. "Sorry, boss, only the essentials here".

"You call an air-conditioner essential?", Zack teased.

"Hey, my 'vette has one. This is California, for Pete's sake. *Everybody* has air-conditioning!"

"Shucks, and tomorrow is Thanksgiving! That means we won't be able to airlift this beauty until Monday. That's almost a week to wait!"

"Courage, Zack. You've waited this long, you can wait a few days more".

"I guess I'll have to", moaned Zack. Then he brightened and said, "Unless I could bribe one of those hot-shot transport pilots to come out on Friday!"

"Not a chance. I already tried it. Besides, you'd need a driver".

"Why? I've driven fire engines since before you were born!", said Zack indignantly.

"Not out the back of a moving airplane, you haven't".

"Oh, I hadn't thought of that. So, what are you doing Friday, Jack my boy?"

"I think there's a bowl game on".

"I'll make a deal with you", said Zack slyly. "I'll let you be the first guy to drive this here shiny new truck out the back of a plane. That is, of course, if I can pry you away from your precious game".

"Is that all?", said Jack with a hurt look. "Aren't you even going to offer me a raise or a bonus or anything like that?"

"Don't press your luck! I guess I could ask Tobias over in the 502nd if *he* wants the honor".

"I'm in", said Jack simply. They arrived back at the garage at that moment. Jack eased the truck through the door and Zack got out to close it. As Jack was getting out, he brushed his hand over the side of the truck. What a beauty, he thought. I just hope it can fly.

Chapter 19

Much to Zack's chagrin, he didn't have any better luck recruiting a pilot to fly Friday than Jack had had, so he spent the weekend fuming. He was at Talon Aerospace by 5 A.M. Monday morning. As soon as Jack and an aircrew had arrived, he rushed them over to the garage. The aircrew was from one of the Heavy Lift squadrons used for the Cat Teams, but Zack was not one to stand on formality. A plane was a plane, as far as he was concerned. He made certain the pilot knew how to do a proper touch-and-go, then loaded the engine up himself. Once the cargo crew had fixed the drogue parachute to the rear of the engine and locked it in for the ride, Jack climbed on board and strapped himself in.

"Don't try anything fancy", cautioned Zack. "Just ease this thing out the back when they tell you to".

"Stop worrying, Zack! Remember, I've practiced this twice with that dinky airbase firetruck. I know what I'm doing. Oh, and by the way, I don't have to do anything until the truck's out. The drogue chute will pull me out the back without any help at all".

"That firebase truck was strapped to a pallet", said Zack with a worried expression. "Do me a favor and don't flip her, OK?"

"With the beefed up suspension on this thing? Not likely", Jack replied. "OK, let's get this show on the road!"

The first turboprop coughed to life and Zack was down the loading ramp and out of the way. The ramp slowly closed up as the other three engines sprang to life. The big transport taxied down the runway, then turned at the end and began to rev up it's engines. Once they reached full power, the plane began rolling down the runway. As the C-130 lifted off, the sun peeked over the horizon, the reflection glistening off the underside of the transport which continued east towards the rising sun. Zack lost sight of the plane after a few moments, then waited expectantly. The dawn of a new day, thought Zack, in more ways than one.

Several personnel arrived in the intervening moments and, once Zack told them what was going on, gathered around and peered out to the east, waiting expectantly.

The C-130 had proceeded fifteen miles east when the pilot, Suzie West, slowly began to bank left. She straightened out when she was lined up on the distant airstrip .

"OK, Howard, drop the ramp", Suzie called into the headset.

"Ramp going down", the loadmaster called back.

"Keep your fingers crossed, Ken", said Suzie as they approached the airstrip.

"And my toes", said Ken. Ken Harrison was used to co-piloting air-dropped equipment. This touch-and-go technique had never been one of his best areas of endeavor. He was glad Suzie was driving. She was one of the best transport pilots he had ever seen. The loadmaster, Howard Parker was not bad either. He had seen Howard sling loads out the back with the grace of an artist. He had seen a few spilled drops, but never one by Howard.

"Ramp down and locked", Howard called back.

" That's a roj", replied Suzie.

"Three miles to target and closing", said Ken.

On the ground, everyone could see the C-130 coming in. The pilot was reducing altitude almost to the point of appearing to land. The plane seemed to drop still lower as it got closer. Once it got over the landing strip, the wheels were practically on the ground. The lowered ramp was clearly visible now.

When the plane was opposite the hanger Suzie shouted, "Deploy load!"

In the back, Howard released the drogue chute and the restraints on the fire engine. The wind caught the chute and it billowed out the back of the plane. The engine was jerked backwards. Jack felt like he had just been tackled. The engine thudded to the ground and Jack put it in drive. The transport pulled quickly away from him down the runway.

"Load clear!", shouted the loadmaster.

"Full power! Engage JATOs! Secure ramp! Raise gear!", Suzie shouted.

Ken slammed the throttles fully forward and flipped a switch on the panel. Fastened on the fuselage near the tail, the rocket packs flared to life, spewing flames backward and slightly downward, giving the transport additional lift. The cargo ramp slowly closed up and the transport shot off of the runway, climbing rapidly away.

Jack pulled the engine up in front of the hanger, parked it, and climbed out as the cheering crowd came surging forward to congratulate him.

"All's I did was put this thing in gear", he protested. "They did all the work", he said as he pointed at the rapidly disappearing transport.

"It was a team effort!", said Zack as he shook Jack's hand. "That was the neatest trick I've ever seen! We sure could have used that at a few fires I've been to!"

"Let's make sure the truck survived the drop before you say too much", said Jack cautiously. "I think we should see how it drives first".

"Looked fine to me when you drove up just now", said Zack. "But if you insist!" He shoved past Jack and slid into the driver's seat.

"Hey, wait for me!", Jack yelled, chasing after the retreating fire truck.

Zack was waiting for Joe when he arrived at his office shortly before 8 A.M. It was all he could do to contain himself as he saw Joe approach.

"Morning Nancy", said Joe.

"Morning Joe", said Zack as he got to his feet.

"Morning Zack. What brings you here this early?", asked Joe as he ushered Zack into his office.

"I just wanted to give you an update on some things. No big deal".

"OK, what have you got?", asked Joe, sitting down behind his desk.

"We've hired on the last of the personnel needed for our demonstration team", Zack said, as he sat down opposite Joe. "I would like to begin training them as quickly as possible in order to have them ready when the last of the equipment gets here".

"Fine. I don't see any problems there. I understand your assistants have been practicing air-landing with the smaller airbase fire trucks. How's that working out?"

"It's good practice. I think they'll be ready for the new pumpers when they arrive".

"Good, good", said Joe, as he started sorting through the papers Nancy had put on his desk. "Anything else?"

"I think that covers all the major topics", said Zack, who stood up and turned to leave. As Zack started through the doorway, he deadpanned, "Oh, by the way. We had our first successful air-landing of a new pumper today". Zack continued walking and had just passed Nancy's desk when he heard Joe shout his name and saw him come running out of the office.

"Did you say you air-landed a *new* pumper today?", he asked excitedly.

"Yeah, why?", asked Zack, wearing his best poker face.

"You're not kidding? You mean one of the new Zephyrs arrived?"

"Yeah, Wednesday of last week", replied Zack, still looking at Joe impassively.

"Why didn't you tell me, you big lug?", Joe shouted in glee. "Where is it now? Out at Talon Aerospace?"

"Last I saw", answered Zack, breaking into a triumphant smile. "And she is a beauty. Want to come see her?"

"Try to stop me!", said Joe as he rushed past Zack. "What are you waiting for? Let's go!"

The two friends hurried down the corridor and out to the parking lot. Zack drove Joe over to the airstrip and parked in front of the garage. Joe hustled inside to see his new acquisition.

"Wow, that's some fire truck!", Joe exclaimed. "How does it perform?"

"Better than any I've ever driven. Want to go for a ride?"

"Sure!", said Joe eagerly.

Zack backed the truck out of the garage and began driving down the tarmac. As they drove, he filled Joe in on the various features of the new pumper. Once they reached the end of the airstrip, Zack turned around and headed back to the garage.

"And you say you've already rolled this pumper out the back of a C-130?"

"Yep, just a couple of hours ago. Came through it without a scratch".

"Excellent! So you can begin training for air-landings now, huh?"

"I planned on starting this morning. The aircrew for this particular engine was getting their plane tanked up as I left to go get you. I suppose they're champing at the bit to get on with it".

"Who drove this thing out the back of the plane this morning? You?"

"Well ... , no", said Zack evasively. "One of my assistants was anxious to try it, and he'd already done it twice with that airbase pumper. I figured I'd let him get first crack at it".

"Of course", said Joe with a patronizing smile. He turned away for a moment, then slowly turned back towards Zack. "So, when are you going to try it yourself?", Joe asked softly.

Zack was quiet for a long minute, then answered, "Soon, I expect. Sooner than I might like to, at least".

"Still fighting that fear, huh? Pieter hasn't been able to help you yet?"

"I'm getting better. At least I don't leave indentations in the upholstery on his plane with my fingers anymore".

"That is a sign of improvement", Joe agreed. "You still have a few more months to master this, of course".

"Yeah", said Zack quietly, a distasteful look on his face.

Joe decided to let the subject drop. They were both silent as Zack pulled up in front of the garage.

"Jack!", Zack called. "You want to load this honey up and show the boss how we deliver fire trucks?"

"Be a pleasure Zack", Jack replied. "Good morning Mr. Talon".

"Morning Jack", Joe replied. "How do you like your new toy, here?"

"Fantastic, ain't it?", Jack said as he got in.

Joe and Zack stepped back while Jack drove the truck down to the waiting C-130. The loadmaster directed him up the ramp, then motioned to the pilot to start the engines. A few minutes later, the ramp was up and the C-130 was taxiing down the runway.

Several minutes after that, the C-130 was flying past the garage again, wheels just inches off the tarmac. The ramp was already down, when suddenly a white chute streamed out the back of the plane's cargo hatch. The Zephyr came bumping out onto the flightline and turned to drive over to the garage, still trailing its chute. The C-130, in the meantime, applied full power and sailed off into the west, leaving four trails of black exhaust behind. The ramp could be seen to close as the plane soared over the western end of the runway.

"They didn't even have to use the JATOs this time", said Zack in amazement. "I kinda wish they had, though. Makes for a more spectacular take-off".

"It seemed like a pretty impressive stunt even without them", said Joe in admiration. "Looks like this means of delivery is feasible, doesn't it Zack?"

"You bet", Zack replied. "I was telling the guys at the first run this morning that I wish we had had this sort of system available when I was fighting fires before. It seemed to take hours to get any equipment up to the fires by roads".

"I wonder if we could land these out in meadows?", mused Joe. "That might cut delivery time even more".

"Let's ask a pilot", suggested Zack. "Suzie, could I talk to you for a minute?", Zack called over to a pilot.

"Yes sir, may I help you?", she asked as she walked over.

"This is Joe Talon", said Zack. "We were wondering if these transports could land in a field or meadow okay?"

"Suzie West", the pilot said, as she extended her hand. "Sure, we did a lot of open-field landing in Germany for the REFORGER exercises. We landed several companies of Sheridan light tanks onto a grass field as part of that operation. The fields shouldn't be too wet or soft, though. Are we going to be doing that here?"

"We were thinking about it", said Joe. "It would cut the time of delivery down considerably for forest fires".

"You might want to have some LZ personnel go in ahead of the transports to check the field", said Suzie. "They could be air-dropped before we got there and advise us over the radio about ground conditions. Might save you a lot of headaches and damaged equipment".

"What are LZ personnel?", asked Joe.

"People who have experience with air-landing techniques and know what to look for in a landing zone", replied Suzie. "Paratroopers call them "pathfinders". I've talked to a few since I've been here. I can get some names for you if you'd like to talk this over with them further".

"That's not a bad idea", said Joe. "OK, Zack. Get the list from this young lady and give them to Pieter. You two guys can figure out how you want to take care of this. I think it might be a useful addition to our capabilities".

"You got it, Joe", replied Zack. "Well Suzie, what say we take a walk over to my office and talk a spell?"

"I'm available", Suzie answered. The two of them walked out the door as the   C-130 came taxiing back over in front of the garage. Once the props had stopped, the six crewmen emerged from the plane and walked over to the garage.

"Do you want to load the truck back up again?", one of the loadmasters asked Jack.

"I think we're going to check everything out structurally before we take it up again", replied Jack.

"How long before you need it loaded again", the pilot asked

"Probably not until tomorrow", replied Jack.

"OK, we'll take our bird over and park her, then", said the pilot. The pilot and co-pilot walked back over to the plane, while the other four crewmen walked towards the hanger. After they were gone, Joe turned to Jack.

"You've delivered this thing twice, now?", Joe asked.

"Yes sir, both today", Jack replied. "I'd kind of like to give her a complete checkup before we drop her anymore".

"Looks sound to me", said Joe. "But I guess it's best not to take chances. Do you know when you'll do this again? I'd like to have some of my staff on hand for the next one".

"How about after noon tomorrow?", replied Jack.

"Say about 1 P.M.?", asked Joe.

"That would be good", agreed Jack.

"I'll have them out here tomorrow at one, then", said Joe as he turned to leave. "Don't go without us, OK?"

"OK", replied Jack, getting into the fire truck. He began to drive over to the hydraulic lift as Joe walked out.

The air-landing the next afternoon came off flawlessly. Allen Sims, Jerry Porter, and Dave Albrecht accompanied Joe to the demonstration and were suitably impressed. Joe had an executive staff meeting which included Allen, Jerry, and Dave, along with Zack and Pieter. They discussed plans for the future and set a date in January for a small demonstration of air-landing a single engine company, a company of firejumpers, and a coordinated effort by these units along with a squadron of firebombers in containing a small fire on the practice field. Once the overall plan was established, the meeting broke up. Zack and Pieter went back to the Training Center to brief their respective staffs and establish detailed training plans in preparation for the event.

The weeks sped on to Christmas. Joe once again joined Jerry and Diane Porter for Christmas, then the executive staff and their wives trooped over to Joe's place for New Year's Eve and New Year's Day.

The days dragged on into the middle of January, or so it seemed to Joe. From Zack and Pieter's perspective, they were going by too quickly. The next six engines had been delivered to the Training Center and were being integrated into a company totaling five pumpers, which made up the 501st Engine Company. The other two engines were used to train ground personnel, while the 501st practiced air-landings. Bergway Chemical had sent the first technicians out with the new mixers to be installed in the firebombers themselves. Pieter would begin testing the system after the demonstration January 14th.

Chapter 20

Joe arrived at the Training Center at 7 A.M. on the 14th. The ground crews were already prepping the planes and pumpers. Pieter was just arriving as Joe pulled in.

"Morning Pieter", Joe shouted as he got out of his car.

"Good morning boss", Pieter called back. "Here kind of early aren't you? The demonstration isn't scheduled to begin until ten".

"I probably couldn't keep my mind on my work anyway. I figured I'd come over here and watch you guys get ready".

"I won't have much time to chat today, I'm afraid", said Pieter as he walked over. "I'll have my hands full getting the last-minute details ironed out".

"I understand. I'll stay out of the way, I promise".

Pieter and Joe continued to talk as Pieter headed for the Training Center office.

"How's the mixer installation going?", asked Joe.

"We've had a few hang-ups, but nothing serious. The real test will come when we try to mix the retardant into the water. If it can do that reliably, then I'd say we're home free. I won't be able to give you a better answer for a few days, though".

"That's OK. It's not tremendously important for now anyway. You think your crews are ready for today's exhibition?"

"That remains to be seen. We've drilled enough over the past couple of weeks that we should be able to pull it off blindfolded, but we'll see".

"I think I'll go over to the garage and see how Zack's doing. If I don't see you again before ten, good luck!"

"Thanks Joe ", said Pieter, who walked into the Training Center office. Joe wandered over to the garage and found it to be in an uproar. Hoses were rolled out everywhere, crews were shouting instructions to each other, motors were being revved up, and pumps pressure-tested. In the midst of it all was Zack. Seeing this situation, Joe decided it was better to step into the lounge and watch, rather than disturb Zack, who was obviously very busy.

Meanwhile, over in the firebomber hanger, Bob Mitchell and Dick Morrison were just walking in when a mechanic came over with a scowl on his face.

"You guys should have that mechanic of yours defanged before he hurts somebody!", the mechanic said heatedly.

"Why, what happened?", Dick asked.

"I was checking the air pressure on your plane's tires and the old codger started yelling at me!", replied the mechanic. "I've never heard half the names he was calling me. When I asked him what was the matter, he yelled that your plane was off-limits to everyone but him. What does he think he is, your private mechanic?"

"Sorry", said Bob. "We'll go try to cool him down. It won't happen again".

"Pat, have you been beating up on your associates again?", asked Bob as they approached their plane.

"Now donah git after me about that, lads", said Pat defensively. "I only want to make sure that no dunderhead mucks up your plane. After all, it's my responsibility to look after you, not theirs!"

"These guys are all trained mechanics, Pat", said Dick. "You can't treat them like they're wet behind the ears. Some of them might even be as good as you!"

"I have me doubts", said Pat sourly. "Ah donah think most of them have a bit o' sense. An' I donah plan to give them a chance tah prove it wit' your plane!"

"You ever notice how his brogue gets worse when he's angry?", Dick said to Bob with a grin.

"I just wish we could get him to behave himself", said Bob with a sigh. "OK, Pat. You can have the plane to yourself, just don't go snapping at any VIPs who might get too close. Remember, the *big* bosses are here today".

"That I will", said Pat, his face brightening. "An' you needn't worry about your plane. She'll be in fine fettle when you need her!"

"That should be in about an hour", said Dick. "Have you checked everything yet?"

"I've not yet finished. I was too busy chasin' away the pests!", Pat said, scowling at the other mechanic.

"I'll talk to the shop boss and smooth this out", Bob said to Dick. "In the meantime, why don't you give Pat a hand checking the bird out?"

"Will do", said Dick.

At 9 A.M, Pieter assembled his crews in a hanger for a final briefing, while Zack herded his personnel into the Training Center auditorium. Joe tagged along with Zack's group in order to listen in. Once everyone was clear on the plan of action, the two gatherings broke up and the personnel went back to finish up their last-minute chores. Hoses were coiled onto the firetrucks, planes were taxied out onto the airstrip for fueling, and airbase fire crews, under Zack's watchful eye, began setting the controlled fires on the training ground.

Bob and Dick came walking back to their plane after the briefing. Pat was standing off to one side beaming at them. As they approached, Bob could see something written in flowing gold letters on the fuselage just below the cockpit windows. When they came up along the plane, Bob and Dick both gasped. The name 'Gertie's Garters' had been painted on the side.

"I hope ye donah mind me namin' your plane for ye", said Pat sheepishly. "I just thought, well, Charlie would ha' liked it".

"That solves one problem Dick and I had been wrestling with for the last couple of weeks, Pat", said Bob. "What to name our plane. That name suits me fine. How about you Dick?"

"OK by me. We'll think of Charlie whenever we see it. I like that".

"I wanted it tah be a surprise, so I painted it on yesterday, then covered it wit' a piece o' blue fabric this morning, just so's I could surprise you lads", Pat said proudly. "It willna wash off when yah go in the water, you see."

"You thought of everything, didn't you Pat?", said Dick in wonder.

"Aye, that I did!", said Pat. "Well, enough o' this chit-chat, you lads had best be off. An' good luck to ye both today!"

Both pilots thanked Pat, then climbed aboard their plane. After the pre-flight check was completed, the engines roared to life and Bob taxied 'Gertie's Garters' out onto the runway.

As the plane moved toward the fueling station, Pat spoke quietly to himself, "They're good lads, Charlie. I'll keep an eye on them an' pray God brings them home safe. Hail and farewell, old friend." Pat wiped a tear from his eye and walked slowly back into the now-peaceful hanger.

As ten o'clock approached, the firetrucks were carefully loaded onto transports and firejumpers embarked their planes. At five minutes till ten, the first transports taxied out onto the flightline and awaited permission to take off. Joe was now in the small bleacher that had been erected in front of the firebomber hanger. Along with Jerry, Allen, Dave, and a few staff members, he waited expectantly for the exercise to commence.

"What exactly are we supposed to see?", Jerry asked Joe.

"First, firejumpers will parachute in while the pumpers are air-landed on the airstrip. They are all supposed to converge on the north side of the fire and seal it off. By that time, the firebombers will have tanked up and will begin laying a cordon of retardant around the fire. They will contain three sides of the fire, leaving the last side for the ground personnel to handle".

"Sounds complicated", said Dave. "Why aren't the Cat Teams being used?"

"This operation doesn't really warrant their use. If we were fighting a fire out in the wilds, they would be off somewhere constructing firebreaks. Here, we've got more than enough personnel and equipment to cover this fire. The Cat Teams would simply be in the way".

"I was under the impression that we did not have the new retardant mixers in the firebombers themselves", said Allen. "What are the bombers using for their retardant?"

"Class A Foam", replied Joe. "It's a short-term retardant. It's better than water, but not nearly as good as the long-term retardant. It will make a firebreak which will stop the fire long enough to finish it off with ground crews. Canadair provided the planes with a mixer system which allows us to reload up to twenty times with water and mix the retardant in automatically".

At precisely 10 A.M., the first aircraft roared down the runway, followed at short intervals by several more. First the five firebombers took off, so that they could load up with water at the nearby reservoir. Pieter led these aircraft out, followed quickly by the next squadrons, the transports. The five firejumper planes went aloft first, closely followed by the five firetruck transports. A total of almost four hundred personnel were now airborne.

Zack had the brushfire well under way. Smoke was beginning to drift upwards and slightly south of the fire, fortunately for the onlookers who were several hundred feet north of the fire. The airstrip itself formed an impassable barrier to the fire even if it did start moving north, so that the facilities and the audience were not put in danger.

The controllers in the airbase tower had been doubled to handle the increase in traffic. Controllers were calling off headings and altitudes to the swarm of aircraft as each squadron began lining up for their part in the operation.

"Pathfinder leader to Pathfinder flight", Pieter called into his headset. "Begin loading". Pieter dipped the 'North Star' down into the water for a few seconds until the indicator showed both tanks full. He pulled back on the yoke and soared over the dam, followed by each trailing plane in turn, until all five were filled up.

"Pathfinder leader to Talon tower, what are our holding box coordinates, over", Pieter called over the radio.

"Pathfinder leader, this is Talon tower, turn to three-three-zero and climb to twenty-five hundred feet", the tower controller replied. Proceed to grid zero-five-zero and orbit, over".

"That's a roj, Talon tower", Pieter replied. He verified that each plane in his squadron had received the instructions, then the planes proceeded to this holding point to orbit until the transports were in position.

"Talon tower, this is Ace Movers leader requesting approach vector to Drop Zone, over", pilot Rich Reasoner called over the mike.

"Ace Movers leader, this is Talon tower, turn to one-two-zero and descend to twelve hundred feet", replied the tower. "Wind bearing three-one-five degrees at five knots, over".

"That's a roj, tower", Rich replied. "Ace leader to Ace flight. OK boys, you know the drill. Drop 'em quick and let's get out of there!"

The five troop transports turned to their approach vector and began descending in echelon formation. Ahead, the smoke from the fire could be plainly seen. "AQMD is not going to be happy about this", mused Rich. "How far to DZ, Harvey?"

Harvey Simpson, the co-pilot, punched a few keys on his keypad and checked his computer screen. "Eight point eight miles and closing", he replied. "Altitude nominal, wind nominal. Looks like a good day for a drop".

As the red lights went on in the cargo portion of each troop carrier, the jumpmasters started preparing the firejumpers for their exit. The assistant jumpmasters checked each stick of firejumpers as they stood up and folded their seats, then they moved into line and the next stick of firejumpers was checked.

"Slowing to one-two-zero knots, altitude three thousand feet", Rich intoned.

"Approaching LZ, range one-point-eight miles", Harvey called off. "Showtime, gentlemen".

Flaps came down and the blast-deflectors on the rear of each wheel-well were extended from the fuselage. These would cut down on the turbulence encountered by the firejumpers as they exited the planes. The side doors were opened and static lines given one last check as the first pair of jumpers stood in the doors. Once they were over the LZ, the first pair went out the doors of each transport, followed at one second intervals by another pair until half of the sixty men had exited each plane. The doors were then closed and the flaps and blast-deflectors tucked in. Rich applied full-power and banked right. Each plane in the squadron completed its first pass and followed him. It was now the turn of the transports carrying the firetrucks.

"Roadrunner leader, this is Talon tower, over", the controller called out.

"Talon tower, this is Roadrunner leader, over", Wally Pritchard, pilot of the lead plane in the pumper transport squadron, called into the mike.

"Roadrunner leader, you are cleared for approach to airstrip", the tower controller responded. "Wind bearing three-two-zero at five knots, over".

"Roger that tower, beginning approach now, out", Wally replied. "Roadrunner leader to Roadrunner flight. Beginning air-landing op now, acknowledge". Each pilot in the squadron acknowledged the message, then began descending behind Wally's plane, 'Lancer'.

Joe and his guests had been watching the first group of firejumpers descending on the landing zone. Since each paratrooper had a controllable canopy chute, they were able to adjust their trajectories on the way down, enabling most of them to land within the Landing Zone. Two or three chutes failed to open properly, and the firejumpers had to use their reserve belly chutes, causing them to end up just outside of the LZ. The last of the parachutes had come to earth when a line of C-130s appeared from the east and began descending on the airstrip.

"That should be the transports with the fire engines", said Joe. Everyone watched as the lead plane slowly approached the end of the airstrip.

"Loadmaster, drop ramp!", Wally shouted into the headset. The loadmaster, Charles Dykstra, activated the loading ramp, which began to descend. Simultaneously, Kevin Pritchard, Wally's brother and co-pilot, lowered the flaps to reduce speed further.

"Ramp down and locked!", Charles called over the intercom.

As the C-130 came opposite the hangers, Wally shouted into the headset, "Deploy load!"

The drogue chute streamed out behind the firetruck as the loadmaster released the restraints. The truck, being driven by Jack Bazranian lurched backwards and out the door. Once the truck hit the ground, the loadmaster called into the intercom, "Load clear!"

"Throttle up to Full power! Raise ramp! Engage JATOs!", Wally commanded. Wally's brother pushed the four throttles up to maximum while firing off the JATO packs on either side of the fuselage. Charles was already raising the ramp as the JATO packs ignited, causing the plane to jump slightly and rapidly accelerate.

To the rear of the plane, Jack was quickly driving over to the side of the flightline as the transport bolted skyward and the next transport came over the east end of the airstrip. Jack's crew got out and hastily bundled up the drogue chute just as the second fire engine thudded onto the tarmac.

"That is what I call rapid delivery!", Allen said to Joe.

"That's the idea", Joe replied. "It sure beats driving our equipment up to the fires, doesn't it?"

"Yes indeed", Allen answered.

As they were speaking, the fourth transport appeared over the east end of the landing strip.

"That guy seems to be coming in a bit higher than the previous planes", observed Dave.

"He is at that", Joe remarked, a hint of apprehension creeping into his voice. As they watched, the plane drew up opposite to the hanger and the Zephyr dropped out the rear - literally. It bounced high off the ground once, blowing the front right tire, then swerved off to the side and rolled over completely, ending up on its right side.

The pilot of the transport following close behind the fourth transport uttered a curse, then shouted, "Full power! Close ramp! Climb, baby, *climb*!"

Joe watched in disbelief as the careening fire engine came to a halt lying on its side. His look changed to one of horror when he saw the C-130 coming up fast from behind the truck. The crews of the other three trucks rushed over to help their comrades, as the engines on the fast-approaching transport roared up to full power and the plane raced over the fallen fire truck with only a few feet to spare.

"That was too close!", said Joe as he slumped into his seat. Allen glanced at Jerry and Dave with a knowing look. They would be in need of a replacement pilot, it would appear.

Over at the crash site, the ground personnel were helping their friends out of the wreck. Miraculously, the only injuries were scratches and bruises. The double roll-bars and seat-belts had served their purpose quite well. The truck, however, was a write-off. The second wave of firejumpers were descending on the DZ as the three serviceable fire trucks combined to drag the wrecked one off of the flight line. Once the wreck was clear and the last of the firejumpers had landed, the fifth Roadrunner transport landed its engine, then roared off the airstrip to form up with the rest of its squadron.

"Looks like everybody got out OK", said Joe thankfully. "I think Pieter is going to have to have a little talk with that transport pilot, though".

At that moment, the tower gave Pieter clearance to begin his first bombing run. Zack had the brushfire up to a good sized spot-fire by now and Pieter would need his entire squadron dropping in order to contain just one side of the blaze.

"Talon tower, this is 'North Star'", Pieter called over the radio. "We are beginning our attack run".

"Roger that, 'North Star'", the tower replied. "Be advised that wind is five knots at bearing three-two-five".

"Copy that, tower", replied Pieter. "'North Star' out. Pathfinder leader to Pathfinder flight, begin bombing op".

Pieter took his plane down to 200 feet and approached the fire from the northeast, then adjusted his flight path to due west just in front of the leading edge of the blaze.

"Punch us up a winner, Ralph", he told co-pilot Ralph Gautier.

"OK, Pieter", Ralph answered as he began ranging the distance to the fire. Once he had entered the information into the computer, he punched the 'salvo' button. "It's set", he said.

The bombay doors opened as they approached the fire, and the gelled water spilled out onto the dry grass. Pieter applied full power and kept his plane level after the retardant was dispensed. Each plane followed in line, dropping just as they reached the center of the previous drop, neatly linking the five loads together. When the second plane had dropped, Pieter began to climb and turn back towards the reservoir to reload.

"Looks like a good pattern", Pieter said to Ralph as he banked left.

"That finishes one side", replied Ralph. "Two more like that and it's Miller time!"

"We'll worry about that when we've done the job", said Pieter cautiously. Then he spoke into the mike, "Well done, Pathfinders! Let's go back and do it again".

The five planes headed off to reload as the firejumpers and the remaining fire trucks converged on the north side of the fire.

"Looks like they've stopped the head's progress", said Jack as his pumper approached the fire. "Let's see what we can do about the base".

The ground personnel spread out and began hosing down the fires closest to them. The firejumpers checked the brush and clumps of grass to make sure there were no embers, then proceeded onto the next cluster of flaming grass. By the time the firebombers came around for their second pass, the engine company and firejumper company had pushed more than thirty feet into the base of the fire.

"Zack's people appear to be having fun", Dave said to Joe. "I didn't realize they could move into a fire that quickly".

"I imagine that progress will be slower on hills or in amongst trees", said Joe. "In grass, though, I guess they can move pretty fast. It helps when you know the game-plan too. Having four more companies of both engine crews and firejumpers, not to mention the two Cat Teams and airbase firefighters, makes for a confident Ground Boss"

"The deck is stacked fairly heavily against the fire at that, isn't it?", chuckled Dave.

"Let's just say Zack's not taking any chances", answered Joe. "It would be even better if those engine crews had their fire trucks, but I guess we can't have everything".

"And now it appears that we will be one engine behind", said Jerry.

"You did have to bring that up, didn't you?", said Joe ruefully. "I wonder whether they can repair it, or if we simply write it off?"

"If it was made of steel, I'd say you might be able to salvage it", replied Dave. "But with that composite stuff, I'm afraid they may just have to scrap the whole thing".

"It would appear that we have just discovered the first major shortcoming to our High Tech approach to firefighting", said Jerry. "We cannot repair extensive damage as easily as if it were common steel. You may have to look into a field repair system for these new machines, Joe".

"Not me", said Joe. "I have more important things to do. No, what this requires is someone with some technical knowledge. Someone with a flair for improvisation. Someone with the ear of the money managers. Someone .... like *Dave!*"

Dave nearly fell off the bleacher at that. "Wait a minute!", he protested. "I don't have time for this! You've already got me doing fifty-'leven things as it is! No, you're going to have to get someone at Caprock to ride herd on this problem. I'm booked solid".

"Well, I guess I should let them do it anyway", said Joe resignedly. "After all, they are the ones who came up with this witches' brew in the first place. OK, Dave, you're off the hook".

"Thank heavens for that!", said Dave.

As Joe and his associates finished talking, Pieter led his squadron in for the final drop on the west side of the fire. The ground crews had now sliced through better than 100 feet of grass and were rapidly approaching the center of the fire.

"Pathfinder flight, this is Pathfinder leader", Pieter called into the mike. "Set up for a linked salvo drop this time".

"I thought we needed a Hawkeye airborne to do that?", said Ralph incredulously.

"I took the liberty of having Dave Albrecht install a system like the Hawkeye uses for interrogating our beacons in the tower", answered Pieter. "It will act like a Hawkeye for this exercise".

"Pretty slick, Pieter", Ralph replied with a smirk. "We get to see if this fancy system really works, huh?"

"You got it", replied Pieter. "And we get to do it *before* we do a demonstration to outsiders. All I need is to have this gizmo foul up in front of God and country in order to ruin my meals for a week!"

"We'll also have to rely on the TRIDINT's Forward Looking Infra-Red pods for this pass", said Ralph. "Looks like we get to try out everything today!"

"Everything except the most important thing", said Pieter. "I wish we had those retardant mixers on board. I'd like to see how those perform".

"That's your assignment for the next couple of weeks, Pieter", said Ralph with a laugh. "Don't get so anxious! You've got plenty of time to do that in".

"Not with April just around the corner I don't", replied Pieter, a worried look crossing his face. "If everything was working fine now, then I could relax. As it is, though, there's still too many unknowns".

"I don't think the boss has even mailed out any invitations yet", said Ralph. "He could probably postpone the demonstration if necessary".

"Well, I guess I shouldn't worry too much", said Pieter. "I still need to talk to Dave about that low-level avoidance system".

"What's that?", Ralph asked.

"Tell you as soon as we plaster this fire", replied Pieter. "OK, we're lined up for a south-to-north vector. We'll want to drop about thirty feet to the west of the fire. Get me a range on the base of this western flank".

"TRIDINT indicates... about five hundred feet from the head", said Ralph, staring into the display.

"Program a salvo about 50 feet from the base, then press the 'Master Link' button so when we drop, everybody else drops. That should seal up this flank".

Ralph quickly punched in the location, then pressed the 'salvo' and 'Master Link' buttons. The 'link' light began flashing. "Looks like we're ready. That TRIDINT equipment works pretty good. It looks like pea-soup out the window with all this smoke, but the fire shows up perfectly on the display".

"It makes the job easier by half, doesn't it?", mused Pieter.

As the 'North Star' passed over the leading edge of the fire, the other four aircraft reduced altitude to match and lined up on the fire. When Pieter's plane was near the trailing edge, his bombay doors opened automatically and gelled water streamed out. At almost the same instant, the bombay doors on each of the other four planes also sprang open, flooding the field below with a continuous line of retardant. The last flank of the fire was now fireproofed.

"Now that's what I call the easy way to contain a fire!", crowed Pieter. He banked left for a look at the fire. "Looks like the boys on the ground have a handle on this one. What say we head for the hanger?"

"Sure, why not?", replied Ralph.

"Pathfinder leader to Pathfinder flight, return to base. Well done everyone", Pieter called over the radio.

"Now what was this about some kind of avoidance system?", said Ralph.

"Oh yeah", replied Pieter. "Dave was telling us about a system the military was working on for their helicopters and aircraft to keep them from running into power lines and other low-level obstacles. I guess they had problems with such things when they invaded Panama a few years back. Dave said he could get the folks at Talon Electronics to rig up something like that for us".

"What danger is there of running into power lines in the forest?", asked Ralph. "I thought we would be well away from any kind of lines out there".

"You can't always tell", said Pieter, banking around for his final approach. "I was telling the staff a story about a guy who flew right into a high-power line when we were fighting a fire one time. All's you have to do is touch one of those things and you're history".

"So Dave is working on something like that for us, huh?", asked Ralph. "I wonder when he plans to have it done?"

"That's what I've got to talk to him about", replied Pieter as they touched down. "If we're going out to do a demonstration, it's most likely going to be around built-up areas If we do it at night in order to show off our night-fighting capabilities, then we'll definitely want that kind of system to keep us from getting clotheslined. I think I'll go find Dave once we park this thing".

"Close up your ranks", Jack yelled at his engine company. "Make sure you don't miss any smoldering grass, otherwise this could restart behind you!"

The firefighters moved steadily forward flanked by the four remaining pumpers. Each pumper was providing four hoses discharging over 300 gallons-per-minute of water onto the fire.

Smokechaser teams of three or four men followed along behind the main front, checking for smoldering brush or grass and extinguishing any embers which had been missed. By the time the bombers dropped their final line into place, the center of the burned area had been reached by the ground crews. In less than an hour, the firefighters had reached the southern edge of the fire and completed the job of extinguishing it.

"Looks like you've killed this bugger", said Zack as he walked over by Jack. The fire crews were putting out the last pockets of fire as they spoke.

"It appears that way, doesn't it?", said Jack with a grin. "So, what do you think, boss?"

"I wish we could carry more water in these pumpers", said Zack. "They were practically out by the time you reached the firebreak".

"There may be streams to reload from at an actual fire, or fire hydrants, if we're up in the residential areas", said Jack.

"Maybe", replied Zack. "And then again, maybe not. We'll have to develop our tactics based on the idea that we won't have any additional water available. That way, if we do have water near the fire, we're okay. Otherwise, we're trained to go without".

"Seems reasonable, said Jack. "So what's next on the agenda?"

"Post-operational assessment", said Zack. "Get everybody cleaned up and back to the training room. I want to go over ways to improve our efficiency and listen to complaints and suggestions from the line crews while this is still fresh in their minds".

"OK, I'll pass the word", said Jack. Zack walked over to talk to some of the other commanders.

Forty-five minutes later, the ground crews assembled at the Training Center auditorium for their debriefing. Simultaneously, the air crews were gathering over in the firebombers hanger for a similar debriefing. Once all the business of the day was covered, the crews finished straightening up their gear and headed for home, while Pieter and Zack drove over to Talon Industries to meet with the remaining executive staff there.

"What's the status on the Zephyr that got dropped?", asked Joe after the meeting began.

"We're going to ship it back to Caprock and see if they can do anything with it", replied Zack. "The body is pretty badly damaged, but the frame may still be salvageable".

"What about the crew?", Joe asked.

"Everybody got out OK", said Zack. "I think the most serious injury was a sprained wrist on the driver. All the other injuries were confined to bruises and minor cuts. Nobody had anything broken".

"At least the roll-bars worked right", said Dave.

"And the pilot of the transport?", Joe asked Pieter.

"He's going to be switched over to piloting a Cat Team transport", Pieter answered. "There was a female pilot who did a dandy job on air-landing our first pumper, Suzie West. I believe you and Zack have met her, Joe".

"Yes, I believe we did at that", said Joe. "She knows how to land these things *carefully*?"

"I'm told she was one of the best pilots in the 464th Tactical Airlift Wing", said Pieter. "I'd say she qualifies for the job. In order to keep the pilots happy, we simply swapped the crews of both planes in their entirety from one squadron to the other. Both pilots had expressed a desire to keep their crews with them".

"I hope that guy has better luck dropping Cats", mused Joe. "I want to hear your individual opinions of how the operation today went. Why don't we lead off with you, Zack?"

"Other than wrecking one of my trucks, I'd say the operation went off without a hitch", Zack answered. "The fire was quickly contained and the ground crews didn't miss any spot fires while they were cleaning up behind the fire line".

"What did you think of your fire trucks' performance?", asked Dave.

"Very good", replied Zack. "They were able to keep a constant stream of water coming from all four outlets, plus being on the scene quickly with the air-landing capability. In time of need, we may be able to air-land them in meadows or fields, allowing them to get to the fire even faster. I can think of several Forestry people who would want to have engines like that in their fire lines".

"So we might have a shot at marketing these as well?", asked Joe.

"I don't see why not", answered Zack. "If I had the option on buying such a machine, I'd jump at it. The price-tag may be too high, though".

"We might defray the costs on some of the more expensive items by adding profit to the less expensive ones", said Jerry. "If we were to raise the price on the retardant, for instance, it would not show up as a major expense for small orders, but would add up to a considerable profit overall. I will have some of my people look into this further, if you wish".

"Yes, do so Jerry", said Joe. "Anything else, Zack?"

"I think we should also begin thinking about how we're going to coordinate firefighting operations", said Zack. "We plan to use an air-traffic controller up in the Hawkeye, but we need to have our Air Boss where he can see what's going on. It seems to me the Hawkeye would be the best place for that. Are you going to be the nominal Air Boss Pieter?"

"I'm not sure, yet", Pieter answered. "I'd like to be able to fly bombers during the ops, but there is the need for someone to coordinate air-ops. How about if we recruit someone from Forestry?"

"I'm open to suggestions", said Joe.

"There was one guy who worked out of Ukiah", said Pieter thoughtfully. "Oh what was his name?"

"So you want to stay in the driver's seat Pieter?", asked Joe.

"I think so", Pieter replied. "My first love is flying, not being a traffic cop".

"That's settled, then", said Joe. "I'll want a list of candidates who could fill the position by February at the latest. We'll need time to get him up to speed on our firefighting techniques, especially the capabilities of our bombers. I leave it up to Pieter and Zack to come up with the list. Get it to me ASAP, OK?"

"OK Joe", said Pieter. "I just wish I could remember that guy's name. Well, it'll come to me, I'm sure".

"I think we'll also need an overall Fire Boss who has knowledge of the total operation", said Zack. "I figured I could fill that position and put Jack Bazranian in my present position of Ground Boss. He's got several years of experience and I think he'd perform the job very well".

"I'll approve it if that's your decision", said Joe.

"Fine", replied Zack. "Oh, and one other thing that struck me when we were out on the practice field. We need some sort of command-control station for the Fire Boss and his staff. This would need to have communications gear for talking directly to the aircraft and the engine companies. Can something be put together that we could air-land at the fire?"

"Dave, that sounds like your department", said Joe.

"It goes along with something I've been thinking about for a while, anyway", said Dave. "I had already drawn up some preliminary sketches of a command vehicle which we could airlift in and drive out again. We might want to have a couple, actually. One for the overall fire commander and one for each of the other two commanders; the Air Boss and the Ground Boss. I could have the Hawkeye's displays, including the radar track, download in real-time to the Command Control Centers. That would allow the Air Boss staff to remain on the ground, making it a lot less crowded up in the Hawkeye".

"Now that sounds like a great idea!", said Joe. "My staff could even come along and see how each facet of the operation was going. I like that!"

"Just as long as you don't get in the way", growled Zack. "I don't want to have to nursemaid a bunch of camp followers every time we go to a fire. I imagine you are going to want the press to be on hand for our operations until the novelty wears off. You had best keep them away from me when I'm fighting a fire, else their papers may need some replacement reporters".

"Well, maybe we could bring along an extra vehicle which would be for the use of Joe and his staff exclusively", said Dave quickly. He saw Joe's face flushing slightly after Zack's rebuke. "That would also give us a redundant CCC vehicle in case one of the others suffered the fate of our bouncing firetruck today".

"Would that satisfy you, Zack?", Joe asked coolly.

"Yep, it never hurts to have too many radios along", Zack replied unruffled. When it came to the business of fighting fires, he didn't pull any punches with anybody, boss or no boss. He had seen too many media circuses at hi-profile fires and he wanted no part of that when he was running the show.

"One thing for all of you to bear in mind", said Joe. "I plan to advertise our operations from the beginning. This organization has cost a ton of money to build up and we've seen absolutely no profit from it as of yet. The only hope of keeping the organization running is to sell our inventions and expertise to other people. The best way to get free advertising is to invite the press along to give us coverage. Otherwise, the stockholders are going to be shouting for my head on a plate at the next annual meeting. Some of them have already expressed misgivings about the time and money we've invested in this operation. I will have to have something positive to show for our efforts by the end of this year, or we may all be out looking for new jobs".

The room quieted down for a few moments as Joe let that sink in. "Anything else Zack?", Joe asked.

"Nope, I think that covers everything", Zack replied.

"Pieter, what have you got?", Joe asked.

"The bombing ops went off without a hitch", Pieter began. "We tried Dave's drop-linking system on our last drop and it seemed to work flawlessly. We were able to drop a perfect overlapping pattern of retardant. The Class A Foam worked fine for today's exercise. The TRIDINT equipment worked great and we were able to see all the way down one flank of the fire just as clear as day. Aside from the one fire engine mishap, the remainder of the air-transport missions went fine. Most of the firejumpers landed within the Drop Zone and no one suffered any injuries. Time to delivery was minimal, even with the need for a second pass in order to drop the full load of firejumpers in the DZ".

"I think that fifth transport pilot deserves a medal for avoiding the wreckage on the runway", said Joe.

"Would you consider a bonus?", asked Pieter expectantly.

"Done", said Joe. "Jerry, I want a 20% raise in that pilot's salary, effective immediately. I also want a 20% decrease in the salary of that pilot who created that little mishap. Take care of that will you?"

"Certainly", replied Jerry as he leaned over and whispered something to Pieter, then began writing.

Pieter spoke up a moment later, "Joe, do you think it's a good idea to reduce the pilot's salary in addition to changing his squadron? That's kind of like kicking the poor guy when he's already down".

"Would you rather I just fire the guy and be done with it?", asked Joe, a hint of anger in his eyes.

"No, I guess not", said Pieter dejectedly. He'd seen the exasperated look on the pilot's face after he had landed. He didn't think this double-dose of punishment was necessary, but it wasn't his decision to make.

"OK, Pieter", said Joe after a moment. "Any other items?"

"One more thing which I keep on forgetting to ask Dave about", said Pieter. "Have you given any thought to that low-level avoidance system you had mentioned earlier?"

"Not really", said Dave.

"Uh-huh. Do you think you could have that ready by April?", asked Pieter.

"We're still finishing the outfitting of the Hawkeyes", Dave replied. "I don't see how I could get it done in time. Tell you what, I'll turn it over to the whiz kids at Talon Electronics, see what they can come up with. I doubt they can have it by April, though".

"Oh well", said Pieter. "I was hoping you already had people working on it".

"Sorry", replied Dave. "I've been too busy with everything else. I'll tell them to try and hurry it up, but unless we buy an existing system, I don't see how we can have anything other than a crude prototype ready any sooner than June".

"Just do the best you can, Dave", said Pieter. "I don't want some kind of cluj that breaks down at the wrong moment. Better to have our pilots cautious without it than overconfident with it. It might fail at just the wrong time and kill a crew".

"I'll see what I can do", replied Dave. "Do you also want me to look into a Heads Up Display unit for the bombers? It might make the pilots' work a whole lot easier if they could keep looking straight ahead, instead of constantly glancing at this display, that gauge, and so forth".

"Just as long as you don't get carried away", cautioned Joe. "Remember, we don't want to overload our pilots with too many gadgets".

"Or our service personnel, either", Pieter chimed in.

"That's the beauty to a HUD system", said Dave, who was getting enthused again. "They reduce all the fishing around the pilot has to do in order to fly the plane. They put all of the pertinent information right there in front of his eyes so he doesn't even have to look away from the windshield. I'll see if I can get a tour arranged over at Talon Aerospace. We're working on one there for that C-35 transport plane".

"Sounds good. But I'd like to see one before I commit to it", said Pieter.

"When will the Hawkeyes be operational, Dave?", asked Joe.

"I hope to have the first one finished by the end of next week", Dave replied.

"That will be one of the critical links in this operation and in the April demonstration", said Joe. "I want everything triple-checked and fully proofed-out before the demonstration takes place. The last thing we need is a mid-air collision during our ops".

"I have a couple of Talon Electronic's best field engineers cross-checking all the systems as I go", said Dave. "We should be able to catch any bugs that way".

"And Pieter, I believe you have an important set of tests to run yourself", said Joe.

"Yep, I'll begin checking out the retardant mixer tomorrow", said Pieter. "I hope it works as well as they say. We only have a few weeks left to fix it in if it doesn't work right".

"Time is getting exceedingly short", said Jerry. "Allen and I have still made no progress with the various contractors on manufacturing the equipment ourselves. Therefore, I would say that we will be restricted to the snail's-pace of equipment acquisitions as they now stand".

"Well, the only pacing items for the project now are both in-house items anyway", said Joe. "*If* the retardant mixer works and *if* we can get enough fire engines in time, we may have a shot at it".

"One suggestion I have in case the retardant mixer doesn't work is that we tank up the bombers with pre-mixed long-term retardant for the first drops, then use the short-term Class A Foam for any remaining drops", offered Pieter. "That way, we can bomb the head of the fire with the best stuff first, and close up the flanks with the poorer stuff. We could drop retardant each time, just not long-term all the time".

"Let's hope that mixer works right, then we won't have to consider any options", said Joe. "How are our force-levels as it stands now, Pieter?"

"We presently have fifteen firebombers operational", began Pieter. "We expect to receive the rest of the first lot of thirty planes by the end of March, just in time for our April show. The transports have all been delivered now. We have them divided up into twenty-five for the five engine companies and five firejumper companies to share; ten planes for the two Cat Teams; five KC-130s to be used for aerial refueling; and an additional three C-130s for spares. Since you guys are planning on air-lifting some additional CCC equipment, I will probably use those extra planes for that task. Once Dave has the electronics installed on the two Hawkeyes, and the electronic upgrades bolted into the late-arrivals, we plan to have a total of twenty-five firebombers active, with five spares; two Hawkeyes; five tankers; and thirty-five C-130s, with three spares. That gives us a total of 67 active aircraft".

"Zack, what about the ground crews?", asked Joe.

"Right now, we have a total of 1500 firejumpers divided up into five companies of 300 firejumpers each on the line, plus about forty support personnel", Zack said. "We also have mechanized crews broken up into two Cat Teams consisting of eight men each, and five engine companies which will eventually total twenty-five engines and 130 total personnel, counting engine crews and command staff. Our projected force totals are for approximately 1700 personnel, which would be roughly equal to about two reinforced battalions".

"How about support personnel for the aircraft, maintenance types and the like?", asked Dave.

"We haven't done any detailed counts for the size by April", said Pieter, "but our estimates are that we will have about 40% of the air-crew strength in total maintenance personnel. That would figure out to about 300 air-crews and around 120 ground personnel. The garages constitute another fifty personnel tops, so we're talking a grand total of about 2200 personnel".

"That's a fair number of bodies", said Dave. "We should be able to put a dent in a fire with that much equipment and personnel".

"It all depends on how you use them", cautioned Zack. "We have to conserve our resources during a fire because we never know how long it's going to burn. Today, we knew exactly what we were up against and precisely how to control the fire, everything was calculated ahead of time. Even in those ideal circumstances, we were getting pretty slim on water supplies. In a real fire, you won't know for sure what the weather is going to do. You can't be certain the dispatcher won't pull your air-support away for another, more critical fire. And when night comes it gets downright dangerous fighting a fire in the hills. Don't get overconfident or you may find out just how deadly an adversary a fire can be".

"And how", seconded Pieter quietly.

"Does anybody else have anything to add?", asked Joe after a moment. "No? OK, you all know your assignments. Let's set a tentative meeting date of two weeks from now. Thank you all for coming".

Chapter 21

The next morning, Pieter was at the hanger by 8 A.M. He stopped by to check on the progress of the Bergway Chemical people who were overseeing installation of the mixer and retardant tanks on his plane.

"Good morning gentlemen", Pieter said as he joined the group huddled around the plane. "How goes the battle?"

"We havena' started yet", replied Patrick. "This isna' goin' tah be an easy task, you know".

"Well, I'm here to help", said Pieter. "I'll be in my office if you guys need anything".

The remainder of the morning was relatively peaceful, at least in Pieter's office it was. In the hanger, several of the maintenance personnel got an education in the finer points of Irish profanity. Patrick was fit to be tied by the end of the day, as Pieter found when he came out late in the afternoon to see how the project was coming along. Pieter quickly came to regret his visit.

"Ye canna put that hose over there ye nitwit!", Patrick was shouting at a Bergway technician. "Ha' ye no common sense in that empty head o' yours?"

"Problems Patrick?", Pieter asked as he approached.

"Aye, ye could say that!", shouted Patrick. "These twits ha' no idea about this plane, let alone how ta put this new tank intah her belly!"

"Patience, Pat", said Pieter. "Remember, not everyone is a mechanical genius like you. These guys probably know a lot more about chemical mixers than they know about planes. That's why you're here, to help them interface this new gear with the plane. If you can't hack the job, then I'll assign someone else. Is that what you want?"

"Nay, I donat", replied Patrick more quietly. "Nobody touches this plane but me. Ah suppose we can work better together".

"That seems reasonable", said Pieter. "Well, I'm off. See you gents tomorrow". As Pieter walked out the hanger door, he heard the group behind him speaking more quietly. He had averted a crisis this time, but how long the calm would last was uncertain.

Pieter got his answer when he arrived at the hanger the next morning. Pat was already swearing up a blue streak and it took several minutes for Pieter to calm him down. After Pieter brought over a pair of ground crewmen to help, the belly tank was finally properly installed. Patrick had continued to glower at his two fellow mechanics for the rest of the time they dared to touch 'his' plane, but cooled down when the tank was finally in place.

"When will she be ready to take aloft?", Pieter asked, once they finished hooking up the last cables and hoses.

"Not until I say so!", said Patrick defiantly. "No sooner than midday at the earliest".

"OK, well let me know when she's ready", said Pieter, who retreated to his office.

Shortly after 1 P.M., Patrick came sauntering into Pieter's office. "Your carriage awaits, yer lordship!", Patrick said with a weary smile.

Pieter practically knocked his chair over backwards when he jumped up. Ralph was already in the cockpit making the pre-flight checks.

"Hiya, boss!", Ralph said as Pieter climbed in. "Feel like snuffing a few burn-barrels?"

"You betcha!", said Pieter enthusiastically. "Let's fire this bird up and see how she dumps now".

The engines roared to life and the plane was soon taxiing over to the fueling pad. Once Pieter had gotten clearance from the tower, the plane raced off the end of the runway and banked right, towards the nearby reservoir.

"From what Patrick and the technicians told me, this works the same as the Class A Foam additions", said Ralph. "Should be a piece of cake".

"We'll soon find out", said Pieter. The plane began descending into the reservoir. A few seconds later, with the retardant tanks full, the plane soared over the dam at the end of the reservoir and headed for the training field. The ground crews had set three burn barrels on fire and were in the process of lighting a fourth when the bomber began its attack run.

"Let's take them two at a time", said Pieter. "Get set up for the pair on the left first".

Ralph punched up the range on his TRIDINT readout, then fed the coordinates into the ballistic computer. Once this was completed, he pressed the 'salvo' button. "Ready", he said.

As the plane neared the pair of barrels, the bombay doors opened and red retardant streamed out. When the plane was past the end of the field, Pieter banked left for a look.

"Hot dog, it worked!", he yelled. "Let's load up again and see if we get lucky a second time".

Five minutes later, they were on their next approach run, this time for the second pair of barrels. Ralph entered the coordinates as before and the bombay doors opened once again. This time, however, only water dropped out. When Pieter banked left to observe the results, he was less than pleased.

"What happened to the retardant?", he asked incredulously. "All's we dropped was water, no retardant!"

"Maybe the mixer jammed", offered Ralph. "Let's try it again. A second reload might break the plug loose".

"It's worth a try", agreed Pieter. "I hope it works this next time".

The plane skimmed across the reservoir a third time, then proceeded towards the training field again. Ralph punched in the coordinates and set the salvo up. "Keep your fingers crossed", he said as the plane crossed over the edge of the field. The doors opened again and once again only water fell on the now-quenched burn-barrels.

Pieter cursed as he came around again for a look. "I think we've got a problem here".

"Personally, I would have been surprised if this thing had worked perfectly anyway", said Ralph. "Something as complicated as this is bound to have teething problems. At least we have a couple of months to get them fixed. Plus, the technicians are here to do the fixing".

"Still, I had hoped it would work right the first time", groused Pieter. "It would have been one less thing to worry about later".

"Sure. It would be nice to have all of our planes here and all of the crews fully trained, too", said Ralph. "But we don't. We'll just have to be grateful for those things we do have".

Pieter landed a minute later and taxied over to the hanger. Once there, he explained the problem to the technicians, who proceeded to tear into the belly tank, under Patrick's watchful eye. Two-and-a-half hours later, Patrick came and got Pieter for another try. The results were the same as before. One perfect drop, followed by nothing but water after that. Pieter was not a happy camper. He finally went home that afternoon under a black cloud. The technicians were baffled and could promise him nothing until the next day.

The next day, the results were no better. The days stretched into a week, then two. Pieter had finally had enough.

"I thought you boneheads knew what you were doing!", he shouted at the technicians. "Fine lot of help you jokers are. I have a schedule to keep, and you guys aren't helping me one little bit. There have to be five squadrons of these planes fully equipped in eight weeks time. I wonder now if you can even solve this little problem on *my* plane by that time!"

"You know, Pieter, there was a wise young lad who told me to calm down and be patient a fortnight ago", said Patrick quietly. "It sets me wonderin' whether that might not be good advice for yer lordship as well?"

"I'm perfectly calm!", shouted Pieter, his face as red as a beet. "I'm in complete control of my emotions! You should see me when I really get mad!"

Patrick began chuckling softly to himself. Pieter, pausing long enough to hear Patrick, turned to face him for the first time in the conversation and saw the merriment in his eyes. Pieter's anger began to fade away as he realized the absurdity of his actions. Soon he and Patrick were both laughing heartily together, joined by the more nervous laughter of the Bergway technicians.

"OK Patrick, you old leprechaun, you've made your point!"

"An a good bit o' fun I had doin' it, too!", said Patrick with a chuckle. "This time more than most".

"OK, let me pull my foot out of my mouth so I can go back and hide in my office", said Pieter. "Come get me when you guys are ready".

"Will do", said Patrick. Ralph walked up to the group, casting puzzled glances at Patrick and Pieter.

"Well now lad, are ye ready to work?", Patrick asked Ralph.

"That's what I'm here for", said Ralph. "What was all the laughing about?"

"Just a wee bit o' attitude adjustment, that's all", said Patrick with a sly grin. "Give us a hand here laddie".

Thirty minutes later Ralph climbed into the bomber and began the pre-flight while Patrick went and got Pieter. Twenty minutes later, the bomber was closing on a pair of burn barrels. Another pair stood off to the right side, red stained and still steaming from the first bomb run a few moments before.

"Coordinates locked in, salvo selected", Ralph intoned. I hope to God this thing works this time, he thought, otherwise I may have to find out if my parachute works from this altitude. He glanced over at Pieter whose attention seemed to be tightly focused on the burn barrels ahead. The plane quickly ate up the distance to the target. As the plane neared the barrels, the bombay doors opened and dumped the load. Pieter continued on straight and level to the end of the practice field, then banked left, straining to see the barrels. The plane slowly came around and Ralph craned his neck to see out Pieter's side. Finally, the plane came around enough for a look at the barrels. Across both sets of barrels stretched the hoped-for red stain.

"It worked!", yelled Ralph. "They finally fixed it!"

"Looks that way", said Pieter in quiet satisfaction. "Let's try it a couple more times just to be sure, though".

Pieter wheeled the plane back around and headed for the reservoir. A few minutes later, he made a third drop. Several minutes after that he made a fourth, followed by a fifth. In each case, the red retardant cascaded down onto the targets without fail. When Pieter landed after the fifth drop, he leaped out of the plane and ran over to shake the hands of the technicians, then set up a retro-fit schedule for the other planes. Joe got the news that evening. Another hurdle was now behind them.

The maiden flight of the first Hawkeye took place in late February. Dave Albrecht flew along with the air crew to act as technician in case anything went wrong. The plane performed flawlessly, but the electronics still needed some fine-tuning. Pieter had hired several Air-Traffic Controllers who had worked aboard Hawkeyes in the Navy. They had been training on the ground with the equipment Dave and his associates at Talon Electronics had put together. The ATCs adapted to the new equipment very quickly, and by the time of the second flight of the Hawkeye, the simulated traffic (generated from a computer on the ground) was handled perfectly. Pieter set up a real ATC exercise using two bomber squadrons and two transport squadrons. No mishaps occurred, although some minor miscommunications did. After evaluation of the operation, Pieter deemed the crews ready to operate as a team.

"What do you mean they don't want to come here?", Joe shouted angrily.

"They wish to observe the operation Mr. Talon", said Hans Zwickau, the spokesman from the Los Angeles County Supervisors. "It's simply that they wish to have the operation staged in a place of their choosing. It was felt that you are too familiar with your training area, here, and that a demonstration in an unfamiliar area would serve the purpose of more fairly evaluating your claims".

"I see", said Joe coldly. "So where is the exercise to be held, then?"

"We shall give you the location one day in advance of the exercise, sir", said the spokesman.

"*One day*?", shouted Joe. "We need more time than that to plan and prepare!"

"You would probably not get any more notice than that for a real fire, Mr. Talon", the spokesman replied pleasantly. "One day will give your people sufficient time to prepare. I have been assured of this by our friends from Forestry".

"Mr. Zwickau", Joe began.

"Hans, Mr. Talon. You can call me Hans".

"Mr. Zwickau", Joe continued, "this organization is brand new. We have hardly had time to fully test the individual systems by themselves, let alone as an integrated whole. One day gives us less time than we need to prepare our battle plan. Can you give us at least two days, that isn't too much to ask is it?"

"Mr. Talon, we are prepared to give you all the time you need", said Hans with a smile. "You are the ones who have proffered this organization as being quite capable of handling any situation within the normal constraints of a wildfire. We have only set a limit on the length of time from first spotting of the area the fire is in to interdiction of the fire by your personnel. If you require more time to prepare your organization for fighting fires, then you have it. But insofar as our disclosing the location of this training fire, we are not prepared to give you any details until the day before you are to put it out. Is this clear?"

"Crystal", said Joe softly. "Understand this, though, Mr. Zwickau. If any of my personnel are injured or killed because of this ridiculous restriction, I will hold you and the County of Los Angeles personally responsible, is *that* understood?"

"You will have no recourse in this area, Mr. Talon", Hans replied pleasantly, "because before we agree to this operation, you will sign a waiver absolving us of all responsibility for any mishaps. I have the documents with me, if you would like to look them over".

"You seem to have anticipated my reaction, sir", said Joe warily. "Yes, I would like to see the document. In fact, if you don't mind, I'd like my staff to have a look at it. Do you suppose my secretary could make a copy of it?"

"No need Mr. Talon. I took the liberty of having two extra copies made up for your perusal".

"Are you a lawyer, Mr. Zwickau?"

"As a matter of fact I am, Mr. Talon. Does it matter?"

"No, I don't imagine it does. But I think I'll warn my lawyers to be extra careful in interpreting this document. You seem to be quite adept at outmaneuvering your opponents".

"A bad habit left over from competing in chess tournaments when I was younger, I'm afraid. Do you play chess Mr. Talon?"

"Can't say that I do. I get my entertainment from making money through business deals".

"Ah yes, so your portfolio indicated", said Hans thoughtfully.

"My portfolio?", said Joe in surprise.

"Why, yes. I scanned a portfolio of information about you before undertaking this rather delicate mission".

"What conclusions did you draw about me?", asked Joe, his eyes narrowing.

"I perceived a keen intellect which is always more interested in a challenge than in a walkover", answered Hans.

"Hence, your hard-sell of the time-frame", said Joe with a look of realization crossing his face. "I believe I also perceive a keen intellect at work here, Mr. Zwickau".

"I'll take that as a compliment", said Hans with a smile. "And might I say I was most impressed with your business dealings in acquiring this empire of yours. Few men would have been able to revive half the companies you have pulled out of bankruptcy".

"Thank you very much, Mr. Zwickau", said Joe. "If you hadn't behaved as such a scoundrel at the outset of this meeting, I might have even said I liked you".

"I have my job to do, Mr. Talon", said Hans. "The time-frame was imposed by the Supervisors, it's true. But they did leave some room for negotiation upwards to three days of time, if required

"*What*? You mean we've been haggling over nothing? What's your game, Hans?"

"Why, employment, Mr. Talon", said Hans with a grin. "I am offering my services to you. I have already demonstrated my capability to manipulate an audience, and a difficult audience to divert, if I may say so".

"I think I'll say thanks for your backhanded compliment."

"And as I have already indicated", Hans continued, "I excel at strategy and tactics in the legal world. I could be an invaluable asset to you and your corporation, especially in regards to getting the ear of high-level city and county personalities. I have also had some dealings with the media, and would be able to render advice or direct aid in dealing with them".

Joe's head was swimming from the way this meeting had turned around. One minute, he was ready to punch the spokesman in the face, the next his mind was caught up in the prospects of hiring this brash young lawyer to work for him. It would give him an invaluable 'inside track' with the L.A. politicians. Someone who knew all their idiosyncrasies first-hand. "How much do you want a job here?", Joe asked after a moment's consideration.

"As I say, I have admired your organization in general and you in particular ever since I was given this task. As such, I'm very interested in a job here".

"Let's use this interface with the L.A. County Supervisors as a test case, then", said Joe. "If you can deliver on our getting some big-shots out there for our little wienie roast, *and* the delay from target designation to interdiction of three days, then I'll consider your offer".

"An equitable arrangement. I will accept that as confirmation of your intent to hire me, then. Are there any further questions you have for me before I leave?"

"The only one that occurs to me is this: Are there any more like you out there?"

"None whom I am aware of", said Hans with a smile.

"Good. I was afraid I was going to have to have my senior staff screen any callers from here on", said Joe in exasperation.

"It was a pleasure meeting you, Mr. Talon", said Hans as he rose to leave.

"Aside from feeling like I just got off a roller-coaster ride, I guess I'd have to say the same about you, Mr. Zwickau", Joe replied as he extended his hand. "I look forward to seeing you again with the Supervisors' answer. At least, I think I do".

After Hans left the office, Joe eased back down into his chair. Now there was a young man to keep an eye on, Joe thought. He wondered how Hans' chess tournament tally sheet looked. Probably very few defeats, he decided. Another new face in the ranks? Perhaps. He'd see what Hans could whip up first.

Hans proved as good as his word. A few days later, he arrived back at Talon Industries with the news: The entire L.A. City Council and L.A. County Supervisors would be on hand to see the demonstration. In addition, several State of California officials would be there. A few of the dignitaries represented the various government agencies involved in fire-fighting, including the U.S. Forest Service, Bureau of Land Management, and the California Department of Forestry. Joe could feel a knot form in his stomach after Hans left. He and his people were taking an awful chance. If everything went off without a hitch, it would be a major feather in his cap. If not, then his investment could come to naught. So much yet to do, Joe thought.

He wished Martha were still here to talk things over with. She had always provided him a shoulder to lean on in times of stress. Joe found himself remembering her face, the touch of her fingers, the way sunlight shone on her hair. All gone. Well, he decided, he had gotten along before he met Martha, and he supposed he could get along now. Somehow...

Both Pieter and Zack sped up the training programs the day after Joe's announcement. They also felt the burden of responsibility and were not looking forward to the timetable as outlined by Joe. So few weeks left in which to get ready. So much to do and so little margin for error. The last additions of equipment and personnel arrived. The last bombers had mixers installed only days before the demonstration was scheduled to take place. Both Hawkeyes were now outfitted and final systems testing was underway. The last of the twenty-five pumpers arrived and was immediately swarmed over by the eager crews.

The first mock-up for a CCC vehicle also arrived. The composite body had not yet been formed (all composite work was being dedicated to making fire truck bodies), so this one was put together with sheet-steel. Once it was painted, it didn't look quite so awkward. Dave's technicians quickly bolted in the electronics for rudimentary communications, but didn't have time to put in all the systems eventually planned for the vehicles. It would be several months before those systems could be installed, but Zack and Pieter were satisfied with what Dave was able to accomplish in the meantime.

In addition to the arrival of the new vehicles, there was a new addition to the staff. One day while Joe was signing off some paperwork, Zack and Pieter came into his office with a short, stout little man wearing a wide grin on his face following behind.

"Joe Talon, meet Abner Hollis, our new Air Boss", said Pieter.

"Pleased to meet you, Mr. Talon", boomed Abner as he extended his hand.

"Welcome, Abner", said Joe as they shook hands.

"Abner has been riding herd on us bomber pilots for as long as I can remember", said Pieter. "I met him at my first fire almost thirty years ago, up in Ukiah. He may not look like much, but he's the best in the business, as far as I'm concerned".

"I may not look like much?", bellowed Abner. "Why I'll clean your clock any day of the week you mangy horney toad!"

"And he has a pleasing disposition to boot", added Zack with a chuckle.

"Well, it looks like it's a good thing your organization hired me, Mr. Talon", said Abner, giving Zack and Pieter a skeptical look. "With guys like these running your operations, you're going to need all the help you can get!"

"My very thoughts. And please, call me Joe".

"OK, Joe", said Abner with a smile. "So, what's the game plan?"

The remainder of the morning was spent going over the pending operation and with familiarizing Abner with the equipment and the personnel. By the end of the day, Joe was sure Pieter and Zack had made the right choice for their Air Boss .

Finally, one week before the scheduled date, everything was in readiness. Parachutes were packed, equipment was put into intense maintenance cycles to insure proper performance the following week, and the personnel who were not directly involved in final maintenance were going over their last classroom assignments and computer simulations. Three days before the deadline, Joe received the long-awaited location for the demonstration.

"Hello Mr. Talon", greeted Hans over the phone.

"Hello Hans", Joe replied pensively. "Well, what's the address?"

"You should be receiving a FAX of the latitude and longitude right about ... now", Hans replied.

Sure enough, the FAX machine chattered to life and began printing out the coordinates and ground rules for the demo. When the message was complete, Joe took it out of the machine and examined it closely.

"I've got the FAX", said Joe when he returned to the phone, "but I don't have a map here right now. What is the name of the area?"

"It's a series of old fields up near Sunland which L.A. used to use for a combined Police-Fire training area years ago", replied Hans. "It covers about two-hundred acres and should be ideal for your operation. L.A. has already sold off several acres of the original parcel for real-estate development and will probably sell this remaining land soon, as well. What better way to clear the brush than to have a controlled wildfire burn it off?"

"OK. But are you going to have sufficient fire equipment on hand in case it gets out of control?"

"Indeed we are", replied Hans reassuringly. "There will be four companies of L.A. City Fire Department on hand in case your people run into any difficulties".

"I see you've limited the size of the force we can use to only two squadrons of firebombers and two companies each of engines and firejumpers. Why is this?"

"Our advisors told us that this would be sufficient for controlling a fire of that size on two sides. I'm afraid they don't yet trust you to be able to deliver on all of your promises, so they've hedged their bets by allotting two sides of the fire to LAFD to control, while your people handle the other two sides. With several LAFD companies on hand, they figure there shouldn't be any problems even if you fail to show".

"It's nice to be appreciated", Joe grumbled.

"I wouldn't get too put out by them", said Hans. "They're used to outside organizations promising the moon on a string and L.A. getting saddled with a piece of cheese. If your organization can control two sides of the fire, then they'll assume that you can do an even better job with all of your planes and companies involved".

"I see", said a more subdued Joe. "I was just hoping for more involvement and control over the situation by our units".

"My apologies. Do you accept the arrangement as it stands, then?"

"We accept. We'll be there, don't worry".

"I'm not worried at all. Remember, I know all about you!"

"Only what's published, you mean. Thanks Hans".

After he hung up the phone, Joe called a staff meeting of his fire personnel. The meeting was heated, with arguments and opinions being thrown out from all involved, but everyone finally settled down and detailed operational planning began. By that night, all of the senior staff knew what they had to do.

The following day, the remainder of the crews were briefed and individual assignments for the units taking part were made. There was a good deal of disappointment from the crews not taking part, but that couldn't be helped. Everyone from the Fire Boss down through the ranks had trained and fully expected to go into battle together, as a unified team. Now, only a portion of the men and women would be getting to show off their abilities. The senior staff assured the non-participants that they would get their chances soon enough. None of them realized how soon that would be.

Chapter 22

Joe hadn't slept well all night. When he awoke for the sixth time at 4 A.M., he decided to just stay up. He couldn't put his finger on it, but something was bothering him. He ate a light breakfast, then drove himself over to Talon Aerospace. When he got there at 5:30, the crews were already beginning to arrive. Zack and Pieter came in just behind him, then went to attend to their tasks. Joe wandered around the Training Center and watched pensively as the base began to come to life.

By the time the sun had peeked over the horizon, several aircraft had already moved over to the fueling pad and tanked up. Fuel bowsers circulated amongst several other planes. Fire trucks were given their final checks and loaded onto the transports. Once again, the Cat Teams were left out of the hustle. There would be no need for bulldozers where the fire was today.

Abner saw Joe loitering around the office building around nine-thirty and poked his head out the door of the office.

"Mornin' Joe", Abner said. "Excited?"

"Apprehensive is more the word. Something is bothering me but I don't know what".

"I wouldn't worry. Zack and Pieter have gone over every detail a hundred times. I don't see how they could have missed anything".

"That's what they said about the Titanic", Joe replied ruefully. "No, I don't think it's anything in our preparations it's just .... I don't know. Maybe I'm getting paranoid or something".

Dave walked up a moment later and greeted Joe and Abner. He looked at Joe, then said, "You look concerned about something, Joe. Things not to your liking here?"

"As far as I can tell, everything appears to be proceeding as planned", Joe answered absently. "That's what bothers me. I think I'll go talk to Zack and Pieter for a minute".

"Pre-mission jitters", Abner pronounced after Joe had left.

"I'm not so sure", said Dave. "I've seen him like this before. There were a couple of times during his corporate takeovers when this, I don't know, sixth sense I guess you'd call it, kicks in. He's seldom been wrong when he felt this way. Something unforeseen has always happened. LFP, Jerry calls them.

"One time he was just about ready to close a deal on a factory. There was no competition worth considering, according to his advisors. He had a funny feeling that someone was going to put up a bid for the company, though, and instructed his advisors to liquidate some of his assets to free up some additional cash, just in case. He was bang on target. Another big corporation had been secretly negotiating behind the scenes and had agreed to act as a 'white knight' on behalf of this company Joe was after. They pushed the bid up way above where it had been before. If Joe hadn't gotten that extra cash freed up, he would have lost out on the bid. He won, barely, and gained an even more respected reputation in the business world. That company later became Bergway Chemical. Funny thing is, the so-called 'white knight' *did* manage to buy up another chemical plant a couple of years later and you know what? They raped the company's retirement plan, laid off most of the people, and sold the facilities off to a foreign concern. Funny, isn't it? Their savior turned out to be exactly what Bergway had feared Joe to be".

"Interesting story. What does LFP mean?"

"Left-Field Prediction".

"Now you're beginning to get me worried", said Abner with a nervous laugh.

"Pieter, can I have a word with you?", Joe asked when he reached the hanger.

"Can it wait? We're getting close to departure time and I still have a lot to do".

"OK, go take care of business and meet me at the office in thirty minutes", Joe replied. He passed along a similar message to Zack.

Half-an-hour later the three, joined by Abner and the executive staff, met in the training office.

"Guys, I don't know how to put this but I think we're going to hit a snag today", Joe began. "What I'd like to do is to keep the extra personnel here just in case we need them".

"I doubt we will", said Zack, "but it doesn't hurt to have them hang around awhile".

"Could we get the equipment loaded up on the remaining transports?", asked Dave.

"If there is a problem, we don't know what form it will take", Pieter said. "If we load up equipment and then need more firejumpers, we'll run into a delay pulling the equipment out and putting the paratroop inserts into the transports. It ordinarily takes almost two hours to put a paratroop insert into a C-130 and bolt it down. We've been experimenting with methods of using more personnel to bolt it down in less time and we've managed to cut the time in half. But if we put one in now, then have to pull it out to put fire engines on board, that will be a pretty hefty waste of time. We can secure a fire engine more quickly than a paratroop insert".

"Plus, fire engines will be more effective at a brushfire than firejumpers", Zack added. "I think it would be best if we make sure the transports are fueled and the equipment ready to load on a moment's notice."

"I guess you had better start refueling the transports after the strike force has finished, then", said Joe. "Do you think the refueling tankers should be filled up first?"

"Probably best to do them first", replied Pieter. "They can refuel anyone in the air who's not finished fueling if we have to scramble the remaining squadrons".

"It's a good thing the klaxons weren't pulled out when this base went from being a Continental Defense airbase to a private airstrip", mused Pieter. "We might need those horns today".

"Pass the word along to the personnel we're leaving behind to stay put", said Joe. "Tell them whatever you want, just make sure the company and squadron commanders know what to do if those klaxons sound".

As the appointed hour approached, the aircraft began taxiing out to the holding areas and the refueling squadrons finished tanking up. The transports remaining behind began to tank up at this time.

The Hawkeye being used for the operation today, Hawk One, took lead position in the line. When the hour had come, it taxied onto the runway and cranked up to full power. The twin-engined turboprop with the ungainly saucer-shaped radar on top began rolling down the runway at precisely 11 A.M. Following the Hawkeye was a lone transport, one of the spares, which was carrying the Command, Control, and Communications vehicle. Joe, Zack, Abner, and their immediate staff members were strapped in on board the CCC vehicle (Zack being the most reluctant member there). They would be the first vehicle on the scene, which would allow them to direct the firefighters as the remainder of the aircraft arrived.

Many miles away, outside of Sunland, L.A. City Fire Department personnel were lighting the control fires for the exercise. Four companies of L.A.'s finest were lined up to contain any problems that might occur when these 'green' Talon crews started tripping over each other. Behind the fire companies stood a new development of townhomes which was building next to the vacant fields. There was a wide expanse of brush-covered ground between the distant control fires and these skeletal structures. The fire, if it got out of control, would never be able to reach them. Even a full-blown firestorm would be hard-pressed to win through so many men and so much equipment. No, there was no danger. It would be an amusing morning looking at these greenhorns trying to put out this little blaze. It certainly beat waiting around the fire station for a call to a fire in a dangerous condemned tenement building or some other life-threatening situation. Today was a day to catch some rays and open air while watching the equivalent of a football bloopers escapade - and get paid at the same time!

At the same moment that these thoughts were dancing through the heads of the fire crews, a minor fire at a Signal Hill oil refinery started to get out of control. The refinery fire chief saw that this situation was getting ugly and decided to call for help. Too late. The spreading flames reached a fuel line and ruptured it. A stream of burning fuel spouted onto a cracking tower and set it ablaze. An explosion rocked the refinery.

The first squadron of firebombers began taking off at Talon Aerospace. Pieter led the line out in 'North Star', followed by the rest of the 201st Firebomber Squadron (Pathfinders). Behind them came the 202nd Firebomber Squadron (Ridgerunners). Next came the transports, 101st Lift Squadron (Ace Movers) followed by the 102nd (Roadrunners), both carrying engine companies (the 501st and 502nd, respectively). Finally, the last two transport squadrons lifted off, the 103rd Lift Squadron (Knights) carrying the 701st Firejumper Company and the 104th Lift Squadron (Roadhogs) carrying the 702nd Firejumper Company. The remaining personnel cast envious glances in the direction of the vanishing transports, then returned to the hangers and shops.

While the last Firebombers planes were lifting out of Talon Aerospace, the four LAFD engine companies watching the slowly spreading control fire outside of Sunland received a plaintive call from home. There was a major refinery fire underway in Signal Hill and their presence was urgently required there. The battalion chief replied that they had a fire to baby-sit and would come as soon as they could.

Joe and his staff were discussing the plan of assault when their plane's flight engineer knocked on the door to the CCC vehicle. Joe unstrapped himself and opened the door.

"Sir, we've just had a report of a refinery fire in Signal Hill", said the flight engineer. "Looks like they're pulling in every engine company in the county to try and put it out. We may lose our LAFD backup on that Sunland fire real quick if that's true".

"OK, thanks", said Joe. The flight engineer left to return to the flight deck. The van was buzzing with conversation even before Joe strapped himself back in.

Dave turned to Abner and mouthed the letters LFP along with an
I-told-you-so expression. Abner nodded.

"Looks like your hunch was right, Joe", Zack remarked. "Good thing we kept the extra crews around".

"So it seems", Joe replied. "Abner, what's the status of our remaining aircraft?"

"As of departure, the refueling squadron's tankers were fully loaded and the remaining transports were beginning to tank up", Abner stated. "I wish we'd tanked the firebombers first. We won't need the full range of those transports, but we'll want to keep the firebombers aloft as long as possible. That was a major oversight on my part".

"Perhaps", said Joe calmly. "But at least the refueling tankers are ready to go. We can use our contingency plan and refuel the firebombers in the air. By the time they arrive over the fire, they'll be tanked up. In the meantime, I want the remaining engine companies airlifted in to that Signal Hill fire."

"Airlifted?", asked Abner in puzzlement. "Why, by the time we get the transports back from the Sunland fire, pull the paratroop inserts out of them, and fly the pumpers to Signal Hill we could have practically driven them there, even with rush-hour traffic".

"Yes, but it wouldn't get us the press I want", replied Joe. "Unless we make a splash with this outfit we don't stand a chance of turning a profit. I want our name on everybody's lips and in front of their faces as much as possible. Firebombers Incorporated has to become synonymous with firefighting if this organization is to survive".

Abner said nothing more, but looked at Pieter and Zack to see what their reactions were. After a moment, Zack cleared his throat and said, "Long Beach Airport is fairly close to Signal Hill. We can airlift our engine companies into there. They don't have snorkels or extendible ladders like the city rigs have, but they can still provide hoses for the fire crews to use on fires that are close to the ground. It would free up some of the city equipment to fight fires where their extra reach could be important".

"What about firejumpers?", Joe asked.

"No, they aren't really trained in fighting fires in close quarters, especially not in buildings of that sort. I think they would simply get themselves in trouble. I think we should send them to the Sunland fire. The five squadrons of firebombers should be able to contain the fire there until our transports have a chance to airlift the remaining three companies of firejumpers in. Those two initial companies of firejumpers are going to be mighty busy for awhile".

"Why not use the Heavy Lift squadrons to deliver the engine companies, while we send the Lift squadrons used here back once they're empty to transport the remaining firejumpers to Sunland?", asked Abner, beginning to join in with the spirit of the discussion. "That would give us two squadrons already outfitted for firejumpers".

"I agree", said Zack. "We could put inserts in the remaining transport squadron fairly quickly".

"The inserts could be put in while the other two transport squadrons load up and lift off", said Abner. "The last transports would only be a little behind the rest".

"As soon as we get on the ground, I want all the remaining squadrons scrambled", said Joe. "Pass along the plan as we've just discussed and tell those firebombers to step on it. We don't have time to pussyfoot around with this Sunland fire, especially since we have less ground support now. I don't want to disappoint our audience, and at the same time I don't want to miss out on this opportunity to help out with that refinery fire".

"Red light's on", said the driver of the CCC vehicle. "Six minutes to LZ".

"Everybody check your restraints one last time", said Abner. "We don't need the complications of injuries on top of all the other problems this morning".

A few minutes later, they could feel the plane begin to descend. Ahead, the smoke from the control fires was plainly visible to the pilot. Burbank Airport had already been advised of the pending operation and the controllers there had rerouted all north-south traffic onto the east-west runway.

The assembled dignitaries watched expectantly as the first transport came into view. The plane seemed to approach ever so slowly, continuing to dip closer to the ground. A section of open ground south of the base of the fire had been selected as the best place to land. Pieter had taken the opportunity to send a crew of air-landing experts from his staff to test the ground for firmness early that morning. They had reported that, barring any rainstorms, the ground was quite capable of supporting several landings by the transports.

High above the fire the Hawkeye now orbited at 10,000 feet, its TRIDINT equipment taking in the scene below. The controllers were directing the transports and the firebombers on the terminal leg of their flight. The CCC transport was the first to arrive, as planned. To Joe, who had never been through an air-landing operation before, the experience was unnerving. One moment, all was peaceful, aside from the thrum of the turboprops, the next moment, they were jerked roughly backwards and began bumping and lurching across the ground. The CCC driver quickly steered the now earthbound vehicle over by the waiting dignitaries as the first firebombers approached. Joe and his staff climbed out of the vehicle as Zack and Abner began powering up the communications gear in order to coordinate the operation.

"Good morning, Mr. Talon", said Hans quickly. "I'm afraid we will have to forgo the introductions for the moment, as we have a major crisis looming".

Before Hans could continue, Joe broke in, "Yes, I've heard about the refinery fire, Hans. I expect your LAFD crews are needed there right away, and let me take this opportunity to offer the services of our organization. We can have three companies of pumpers at the fire in Signal Hill within thirty minutes, if that would be of assistance".

"Thirty minutes?", asked one of the fire officials. "How can you get them there from San Bernardino so quickly, Mr. Talon".

"The same way we're getting our personnel to this fire, gentlemen", Joe replied. "We airlift them to Long Beach Airport. Oh, that reminds me. Would it be possible for someone here to give the controllers at Long Beach Airport the word that we're coming? It would probably expedite our arrival at the refinery if we could bypass all of the usual delays involved in lining up with the commercial traffic".

Once the shock of Joe's statements wore off, several city and county officials rushed over to their cars and began alerting the pertinent people by car-phone about what was happening. In the meantime, Zack and Abner had sent word back to Talon Aerospace to scramble all the remaining squadrons as per the plan they had devised on the flight to Sunland.

Patrick was just finishing his third cup of tea for the morning, listening to the complaints of the crews who had been left behind, when the klaxons sounded. "What the devil is all that racket?", he shouted as the crews rushed out to their planes. He saw one of the squadron commanders running past.   "What's all the ruckus about?", Patrick shouted at him.

"We just got a call from the boss that we've got to get airborne pronto", the pilot yelled as he ran to his plane. "Something about a fire in Signal Hill. He said the tower would brief us after takeoff".

After the pilot had run past, Patrick saw the firebomber crews rushing to their planes and doing a quick pre-flight. Fuel bowsers pulled away from beside several of the aircraft, sometimes before refueling had been completed. One by one, the planes fired up their engines, then taxied over to the flight line. While the firebombers were assembling into their squadrons, engine companies were loading into the transports, where the ground personnel worked feverishly to tie them down. The first engine company, the 503rd, loaded onto the remaining Lift squadron, the 105th (Long Haulers), while the other two engine companies, the 504th and 505th, loaded into the transports normally used for the Cat Teams, 401st and 402nd Heavy Lift Squadrons (Alleycats and Tomcats).   The remaining firetrucks were racing past on their way to the waiting transports as companies of firejumpers double-timed past the hanger to get outfitted for their pending departure when the transports returned from Sunland. The necessary inserts were being wheeled out as the refueling tankers, followed closely by the first squadron of firebombers, the 203rd (Night Hawks), began lifting off.

To the north of Sunland, the first firebombers were beginning to tank up at Lake Castaic. Traffic around the lake slowed to a crawl as people gawked at the twin-engined, royal-blue planes dipping down into the water, then climbing skyward. Each plane tanked up, then turned back south toward Sunland. An enterprising motorist who had a camcorder along pulled over to the shoulder and began filming the exploit.

Meanwhile, Joe had begun discussing the plan of action with the dignitaries. "I understand your problem, gentlemen", Joe began. "We have already taken action to assist your fire department at both this demonstration fire and the more important Signal Hill fire. As we speak, three additional squadrons of firebombers are lifting out of San Bernardino and heading to this location. As soon as they have departed from the airbase, three transport squadrons carrying fifteen fire engines will depart for Long Beach Airport. Once those squadrons land, you will have three additional companies of pumpers at your disposal. We have conferred with your fire personnel here as to radio frequencies to be used to direct our engine companies".

"Can you stop this fire with two companies of ground personnel and a few air-tankers Mr. Talon?", one of the County Supervisors asked.

"No sir, but we can slow the fire down until the remaining forces arrive", Joe replied. "Our firebombers can drop retardant repeatedly, merely needing to reload with water from Lake Castaic in order to prepare them for another drop.

"As soon as our transports have dropped off their cargoes here, they will return at maximum speed to our airbase outside of San Bernardino and embark the remaining three companies of firejumpers. Once they arrive, we'll have over 1500 men and women on the ground, plus ten pumpers and twenty-five firebombers. That should be sufficient to snuff a blaze of this size in no time at all".

"Mr. Talon, does this mean you can handle this fire without need for our fire companies?", the LAFD battalion chief asked.

Joe looked at the expanding brush fire, then back to the audience. He felt his stomach beginning to tighten up as he said, "I believe we can, yes". He hoped they could anyway.

"Then I would like to withdraw my engine companies and send them to Signal Hill where they are really needed at the moment", said the chief.

"Be my guest", said Joe. Several people followed the chief back to his car and they seemed to have a rather animated conversation. After a few moments and a final angry gesture by a County Supervisor at the unfinished houses, the battalion chief climbed into his car and led his waiting engine companies across the field to the nearby road. They soon disappeared in a cloud of dust. Well, Joe thought, we're on our own now.

One of the Forestry officials started to ask a question, but his words were drowned out as the first transport squadron roared overhead. The planes descended one by one into the field beyond.

"Full flaps, lower ramp!", Suzie West commanded.
"Ramp down and locked", came Howard Parker's reply a moment later.

"You ever done an open-field LAPES op Ken?", Suzie asked as she lined up on the Landing Zone.

"Only on simulators", Ken replied. "Is it that much different from landing on an airstrip?"

"I try to slow down a bit more", replied Suzie as she checked her flaps and tapped the throttles a little lower on the outboard engines. "If you go too fast on one of these landings, you can cause the vehicle driver a whole world of hurt. What with all the chuckholes out there, he's liable to crack-up if he's dropped too hard. I just hope they had somebody with his head on straight doing the LZ assessment".

"How many of these have you done before?", Ken asked nervously.

"A couple for REFORGER ops several years ago", answered Suzie. "I don't like them as well as the airstrip LAPES ops, but they're doable".

As the plane came in over the dignitaries, Suzie eased down practically onto the ground. She had nearly reached stall-speed when she shouted into the intercom, "Drop load!"

"Load clear!", Howard replied once the pumper had hit the ground.

"Full power! Raise ramp!", Suzie shouted.

Ken slammed the throttles up to maximum power and Suzie pulled back on the yoke to gain altitude. The big plane lurched forward from the combined loss of mass and the surge in power. The dignitaries gasped in amazement as the sleek Zephyr emerged from the back of the C-130 which climbed rapidly skyward.

"Piece of cake!", said Suzie exultantly. The plane was quickly gaining altitude and speed.

"Hawk One this is Ace Movers leader requesting instructions", Suzie called over the radio.

"Ace Movers leader, RTB ASAP and embark firejumpers, acknowledge", replied the Air Traffic Controller.

"Return and reload, acknowledged", replied Suzie. "Looks like we've just begun, Ken!"

"Looks that way", said Ken, gazing down at the fire. Suzie was banking right to come back around on the north side of it, away from nearby Burbank Airport. Good idea, thought Ken. They didn't need to run into any 737s today.

The dignitaries watched as the first engine drove over by the fire and the crew detached the parachute, then began unloading the hoses in order to begin containment on the base of the fire. They moved quickly to prep the engine as each successive transport roared overhead and deposited its cargo on the field, then rocketed away. Finally, all ten engines were on the ground and the two companies began to form up. By this time, the first firejumper transports arrived over the Drop Zone.

"Road Hog leader, you are cleared to begin op", the ATC called over the radio. "Wind is five knots bearing one-eighty with gusts to ten knots".

"Roger that, Hawk One", replied the pilot. In the back of the plane, the assistant jumpmasters already had everybody in the first wave of jumpers on their feet. When the pilot hit the indicator, the jumpmasters began their routine. Blast deflectors were swung out and flaps dropped. The first pair of firejumpers went out the doors several hundred feet ahead of the DZ and drifted towards it while directing their paths of descent with their controllable canopies. With half their loads discharged, the two transport squadrons quickly swung around and passed over the DZ a second time, discharging their remaining firejumpers. Blast deflectors were pulled back against the hull and flaps were raised again. Once this was done they banked hard right and brought engines up to full throttle for the return trip to base and their next loads.

"As you can see gentlemen, we can deploy to a fire very quickly", Joe told the dignitaries. "We now have two engine companies and over 600 ground personnel at this fire, with an additional 900 personnel waiting for our planes to return and embark them. They should be here in a little over an hour. In the meantime, we have ten firebombers overhead with which to channel and delay the fire until the other planes and ground personnel arrive".

One of the Forestry officials returning to the group asked, "Mr. Talon you claim that you will be dropping retardant on each pass. Will this be Class A Foam?"

"No sir, it will be a long-term retardant of our own formulation called BC2000", replied Joe.

"But how can you refill from a reservoir and drop long-term on the fire? Is this BC2000 being mixed in transit?"

"Yes sir, it is", answered Joe. "We have come up with a chemical compound which can be mixed with water as the tanks are filling. The resulting mixture is the equivalent of a long-term retardant. It takes up approximately the same amount of room in its unmixed form as Class A Foam, but conveys the properties of a long-term retardant to the mixture",

"Amazing", said the Forestry official. "Would you be willing to allow us to try this chemical out on our aircraft?"

"As long as we have a written understanding that Talon Industries keeps the formula a secret and that you buy any future quantities from our subsidiaries", replied Joe. *Bingo!*

"Hawk One, this is Pathfinder leader requesting attack coordinates, over", Pieter called over the radio.

"Pathfinder leader, you are cleared to begin attack run at grid one-zero-one", replied the ATC. "Axis is roughly west to east. Wind is bearing two-ten degrees at six knots. Be advised, all LAFD support has been withdrawn. Suggest you use staggered trail delivery until additional squadrons are on station this location, over".

Pieter was taken aback by the sudden change in plan, but decided the ATC knew what was going on better than he did.

"That's a roj, Hawk One", Pieter replied. "Pathfinder leader commencing attack run, out. Pathfinder flight, this is Pathfinder leader. We've got to fight a delaying action for now. Set your drop systems for a linked split drop and follow me in, acknowledge".

One by one, the four pilots acknowledged Pieter's transmission and followed 'North Star' down.

"What do you think is going on?", Dick asked Bob.

"Don't know", said Bob as he trimmed his speed and lined up behind 'North Star'. "Sounds like we've lost some ground support. Judging by what the ATC said, I'd have to assume LAFD had more important business to attend to".

"Looks like our 'Baptism of Fire' is going to be a little bumpier than we figured", said Dick while he programmed the drop system as commanded by Pieter.

The squadron commander behind Pieter received similar instructions from the ATC. His planes orbited while Pieter's squadron began their drops. Once the Pathfinders had cleared the area, the Ridgerunners would take their turn.

Many miles away, at Talon Aerospace, three squadrons of C-130s carrying the 503rd, 504th, and 505th Engine Companies began lifting out of San Bernardino. The four returning squadrons of transports spotted the three outbound squadrons of firebombers and tankers midway between Sunland and San Bernardino. Several irreverent comments were made between each group as they passed going in opposite directions. The transports were now operating with throttles wide open and closed on San Bernardino at nearly 400 miles per hour.

"Night Hawk leader, you are cleared to begin refueling", the tanker refueling operator called over the radio. He had already extended the refueling boom from the rear of the KC-130.

"Confirmed, tanker", replied the CL-415 pilot. He eased his plane up to the boom and gently inserted the probe into it. His squadron was first in line for refueling and the other four planes were also hooking up with the other tankers.

"We've got a green light, Night Hawk leader", called the tanker. "Beginning transfer".

"Fill her up and check the oil, will ya?", the firebomber pilot called back. "And step on it. I'm in a hurry!"

"Hold your horses, pal", the boom operator replied. "What's the matter, you on your way to a fire or something?"

"Could be, if they don't put it out before we get there", the firebomber pilot replied. A few moments later, his tanks were topped off and he dropped away from the boom. All of the planes in his squadron were now fully fueled. As his squadron moved ahead of the tankers, the Linebackers pulled in for their turn. The last squadron, the Black Widows, would be tanking last.

"From the coordinates given by the ATC, we're supposed to hit the east end of the fire first, Pieter", said Ralph. "Ah, I see why too. There's a new housing development going in about 500 yards from the fire".

"Yeah, but even with a staggered drop our retardant won't cover the whole line in front of those frames", said Pieter. "Move our projected drop back about ·a hundred yards. We can connect up linearly with that line on our second drop" .

"Will do", said Ralph. He fed the new coordinates into the computer and selected the 'Master Link' switch, then set the drop selector for 'split'. The 'Ready' light began blinking a moment later. "OK, get us a bullseye!"

Pieter dropped down to fifty feet and chopped speed to less than 95 knots. "Here we go!", he shouted as the plane ate up the distance to target.

On the ground, the County Supervisors were getting very worried. The fire was getting closer to the housing development and the firefighters were only working the backside, not the advancing front. One of the Supervisors began to complain to Joe as a firebomber suddenly loomed out of the billowing smoke a mere fifty feet overhead, less than a mile away. Joe saw the picture of a rugged mountain man in buckskins cradling a flintlock rifle in his arms emblazoned on the tail and realized it was Pieter leading in the Pathfinders squadron. A stream of red retardant could be seen issuing from the right-side bombay door. As they watched, the left-side door opened and began dropping a steady stream of liquid. By the time the plane reached the onlookers, the retardant was down and Pieter applied full-power, then banked north for a return to the reservoir. He was followed at intervals by the other four aircraft in the squadron, who had already dropped their loads before emerging from the smoke.

"Mr. Talon", the Supervisor said angrily, "your people are not tackling the fire at the forefront. We have this housing development to protect. Do you intend to put any personnel in the path of the fire or are you going to rely on this... this flying circus of yours to stop it?"

"We have too few people on the ground to handle the fire head-on, sir", Joe replied calmly. "Therefore, yes, I am relying on my firebombers to control the fire's advance. I believe your associates from the two Forestry outfits can vouch for using retardant to stop the fire".

"If you have enough retardant deposited, then it should be sufficient", said the Forestry representative. "But your planes are not dropping salvoes, from what I can see. They are apparently dropping lighter concentrations of retardant than I would recommend in such a situation".

The Supervisor turned back to Joe with a self-satisfied grin on his face which quickly twisted into a scowl. "Mr. Talon", he said, "I must ask you to place your people in the path of the fire. We must save these structures if at all possible".

Joe looked pensively at the approaching fire, then motioned for Zack to join them. "My Fire Boss would be the best person to explain our strategy to you said Joe. "I'm afraid I'm a neophyte at this business compared to him".

"Gentlemen", Zack greeted as he walked over. "Is there a problem here?"

"I can't seem to convince these gentlemen that we know what we're doing, Zack", Joe said.

"We are fighting a delaying action until additional support units arrive", said Zack succinctly. "These firefighters and pilots are trained, but not seasoned. If these were veteran firefighters, I would put them in the line of the fire. With airdrops occurring along that line, I don't want to risk injuries to the ground personnel from our retardant drops. We have three firebomber squadrons on the way, along with an additional 900 ground personnel. That will give us sufficient forces to contain this fire in approximately one hour", he concluded, looking at his watch.

"Are you sure your firebreak will hold, commander?", asked the Forestry spokesman.

"It will delay the fire enough until our additional forces arrive", replied Zack. "The two squadrons which just dropped screened the development for three-quarters of its length. They will overlap this line on their next drop, completely fireproofing the center and slowing the fire on the west side. Once the additional squadrons arrive, they will finish reinforcing the flanks of this line and will begin laying the firebreaks on the left and right flanks of the fire. By then, the additional firejumpers should be on the ground and a general advance into the center of the fire can commence. I am confident that, barring any unforeseen circumstances, we're covered".

"What sort of unforeseen circumstances do you refer to?", asked the Supervisor sharply.

"Sudden wind shift or speed increase, encountering an incendiary, such as a gas line, or other similar problems", replied Zack.

"It seems that we have no choice in any case", said the Supervisor bitterly. "Let us hope you can stop it in time". He looked forlornly over at the unfinished houses and sighed heavily.

Zack returned to the CCC van and checked on the progress of the incoming squadrons. Joe followed him over.

"Abner, what's the story on our reinforcements?", asked Joe.

"Hawk One has reported three firebomber squadrons inbound, Joe", Abner called out of the CCC van. "The last squadron is loading up with water at Lake Castaic now and the rest should be here in about fifteen minutes".

"OK, thanks Abner", Joe replied. Joe hurried over to the crowd and shouted: "Our planes will be here in under fifteen minutes, gentlemen". Several heads turned and began scanning the sky expectantly.

The first transport planes began to land at Talon Aerospace a few minutes later. The first squadron (Ace Movers) quickly taxied over to the hangers where the inserts for their planes were brought forward and the next transport squadron (Knights) rolled up to receive the firejumpers, who were drawn up in their companies. The jumpmasters shouted at the firefighters to pick up their feet as they rushed to board. The last personnel of 703rd Firejumpers Company were boarding just as the last squadron of transports (Roadhogs) rolled up to the loading area and began embarking the 704th. The Knights taxied out to the flightline and Ace Movers began loading firejumpers.

The Hawkeye directed the three incoming squadrons of firebombers to reinforce the firebreak along the head of the fire while the original two squadrons tanked up at Lake Castaic. Meanwhile, far to the south, the Long Beach Airport controllers were getting a surprise.

"Supervisor!", one controller called out, "I have multiple incoming aircraft in my zone. I count twelve, make that fifteen aircraft approaching in a relatively tight formation".

"We were told to expect them", said the supervisor as he came over. "Put all of your westbound traffic into holding patterns. These newcomers are to be granted priority landing privileges".

"OK, but we're going to have a lot of angry airline passengers", said the controller. "What are their call-signs?"

"They consist of three separate squadrons, five planes each" replied the supervisor. "IDs are Alleycat leader, Tomcat leader, and Long Haulers leader. Assign them runway two-five left".

"You've got to be kidding", said the controller. "What nuthouse did these guys just come from?"

"Unknown", replied the supervisor. "But I wouldn't recommend offending them. Their clearance came from *way* up the chain of command".

"Oh", the controller said quietly. Once the supervisor had left, he toggled his mike, "Alleycat leader, this is Long Beach Tower, you are cleared to land on runway two-five left. Wind is seven knots bearing one-eight-zero, do you copy?"

"Copy that, Long Beach Tower", replied the pilot. "We are beginning our descent now, out".

Looks like the circus is coming to town early this year, the controller said to himself.

"Ace Movers leader you are cleared for takeoff", Talon Tower called over the radio. "Wind is ten knots bearing two-three-five. Step on it guys, you're late!"

"Affirmative, tower. Ace Movers departing Gateway", Suzie replied into the mike. "Let's put the pedal to the metal, Ken!"

"Raising power on two and three", Ken replied. The center pair of throttles were advanced to the stops and the outside pair nearly that far. The four Allison turboprops increased in power. When maximum revs had been reached, Suzie released the brakes and the plane began rolling down the airstrip. The props were adjusted for optimal blade angle and the plane picked up speed. Suzie steered the plane using the nose wheel while she adjusted the throttles. Ken handled the rudder and watched the gauges and indicators. Once the plane had reached 80 knots, the rudder took over steering, allowing Suzie to increase the outside throttles to full power (they had been held back to prevent loss of control in case of an outboard engine failure).

"We're up to 100 knots", said Ken, as the C-130 thundered down the runway.

"Right, prepare to rotate", replied Suzie. As soon as they reached 110 knots, the nosewheel lifted off the ground, followed shortly by the remaining landing gear. Four black exhaust trails followed behind the transport as it faded into the west. The next transport was off the ground 10 seconds behind Suzie and soon the entire squadron was airborne and enroute to Sunland.

The first transport from 401st squadron (Alleycats) touched down at Long Beach Airport and taxied over by the terminal. Soon, all fifteen aircraft had landed and disembarked the three engine companies. After a quick check by radio with the fire chief in charge of the refinery fire, the Zephyrs engaged their lights and sirens and raced off to Signal Hill. Several reporters who had been on hand to cover the arrival of a local sports team had seen the odd spectacle which had just taken place. They rushed over and mobbed the unprepared aircrews as the latter were checking out their planes.

The fire was nearly on top of the incomplete line of retardant as the second wave of firebombers descended on it. The three squadrons of latecomers made up for their tardiness by finishing the firebreak just as the fire reached it. One after another, the Night Hawks, Linebackers, and Black Widows dumped retardant by squadrons. By the time Pieter led the Pathfinders and Ridgerunners back for their next drop, the fire had been stopped dead in its tracks.

"Hawk One, this is Pathfinder leader", Pieter called over the radio. "It looks like the head of the fire is now contained. Suggest we begin work on the flanks, over".

"Pathfinder leader, we concur", replied the ATC. "Come left to new course zero-one-five and move to grid one-one-two and orbit at 1000 feet, acknowledge".

Pieter acknowledged the new position, then the ATC directed the two squadrons to follow him. Once they had all begun to orbit, Pieter was contacted by the ATC again.

"Pathfinder leader, you are cleared to begin attack run at coordinates zero-nine-nine", called the ATC. "This is a north-to-south approach vector, winds are seven knots, bearing two-two-five degrees, acknowledge".

Pieter confirmed the coordinates, then turned to Ralph and said, "Set us up for a linked salvo, Ralph. Put it about twenty yards to the left of the fire".

"One linked salvo coming up!", said Ralph cheerily. The pressure was off now. They had held the fire until help arrived. Now it was merely a matter of corralling the rest of the fire, then squeezing it out. He punched up the coordinates on the TRIDINT screen, then entered the range into the computer and pushed the appropriate buttons. A moment later he was greeted with a flashing 'Ready' light. "Ready whenever you are!", he told Pieter.

"Right", said Pieter as he concentrated on keeping on target. "She's handling pretty good today. Not too many thermals".

Joe saw the planes approaching from the north about two miles out, which was difficult with all of the smoke in the air. They looked like they were coming in too close to the gathering, so he suggested everyone should move back a bit. They were all glad they did, as the second squadron to drop aimed their retardant fifteen yards farther to the left than Pieter's drop. With the spread from the prevailing breeze, the CCC van received a light dusting with retardant, but almost no wisps reached the dignitaries. The Supervisor was looking a bit more relieved now and had begun talking pleasantly with Hans, who was obviously enjoying this sudden turn of events.

The last firebombers were departing to reload just as more aircraft droned overhead. The first transports from the 103rd Lift Squadron had arrived and were already beginning to drop their firejumpers. Their tired and dirty comrades on the ground sent up a cheer when they saw the sky filled with parachutes behind them. The new arrivals quickly bundled up their chutes and hoofed it over to join the ranks of their cohorts. The transports came around for their second passes a few moments later. There were now over 1200 firefighters on the fire line along with ten pumpers and their crews.

Jack Bazranian, the Ground Boss, decided to begin an envelopment movement with one of his engine companies and the two newly arrived companies of firejumpers. Since the firebombers had just pounded the fire's right flank, that would be the flank to invest first. He moved his rightmost engine company, the 501st, over to the flank and spread out the 502nd to cover more of a front. The two newly arrived firejumper companies, the 703rd and 704th, moved over to roll up the flank of the fire.

"Six minutes to LZ", Ted Cook, navigator for 'Double Trouble', told Suzie West.

"Red light on", Suzie commanded. "Hawk One, this is Ace Movers leader requesting approach to LZ, over".

"Ace Movers leader, you are cleared to descend to 3000 feet and steer two-seven-one", replied the ATC. "Winds are eight knots bearing one-niner-eight degrees, gusts to ten knots, acknowledge".

"Acknowledged, Hawk One, out", Suzie said over the radio. "Ace Movers leader to Ace Movers flight, decrease altitude to 3000 feet and follow me".

As the transports approached the LZ, the crews were amazed by the activity on the ground. The fire had shrunk since they had left and was being slowly surrounded by red barriers.

"Looks like somebody kicked over an anthill!", said Ken, peering out the side window at the activity below.

Suzie reduced altitude and throttled back on the engines. "I don't even know if they need this last shipment", she mused. "I guess there's no such thing as too many firemen at a fire, though. Let's send a few more down".

In the rear of the plane, the jump indicator came on and the assistant jumpmasters put the first pair of firejumpers out the doors. Pairs of firefighters followed at even intervals until thirty had departed. Suzie continued on straight until the last transport had finished, then slowly turned northward to bring her planes around for another pass.

Jack had begun his flanking maneuver by the time Ace Movers arrived on the Landing Zone. More parachutes began sprouting in the sky, then descended slowly to the earth. Soon, another three hundred firefighters joined the ground battle. Once the transports cleared the area, Abner turned the Night Hawks, Linebackers, and Black Widows loose on the left flank of the fire.

"Looks like the 705th has just arrived", said one of Jack's assistants. "Want me to go get the company commander?"

"Yeah, bring him over here", said Jack. "We'll see if they can start an enveloping movement on the fire's left flank. We could roll it up from both flanks and snuff it out even quicker!"

"OK, I'll go see if I can find him", said the assistant.

Now this was more like it, thought Jack. The only thing that could sweeten this would be if we had more engine companies in the line. But with five squadrons of firebombers and seven companies of ground troops, this bugger is already licked.

"Hello Jack!", said the commander of the 705th Firejumpers Company as he walked up. "How goes the battle?"

"I think we might just win this one", replied Jack with a grin. "What shape is your company in, Doug?"

"Spoiling for some action", Doug replied. "Where do you want us?"

"I want to see if we can roll up the left flank of this thing", answered Jack. "The firebombers just worked that flank over, so you should be able to swing around it and cave in the side. Let's see if you can roll it all the way up to the center. I've already got two reinforced companies pushing in from the right flank".

"No problem", said Doug. "I'll take my company over there and get started. Anything else?"

"Nothing that occurs to me right now", said Jack, "but if I think of anything, I'll let you know".

"OK Jack", replied Doug. "See you in a little while. Buck", he yelled over to a burly firejumper, "form up the company. We're moving out".

"Yes sir!", the assistant replied. "OK, you heard the man. Form up by columns and march!"

Jack watched as the scattered group of firefighters formed into a well-ordered formation and began heading over to the east. Watching them move out of sight through the smoke, he wondered how the engine companies were fairing down in Signal Hill. He decided he had enough to worry about right here and turned back to shout some orders to an engine crew on his left. Overhead, the last plane of a departing squadron of firebombers was climbing to join his buddies, who had headed off to Lake Castaic to reload.

Down at the refinery in Signal Hill, the three engine companies from Firebombers were hosing down a cracking tower while attempting to keep the flames from the burning building, which was dangerously close to it, from spreading to the tower. So far, the only explosions had been on the other side of the refinery. The battalion commander, Clancy Peterson, had never seen a fire like this. Off to his right, the entire refinery complex seemed to look like an image right out of Dante's Inferno. There were twelve companies on the scene and more were arriving every few minutes.

Since their trucks didn't possess the snorkels or extension ladders with which the other engines were equipped, Clancy's battalion had been assigned this supporting role of preventing the spread of the fire. The other companies' trucks were being used to get above the burning buildings. This was fine with Clancy. He was not interested in getting any closer to potentially explosive buildings. He had chosen to be a firefighter ten years before based on the premise that he would fight fires in the woods, not in multistory buildings (to which he now added burning refineries). He would be very happy to leave this fire behind.

As Clancy was mulling over these thoughts, several engine companies arrived. Clancy saw the fire chief, who was talking to the commander of the new arrivals, pointing over in the direction of the burning building adjacent to Clancy's cracking tower. Good, he thought, somebody to finally put out that roman candle and relieve Clancy of a major headache. The battalion chief hopped into his car and led the companies of LAFD engines over by the Firebomber companies.

"Hi, I'm Clancy Peterson", said Clancy as the chief's car pulled up next to him.

"Hello", said the battalion chief as he got out. "My name is Butch Thomas. Say, you guys really get around. I saw one of these fancy engines pop out of a plane up in Sunland a little while ago".

"Yeah, that was where the rest of the companies went", said Clancy. "They had all the luck. Some little brushfire to snuff out. Probably took them all of five minutes, while we're stuck here hosing down a timebomb!"

"When I left, they had their hands full", said Butch. "We pulled out and they were left holding the bag on a two hundred acre fire we had just set. They only had two engine companies and some smokejumpers to control it. Oh, and a handful of planes, too. Not a pleasant situation. You should be glad you got this assignment. At least we've got enough muscle to put a wrap on this".

"Maybe, but at least they don't have to worry about anything exploding where they are!", said Clancy tensely. "You guys *are* going to hose that building down, aren't you?"

"That's what the chief wants", said Butch. "And what the chief wants, the chief gets!"

"*Now*, right?", said Clancy with a laugh.

"You got that right", said Butch. "Well, enough of this chit-chat. I think my guys need me to show them where to start. 'Scuse me, Clancy".

"Good luck, Butch", said Clancy. "And remember, no smoking, huh?"

"I'll try to remember that", said Butch as he walked away.

The fire in the building was under control in less than ten minutes, which made Clancy *very* happy. Butch and his crews began working down the line of buildings and gradually moved on to link up with several other fire companies who were dousing a cracking tower which had started to catch fire.

The chief called up Clancy and informed him that the situation was now under control and that the Firebombers engine companies would be relegated to the role of strategic reserve. Clancy pulled his engines back to the center of the refinery, well away from the fires, and waited for another assignment. He figured the chief knew the Firebomber crews weren't trained in fighting this kind of fire, nor did they have the special breather gear and thermal suits to work inside the buildings. Clancy was grateful that the chief had pulled them back.

Up in Sunland, the firebombers were dropping their last loads directly on the head of the fire, driving it further back from the housing development. The advancing ground troops were now closing in on three sides and the area still burning constituted less than fifty acres.

Zack stepped out of the CCC van and stretched. "Looks like this one is pretty close to dead. It was nip-and-tuck for awhile, though".

"Yep, but we won", said Joe with a smile. "Any word from the boys in Signal Hill?"

"I've been monitoring the channels they should be using, but nothing from them directly", replied Zack. "It sounds like a real mess down there, though. Personally, I'd rather be here than there".

"Me too", said Joe. "Especially since it looks like this one is history".

"Mr. Talon", said a County Supervisor from behind. "I just wanted to say I was sorry for blowing up at you a while back. We all appreciate the job your people did here today. On behalf of the City Council and the County Supervisors, I wish to say 'thanks'. We were all impressed with your organization's performance here today. As soon as we process the paperwork, you will be given permission to operate anywhere in the Greater Los Angeles area. I'm sure that if the mayor were here, he would concur".

"That's most kind, sir", said Joe as he shook the Supervisor's hand. "We were just glad to be of service. We will be on call from now on if you need a wildfire fought somewhere. We have also developed several new items and tactics which might interest you and your respective fire agencies. Please feel free to inspect our equipment and ask questions of our personnel. I believe we have a lot to offer".

"We were wondering if you would be open to a presentation at City Hall in the near future", said one of the City Councilmen. "We could put out the word and have quite a few big names in the firefighting business there. We could also invite representatives from local and federal government agencies, if you like".

"That sounds worthwhile", said Joe. "Set the date and I'll send out a delegation of our people to make the presentation. I believe it would be mutually beneficial if you could invite as many different groups as possible".

Jerry walked up to Joe when the dignitaries had left. "Success Joe?"

"Success!", said Joe with satisfaction. "I always did like a good game of poker, especially where I won big-time. I think we just gambled the store and won".

"Hopefully we can gain some lucrative contracts from this operation", replied Jerry.

"They'd like a presentation at City Hall soon", said Joe. "I think we'll want to acquire the services of Mr. Zwickau to prepare our team for that task".

"Ah yes, the brash young man you spoke about. Do you think he will succeed in doing a proper job of hawking our wares?"

"I'll let you arrange for that. Retain his services and help him to prepare our people for the pitch at City Hall. Then I want a dry run set up for the executive staff to view ahead of time".

"Very well. I will approach him with our offer now, if that is acceptable to you".

"Have at it". As Jerry walked away, Zack popped his head out of the CCC van. "Joe, the planes have dropped about all the retardant they can without hitting our ground personnel. I'd recommend that we disengage the firebombers and send them home. Is that okay with you?"

"Whatever you recommend. Oh, by the way. What's the status of that fire down south. Could they use our planes at the refinery fire?"

"According to the radio traffic I'd heard, they have that one stalled already. I just contacted our commander down there and he said all three companies of pumpers had been put in reserve. I doubt they need any additional help. Besides, firebombers aren't much help in a vertical fire like that. They need personnel who can go into the buildings".

"OK, send the bombers home, then", said Joe.

"Pathfinder leader, this is Hawk One", the ATC called over the radio a few moments later. "You are to cease bombing operations and return to base, over".

"Acknowledged, Hawk One", replied Pieter. "Pathfinders returning to base, out".

"Miller Time?", asked Ralph with a grin.

"You betcha'", agreed Pieter. "From what I saw today, I think we're ready for a stand-up fight".

"All's we need now is a fire", said Ralph. "I wish there was one going now. I'm ready to do this again!"

"Be careful what you wish for, buddy", cautioned Pieter, "you may get it!"

Less than an hour later, most of the firebombers had landed at Talon Aerospace. The firejumpers finished stamping out the last of the brush fire, then double-checked the field for any smoldering embers. Once this was done, Zack realized they had overlooked one very important point: they hadn't provided a means of transportation home for the firejumpers. He made some quick phone calls to a pair of local bus chartering companies, then sent the engine companies home. While the busses were on the way, Jack took the opportunity to have the three companies who had arrived late recheck the field for embers while the two companies who had parachuted in first were allowed to take a breather. By the time the busses arrived, the field had been thoroughly rechecked.

The refinery fire was practically extinguished by nightfall. The fire chief released the Firebomber engine companies and sent them on their way with his thanks. By 7 P.M., the transports carrying the three engine companies touched down at Talon Aerospace. Joe had left orders for everyone to go home and get a good night's sleep. There would be debriefing meetings held the next morning. He expressed his gratitude for the way everyone had handled themselves, feelings which were seconded by the command staff. They had passed their first major test with flying colors. In addition, Joe had gotten the positive notoriety which he had wanted, as he found out when he arrived home that evening and turned on the news.

"In the headlines tonight, a spectacular blaze at the Ajax Refinery in Signal Hill took place today", the newscaster stated. "Over twenty engine companies and some 950 personnel battled the blaze for several hours before finally bringing it under control. In the midst of it all was a contingent of three engine companies from a new firefighting organization called Firebombers Incorporated. Our reporter, Linda Alcado, spoke to Los Angeles County Fire Chief Roland Gilson at the scene of the fire."

The picture changed to one of a burning refinery complex. Several fire engines with snorkels were spraying water and foam on the burning buildings. The words 'Taped Earlier' were displayed at the bottom of the picture.

"Shortly before noon today, a fire broke out in this refinery in Signal Hill", said the narrator. The camera changed angle to show her in front of the refinery. "Nearly twenty city and county engine companies responded to the alarm before it was brought under control. In addition to these firemen, three engine companies which were not under local jurisdiction also responded. An organization calling itself 'Firebombers Incorporated' apparently airlifted fifteen fire engines to the fire. We talked with the man in charge of the operation, Chief Roland Gilson, about the fire in general and these newcomers in particular".

The camera view changed to one showing an older fireman waiting off to one side who was motioned forward by the reporter,

"Chief Gilson, what was the cause of this fire?", asked Miss Alcado.

"As far as we can determine at this time, an electrical box overloaded in a storeroom, setting the room on fire", answered the chief. "The refinery fire department arrived at the fire too late to prevent a fuel line from rupturing. The burning fuel ignited a cracking tower and several adjacent fuel lines, causing a catastrophic fire. We were called in approximately twenty-five minutes after the initial fire started".

"And what is the status of the fire at this time?", asked the reporter.

"We have the fire under control and are extinguishing the remaining isolated fires in buildings located near to the center of the blaze", replied the chief, who pointed to the buildings behind him.

"And what do you know about this new firefighting outfit, Firebombers Incorporated?", Miss Alcado asked.

"Not very much, I'm afraid", replied the chief. "I was contacted by my superiors and told these people were on their way and to integrate them into the plan of action".

"And how did they perform, chief?"

"They were not equipped for extensive operations at this kind of fire", Chief Gilson answered, "but they handled their assignment competently and helped us to hold the line until better-equipped personnel could arrive. I understand from one LAFD battalion commander who arrived at a critical moment during our fire here that members of this organization relieved his units from watching a control fire in Sunland. He stated that the units which took over the Sunland fire containment were airlifted into the fire. That, by itself, helped to turn the tide. Without his engine companies, the situation would have gotten much worse".

"Sources at Long Beach Airport told us earlier that the three companies who fought here were also airlifted to that airport, chief. Do you know anything about that?"

"My superiors indicated only that they would be available to us, not their method of delivery. Needless to say, they drove into the refinery", he added with a smirk.

"Thank you Chief Gilson", said Miss Alcado. She stepped away from the chief and the camera panned over to show several sleek royal-blue Zephyrs in the background. "We also spoke with the man in charge of this contingent of fire engines from

Firebombers Incorporated, Battalion Commander Clancy Peterson, about their involvement here".

"Commander Peterson, when did your organization begin operating?", asked Miss Alcado.

"Well, we began actual firefighting operations today", said Clancy, who was obviously very nervous.

"So this is the first fire your organization has fought, then?", asked the reporter.

"Actually, there are two fires that our organization is currently fighting", answered Clancy. "There is also a demonstration fire up in Sunland which most of our equipment is at right now".

"By demonstration fire, you mean one which was deliberately set?", she asked.

"Yeah, the LAFD set that one so that we could show how well we fought fires", replied Clancy. "We were trained to fight primarily brush fires, not fires like this". Clancy motioned to the refinery behind him.

"Do you know the details of this fire up in Sunland, Commander Peterson?", asked the reporter.

"No, I'm afraid I don't", Clancy replied. "You could call our headquarters out in San Bernardino if you want more details on it, though".

"How large is your organization, Commander?"

"Uh, I don't have a complete head count", said Clancy, "but I think there's around two thousand of us".

"That's a fairly good-sized organization", she said. "Where have you received your funding for this many people?"

"It's all funded by Talon Industries, I think", said Clancy. "Don't quote me on that, though. They might be getting support from other sources that I don't know about".

"So, this is a privately funded organization - to the best of your knowledge?"

"As far as I know, yeah".

"One final question, Commander Peterson", said Miss Alcado. "We have unconfirmed reports that your engine companies were all airlifted into Long Beach Airport, is that true?".

"Yeah, that's right. We're an integrated firefighting force which airlifts its personnel and equipment to the fire. We arrived by C-130 transports. The engine companies up at the Sunland fire were flown into that fire, too. The other firefighters got there by parachuting in.

And the planes that we get our company name from are firebombers. They drop loads of retardant on the fire".

"Thank you for your time, Commander, and good luck", said Miss Alcado. The camera focused in on her face. "And there you have it. A new firefighting force has made a spectacular debut. It should prove interesting to watch its progress during the coming fire season. This is Linda Alcado, reporting from Signal Hill. Back to you in the studio".

The picture changed back to the anchorman in the studio. "Earlier today, our reporter John Nelson was at Long Beach Airport on assignment when the planes Linda just mentioned touched down. Here is a taped report from John". The picture changed to a view looking toward the passenger terminal at Long Beach Airport. In the background were several C-130s sporting the markings of Firebombers Incorporated and the gaudy tail-markings of the 'Alleycats' Heavy Lift Squadron. The camera view sharpened and focused in on one of the pilots talking with a reporter.

"I have here Firebombers pilot Steve Guzman", said the reporter. "Mr. Guzman, you just flew your planes in here a short while ago. Would you mind letting us in on what you are doing here?"

"Sure", replied Steve. "We just delivered three engine companies they needed at a fire over in Signal Hill".

"Where did you fly in from, Mr. Guzman?"

"We have a base out in San Bernardino at Talon Aerospace".

"And you brought these fire engines in on whose request? The city's? The county's?"

"Nah, we brought them in because our boss told us to", said Steve with a grin.

"And who is your boss?"

"Well, my boss is Pieter Van Vrees, but the guy in charge of everything is Joe Talon".

"The corporate raider? The man who runs Talon Industries?"

"The same".

"So you're part of a private organization, not affiliated with the county or state governments?"

"That's right."

"What are your plans now?"

"We wait for the trucks to come back, then we go home", answered Steve matter-of-factly.

"I mean, what are your plans for the future?", asked the reporter, who nearly succeeded in keeping a straight face. "What does this organization plan to do now?"

"Fight fires! Wherever we're told to".

"Thank you, Mr. Steve Guzman, pilot for Firebombers Incorporated", said Mr. Nelson. The camera panned right and focused on the reporter's face. "As you can see, we've moved into a new era of firefighting. No doubt we will be hearing more from Firebombers Incorporated in the very near future. This is John Nelson reporting from Long Beach Airport".

The TV picture switched back to the studio again. "An amateur photographer was able to shoot some film of more of the Firebombers Incorporated aircraft in action up by Lake Castaic today", said the anchorman. The picture changed to a somewhat shaky film of several firebombers gliding across the reservoir, then climbing out over the dam and banking to the left.

"As can be seen, these aircraft were some of the bombers referred to by pilot Steve Guzman at Long Beach Airport", narrated the anchorman. "A total of ten of these retardant-dropping aircraft were filmed by Mr. Robert Lee of Garden Grove as he was driving home from Bakersfield. They were apparently fighting the fire set in Sunland by L.A. City Fire Department personnel. Our reporter Nancy Chen has this story from Sunland. Nancy?"

The screen switched to a reporter standing outside a house. Behind the reporter was a crowd of people. The caption 'Live from Sunland' was printed at the bottom of the picture.

"Late this morning, this foothill community was disturbed by the sound of aircraft engines overhead", Mrs. Chen began. "Toni Marchek was doing the lunch dishes when she heard a commotion and went outside to see what was going on".

A taped conversation was shown next. A middle-aged woman was pointing off to the southwest as she spoke to the reporter.

"I was doin' the dishes when I heard all these planes outside", Toni said. "We're right under the Burbank Airport flight path, so I'm used to hearing jets and sometimes these little private planes, but these were *big*! I ran outside to see what was goin' on and what do you know, but here comes a long line of big blue planes flying along about a mile or so south of here. I took a look over where they were flyin' and I see smoke. I thought 'Oh my gosh, there must be a big fire over there!' I seen pictures of these guys fightin' forest fires with planes that drop that red stuff to put out the fires, so I figured that's what these guys were doin'. Then I saw a bunch of planes flyin' over way up there. They looked smaller than these big guys, but they seemed to be flyin' in formation, so I thought, 'Maybe they're filmin' a war movie, or somethin'. I wanted to go over and watch, but I had my baby to watch and my oldest was due home from kindergarten soon, so I couldn't leave. Those planes kept on buzzing the place for a couple of hours, though".

"We talked to several other neighbors who lived in this neighborhood, and they all gave pretty much the same story", said Mrs. Chen. "Reports of upwards of eighty aircraft were involved in this operation, although none of this has been officially confirmed as of yet. From what our sources have been able to tell us, the former L.A. City Field Practice Area, an area which the city has been anxious to see developed, was set on fire shortly before noon today. This was a controlled burn, designed to demonstrate the effectiveness of a brand new firefighting organization called Firebombers Incorporated.   At one point, the fire did threaten a new housing tract which was under construction at the far end of the field, but the Firebombers personnel apparently gained the upper hand on the blaze before any damage was done. City and County sources confirmed that much of the story, but have been unavailable for any more detailed comments on today's surprise operation. This is Nancy Chen reporting live from Sunland, back to you Chuck".

The screen filled with the face of the anchorman. "Many people said that they thought that a movie was being filmed when they saw wave after wave of aircraft fly in and drop paratroopers into the fields beyond", he said. "One elderly woman called the police and reported that she thought a Russian invasion was underway. Police and fire department switchboards have been deluged by calls all day from anxious or simply curious citizens seeking more information on the unusual events. Joseph Talon, the man who has been credited with the founding of this new firefighting organization has been unavailable for comment. In other news today, fighting heated up in Central America..."

Joe jumped around the channels taking in the reports of the day's events. While he was watching another report on the refinery fire, the phone rang.

"Joe, did you see the news tonight?", asked Pieter over the phone. "You're famous!"

"Looks like we're all famous, Pieter", said Joe in amusement. "I imagine we're going to be inundated with reporters for awhile. Better hire yourself a bodyguard!"

"More like three or four of them!", said Pieter. "I'd say you got your positive notoriety. All's you need now is a good adman to push your products!"

"Already got one lined up!", said Joe.

"I should have guessed! What time do you want to meet tomorrow?"

"Probably after lunch, say about twoish?", replied Joe.

"Fine, I'll spread the word when I get to work in the morning", said Pieter. "Looks like we're on our way!"

"Maybe. Better let your answering machine screen your calls for a few days", said Joe. "I have a hunch every hack writer and reporter is going to want to talk to you, me, and the rest of the staff".

"All right, boss. See you in the morning".

"Night Pieter". A short while after he had hung up the phone, it rang again.

"Mr. Talon, this is Joey Burton from CNN", said the voice on the other end. "Could you spare a few moments of your time to answer some questions?"

"I suppose so", said Joe. And so it begins, he thought.

Chapter 23

The airbase was buzzing with excitement when Pieter, Abner, and Zack got there the next day. Reporters were swarming all over the place, asking questions, taking pictures. Several of the aircrews and ground crews posed in front of their planes. The Cat Teams and engine companies had rolled their equipment out onto the flight line for photographers to take pictures of. It was well past nine before the bosses managed to get the media circus under control and clear the runways.

At 10 A.M. the debriefings began. They lasted until noon, at which time everybody headed out for lunch. Only a few reporters were left by then, since most now had enough material to write their stories.

Joe was met by a phalanx of reporters and photographers at Talon Industries that morning. After he had answered all of their questions (or at least, all of the questions he intended to answer) he waded through the mob and managed to get in the door to the office building. The security guards finally turned the reporters away at the elevator after Joe had promised to hold a press conference as soon as a presentation had been put together.

When Joe reached his office, Nancy was fit to be tied. She hadn't been able to get off the phone for the past hour. All of the lights were flashing, and when she managed to finish one call, another one appeared to takes its place. She just waved to Joe as he walked into his office. He could see it was going to be a busy day for everyone.

Joe finally managed to tear himself away from the phone just past 2 P.M. He hurried down the hall towards the conference room, his stomach growling from lack of food (he hadn't been able to get out for lunch). He rushed through the door just as Zack was sitting down. Once he had taken his seat, Joe started the meeting.

"Gentlemen, we seem to have the tiger by the tail", Joe said with a smirk. "I'm not sure whether we dare let it go, now!"

"I believe we should be able to keep it happy by feeding it at regular intervals", said Jerry.

"Which brings us to your task of hiring our PR man, Jerry", said Joe. "Have you signed up Mr. Zwickau yet?"

"I have been unable to reach him today to conclude the deal, but I will keep trying", Jerry replied.

"I'm kind of surprised he hasn't called us", said Joe with a chuckle. "He seemed to be reveling in the limelight late yesterday, after we turned the fire around, that is. Don't worry, Jerry, I'm sure he'll pop up soon. Now, onto other business. Let's hear some evaluations of the operation yesterday. We'll start with you, Zack".

"As far as I'm concerned, everything went pretty smoothly", said Zack. "The Ground Boss didn't divide his forces quite as well as I would have liked for fighting the flank fires. He put two reinforced companies on the right flank and only one on the left. Other than that, he did good.

"One recommendation my crews who fought that refinery fire made was that we issue breathing gear and thermal suits to our people for work in buildings. For that matter, they should be trained in firefighting techniques in urban areas. It's beyond my expertise, though, so we'd have to hire someone to train the crews. Not every crew would have to be trained, half our ground personnel would be enough. As long as we have some people equipped for it, that would be satisfactory. Assuming they were along with the units during a building fire, that is.

"Another thing we might consider is equipping our smokechasers with extinguishers containing that BC2000 retardant. They could snuff tougher spot-fires than the existing extinguishers do, allowing the line to advance faster and requiring less engine support. They could reload from the pumpers or streams and keep moving. Other firejumpers could carry reloads of the concentrate in their packs so that the smokechasers wouldn't need to carry so much themselves."

"I don't see why it wouldn't work", said Pieter. "If we can do it in the planes, why not do it on a smaller scale for the ground troops".

"Anything else, Zack?", asked Joe.

"Not that I can think of at the moment", replied Zack.

"OK Pieter, what have you and Abner got?", Joe asked.

"Yesterday, we had our first operational aerial refueling on the fly", said Pieter. "It came off without a hitch. We were able to tank up three full squadrons of firebombers between here and Sunland, with time to spare, no less!"

"One thing I was wondering about", Abner asked. "Could we pass concentrated retardant from the tankers to the bombers through a similar refueling line? As it now stands, we're limited by the amount of retardant we can carry, not by crew endurance or fuel considerations. If we could somehow transfer reloads of retardant concentrate to our planes, then we might be able to keep them aloft much longer".

"What do you think, Dave?", Joe asked.

"I'm afraid I'm not the man to ask", said Dave. "You'll have to spring that idea on the folks at Bergway Chemical, Abner. They could probably give you a better answer as to its feasibility".

"Just a thought", said Abner. "It would be nice to be able to make more than 20 drops before landing".

"One thing that did slow down our response time when we needed to get more troops on the scene was the need to reuse transports already committed to the first wave", said Pieter. "Have you considered buying some more transports and having dedicated truck transports *and* troop transports, Joe?"

"You guys can spend my money faster than anybody, can't you?", said Joe sarcastically. "Let me put you off for the moment on that topic. If we make enough profit on marketing our products and ideas, then I'll consider purchasing more planes".

"You asked for ideas", said Pieter with a hurt look on his face. "That was just an idea, nothing more".

"Sorry", said Joe sheepishly. "I'm afraid I'm not in that great a mood. The media has been monopolizing my time today. I didn't even get lunch yet!"

"I've got some used chewing gum you're welcome to", said Zack, pulling a wad out of his mouth and smiling.

"Comedians", Joe sighed. "The world is *full* of comedians! No, what I'd like now is a nice steak sandwich and some onion rings".

"Why don't you order out?", asked Dave.

"Have you *seen* the phone lines today?", asked Joe. "The switchboard is jammed with calls. I'll be glad when we finally modernize the phone system around here. Anyway, where were we? Oh yeah, Pieter's idea about extra squadrons. I'll give you a strong 'maybe' on that item. Let's move on. What else?"

"We should probably order some more of those CCC vans", said Zack. "That worked out pretty neat yesterday, even as much of a cluj as it was".

"We've got three more ordered", said Joe. "They're in the pipeline now".

"When do you expect to see them?", asked Zack.

"Not for a while yet", Joe replied. "Caprock is still tooling up to make the bodies from composite. I told them not to make a big production out of this, since we only want four, five at the most. Plus we don't want to take away much effort from the Zephyr fabrication line".

"You might wish to consider selling the CCC vans along with the Zephyrs themselves", said Jerry. "This would allow you to pay off the tooling costs for building the ones you truly needed".

"I hadn't thought of that", said Joe. "OK, when Hans makes his presentation, we'll see how many people are interested in this item. If we get enough customer interest, I'll consider opening up a line just for the CCC vans. Pieter, you look like something's troubling you".

"Just an idea that's been buzzing around in my head", Pieter replied. "What if we have a couple of planes assigned strictly to the Hawkeye for spot-fire extinguishing? They wouldn't be part of any specific squadron, just floaters which could be directed by the command staff or the ATC onto any potential threats. We had a few periods yesterday where all the squadrons were reloading. If something had flared up while they were away, we could have been in trouble. With a pair of unattached orbiting firebombers, we could at least delay a problem until the regular squadrons got back. I think it would be a good idea to attach them to the Hawkeyes directly, maybe incorporate the Hawkeyes, the pair of floating firebombers, and the planes carrying the command staff all into one large squadron. We could call it 1st Composite Squadron".

"How many planes would you project for this 'composite squadron'?", asked Joe.

"We have two Hawkeyes", said Pieter. "Add to that the two firebombers, which we could call the Tag-Team, and three or four transports for the command staff vehicles. That would be a maximum of eight planes".

"Are you planning to use existing spares to make up this new squadron?", asked Joe.

"We don't have four spare transports yet, but we could get by with the three we do have for the moment", replied Pieter. "Ground Boss and Fire Boss could double up in one CCC van, while the Air Boss and your VIPs could have the other two CCC vans. That would take care of all our spares as it stands now. We also have three spare CL-415s, which we would be able to steal two planes from".

"What about aircrews?", asked Abner.

"We would have to hire some more for the additional planes, but we shouldn't have any problems actually finding them", replied Pieter. "We had to turn away several qualified crews simply because we didn't have enough planes to go around. Most of those we turned away were told that we might be needing more crews in the future. Almost all of them expressed an interest in hiring on at a later date".

"When do you plan to start hiring the extra people, then?", asked Joe.

"As soon as you give me the go-ahead".

"You got it! Allen, what about the legal perspective on our operation yesterday?"

"It was fortunate that none of the housing units bordering the fire were damaged", said Allen. "As spelled out in the contract, we would have been liable for any damages resulting from our inability to protect them".

"Can we draw up some sort of contract for future operations which would keep us out of trouble like that?", asked Joe.

"I have already set my staff to task writing up a document which would absolve us of the bulk of the liability in the event of a similar incident", Allen answered.

"Good, keep me posted", said Joe.

"I also have some new information on another matter to discuss with you at your convenience", said Allen.

"See me after the meeting", said Joe. Allen nodded and went back to reading a document. "Dave, I believe you were going to set up a demonstration over at Talon Aerospace of that Heads-Up Display unit?"

"I'm glad you reminded me of that", said Dave. "I'll see if they can show us one in, say, three weeks?"

"And what about that wire-avoidance system you had promised me?", asked Pieter. "Have they done anything on that over at Talon Electronics?"

"I haven't checked lately", said Dave evasively. "I'll check with them right after the meeting".

"If you can get an outside line, you mean", Joe teased. "While you're at it, see if the phone company can get us some more phone lines".

"I thought that stuff would fall to Jerry", complained Dave.

"Not if I assign it to you", said Joe more seriously.

"OK, OK, I'll see what I can do!", said Dave, a look of frustration passing over his face. "Isn't anybody even going to compliment me on how well the electronics worked yesterday?"

"All together, everybody", said Joe. *Thank you, Dave!*" The other people at the table joined in on the chorus, following it with a great deal of laughter. Dave looked downright sullen by the time everyone had stopped.

"Thanks for nothing!", Dave said glumly.

"Seriously though, Dave is right", said Joe. "You *all* deserve thanks for your performances yesterday. Everybody did a magnificent job. I couldn't have asked for a smoother operation, especially considering the rapid change in plans.

"Because of you all, this organization is now a feasible, moneymaking proposition. In another year, we may be able to consider expanding operations into other states, possibly even into other countries".

Everyone around the table brightened at Joe's praise, even Dave, who said, "Yeah, well there's still some improvements I can think of to the electronics. For instance..."

"Just get the gear you've promised me done first", growled Pieter. "Then you can start thinking about your wonder-toys".

"OK", replied Dave quietly. "I'll get on them first thing tomorrow".

"Jerry, how are our bids to manufacture this equipment going?", asked Joe.

"Not very well, I am afraid", answered Jerry. "The manufacturers are still only willing to provide us with finished products. I hope to be able to cultivate some friendly sources within the manufacturers' ranks to push our bids along. So far, however, I have been unable to make any worthwhile progress".

"If it's a matter of money with these 'friendly sources', don't try to get them cheap", said Joe. "I want to get licenses for manufacturing everything here. I'll even go so far as to build a new facility if necessary. Assuming, of course, that our presentation at City Hall draws in enough interested parties for us to begin making a substantial profit on our products and services".

"I shall tell my people to redouble their efforts in recruitment", said Jerry.

"Well, is there anything else?", asked Joe. No one spoke up. "All right, then. Let's get back at it and, once again, thanks for the jobs you all did out there yesterday. Here's to many more successes!"

Once Allen stepped outside the conference room, Joe steered him off towards his office. Joe closed the office door, then sat down at his desk. "So, Allen, what do you have for me?"

"My operatives have traced your Mr. Holmstead to Germany", replied Allen. "They have located a boarding house where he is staying in Heidelberg. The house has been staked out now since late last night, our time".

"Have they seen Mr. Holmstead yet?", asked Joe excitedly.

"Not that I have been told", answered Allen. "But they should be able to intercept him as soon as he does appear".

"Have you found out anything on his background?", asked Joe.

"Nothing conclusive", replied Allen. "We have been able to find out from the authorities here that he is wanted in connection with two other arson jobs, both involving deaths".

"So this was not his first such job", said Joe thoughtfully. "Have you researched the deaths of the two witnesses from the Ethan Davis' hearing?"

"No, do you wish me to?", asked Allen.

"Yes, I would like to find out if there is some connection between their 'disappearances' and this Holmstead fellow. If my hunch is right, he may have been the cause of their disappearances".

"Do you wish me to find out more about the two prior arson jobs which the police credit to Mr. Holmstead?", asked Allen.

"Yes, find out all you can. Who knows, there may be some connection between the arsonist, Davis, and the witnesses. If we could tie them all together we might have some interesting evidence with which to prosecute Mr. Davis. It may be too much to hope for, but let's not overlook such an opportunity".

"If we locate this Mr. Holmstead at the boarding house, what action do you want taken?", asked Allen, a slight gleam in his eye.

"Tell your people to question him as far as they can within the law", said Joe. "No kidnapping, no rough stuff unless provoked. I don't want an incident in which the authorities jump down our throats. Keep it all decent and above-board".

"As you wish", Allen replied. "I know that you would like us to speak to him before the authorities do, but once we have questioned him, do you wish us to turn him in?"

"Absolutely!", said Joe. "I want him nailed to the wall, if he's guilty. Just try to make sure you're right before you blow the whistle".

"Rest assured, we will be", replied Allen.

"Keep me informed, and let me know the moment this brigand shows up", said Joe. "And now, I think I'll go get some lunch".

"Bon appetit!", said Allen as he walked out the door.

The next day, Joe was signing off papers in his office at 10 A.M. when Allen phoned over to talk to him.

"Has our friend showed up yet?", asked Joe.

"Unfortunately, yes", replied Allen. "He appeared about an hour-and-a-half ago. One of my people was stationed just inside the stairwell, assuming the fellow would take the elevator. He was struck from behind and, when he regained consciousness, found that his pockets had been rummaged through and his wallet stolen".

"The arsonist?", asked Joe pensively.

"Undoubtedly".

"What did he find?"

"My most recent cable to our operatives", replied Allen. "I believe he knows he is being followed now. This will make the task of finding him doubly difficult. By the time my operatives entered his room, he had cleaned it out and departed. They are beginning a search of the airport and train stations, but it does not look hopeful".

"Great, just great!", Joe shouted. "Well, tell them to keep at it. Maybe you should send someone who is better qualified to deal with this snake, Allen".

"I assure you, these are two of my best operatives, sir", replied Allen stiffly.

"How about doubling up the team, then?", asked Joe more calmly. "Send another pair of operatives over to track him. And try to impress on these guys the importance of this task".

"Understood, sir", answered Allen. After Joe hung up, Allen decided it had been wiser to call Joe. He didn't think he would have wanted to have seen him face to face.

"Man, did you get a look at that blonde?", Jose Gomez asked George Ostermann. "What a sweetheart!"

"Yeah, I wish there were more reporters who looked like her. Whew!" They had just brought their equipment back in off the practice field where they had been driving around for the press.

"I wish they'd give us something to do besides just driving around the field showing off!", groused Manuel Hermosa. "I want to get in on some action! All's we been doing is sitting here waving to the planes as they fly off to fight fires while we go back to polishing doorknobs!"

"Hey, man, you're never satisfied!", replied Jose. "You got no work to do, a steady paycheck, and babes as far as the eye can see. And you're mad because you ain't got nothin' to do? Man, you're one crazy dude".

"He does have a point, though", George cut in. "I mean, the rest of the guys get to go to those two fires where the press made a big deal of it, and we're stuck back here doing nothing. Even our transports got in on the action! Where are we? Sitting here with nothing to do but stare at each other! I'm tired of having friends ask me which fire I was at and all I can say is 'Uh, well... I fought a couple on the training ground. It stinks!"

"I like getting my picture taken as much as the next guy, but we haven't done anything yet to talk about", said Manuel. "Did you see that one guy who came into the garage yesterday? He was looking around for the guys from the 504th Engine Company. He wanted to interview them about that refinery fire. When I told him we were one of the Cat Teams, he didn't even want to find out what we did! That burns me up!"

"So what?", said an exasperated Jose. "We get almost the same deal without doin' anything but practice. I say the rest of these guys got the raw deal, not us".

"Well maybe when you get your head on straight you'll understand what we're talking about!", replied Manuel, who stomped away in disgust.

"Weird dude", said Jose quietly. "Where's that blonde, George? I think I'll go see if I can get an interview, know what I mean?"

"Yeah, well good luck, pal", said George. "Why don't you find out which units she's trying to interview. Maybe you could act as a tour guide or something that way".

"Yeah! That's the ticket!", said Jose with a smile. "Thanks, I'll try it!"

This was the third straight day of visits by reporters and cameramen, all of whom had wanted action shots of the Cat Teams and engine companies practicing. Requests to have repeated take-offs by the transports or firebombers, and air-landings of equipment had been denied by the higher-ups.

Zack stopped by Joe's office towards the end of the day. Allen was already there, looking over some briefs.

"Say Joe, when are you planning on having a demonstration?", Zack asked expectantly.

"In another week or so", Joe replied. "Why?"

"Those reporters are driving me crazy out at the Training Center", Zack answered as he settled into a chair. "Everybody wants to ask questions, and the more questions I answer, the more they have left to ask. I can't get any work done and the crews are so distracted that they can't even practice on the training field, what with all the shutterbugs running around the place".

"Why don't you turn them away at the gate, then?", Joe asked.

"We do, but they climb over the fences somewhere else on the property", Zack replied plaintively. "The guards can't patrol the whole perimeter and I don't want anybody hurt in a scuffle if the guards take their jobs a little too seriously. I think we could solve this problem if we just gave a demonstration. At least it might cut down on all of these visits".

"Yep, that's what I figure, too", said Joe. "That's why I haven't scheduled one yet. I'm waiting for the media frenzy to reach a peak".

"Ah, I see", said Zack thoughtfully. "When do you think they'll reach their peak? Soon I hope".

"Hans will let us know", Joe answered. "He's helping us gauge the media and also preparing the presentation for City Hall in mid-June".

"I thought he was still working for L.A. County", Zack said, a critical look in his eye.

Joe looked over at Allen, who looked up from studying his paperwork. "Officially, he is", said Allen, "although unofficially, he is also being retained by us".

Zack cocked an eyebrow in concern and said, "Isn't that a little unethical?".

"Just a little", Allen replied. "We would like to retain him exclusively, but he feels he can do us more good working in the L.A. County Supervisors' office for the moment. He has deferred becoming a full-time Talon employee for a few more weeks".

"I still don't like it, Allen", Joe remarked. "This situation could jump up and bite us if we aren't careful".

"These were the only conditions under which we could retain Mr. Zwickau's services", Allen stated. "He refused to cut all ties to the county just yet. He promised to do so as soon as he felt it was propitious".

"I also wish he'd hurry up with that presentation", Joe groused. "It has to be ready soon if Jerry and his staff are to have a chance at polishing and rehearsing it".

"Mr. Zwickau seems highly competent", Allen said smoothly. "I have reviewed his case record and reviews and found them to be exemplary. I believe he would fit well on the legal staff here even if his media presence is found to be lacking".

"We'll see", said Joe skeptically. "I still get a bad feeling about this situation, though".

"On another subject, Pieter was saying something about expanding operations", said Zack. "What are your plans along those lines?"

"Well, it occurred to me that other areas of the world have forest and brush fires", Joe began. "Why not market our products and services worldwide. That would open up an even bigger customer base for us. That is, providing that we can make a big enough splash here".

"Hence, the need for generating media frenzy", Allen observed.

"I see", said Zack. "So you're thinking of setting up more bases like this one across the country?"

"Initially", Joe replied. "Then we may consider opening some worldwide. It's too early to tell yet, but I think this fire season will give us a pretty good idea of what potential this organization has. The combination of our firefighting services and product lines could make this a very lucrative business".

Zack nodded his head, a look of realization crossing his face. "And the demonstration followed by the presentation at City Hall is the key".

"Exactly!", said Joe. "So let's hope we don't stub our toe on either one".

Joe finally gave the press a date for a demonstration a week later. The following Monday appeared to be a good time, he said. The media ate it up. As soon as the word got around, several important politicians, celebrities, and others were flooding Talon Industries with requests for tickets to the demonstration. Hereagain, Joe played the situation to his advantage. This rehearsal would be without any actual fire. The winds might whip around the smoke and blind the audience, something which Joe didn't want to have happen. Once again, the bleachers would be erected across from the practice field on the north side of the airstrip. It was planned to land all of the equipment this time, including the Cat Teams. The shortage of transports, though, forced Joe to scale back his plans a bit. It was decided to land three engine companies and three companies of firejumpers. One squadron of Cat transports would be used for hauling an engine company, which meant that one Cat Team would be left out of the operation again.

"The only fair way I know of resolving this is to flip a coin on it", Zack told the two Cat Teams. "I'll flip it and Panther leader will call it. Ready?"

"Heads!", George called when Zack flipped it. Everyone held their breath waiting for the outcome. The coin hit the ground and it was ...

"Tails!", shouted Manuel in disgust. "I can't believe it! We lose again?"

"Sorry, guys", said Zack as he picked up the coin. "If we have another demonstration, I promise I'll include you guys in it, OK?"

"Sure, fine", grumbled Manuel.

When Zack had walked out of earshot, George cursed under his breath. "I get the feeling somebody up there doesn't like us?", he said. "Well, looks like it's time to polish some more doorknobs, Manuel".

Manuel simply gave him an angry frown, then looked over at a smiling Jose. "What are you so happy about?", he snapped.

"This is great!", said Jose enthusiastically. "Now I can go over to the stands and scope out the chicks while the rest of these guys are out on the field. I'll have them all to myself!"

"I guess there's got to be one in every crowd", said George to Manuel. "Is this guy ever upset about anything?"

"Oh, I know how to bring this homeboy back down to earth", said Manuel with an evil grin. He turned to a smiling Jose and said, "Hey lover boy! Remember what the man said? We get the call for sure next time. That means jumping out of an airplane, your favorite pastime!"

Jose's smile slipped a bit, but he gamely replied, "Maybe so, but not this time!"

Chapter 24

Expectations were high the following Monday. The command staff had carefully briefed everyone and warned them to be on their best behavior, since there would be VIPs and press all over the complex. Zack had set up a series of burn-barrels for the bombers to target and the obstacle course fire-pits were lit. People began arriving hours early. Several pieces of equipment and their crews were put out on display off to the side of the bleachers. This gave the early-comers an opportunity to be photographed in front of the equipment along with the crews, which boosted crew morale immensely. Since Team Panther was not going to participate in the operation, all of their equipment had been put on display. Jose was in seventh heaven with all the attention (not to mention phone numbers) that he was getting.

As showtime approached, it was discovered that there was an overflow crowd present, and more coming. Fortunately, Jerry had had the foresight to order up more bleachers. Even then, there was not enough seating for all of the people who showed up. Zack and Pieter had some of the employees help them carry chairs out from the training rooms, which eased things considerably.

Few of the executive staff had slept well the previous night. Joe was tied up in knots from a mix of both fear and elation. The image of the Zephyr crashing onto the tarmac weeks before kept flashing through his mind. He made sure Pieter and Zack were well aware of the importance of this operation, and made them promise to impress this on their crews. There was a great deal riding on the success of this demonstration today, he realized - possibly more even than on the impending City Hall presentation.

The planes were finally loaded and the crews did one last pre-flight check. Ground crews removed the chocks from wheels and verified that the planes all looked fine. Bob and Dick were slightly delayed as Patrick clucked over 'one last thing' he wanted to check. They hurried to catch up with the rest of their squadron when Patrick finally finished. Soon, the taxiways were crowded with a long line of idling aircraft.

At precisely 10 A.M., the first aircraft, a Hawkeye, began rolling down the runway. A cheer went up from the assembled throng as the twin-engined plane lumbered into the air. Next came all five squadrons of firebombers, led, as always, by Pieter and Ralph in 'North Star'. Once they were airborne, the five squadrons of transports lifted off, closely followed by the two Heavy Lift squadrons. A total of 61 aircraft were now in the air.

"Most impressive!", gushed one of the dignitaries to Joe, who was seated next to her. "Tell me, Mr. Talon, what do all the symbols painted on each plane mean, exactly".

"They indicate which unit that plane belongs to, ma'am", said Joe. "For instance, the last squadron to leave had the picture of a tomcat on the tail, which represents the name of the squadron, 'the Tomcats'".

"How interesting!", she exclaimed. "I noticed several unusual symbols and pictures on different planes. One had a picture of a running wild boar and the name 'Razorback' written below it. Who selected these symbols for the squadrons, pray tell".

"Each of the squadrons were assigned a name by the commander of the air group, Pieter Van Vrees", Joe replied. "The crews were then invited to pick a name for their own planes, like the one you saw. Some of the others are 'Candle Snuffer', 'Moonbeam', and 'King Cobra'".

"I see", she said. Several planes began their approach to the airstrip. "What are these planes doing now?"

"They are going to land equipment, in this case fire engines, on the runway", said Joe. "The parachutes you see streaming out the rear of the planes will pull the fire engines out the back, allowing the transport to 'drop off' the equipment without actually having to land. The pilots who were in the military call it LAPES, which is short for Low Altitude Parachute Extraction System".

"My, that is an unusual name", said the woman. "I see parachutes coming out the back of that plane in the lead. Isn't this rather dangerous, though?"

"There is some risk, yes", replied Joe, trying to look unconcerned. "But these crews have been thoroughly trained in this operation. I doubt that they will have any problems". At least I hope they don't have any problems, he thought pensively.

"Have you ever had a mishap doing this?", she asked, turning slightly towards Joe.

"Look, here comes the first group of firebombers!", said Joe excitedly. He breathed a sigh of relief as the dowager turned away. That was one question he hadn't wanted to answer.

Pieter led the Pathfinders in to the target in an echelon formation, each plane slightly left of and behind the preceding plane. This allowed each plane to sight in on a pair of burn-barrels. Shortly before Pieter's plane reached the rightmost pair, the bombay doors opened and a salvo of red retardant fell in a gigantic waterfall onto the target. Each plane took out another pair of barrels until all of the planes had unloaded and turned back towards the reservoir to reload. As the Pathfinders departed, the next squadron, the Ridgerunners, closed on the second row of burn-barrels. Pieter's maneuver was repeated four more times by each squadron in turn until all the burn-barrels were extinguished.

In between these bombing operations, the engine companies were being dropped off. When the last Zephyr was on the ground, Joe breathed a loud sigh of relief, which was drowned out by the 'oohs' and 'aahs' of the assembled dignitaries.

With the firebombers and equipment transports out of the way, the Team Tiger transports approached the practice field, followed by the troop transports. At an altitude of 3000 feet, the bulldozers and APCs were yanked out the back of their transports by drogue chutes. Right behind the equipment came the crews. A moment of suspense occurred when the parachute of one of the Cat Team drivers failed to open. He executed a free-fall for 500 feet, then used his reserve belly chute. The chute opened and the gasps of the crowd turned to cheers.

Once the Heavy Lift transports had cleared the area, the troop transports began their air-dropping operations. Firejumpers soon filled the sky as the first sticks of firefighters left their transports and their chutes billowed open. By this time the Cat Team members had begun to unstrap their equipment from the pallets. When the last firejumper had touched down, the Caterpillars and M-113s began rolling off of their pallets.

"Looks like everything is going as planned", Abner said to Zack.

"Yep, but now comes the only truly dangerous part to this little carnival", Zack replied. "Let's hope those Cat Team vehicles remain fireproof when they roll through the fire-pits".

"I was wondering why you kept all of your engine companies close to the obstacle course", said Abner. "Now I think I see the method in your madness!"

"Never waste an opportunity", said Zack. "You never know when you might need it".

The vehicles of Team Tiger drove over by the firejumpers and the ramps came down on the back of the APCS. Groups of ten firefighters charged up each ramp and ducked into the interior. Once the squads were secure, the APCs raised their ramps and the Cat Team started rolling towards the obstacle course. To the southwest of the course, partially hidden by the obstacles and the smoke from the burning oil, sat fifteen engines from the three engine companies. They had orders to extinguish the flames at the first sign of trouble. The water cannons on each engine were manned by tense crews. As the Cat Team approached, the water pumps were fired up.

The lead bulldozer clanked over to the first berm and began climbing it. Once it reached the top, the driver eased it down the other side and into the flaming oil. Gasps went up from the onlookers.

"Mr. Talon, is that safe?", asked Joe's companion, a look of alarm crossing her face as the bulldozer disappeared in the smoke and flames.

"That's what they tell me", said Joe. "All of our Cat Team equipment has been fireproofed and is able to withstand temperatures of several hundreds of degrees".

"I can't say that I'd want the job of driving those things through an oil fire", said one man.

When the lead tractor appeared on the other side of the fire-pit, more cheers went up from the crowd. A few moments later, the last vehicle cleared the obstacle course and the Cat Team, accompanied by all three engine companies, began moving over to the center of the practice field. The engine companies started spreading out as they approached the positions of the fully-deployed firejumpers. The ramps on the rear of each APC came down once they arrived by the other firejumpers and the mounted firejumpers ran down the ramps to rejoin their companies.

"Now what happens?", asked the dowager excitedly.

"All of the assembled units will advance on an imaginary fire, executing the sort of operations they would normally use against a real fire", said Joe. He hadn't told his guests about the little surprise. They'd find out soon enough.

"Pathfinder leader, this is Hawk One, execute 'Sideshow'", intoned the Air Traffic Controller. "Ridgerunner leader, follow in Pathfinder flight. Black Widow leader, follow in Ridgerunner flight. All squadron leaders acknowledge".

"Roger that, Hawk One", replied Pieter. "Pathfinder leader to Pathfinder flight, follow me!"

"You think this will turn a few heads?", asked Ralph with a grin.

"It'll wake them up, that's for sure", said Pieter with a chuckle. "Reducing altitude to 50 feet. We want a spot about 1000 yards ahead of the fire line".

"OK, I think I've got a good spot picked out", said Ralph. He punched in the coordinates on the keypad as he read them off the TRIDINT display. He then set the controls for a linked salvo. "Ready!"

"Here goes nothin'!", said Pieter gleefully.

Joe saw the line of firefighters pause and knew what was happening. He covered his ears with his hands. As a few dignitaries saw his actions, they began to ask why, when their questions were drowned out by the roar of aircraft from behind. People turned around to see what was going on behind them just as Pieter's plane thundered over at more than 100 knots only 50 feet off the ground, closely followed by the rest of the three squadrons of firebombers. People were screaming, some in delight, some in terror. Some people ducked as the planes passed overhead. Photographers, who had been taken by surprise, quickly pointed their cameras skyward and began snapping photos. Many expended entire rolls of film in a few moments, having fired the cameras as fast as the autowinders would allow, and had to rummage through their camera bags to find fresh rolls. The entire episode was over in less than 30 seconds. When the last plane had cleared the bleachers, the bombay doors opened on all the planes and the firebombers dropped a continuous line of retardant almost exactly 1000 yards ahead of the ground troops.

"Now that's what I call precision bombing!", shouted one dignitary. Once the crowd had recovered from the shock, hoots and cheers went up from them which deafened Joe more than the aircraft engines had. After the planes had cleared the practice field, the last two squadrons came in from behind the fire line personnel and dropped two flanking lines of retardant which linked up with the long north-south line just laid. The engine companies began spraying down the ground ahead of them as the firejumpers and pumpers started a general advance towards the distant line of retardant.

"I must say, that was truly magnificent!", gushed the dowager. "I nearly fainted when they came over like that! My goodness, it simply takes my breath away!"

Not enough of it, Joe was thinking sourly, but it looks like we've pulled it off. He looked around at the smiling crowd, noticing the excitement on their faces and the brisk gestures towards the advancing firemen. His organization had made an impact, that much was for certain. As the aircraft began landing and the crowd surged over to talk with the personnel, Joe felt an enormous weight lift off of his shoulders. His people hadn't let him down. Now, would it pay off at the presentation? Time would tell.

"Gentlemen, this is a state-of-the-art simulator which we use to train pilots for the C-35 transport", said the engineer. "It incorporates all of the sights and sounds a pilot would experience in the actual transport, without any of the danger of damaging the aircraft".

How would he know what the transport sounded like inside, thought Joe sourly. We haven't even finished building one yet. Joe was in a particularly testy mood today. The Big Show at City Hall was only a couple of weeks away and, although Hans had officially cut ties with L.A. County, Joe's staff still needed more time to practice their delivery and smooth out the rough spots. Time was getting short.

"As you can see, the simulator is completely isolated from the floor by this gyroscopic cage", continued the engineer. "In this manner, the pilot can execute any maneuver, including loops, as in the actual aircraft".

"Do you have simulated flames if he crashes", asked Pieter with a smirk.

"Actually, we don't have flames", replied the engineer, "but the lead software engineer used to program video games and put in a feature where the windscreen cracks to simulate a crash".

"You're kidding!", said Dave. "This I've got to see!"

"We have the simulator reserved for you for the next hour, gentlemen", said the engineer. "We have also taken the liberty of providing a pilot to demonstrate the features of both the simulator and the projected transport.

"I want to go first!", said Dave.

"We should be able to accommodate three people at a time", said the engineer. "Mr. Talon, would you care to try it?"

"Sure, why not", said Joe.

"Mr. Albrecht, you and Mr. Van Vrees can sit in the navigator and flight engineer seats if you wish", the engineer said. "That will give Mr. Talon the best view from the co-pilot's seat".

"I think it would be better for Pieter to sit up front", said Joe "That way, he can see the Heads-Up Display better. That *is* the main reason we're here, after all".

"Of course, anything you say, Mr. Talon", said the engineer deferentially.

The side door on the simulator opened to reveal a pilot already checking over the instruments. "Howdy folks!", he called out cheerily. "Mah name is Jimmy, welcome aboard!"

The threesome stepped onto the darkened flight deck and found their seats. Jimmy showed Joe how to strap in, as Pieter did the same for Dave.

"What would Y'all like to see first?", asked Jimmy.

"The main thing I'm interested in is the navigational display on the HUD", said Pieter.

"Comin' rait up!", said Jimmy. "First, though, we got's to get this crate off the ground". Jimmy toggled the intercom and said, "We're ready to go in here. Y'all can close 'er up". A mechanical whirring sound announced the sealing of the door. Outside, the access ramp withdrew.

"Now, then, we kin do some serious flyin'", said an obviously pleased Jimmy. "Hang on to your hats!"

Jet engine sounds, which had been barely audible before, rose to a more noticeable whine. The simulated runway began moving as though the plane were rolling down it at increasing speed. As they neared the end of it, Jimmy yelled out, "Rotatin'!"

The entire room seemed to tip back noticeably as the noise of jet engines reached a peak, then began to fall away. Jimmy made the simulator continue in a climb until the altimeter read 4000 feet, then he leveled off. The room became level again and the jet noise receded to a soft whine.

"Ah would offer you folks somethin' to drink", said Jimmy, "but ah'm afraid our host out there wouldn't like us messin' up the inside of his purdy little simulator".

"We didn't plan on a very long trip anyway", said Joe. "The main reason we're here is, as Pieter said, to see the HUD. We're thinking of incorporating it into our firebombers".

"Do tell!", exclaimed Jimmy. "Yew mean you fellers are goin' to put this here display on one of them fancy planes I saw flyin' around there a couple of days ago?"

"That depends on how useful it is", said Pieter. "How do I turn it on, anyway?"

"It's that little white button down there at yer side", said Jimmy. "See the one ah'm talkin' about?"

"White button ... , white button .... yeah, I see it!", said Pieter. When he pushed it, numbers and symbols suddenly appeared around the periphery of a series of receding rectangles, all superimposed over the scenery outside.

"What is all this stuff?", asked a shocked Pieter. "It's hard to even see the ground through all of these symbols!"

"Simmer down, mister", said Jimmy. "Tain't that bad once yew get used to it. All them numbers and stuff show the values on yer gauges. See the one up to the right? That one there is your airspeed. The ones below it show altitude, headin', and the like".

"What do all the rectangles represent?", asked Pieter.

"Our flight path", replied Jimmy. "They shows the headin' we want to keep. As long as we's flyin' through the center, we's on the rait course and altitude. If we start missin' the middle and start hittin' the edges, it means we's off course. We kin also set an alarm to go off when we gets off course. Ah don't usually 'cause it makes too much racket".

"So right now we're on course?", asked Pieter.

"Yep, but ah kin get us off course if y'all would like to see what that looks like", Jimmy offered.

"How about using this to make an approach to the airport?", asked Joe.

"Surely, whatever you wants, mister", said Jimmy. He punched a few numbers into a keypad and the rectangles disappeared from Pieter's side of the windshield. Jimmy banked the simulator around hard. Everyone felt like they would fall out of their seats as the flight deck pitched right. Once Jimmy had leveled out again, the rectangles reappeared on Pieter's side, then Jimmy punched a button and they appeared on his side as well, along with the numbers and symbols present on Pieter's HUD.

"This is a lot more complicated than the HUDs I've seen before", said Dave. "It's nice having the two separate HUDs, so both the pilot and co-pilot can fly on instruments like this. What do you think so far, Joe?"

"An interesting system, but will it really be beneficial to our pilots?"

"I think we'd have to ask Pieter that question", said Dave. "Well Pieter, what about it? Do you think this would be an asset to your planes?"

"I'm not quite sold on it yet", said Pieter. "It seems to be pretty complicated, and I could see a whole bunch better if I didn't have all of this clutter in front of me".

Jimmy punched the intercom talk button and said, "Y'all want to give us some fog, please?"

The display quickly went from bright sunshine and green fields to bleak gray fog, completely blotting out the view below.

"This here's where the HUD really comes in handy", said Jimmy. "Ah'd like to see yew fly through this as easy as we will. Watch".

Jimmy lined up perfectly in the center of the rectangles and the passengers felt the simulator begin to pitch forward slightly.

"Keep an eye on that altimeter. Ah'm goin' to turn mine off, so's ah'll be flyin' only with them rectangles". As he finished speaking, he reached over and punched a button on his left. The numbers and symbols vanished from his side of the windshield, but Pieter's still displayed them. The altitude was steadily decreasing, though it was impossible to tell from the view, which remained gray and featureless.

"We're getting pretty low", said Pieter after a few moments of descent. "You had better level out soon".

"Not yet", said Jimmy calmly. He concentrated on keeping exactly in the center of the rectangles, seeming to be oblivious to the potential danger of coming in at this speed without even bothering to check his instruments.

"We're down to less than a hundred feet!", Pieter shouted. "Pull up Jimmy"

"Not till ah lands us", replied Jimmy calmly. A light in front of Jimmy flickered to life and Joe heard the sound of the landing gear lowering, then Jimmy throttled back the engines a little. The nose of the simulator came up slightly. Suddenly, the flight deck lurched noticeably and the sound of wheels contacting pavement could be heard. As the flight deck leveled out and the nose wheel contacted the pavement, Jimmy further reduced the throttles and steered the plane off to the side of the runway onto a taxiway.

"Absolutely amazing!", said Pieter. "A no-instrument landing. In fog no less! I'd heard of systems that could do this, but I'd never seen one."

"Ain't it a kicker?", said Jimmy, flashing Pieter a toothy grin. "Not only that, this here plane kin take off or land without the pilot havin' to do anythin'. Pretty slick, huh?"

"So Pieter, what's your opinion now?", asked Dave.

Pieter unstrapped his harness and turned around to face Joe. "Joe, can I have one of these for Christmas?"

Pieter was pumping Jimmy with all kinds of questions as the four people climbed out of the simulator. The rest of the executive staff was milling around outside waiting their turn and the engineer came up to Joe.

"Did you enjoy your flight, sir?", the engineer asked.

"Yes, it was very interesting", replied Joe. "Tell me, where are these HUD units currently being manufactured?"

"Well, the original source was an electronics firm on the East Coast", said the engineer. "But I believe Talon Electronics is now our sole source for them. Since we haven't completed the first prototype C-35 transport yet, they have not set up an assembly line for our HUD units. The one on this simulator was a prototype, as was the simulator itself".

"So, we manufacture the HUDs", said Joe thoughtfully. "Then we shouldn't have any problem getting all we need. Dave, see whether the staff over at Talon Electronics has made plans for manufacturing these things in quantity yet. If they have, tell them we'll want to equip our firebombers with them once the assembly line is established".

"OK, Joe", said Dave. "By the way, I think Pieter may have just found another pilot for us".

Joe turned to look back at the animated conversation between Pieter and Jimmy, then looked over at Dave and smiled. Like two peas in a pod, he thought.

Chapter 25

The day for the presentation arrived and Joe was not a happy camper. Jerry and his people had barely had enough time to prepare due to delays in Hans handing off information about how to tailor the presentation to appeal to the County Supervisors and City Council members. Hans had advised against postponing the presentation on the grounds that the various officials invited to it had tight schedules and the chances of getting all of these officials together again in the near future was slim. Against his better judgment, Joe allowed Jerry to go ahead with the briefing. City Hall was packed when the spokesman stepped up to the podium.

"Good afternoon, ladies and gentlemen", he began. "On behalf of Talon Industries, I'd like to take this opportunity to welcome you all here today. If any of you failed to get an information packet, please raise your hand now and an usher will see that you get one".

Several hands went up and the spokesman took advantage of the delay to rearrange his papers. When the bulk of the late-comers had been seated and the information packets fully distributed, the spokesman continued with the presentation.

"As you know, suburban brushfires and rural wildfires destroy important resources and prime real estate valued in the tens of millions of dollars each year", said the spokesman. "Add to this the injuries and loss of life which occur and you have a very costly problem. Conventional firefighting resources are usually stretched thin and may react too slowly to the threat when it is identified due to the difficult terrain where many wildfires begin. Therefore, we offer a new organization which can respond more quickly and with greater force, and hence, greater results, than any firefighting unit presently operating in the world. The name of this organization is Firebombers Incorporated.

"This organization was founded to meet a need in the community, the need for a rapid-deployment unit which could quickly knock down a fire before it was able to do substantial damage. At the recent Ajax Refinery fire in Signal Hill, three engine companies from Firebombers Incorporated departed San Bernardino at the same time that four L.A. City Fire Department engine companies were departing Sunland. The Firebombers engine companies were on the scene of the refinery blaze well ahead of the four LAFD companies. And at the same time, Firebombers personnel freed up these selfsame LAFD engine companies from their responsibilities in Sunland so that they could go fight the refinery fire. The FI personnel managed single-handedly to extinguish a two-hundred acre brushfire with an initial investment of only two engine companies and two companies of firejumpers, along with ten retardant-dropping tankers. In addition, the four LAFD companies which FI personnel relieved arrived at Signal Hill just in the nick of time".

A hand came up at this point, but the spokesman simply stated, "Please, hold all questions until the question-and-answer period, thank you. Let me now show you some footage of these brave men and women in action". He motioned for the lights to be darkened and a projector came on in the back of the room.

"This film was taken at a training exercise at the Talon Aerospace Training Center. As you can see, all of the equipment is brought in by plane. Although a landing strip is used in this film, the same operation can be done in open fields and meadows. In fact, the fire in Sunland was fought by personnel who had been inserted by aircraft into a field, not an airstrip. Once there, the equipment and personnel are self-sufficient, needing no further support in order to eliminate the fire. Notice that even bulldozers are airlifted to the site along with Armored Personnel Carriers with which to build firebreaks and transport personnel through areas choked with flames. This film demonstrates the fireproof nature of the vehicles. Notice how they can drive right through flaming pools of oil without any damage.

"This next clip shows how accurate the firebombers themselves are. These burn-barrels were sighted-in by the firebombers while still several miles away. The operation is all automated. The co-pilot need merely type the coordinates in and the on-board computer does the rest. Distance to target, wind conditions, aircraft velocity, these are all taken into account, resulting in a perfect drop every time. Not only this, but each aircraft can be linked to others, allowing a host of aircraft to drop a continuous line of retardant flawlessly. What takes conventional retardant-bombers many passes to do correctly, this organization can do the first time, every time.

"In addition, our aircraft can do something which few other operators can: fight fires at night. Thanks to the special electronics installed on these planes, our firebombers are able to spot fires through smoke, fog, or dark of night as clearly as if it were daytime. Those of you who attended the demonstration out at Talon Aerospace know what I'm talking about, don't you?"

Several heads in the audience began nodding, many of the people were smiling in remembrance of the demonstration at Talon Aerospace weeks before.

"Not only have the tactics of Firebombers Incorporated revolutionized the industry, but they have also developed new chemicals, new processes, and new equipment for use by anyone in firefighting. Bergway Chemicals, a Talon Industries subsidiary, produces the concentrated retardant which the firebombers use with such devastating effect. The electronics on both the transports and the firebombers are state-of-the-art devices which greatly simplify the rigorous and dangerous business of flying aircraft under these conditions. And perhaps the greatest contribution to our community and our country is the employment of so many men and women from our military who would otherwise be without jobs now. Fully one-third of FI personnel are former military personnel.

"All of the transport and airborne control aircraft are military surplus, as are the vehicles in the Cat Teams. This means that they would have been sitting around some military equipment boneyard collecting dust. Instead, they are put to productive use, no longer an asset which would have been taken as a financial loss by our government. The chemicals, electronics, and vehicles which Talon Industries has developed for this organization are available for sale, as shown in your information packets. In the future, Talon Industries will also be publishing training material and conducting seminars on this new firefighting technology.

"Talon Industries is not content to merely rest on their laurels. They are continuing to improve on the techniques and systems which have already proven so effective. New electronics are being developed at Talon Electronics for use in the firebombers and transports currently in use. These electronics will enable pilots to see obstacles such as high-power wires in the darkest of nights or the poorest of weather. New displays for the planes themselves will greatly ease the job of the pilots, making operations which are extremely dangerous at the present much less risky in the future. With these new systems will come new tactics which will further increase the effectiveness of what is probably already the premier firefighting organization in the world.

"We are fast closing out this decade, this century, this millennium. Many people have tried to peer into the future to behold the shape of things to come. But you, ladies and gentlemen, need peer no further than this to see one institution which will

forever redefine the science of firefighting. Firebombers
Incorporated, the firefighting force for the 21st century! Now, I
will take questions".

Reporters began raising their hands in droves, some of them
asking questions before being called on. The spokesman scanned
the crowd, then pointed to a woman in the front row. She stood
and the roar of voices dwindled down to a few murmurs.

"How are these people being financed?", she asked.

"Mr. Joseph Talon, founder and CEO of Talon Industries is
funding this operation completely out of his pocket, miss", he
replied.

"But how can a single man, even one as wealthy as Mr. Talon,
afford such a costly enterprise?", the reporter asked.

"I believe he intends to profit from the spin-offs of products
and services this organization can provide in the future", answered
the spokesman.

"But don't normal firefighting organizations earn income from
actually fighting fires, then being reimbursed by the government?",
she asked.

"Yes, that is the arrangement", replied the spokesman. "And
that will also be a benefit Mr. Talon expects to reap. He would, no
doubt, settle for the standard wage which the government pays to
existing firefighting organizations".

"I see", she said. "Thank you".

As the first reporter sat down, the spokesman pointed to a man
in the third row, who immediately stood up.

"Isn't this a little like using a 747 jetliner to deliver a paper
route?", he asked. "It seems like you people have gone to a lot of
expense to provide a marginal increase in firefighting capacity. Can
you comment on this please?"

"Your point is well taken, sir", began the spokesman. "But, as
I pointed out to the young lady, our organization expects to make
up the initial start-up costs by marketing the innovations which
Talon Industries has developed for use by their personnel. Is there
some point within my explanation which you need clarified?"

"Yes, my question is the following", said the reporter. "With so
many people already involved in firefighting statewide, is there
really a need to have such an elaborate force on call?"

"As I pointed out during the presentation, this firefighting
force, was praised by your city and county officials for its

performance during the recent Sunland and Ajax Refinery fires", replied the spokesman somewhat defensively.

"Those fires were not both real fires", said the reporter more loudly. "The Sunland fire was set by LAFD as a control fire. The fact that it got out of control was due more to the fact that Firebombers Incorporated was unable to respond quickly enough to extinguish it. I would hardly put it in the same category as the refinery fire, which, as I understand it, FI personnel took only a very limited role in fighting. The fire chief on the scene relegated them to a reserve capacity as soon as he had enough firefighters who were *qualified* to fight the fire".

The spokesman was really beginning to get unnerved now. "The fact of the matter is that the Sunland fire was botched by LAFD", the spokesman stated firmly. "They withdrew all of their personnel *after* they had already started the fire! It was left for FI personnel to rectify the situation, which they did magnificently!"

Apprehension was beginning to well up in Joe as he followed the exchange between the two men. He could see that the mood in the audience was starting to turn against the spokesman as he fenced with the reporter. This was a trend which was disturbing to Joe. He was worried where it might lead. "Jerry", he said quietly. "I think you need to pick a calmer spokesman in the future".

"Agreed", replied Jerry soberly. "I think the frantic preparations have frayed his nerves a bit too much. Do you wish me to intervene?"

"No, not yet. Let's hope he gets himself under control soon, though".

"Which they did barely!", shot back the reporter. "Observers whom I interviewed after the fire told me that everyone there, including the Talon Industries executives, were terrified that the fire was going to reach the adjacent housing development, and that the FI personnel only narrowly avoided that very thing!"

"There was never any *real* danger to the development", the spokesman replied, trying to recover his composure. "And what about the four engine companies which were freed up to go to Signal Hill?"

"They never would have *been* up in Sunland if it hadn't been for the demonstration put on for the benefit of the VIPs!", shouted the reporter. "They could have gotten to the refinery fire in less than half the time if they hadn't been occupied with entertaining an industrialist who wants to play fire chief! And from what I understand, Joseph Talon gave their commander his personal assurance that FI personnel could handle the demonstration blaze without any problems."

Jerry could see Joe tense up with the reporter's remark. Joe's face took on an angry set and Jerry decided that he was glad they were sitting this far back. If the reporter had been any closer to Joe, the reporter would be seeing stars about now. And his spokesman would probably soon be looking for another job if he didn't get this situation under control soon.

"I believe we should continue this conversation privately", the spokesman said as evenly as he could. "I think others have questions". He turned away from the still boisterous reporter and picked someone from the other side of the third row. A well-dressed older man slowly rose to his feet and began speaking.

"Sir, isn't it true that a Mr. Hans Zwickau, a former employee of the Los Angeles County Supervisors, acted as the liaison between the Los Angeles County Supervisors and Talon Industries?", the man asked slowly and deliberately.

"Yes, that is true", said the spokesman as he tried to compose himself, not considering what he said. People began to strain to hear the exchange, which was difficult over the din from the outraged reporter down at the other end of the row.

"And isn't it true that he was in contact with Mr. Joseph Talon, head of Talon Industries during the time he was ostensibly representing the interests of the County Supervisors", the man asked.

The spokesman stepped back as if struck a physical blow.

Towards the back of the hall, Jerry could hear Joe groan as the question was asked. Joe looked intently at the spokesman, trying to will him not to answer.

"I ... I have no comment on that question", said the spokesman as he fought to control himself and calm down. "Who else has a question?", he asked as he vainly looked around for a raised hand.

"Perhaps I can help refresh your memory, sir", the older man said firmly. "I have documents which establish beyond a shadow of a doubt that Mr. Hans Zwickau has indeed been working for both L.A. County and Talon Industries at the same time!" He raised a sheaf of papers over his head so the audience could see them clearly.

Several of the Supervisors and City Council members began having an animated conversation at this point. Finally, one of the Supervisors spoke up. "Do you suppose I could see those papers, please?"

The older man walked down to where the Supervisor was standing and handed the documents to him. The Supervisor looked them over for several minutes while a hush fell across the room, punctuated by the low buzzing of quiet conversations. The Supervisor finished reading, then spoke up loudly. "Mr. Talon, Mr. Joseph Talon, are you out there?"

Joe stood up slowly, then said, "Yes, I'm here".

"Mr. Talon, this smacks of the worst sort of collusion and bad business practice", said the Supervisor. "Our lawyers will be in touch with you and we will see you in court on this matter. Henceforth, your organization is forbidden to operate anywhere in the greater L.A. area. I will be conferring with our associates in the other Southern California counties to impose a similar ban, as well as contacting the various forestry agencies on this matter".

Joe didn't reply. He simply turned and started out the door at the rear. Jerry got up quickly and followed him out.

The reporters in the front of the room suddenly jumped to their feet and began to scatter. Some mobbed the Supervisor, some tried to speak with the now mute spokesman, and many tried to chase after Joe. Joe and Jerry reached the car just ahead of them. Joe had Bill, the chauffeur, drive away before the reporters caught up.

Unseen by the crowd, the older man who had exposed Hans slipped out a back door and entered an unoccupied anteroom. He pulled out a cellular phone and began dialing. "Mission accomplished", the older man said over the phone.

"Good job", Ethan Davis replied at the other end. Ethan hung up the phone and turned to the guest in his den. "Everythin' went accordin' to plan", he said with a look of satisfaction on his face. "Those boys are gonna have a lot of trouble gettin' this egg off their faces. The money we discussed'll be deposited in your account in the Caymans tomorrow, as promised".

"Excellent!", replied Hans Zwickau, who smiled broadly back at him from his chair. "It has been a pleasure to do business with you, Mr. Davis".

"Well, that turned into quite a mess, didn't it", said Joe bitterly.

"I dare say things could have gone a good deal better", said Jerry.

Joe said very little on the drive back to his mansion. Jerry had left his car there and departed shortly after they arrived. Once again, the phone was ringing off the hook. Joe refused to answer any calls. He also made sure the gates were closed and locked. He turned on the news and sat down in front of the big-screen TV in the family room.

"Firebombers Incorporated is in the news once again tonight", said the anchorman. "This time, however, the news is not good. Talon Industries made a presentation at City Hall today extolling the benefits of this new firefighting organization, when someone in the audience asked about a Talon Industries employee named Hans Zwickau. It seems that Zwickau was working for the L.A. County Supervisors while also working for Mr. Joseph Talon, CEO of Talon Industries, the parent company of Firebombers Incorporated. The unidentified man who raised the questions produced documents that showed conclusively that Zwickau was indeed in the employ of Talon Industries and L.A. County simultaneously. Zwickau has been charged with collusion by the Los Angeles County Supervisors, who also charged Joseph Talon with various shady business practices, which will be taken up with him in court at a later date. Besides embroiling Talon Industries in a legal battle, the Supervisors have also forbidden Firebombers Incorporated from operating anywhere within L.A. county, and, at this hour, Orange, Riverside, San Diego and Santa Barbara Counties have also agreed to ban their operations anywhere in their areas. Talon and Zwickau were both unavailable for comment on this matter. The person who asked the questions also disappeared from the hall before reporters could question him. In other news today, a teacher's strike appears imminent..."

Joe shut off the TV and started pacing around the family room. He had had a bad feeling about this presentation. Why on earth had he hired Hans? Hindsight was always 20/20, thought Joe ruefully. And where did the information about Hans come from? Joe was sure that Jerry had insisted on Hans cutting ties with L.A. County prior to Talon Industries hiring him. He would have to have that confirmed tomorrow.

In the meantime, perhaps the forestry services would still employ his units. If the Southern California counties saw how well Firebombers Incorporated performed with those organizations, they might just want FI back. Joe would have to get Zack, Pieter, and Abner on the phones tomorrow to see if they could whistle up a deal of some sort with the people at the forestry departments. There was no way to get a call out to them tonight anyway. Even his supposedly private phone numbers were tied up with reporter's calls. In the meantime, Allen and his staff would have their hands full trying to straighten out this mess. And what a mess it was.

Joe had Bill drive him to work the next day. Reporters mobbed Joe both at the gate when leaving home, and at Talon Industries' offices. How fickle the press was, Joe thought bitterly. Last month we were the darlings of the media. Today, we're cads. Same people, different circumstances, completely different opinions. Amazing. Joe had called ahead to have some of the security guards meet him at the car. He had seldom employed bodyguards. If this kept up, they would probably be needed.

"Morning Nancy", said Joe when he reached his office. "Would you please call Allen Sims to my office?"

"Right away, Mr. Talon", she answered.

A few minutes later, Allen came walking in. Joe motioned for him to close the door and have a seat.

"Looks like we've stirred up a hornet's nest, Allen", said Joe as the lawyer sat down. "What kind of damage control can we do for this situation?"

"My suggestion is to state clearly that you had not paid Mr. Zwickau for his services prior to the Sunland operation", said Allen. "If it can be proved that no cash changed hands before that time, then perhaps the worst of the collusion charges can be dismissed, or at least reduced".

"Good thing I didn't pay him in advance, then", said Joe. "What about our business dealings after the Sunland op. Money did change hands at that time".

"I believe we can sidestep that issue for the moment and concentrate attention on the fact that you have been above-board and completely honest with the local officials through that critical time", said Allen. "And under no circumstances would I recommend having any dealings with Mr. Zwickau. Any hint of friendliness between the two of you could be misinterpreted as a sign of a deeper relationship and lend impetus to this case being prepared against you".

"So I shouldn't even talk to Hans if he calls me?", asked Joe.

"Under *no* circumstances should you speak with him!", replied Allen emphatically. "Either contacting him or accepting calls from him would be perilous at this delicate time".

"OK, what else?", asked Joe.

"If you have any favorable documents which would help to proclaim your innocence, give copies to my people and we will release some to the press", Allen answered. "Any evidence which is deleterious should be destroyed. It will be difficult to maintain a semblance of innocence under the present circumstances. If negative evidence is brought to light, it would undoubtedly reinforce the case against you".

"Hans didn't receive any payments until about a month ago", said Joe. "And you're saying to destroy those receipts?"

"Immediately!", Allen replied firmly.

"I don't know, Allen", said Joe as he shook his head. "It seems to me that this action would throw more suspicion on me. People wouldn't know that I had destroyed receipts from the time period following the fires, they would only know from my staff that receipts had been destroyed. I think it would be better to leave well enough alone. We have little to lose by admitting to payments after the event, and a lot to lose by arbitrarily destroying any evidence. No, I think I'll leave the receipts alone".

"I would advise against this policy", said Allen. "You are, however, in charge. I will abide with your desires, but only under protest".

"Anything else I should or shouldn't do?", asked Joe.

"I would suggest maintaining business as usual", replied Allen. "No large donations to charitable causes, as these could be misconstrued as the actions of a guilty conscience being assuaged by giving to the unfortunate. No sudden trips out of the area, as these could be interpreted as attempts to flee from the controversy, once again implying guilt. Basically, maintain a low profile, but no deviation from your normal routine. If you act calm and collected, perhaps people will believe more strongly in your innocence".

"What about the reporters?", asked Joe. "Same procedure we followed when I used to acquire companies?"

"Exactly!", said Allen. "I will assign one of my staff to accompany you on your trips between work and home. They will be instructed on how to field any questions from the press. I would recommend no direct statements by you".

"Yeah, I was also thinking about hiring a couple of bodyguards", said Joe with a look of distaste.

"I would not recommend it. Hereagain, it could be misinterpreted by the public as a sign that you have something to defend yourself against. I seriously doubt that there will be any physical violence perpetrated against you by anyone. Bodyguards would be more likely to create an incident. I shall select one of my former field agents as your legal aid on your journeys. He will have been trained in self-defense, and, therefore, capable of serving both purposes without arousing suspicion".

"Sounds like a plan", said Joe. "Will you be able to assign him today? I had wanted to go out to Talon Aerospace to talk with the command staff about a few items".

"I shall summon him as soon as I leave here", replied Allen. "I am afraid that I have no further news on our elusive arsonist. He seems to have performed an effective vanishing act. My people have redoubled their efforts and hope to trace him within the week".

"I'd be surprised if they find it that easy to do", said Joe. "This guy's middle name must be 'slippery'".

"Nevertheless, we shall continue to search. I shall go make arrangements for your aide, if there is nothing else".

"Nope, I'm done. Thanks Allen". Joe returned to his paperwork. Once it was done, he called out to the Training Center to see if all the command staff members were there. Once he had verified that they were, he asked that they have a meeting at three that afternoon. He then asked Nancy if she could get some lunch brought up from the cafeteria. Joe didn't always enjoy cafeteria food, but he didn't feel like wading through the reporters who still hovered outside waiting for a photo op or interview.

By the time he had finished lunch, Nancy buzzed him and said there was someone from Allen to see him. Joe cleared the lunch dishes off of his desk, then had Nancy send him in. The door opened and in walked a small man who looked to be no taller than 5' 5". He was slight of build, had a dark complexion, and a receding hairline. Yep, looks like a lawyer all right, thought Joe. But a bodyguard? Never.

"Hello Mr. Talon. My name is Horace Kemel. Mr. Sims sent me over as your legal attaché".

"Hello Horace. That's an interesting accent you have. Where are you from?"

"I was born in Athens, Greece. My father was a Turkish diplomat to Greece, my mother was a Greek citizen".

"I'll bet that made for some interesting situations growing up. It's my understanding that there's usually bad feelings between Turks and Greeks. How is it that your parents ever overcame that animosity sufficiently to get married?"

"Actually, they bore no animosity towards each other, obviously, but the families were not on speaking terms, I'm afraid. My first name was chosen as a neutral one, espousing neither Greek nor Turkish traditional names, so as to reduce family friction", replied Horace.

"Did it work?"

"Alas, not as well as they had expected. The fact that my mother had married a Turk at all caused enough damage with the Greek half of the family that my first name became inconsequential. Her father disowned her the moment she told him her mind was made up".

"Allen said that you would also act as my bodyguard for awhile", said Joe as he looked the little man up and down. "No offense, but are you sure you're up to it?"

"Ah yes, my size. I hold a fifth degree black-belt in karate. A leftover from my misspent youth. It was difficult growing up in Greece with a Turkish surname. My father saw to it that I had substantial training in self-defense at an early age. He anticipated the probability of conflict with my classmates as I grew older and laid plans accordingly".

"And was the training necessary?

"Yes, I dare say it was", replied Horace. "However, there were few incidents. After the first few Greek boys were thrashed, the rest either befriended me or, in most cases, simply avoided me. I have kept up with my training since that time, as I find it to be a most enjoyable way to work off the frustrations and rigors of daily life. It provides me with both exercise and self-confidence, something which someone of my stature deems extremely important, both in the legal world and the world outside".

"Allen says that you served as a field agent. Where exactly have you worked?"

"Mostly in Europe and the Middle East. I speak several languages and dialects. That, coupled with my unobtrusive appearance, made me an ideal candidate for surveillance of a delicate nature. People seldom took notice of me, fewer still considered me a threat".

"Have you ever had to put your martial arts skills to use in your job?", asked Joe, intrigued that someone who was obviously so erudite could also be an effective bodyguard.

"Occasionally. I usually try to avoid a conflict, if at all possible. I believe this is one reason Mr. Sims selected me. He knows that I will only use force where it is absolutely necessary. I draw no pleasure out of inflicting injury or pain".

"Very interesting, Mr. Kemel", said Joe. "Well, I think it's time to saunter over to Talon Aerospace. Are you ready to field all those poisoned barbs the media has prepared for me?"

"I believe I will be able to successfully ward them off, yes", said Horace.

Horace was as good as his word. The repeated questions of the media as they left Talon Industries were deftly answered in as neutral a way as could be done. Here was an excellent political candidate, thought Joe with some amusement. Bill drove them out to Talon Aerospace. Joe was relieved to see few reporters there and Bill was able to quickly drive through the gate, leaving the reporters behind. Joe and Horace stepped out of the car and walked over to the training center offices. Joe noticed on the way that none of the personnel he passed seemed too happy. Bad news traveled fast, he guessed. Once inside the building, Pieter and Zack met them. Joe introduced Horace to his two friends.

"Where's Abner?", asked Joe.

"He's on the phone right now", said Pieter. "He should be with us in a minute. The gate guard told us you were coming, and we passed the word along to Abner".

"Let's go over to the briefing room and talk a bit while we're waiting, then", said Joe. They left word with the secretary for Abner to join them there, then wandered into the large room.

"So, what's on your mind, boss?", asked Pieter as they sat down.

"I imagine you've heard about the fiasco over at City Hall yesterday", said Joe.

"Yeah, I heard", replied Zack dejectedly.

"What's done is done", said Joe. "No use crying about it now. What we need to do now is to check with your contacts in Forestry and see if we can get some support from them for operations in the upcoming fire season".

Abner came hurrying through the door as Joe finished speaking. "Sorry I'm late, Joe", he said breathlessly. "What's this meeting all about?"

"I need all of you to contact your friends with the U.S. Forest Service, Bureau of Land Management, and with California Division of Forestry", said Joe. "Find out if they're still interested in what we have to offer. After yesterday's disaster, there's no telling what they think of us".

"I just finished talking to one friend before I got in here", said Abner. "He was concerned that we were going to fold up shop. I told him there was nothing to worry about. There is nothing to worry about, right Joe?", he asked anxiously.

"About us closing up shop? Not a chance!", replied Joe forcefully. "I haven't invested this much time and effort in the organization just to shut it down when we get in a little hot water. As long as we've got customers willing to do business with us, I intend to keep the doors open. But I need to know if we have any customers left, and that's where you guys come in. Like I said, call everybody you know and ask them whether they still want to play ball with us. Then get the answers back to me. Judging by the looks on the personnel I saw outside, a whole bunch of people are uncertain about what we've done and what we intend to do".

"And we intend to keep operating, right?", said Zack.

"Until I say otherwise", Joe answered.

"From the concern my friend up at Sacramento showed, I'd say CDF is very interested in what we can do this fire season", said Abner. "He works at one of the biggest Air Attack bases in the country at Redding. If they're interested, you can bet that the others are too".

"Sounds encouraging", said Joe. "OK, you guys know what to do. I'm going to kick around the facility here for an hour or two. See what kind of mood you can determine and we'll meet back here at, say, 4:30 this afternoon".

They parted at the office doorway. The command staff went to their desks to start calling, while Joe and Horace walked out towards the hangers. It seemed unusual not to see the crews working on planes or personnel training out in the open field. Joe found most of them just standing around in the hangers and garages, talking amongst themselves. When Joe approached the garage, several crews fell silent and started glancing nervously around.

"Hi guys, what's up?", asked Joe as he came over and leaned up against an APC.

"Nothing much today, sir", answered Manuel Hermosa. "When are we going to see some action?"

"I won't lie to you guys", said Joe. "We're in a mess of trouble right now. I've got the bosses calling around to figure out if we're alive or dead as far as the Forestry people go. I say we're still alive, and so does one Forestry guy up in Sacramento. I'll have a better answer for you in a couple of hours, if you want to stick around".

"Will do, sir", said Manuel. As Joe walked away, Manuel shook his head slowly. "He's worried, man. I don't like the feel of this".

"Man, you never like the feel of nothin'", said Jose in exasperation. "If they told you we was goin' into action in five minutes you'd be worried 'cause you had to call your old lady and tell her you wouldn't be home for dinner. Then you'd probably worry that we wouldn't get to the LZ till it was dark. Then you'd probably find somethin' else to worry about once we got there!"

"Did anybody ever tell you that you talk too much, pea-brain?", snapped Manuel.

"Just you, man", replied Jose. "That gives you somethin' else to complain about".

"If you two keep this up, I'm going somewhere else", said George Ostermann. "And I thought *my* brother and I fought a lot. Sheesh!"

Joe and Horace continued meandering past the buildings, noticing the concerned looks on the faces of the men. Sometimes Joe would try to say something to cheer them up, but most of the time he just nodded at them. They knew as well as Joe did that their backs were against the wall. He just hoped the news from up north was not all bad.

When 4:15 rolled around, Joe couldn't stand the suspense anymore. He and Horace walked back over to the offices. He looked into the windows and saw that Abner was not at his desk. He walked in the door and noticed Zack and Pieter were away from their phones also. He hurried into the briefing room and there sat the three friends. They gave him a big smile when he walked in.

"What about it?", asked Joe expectantly. "Are we still in the ballgame?"

"CDF has given you a go-ahead to operate anywhere in California", said Abner. "And they own a lot more wildland than any of the counties down here. I'd say we'll have enough business from them without the south counties even being involved".

"I couldn't talk to everybody of importance at USFS and BLM", said Zack, "but those I could raise were all for our participation in this year's operations. I think that was the prevailing mood with their higher-ups, too. And like Abner said, they own a *ton* of wildland. I wouldn't be a bit surprised if we got *plenty* of business this coming season!"

"Hot Dog!", said Joe. "If you guys will excuse me, I have a few firefighters to give some good news to!" He rushed out the door, closely pursued by Horace.

After Joe had left, Pieter gave Abner a sly look and said, "You think he was excited?"

"Maybe just a little", said Abner with a chuckle. The room suddenly reverberated with a chorus of relieved laughter from the three men. Soon, the entire base was experiencing the same phenomenon.

Chapter 26

"Welcome to the lst Composite Squadron", said Pieter. Around him stood some new and some veteran Firebombers pilots. Bob Mitchell and Dick Morrison had volunteered for the position of one of the Tag-Team firebombers, bringing along their beloved 'Gertie's Garters'. In addition, a new plane was pulled out of the spares and would be piloted by a couple of new hires, Jimmy Rawlins and Tim Ridgeway.

More personnel changes had been made in the existing squadrons, as Suzie West and her crew had transferred (for the second time) into this new squadron, at the special request of Joe. Her transport was to carry Joe's CCC van. Two additional transport crews had been added. Both of the pilots and co-pilots were from 711th Special Operations Squadron. The crews from the two Hawkeyes rounded out the group. Zack was briefing the drivers of the two new CCC vans over in the office complex.

"This is a one-of-a-kind squadron within Firebombers Incorporated", Pieter continued. "You're responsible for getting the command staff to the landing site, directing traffic control, and providing emergency retardant drops in times when the main squadrons are not available. You Hawkeye crews have already been with us for awhile, so I don't have to brief you on how we operate. I included you so that you could get to know the rest of the people in your squadron. Some of you have worked with us before in other squadrons. I'm relying on you to fill in the blanks with the new people if I miss any important material.

"The squadron name which I've chosen is going to be 'the Hunters', since most of this squadron's operations will be in the role of hunting for fires and directing attacks on them. You aircrews will be able to pick the name of your own planes... subject to approval from the staff, of course".

That comment drew a few chuckles and knowing winks from several of the assembled crews. "This is a multipurpose group", Pieter said. "You are probably charged with the greatest responsibility within the entire air-wing. If this squadron doesn't get to the fire, we lose our command structure and our strategic overview of the battle. In short, we're blind, deaf, and dumb.

"You have all been selected because of your proven track-record with us, or outstanding military service, or both. But don't let that go to your heads. We expect exemplary performances from each and every one of you. In fact, the success of our missions depends on it. Are there any questions before I go on? No? Very well then, we'll begin our tour of the facilities here."

For the next couple of hours, Pieter took everyone around the hangers and garages, filling them in on company philosophy and ideals. For the most part, the crews who had been with firebombers for a while already were bored stiff. The newcomers, however, absorbed as much of the new information as they could. Pieter took them over to Talon Aerospace and turned them loose on their own recognizance for an hour so they could get some lunch in the cafeteria or outside.

Jimmy and his co-pilot Tim drove over to a local burger joint. Jimmy had eaten enough of Talon Aerospace's cafeteria food for his interests. He wanted to get something better. While they were waiting for their order, he and Tim struck up a conversation.

"So you say you've been flying planes since you were fifteen?", asked Tim incredulously.

"Yep, ever since mah feet could reach the pedals", Jimmy chortled.

"What kind of flying did you start out doing?", Tim asked.
"Mostly crop-dustin'. Mah family had a little farm up in Macon, Georgia. Daddy never had enough money to have a crop-duster come in and treat his crops, so ah went down to the local airstrip where a friend showed me how to fly for free".

"For free?", asked Tim in surprise. "That was some friend! It cost me just about every penny I could save up to get flying lessons. Wasn't until I was in the military that I finally finished my pilot training. Ran out of money before the instructor ran out of lessons".

"Wull, this here fellar was a friend of mah family from way back", said Jimmy. "He saw ah was crazy to fly, so's he took me up when he wanted to practice hisself. Weren't long afore ah was flyin' as good as him. By the time ah was eighteen, ah was good enough to get a job with a crop-dustin' company over in the next county. Ah could dust mah daddy's crops fer next to nothin. Got purty good at it, too".

"What unit were you in when you were in the military?", asked Tim.

"Thirty-fifth Tac Fighter Wing", said Jimmy. "When ah got mah discharge, Talon Aerospace picked me up and gave me a job flyin' simulators fer them".

"So you were a fighter pilot, huh?", asked Tim.

"More like a fighter-bomber pilot", answered Jimmy. "Mah crop-dustin came in handy fer dropping ordnance on target. Got me a couple citations and a DFC doin' it too".

"That's sure more than I ever did", said Tim as the food arrived. They walked over to the table and started to eat. Around a mouthful of burger, Tim said, "I used to fly S-3 Vikings off of the carrier Saratoga with VS-22".

"A Navy puke, huh?", Jimmy teased.

"Better than being an Air Force puke!", Tim retorted. They both continued talking as they ate. Soon, the hour was almost up and Jimmy suggested they head back for the barn.

Pieter was already waiting there for them. He concluded the tour with a visit to the Training Center briefing room. There, he explained a bit about the tactics of firefighting and spotting fires. By the time he finished, it was nearly quitting time. He herded the crews out the door, then bid them all a good evening.

Over the days that followed, Jimmy and Tim debated about names for their new plane, finally settling on 'Wind Dancer', the name of the last crop-duster Jimmy had flown before entering the Air Force. Soon, they became one of the best crews in the entire organization. Jimmy's ability to bullseye a burn-barrel - even without the computer -became legendary in the space of a few short weeks.

The CCC transport crews drilled hard on delivering their cargoes on target with a minimum of bumps. Soon, Pieter deemed them to be ready to integrate into the organization as a whole. It was none too soon.

"The trial date is set for August 31, 1994", said Allen over the phone. "This gives us several weeks. We shall have our defense formulated by that time, I assure you".

"OK, thanks Allen", said Joe. He hung up the phone, then pulled out his scheduler and entered the date inside. Things had calmed down considerably since that June fiasco.

It was now July and, surprisingly, no fires had broken out where Firebombers Incorporated was needed as of yet. The crews had been training constantly and were sharp as razors, but Zack had warned Joe that they would begin getting stale if they didn't see some action soon. That would change sooner or later, Joe thought. Preferably sooner.

Abner was monitoring a front crossing the coast up north of San Francisco out at the Training Center. "Zack, take a look at this weather report. The radar imaging shows no precipitation. I'd say we've got a potential lightning bust on our hands. What do you say we get everybody off the training field and prep the equipment for departure?"

"Not a bad idea", agreed Zack. "Tell the maintenance crews to give all the equipment a thorough check and send everybody else home for some rest and chow. Let's see, it's four now, that storm will probably be into timber country in an hour. Give it another couple of hours to start some fires and an hour after that before Forestry makes a cattle-call".

"Call them back in at 8 P.M. then?".

"Yeah, that should be about right. Figure an hour to brief the crews, another to load, still another to fuel, and one more to get everybody off the ground. Add two hours minimum transit time and another to load up the bombers at the lakes, that puts us on top of the fires by..."

"About 3 A.M."

"Yeah, about three. Better get Pieter in here and brief him on what's going on. I'll call the boss".

"Joe, it looks like there may be some action up north in another few hours", Zack said over the phone. "I'm standing-down the crews so we can perform some maintenance checks on the equipment, then we'll have a briefing at about eight this evening".

"You think there's going to be fires up north, huh?", said Joe, his excitement rising.

"I think I'd be willing to lay money on it, yeah. In any case, it'll be good practice for the crews even if nothing does come of it. They'll all get a feel for sleeping in the hangers and garages if nothing happens, but if I'm right..."

"We'll be among the first to arrive in force", said Joe excitedly. "What do you plan to send up first, engine companies or firejumpers?"

"Probably half and half again. I imagine engine companies will be the biggest demand item initially, so we'll send three of those, along with two of firejumpers and both of the Cat Teams".

"This will be a first. Both Cat Teams in use at once and everybody going in at night. I'll call Jerry and Dave, see if they're interested in going along".

"Should we expect to see you at eight, then?"

"Yep, I'll be there." After he had hung up the phone, Joe wondered what the next twenty-four hours held. Not for the first time in his life, he wished he had a crystal ball with which to peer into the future.

"Welcome, everyone", greeted Zack when the crews all assembled in the briefing room at eight. Joe could hardly believe he had so many people working for him. And this group didn't even include the maintenance crews, who were not going along and would, therefore, not require a briefing.

"We have a suspicious-looking weather pattern crossing the coast above San Francisco at this time", Zack continued. "This is why we've brought you back. We expect some fires up north before morning. Our plan of action will be to deliver three engine companies and two companies of firejumpers to the site of the fires, then return our transports in order to load the remaining personnel and equipment.

"Both Cat Teams will be inserted into the region, and all five firebomber squadrons will accompany the force north. We could be working out of Air Attack bases from Ukiah, by the coast, as far inland as Grass Valley, and as far north as Redding. Nothing more is known at this time. There is the possibility that there will be no fires, but after conferring with Pieter Van Vrees and Abner Hollis, I believe there is a high probability that we will see some action before sunup tomorrow".

At this point, Joe saw several people turn and smile at their neighbors. Finally, they were going to get to do what they had trained for months to do: fight a real wildfire!

"The first wave will consist of the following units: 1st Composite Squadron; 101st through 105th Lift Squadrons; 201st through 205th Firebomber Squadrons; the 301st Refueling Squadron; 401st and 402nd Heavy Lift Squadrons; 501st through 503rd Engine Companies; 601st and 602nd Cat Teams; and 701st and 702nd Firejumper Companies. The rest of you go in the second wave when the transports return.

"For now, we want you to load up your transports with the necessary equipment, then fuel all the planes. By that time the ground crews will have erected cots and sleeping bags in the hangers and garages for you to rest on. Get some shuteye while you still can. If a fire does break out, we'll have you all back in here before you leave so that you know where to go. After all, knowing where to go might be of some importance to most of you", he said with a grin. "Dismissed!"

Joe worked his way to the front of the room as everyone was leaving. This gave him some idea of what a salmon went through trying to swim upstream against the current. Pieter was talking with Zack and Abner as Joe stepped up by the podium to listen.

"We've gotten scattered reports of small fires over close to Bartlett Springs", said Pieter excitedly. "CDF is mum for the moment, but they may be calling us within the hour".

"Not before we have the planes loaded and ready to go, I hope", said Joe.

"I doubt it", said Zack. "But we'll just have to do the best that we can".

"Where's the front now?", asked Abner.

"Crossing the Sacramento River valley just north of Sacramento", Pieter answered.

"Heading for the Sierras", said Zack quietly.

"Looks like it", agreed Pieter. "I'll bet that phone rings within the hour".

"Sounds like a pretty safe bet to me", said Abner.

"I thought Forestry usually got a call out when they saw a front like this. Before there were any lightning strikes, I mean", said Joe.

"They already have called up several of the contractors and some BLM personnel", replied Pieter. "But they don't want to tap us until they've got something that looks nasty. After all, we can put almost two-thousand guys in the fire-line, plus almost thirty air-tankers overhead. We aren't much interested in little spot-fires. We're designed to fight major fires, those above a couple of thousand acres".

"This waiting is killing me, though", said Joe.

"Better get used to it", cautioned Abner. "That's the way it is in fire season. You see the weather turning bad somewhere, then you loiter around the phone waiting for that call. You almost hate to take a shower or use the toilet because you think that phone is going to ring the second you walk away".

"It usually did", said Pieter with a laugh.

"Or when you're sound asleep", said Zack with a grimace. "I lost count of how many nights I got a call to head out during the summer. I was usually right in the middle of a pleasant dream, too".

"I'd say you'll be wide awake when this one comes in", teased Joe.

"Can't say", replied Zack. "The phone hasn't rung yet". Joe turned and looked expectantly at the phone, which simply sat there. After a few more minutes of conversation, Abner suggested they all go get some coffee at the vending machine outside. Two hours passed.

"You think it's for real, Manuel?", Jose asked excitedly. The Cat Teams were sprawled out on their cots. Manuel was off to Jose's left, George was off to his right. Jose was laying there staring a the ceiling as he talked. "You think we're goin' to go tonight?"

"Feels like it", replied Manuel. "The bosses sure seem to think so. That's good enough for me".

"Wish we had night sights on our ride", said Jose. He lifted up on one elbow to face his friend. "Think we could talk 'em into gettin' us some?"

"I've seen them advertised for about $500 apiece", said Manuel. "Don't seem like much compared to all the money they spent on the rest of this gear".

"Only $500?", said Jose. "That ain't bad. Where'd you see 'em?"

"Some military surplus magazine", answered Manuel. "These were the infantry snoopers, not the APC driver types".

"Don't matter to me", said Jose. "I just don't like the idea of toolin' around at night without bein' able to see, know what I mean?"

"With you driving, yeah I know what you mean", said Manuel churlishly. "You'd probably put us over a cliff!"

"Man, I don't even know why I talk to you sometimes!", said an exasperated Jose as he laid back down on his cot.

"Me too!", George snickered.

"Well Patrick, what's our status?", Bob asked the mechanic.

"She'll get you there and back again", replied the now-filthy mechanic. "I pulled every piece o' hardware off the beastie and gave it a good goin' over just tah be sure. She's as ready as she'll ever be!"

"We'll kind of miss not having you along on this trip", said Dick. "Won't seem the same without you".

"Ah, that's a nice sentiment", said Patrick. "But you lads needn't worry. I can be up there in two shakes of a cat's tail, if need be. We mechanics all got together and outfitted one o' our spare C-130s wit' tools and the like for emergencies".

"Yeah, but who's going to fly you up there?", asked Bob.

"That's the problem we run intah when we finished th' outfittin'", said Patrick, his face changing into a slight scowl. "I havena' figured out that part yet, but I'm workin' on it".

"I suppose one of the transport crews could fly back down and do it", said Bob thoughtfully. "They have to come back down for the extra companies anyway. Why not have an extra crew, from one of the Cat Team transports, for instance, come down with the planes picking up the second wave? They could fly this whole maintenance crew back up".

"What do you say we go bounce this idea off Pieter?", said Dick. "Patrick, you want to come along?"

"Lead on, McDuff!", said Patrick. They found Pieter a few minutes later. He and the rest of the command staff were sipping coffee outside the offices.

"Pieter, we've got a proposal for you", said Bob.

"How much is it going to cost me?", asked Joe warily.

"Shoot!", said Pieter, after giving Joe a wink.

"We haven't got any kind of heavy maintenance crew along with our squadrons when we head north", began Bob. "How about if a spare aircrew is sent back down with the transports picking up the second wave. This aircrew could fly a C-130 with all the equipment in it back up north. That way, you'd have a fully equipped workshop, more or less, plus the workcrew to service any planes that developed mechanical problems the flight engineers couldn't fix".

"Pieter, I thought you said all the spare transports were spoken for!", Joe said accusingly.

"We had two new arrivals a week ago", replied Pieter sheepishly. "I guess I forgot to tell you about them".

"The fact of the matter, your lordship, is that the mechanics have outfitted one o' them spares wit' everything we needs to work on these beasties in the field", Patrick added quickly. "It seems a cryin' shame to leave all this expert help lollin' around down here when there could be jobs needin' doin' up north".

"He does have a point", said Abner. "Why didn't we think of this?"

"I can't imagine why", said Zack dryly. "We've had so few things to do lately".

"OK, Pat", said Pieter, casting an annoyed look at Zack. "You and your buddies can tag along with the second wave. Just be sure you're all ready to go when they are. We're going to be in a little bit of a rush".

"Thank ye, gentlemen!", said Patrick. He walked briskly back to the hangers while Bob and Dick stayed to talk for a few minutes. Their conversation was interrupted fifteen minutes later by a phone call. Abner just about ran Zack down as they both bolted for the door. After they had been gone for a few minutes, Zack came rushing back outside.

"We've got a fire up northeast of Loma Rica!", he said excitedly. "CDF wants us up at Redding ASAP!"

"Time for a wake-up call!", said an elated Joe.

As Joe headed into the office, the rest of the command staff, along with Bob and Dick, went around the complex rousing the personnel and herding them back over to the briefing room.

"We have what looks to be a major fire shaping up in the foothills of the Sierras northeast of Sacramento", said Zack. "The operation will unfold like this. All firebomber squadrons will fly in empty and tank up with water up there. The flight plans you've just received detail your water sources as either Englebright Lake or Collins Lake on the way in, then at Bullards Bar Reservoir once we're on station.

"The lst Composite Squadron will head for Redding, where the CCC vans will be dropped off. The command staff will coordinate with CDF. The Hawkeyes will perform traffic control and assign safe orbital coordinates for the transports until we know where CDF wants the ground crews put down. By that time, the firebombers should be tanked up and ready to go. They will be assigned holding orbits by the Air Traffic Controller. I want the refueling squadron to top off the firebombers on the way north. Hawk One will have the duty for the first eight hour shift, Hawk Two will take over after that time. Each Hawkeye will be based out of Redding and will remain on the ground until the shift-change occurs.

"Once the first wave has been delivered, all of the Lift squadrons and 'Thunderbolt' from the 402nd Heavy Lift Squadron will return here to embark the second wave. I want the crew from 'Thunderbolt' to take a specially outfitted maintenance transport back north with the second wave. This plane will carry maintenance personnel and equipment along for servicing aircraft at

Redding. We will give you approach and destination vectors once you reach the area of the fire. Any questions?"

Jose raised his hand. When Zack acknowledged him, he stood up. "Are we goin' to be drivin' in the dark, sir**",** Jose asked.

"Probably so", answered Zack.

"Do we have any night sights around that we could use?", asked Jose.

"See me after the meeting and we'll talk about it", replied Zack. "Any other questions? Departure time is in one hour at.... 12:30 A.M. or, for you military types, 0030 hours. Dismissed!"

Jose weaved his way through the crowd with Manuel tagging along behind. When he reached the podium, Zack came down off the stage to speak with him.

"Now, what's this about night sights?", asked Zack.

"The Army uses these special night-vision goggles called 'night sights', sir", said Jose. "Makes it a whole lot easier to see in the dark. It's tough tryin' to see outside if it's black as pitch, know what I mean?"

"Sounds like the low-light TV systems we use on the firebombers", Pieter remarked. "So they have these for ground personnel too, huh?"

"Yes sir", replied Manuel. "We had some of the snipers and other guys who carried these things to see better in the dark. We had them built into some of the APCs and tanks, too. Made it easier to see when we had night ops".

"Dave, this sounds like something up your alley", Pieter remarked. "Think you can rig the Cat Teams with something like this before we leave?"

"Not on this short of notice**",** Dave replied. "Maybe when we get back I could install something".

"It would sure help us out a lot if you could, sir", said Jose.

Manuel tugged at Jose's sleeve. The two of them turned and melted into the crowd exiting the room.

After they were out of earshot, Zack said, "That's twice tonight we've found things which we hadn't thought of before causing some potential problems. I wonder how many more we'll find before this operation is over?"

"Probably more than we would like to have", said Pieter. He was instantly reminded of an old military saying which stated that few plans survive the first few minutes of action. The same principal would probably operate here.

Jerry and Dave walked over to the transport hanger with Joe. They boarded the transport holding their CCC van and strapped in. Zack and his lieutenants had piled into the 'Fire Boss' CCC van at about the same time. Abner and his staff were the last ones to strap into their van. The transports then taxied out.

"Hawk One, you are cleared for takeoff", said the Talon Aerospace controller. "Wind is eight point five knots bearing zero-niner-zero. Good luck and have a nice day!"

"Copy that, tower", replied the Hawkeye pilot. "First Composite Squadron departing Gateway".

The taxiways were once again crammed with idling aircraft. It was pitch black outside with no moonlight at all. The airbase was lit up like a freightyard, though, and the maintenance crews were all standing in front of the hangers watching the proceedings.

"I've not seen a sight like this since Britain during the war", said Patrick wistfully. "The RAF used to send out thousand-bomber raids at night. Twas quite a sight tah see so many planes at our airbase gettin' ready tah join the rest leavin' other bases around us. Ah, this brings back memories, that it does".

At a few minutes after 12:30 A.M., the ungainly-looking Hawkeye lumbered down the runway and took off. The remaining planes took off at ten second intervals. The sleeping countryside was soon awakened by the droning of aircraft engines heading north in the darkness. Many people who lived near Talon Aerospace came out into the warm summer night to see what was going on. The night was alive with noise and the view was striking as line after line of aircraft flew overhead, their anti-collision and running lights brightly lit. The show seemed to go on forever as still more planes lifted out of San Bernardino. Finally, quiet returned to the sleepy communities as the last of the planes departed over the mountains. Almost seventy-five planes were now in the air.

The maintenance crews returned to the hangers and garages. The second-wave personnel found their way to cots where they laid down and tried to sleep. In a few hours it would be their turn to head north. It promised to be a busy day ahead. They decided that they had better get all the sleep they could now, because it might be the last chance they had for a few days.

Chapter 27

Redding was already a busy place when the lst Composite Squadron arrived. Hawk One and the Tag-Team firebombers had broken off from the main body to take up station over Palermo, down by the fire, while Hawk Two and the three CCC transports set down at Redding Air Attack base. CDF ground crews were tanking up a pair of S-2 bombers while a mechanic worked on an OV-10 spotter. A little smokejumper Sherpa STOL (Short Take-Off and Landing) transport was just taxiing up to the Fire Center when the first C-130 pulled up.

The CCC vans were unloaded from the C-130s once they had found a place to park. The odd-looking command control vehicles attracted a crowd almost immediately. Hawk One was already in contact with the Forestry Air Boss and was directing the incoming firebombers to Collins Lake and Englebright Lake for loading operations. All of the firebombers had finished aerial refueling, so the tanker squadron had diverted to Sacramento Metropolitan Airport to refuel themselves. The transport squadrons were assigned safe orbit zones well clear of the fire zone.

Heavy storm clouds rolled across the sky ahead, the underside of those closest to the fires lit eerily by the blaze. "Looks like an inferno down there", Wally Pritchard, pilot of 'Lancer' in the 102nd Lift Squadron (Roadrunners), said to his brother, co-pilot Kevin Pritchard. "I've never seen a forest fire from this height before. It looks like half of that valley is on fire!"

"Yeah, and we've got the just the thing to snuff it, too", Kevin replied confidently.

"You always were the optimist!", snorted Wally in disgust. "We don't even have one guy on the ground yet and you talk as though this thing was already history!"

"That's because I've seen these guys in action", Kevin replied evenly. "They know what they're doing, and we know what we're doing. We can't miss!"

"Sure, sure. We'll see, but I bet that thing is still burning 24 hours from now".

"You're on!", Kevin exclaimed. "Five dollars?"

"Done!", Wally replied. "'Course it's not up to us whether this thing is licked by then anyway. All's we're gonna do is drop off the guys to do it for us".

"Sorta like watching a football game, ain't it?", Kevin said.

Wally didn't answer right away. He had caught a glimmer of reflected light from a plane down by the fire. "Looks like we're not the only ones who fly at night", he said quietly.

The command staff finally broke free of the crowd of onlookers which had formed when they arrived and made their way over to the Fire Center. When they walked into the building, Joe took the command center in with a sweeping gaze. Uniformed fire personnel were manning communications stations, coordinating the fight in the Sierras. Someone shouted Abner's name. A tall fellow wearing a red vest with 'Fire Boss' emblazoned on it came striding out of the crowd which was gathered around a mapboard.

"Abner, you old sod!", the man shouted. "I thought you had retired from the business and gone fishing!"

"Not me, Henry!", replied Abner as he pumped his friend's hand. "I don't plan to ever retire!"

As the rest of his friends walked up, Abner introduced them to Henry. "This is Henry Luce, California Division of Forestry. Judging by his get-up, I'd guess that he's the Fire Boss at this little barbecue".

"Nothing gets past you, does it Abner?", teased Henry. "Welcome to North Ops, gentlemen. I've heard about your outfit from the guys who went to your presentation in L.A. How much did you bring up with you?"

"Not much", said Abner. "Just twenty-seven air-tankers, five companies of firejumpers, five engine companies, and two self-contained Cat Teams. That totals out to about 1600 ground personnel and twenty-five pumpers, all air-deliverable".

Henry let out a loud whistle. "You boys don't mess around, do you? We've only got about a dozen S-2s, 40 smokejumpers, about five hundred ground personnel, and ten companies of pumpers working this thing now. Shoot, with that much stuff, we can allocate you one entire flank of this fire. That might keep you jumping for awhile".

"How big has the bugger gotten?", asked Zack.

"It's up to 6000 acres and still growing", answered Henry. "We've just labeled it a campaign fire. Must have been more than two dozen lightning strikes since that front rolled in a few hours ago. They're scattered over several thousand acres, what with the winds pushing them along".

"We have along our Command Control and Communications vans", said Joe. "We call them CCC vans for short. You're welcome to use mine for coordinating our units if you'd like".

"Really? I'd like to see one!", said Henry.

"Right outside", said Joe. The group walked out to the van Joe planned to use for his staff. Dave was in his element showing off all of the displays and communications gear he had installed in the van.

"This is the down-link from the radar equipment aboard the Hawkeye", Dave explained. "We have all of our communications relayed through the Hawkeye so that we can talk to units separated from us by ridges. The Hawkeye has one senior controller who is responsible for linking units on the ground to the command staff. This same senior controller can give general orders to the firebomber and transport squadrons, while the Air Traffic Controllers, or ATCs, handle the actual course headings and grid destinations. We call the senior controller our Chief Air Controller, or CAC for short".

"Can I talk to my own units using this equipment, though?", asked Henry.

"If they've got radios, we can talk to them", answered Dave.

"So your Hawkeye can track my air-tankers as well as all of your aircraft?", asked Henry.

"And communicate with them, yes", replied Dave. "Take a look at what the display shows right now. These icons with numbers indicate our planes, which have transponders aboard. The other icons show any other aircraft in the area".

"How many planes can you keep track of?", Henry asked.

"Over a hundred with only one Hawkeye", answered Dave. "We can almost double that by putting both Hawkeyes in the air. They would have to determine a division point, like an airport does".

"So what you're telling me is that you could direct every plane we have at this base, plus your own planes", said Henry. "I'm impressed! Tell me, do you people sell these vans?"

"I think Joe is setting up something like that now", replied Dave. "You might want to ask him about it. I just iron out the technical problems".

"And this display here shows the fire, I take it", said Henry as he moved to the second display.

"Yep, that's the readout from the FLIR equipment on the Hawkeye. All of those different colored splotches show the location and intensity of the fires currently burning within a radius of several miles. The legend alongside the display shows the relative heat of each fire. You can clearly see several hot-spots along what looks to be the leading edge of the fire".

"Uh-huh. With the current wind direction, that should be the head of the fire", said Henry. "Doesn't look like much heat left back by the base. What's that really bright area a mile behind the leading edge, a firestorm?"

"Beats me", answered Dave. "Whatever it is, it's mighty hot. Covers a fair amount of area, too. Let's see... about 150 yards across. I don't think I'd want to drive into that thing".

"Are you able to see the actual fires, or only this graphics display?", asked Henry.

"We can show you whatever you want", said Dave. He was really enjoying this. After months of fighting to get funding for the extra features on the display, it was finally paying off in the form of an interested party. Correction, an interested potential customer. "What would you like to see, visual display, visual display with computer-generated grid lines, or FLIR display with grid lines?"

"How about visual by itself, then we can add in the grid lines in a minute", replied Henry.

"OK, here you go!", said Dave. He punched a pair of buttons and the colorful graphics image disappeared, replaced with one of a low-light TV picture showing a thousand square mile area. The only features immediately visible were the fires themselves and the silhouettes of trees and canyons near the flames. Smoke trails could be seen climbing into the sky, but quickly disappeared when they got too far away from the light of the fires.

"Now add the grid lines", commanded Henry

Dave punched another button, and a series of wavy lines representing the grid coordinates was displayed. This made the fires somewhat harder to see, but allowed one to give precise instructions to aircraft approaching the fire.

"Wait a second", said Henry. "The view is changing slightly. Why is that?"

"Because the Hawkeye is orbiting", said Dave. "The plane flies a racetrack pattern, so as it banks over, the image moves accordingly".

"So the FLIR cameras are fixed?"

"Yep. It was the easiest way we had to install them in the time we had. At a later date, I want to retrofit the Hawkeyes with a moveable camera mount, but I've been too busy lately to get anything done on it. I'm afraid you'll have to be satisfied with a little movement for now. We do have a pair of cameras, one starboard and one portside. If you can't see the area you need from one angle, you might be able to see it from another. We also have the option of communicating directly with the pilot. We can direct him to orbit a specific location if scrutiny of one location is required".

"I like it! Can you also display weather information?"

"Uh, what kind of weather information?"

"You know, temperature, humidity, barometric pressure, stuff like that".

"Well, uh, no, I can't", said Dave timidly. "I never thought about the need for that kind of data".

"Time to start thinking about it", said Henry. "We always have at least one mobile weather station along at a fire. We need to have up-to-the-minute meteorological information. It helps us to know what to expect out of the fire and the weather. We put the gear in the back of a motorhome so we can move it around during the fire. Something you might want to think about adding to your other equipment here. Judging by the complexity of this stuff, a little old weather station shouldn't be that much trouble to install. You might not even want to put one in each van, maybe just the one for the Fire Boss".

"Knowing Joe, he'll want one in every van. Yeah, that wouldn't be hard to do. Thanks for the suggestion Henry".

"My pleasure. Oh, by the way. Can you send encrypted information over these radios?"

"You mean a secure link, like the military uses? No, nothing like that. Besides, our birds don't have any encrypted receivers in them. Why do you ask?"

"We've had problems occasionally with unauthorized people using the same radio frequencies we use. It doesn't happen very often, but we have experienced some problems of that sort".

"Who would want to interfere with a firefighting operation?"

"Who knows", said Henry. "I heard a story once of a pro-golfer who was approached in the locker room by some big beefy guy who said he wanted to shake the golfer's hand. It was during a tournament, so the golfer just thought this guy was a fan. Well, the golfer's hand was swallowed up in this big gorilla's mitt and as they kept shaking, the golfer's hand was being crushed. Pretty soon, the golfer was on his knees begging the 'fan' to let loose, but the guy just kept on crushing the golfer's hand. Finally, another contestant came into the locker room and saw what was going on. He yelled at the guy to let go, at which point the big guy took a swing at the other golfer, then walked out of the locker room. By the time security went looking for the guy, he had disappeared. The golfer went back out and played the worst game of golf anybody could remember him having, because of his injured hand. Most of the people he told this story to figured that somebody had a lot of money bet on this golfer losing, and that they had decided to make sure he would lose big time".

"Is that story true?"

"As far as I know it is. So it just goes to show you, people you don't even know may have an investment in your failure. The same principle applies to firefighting. Some people want to see a section of timber or houses or buildings go up in smoke, all for their own reasons".

"Gee, maybe I'd better think about an encrypter for our radios, then", said Dave thoughtfully.

"Just a suggestion. So, what else can this van do?"

"Zero to sixty in twelve seconds!"

"Not bad, but does it get good gas mileage?"

Abner and Zack had walked over to their vans while Dave was entertaining Henry. They powered up the on-board systems and checked on the situation with the fire and their squadrons. The tankers had refueled at Sacramento Metropolitan and were waiting for orders from the Hawkeye. The ATC had decided that there was no point in the tankers taking off until there was a need for retardant and/or fuel refills on the firebombers. The transports would be heading south as soon as they had dropped off their cargo, so they wouldn't need refueling at this time (unless the higher-ups continued to dawdle on the ground). With a range of over 3400 miles, the C-130s could loiter quite awhile and still have enough fuel for the journey to San Bernardino and back. The transports could always be refueled on the return from Talon Aerospace if need be.

"How many men did you say you have in the air at the moment?", Henry asked Zack as he climbed into the Fire Boss van.

"We've got two reinforced companies of firejumpers, 600 total, three engine companies, which equals 15 pumpers, and four bulldozers in our two Cat Teams", replied Zack.

"What are the capabilities on your pumpers?", Henry asked. He settled into a chair next to Zack and looked at the FLIR display.

"They have the capability of outputting 1750 gpm through the cannon", said Zack. "We've got four pump outlets for hoses and a front-suction arrangement for reloading at streams and lakes".

"How steep a grade can these things take?", asked Henry.

"Up to 45-degrees has been tried", replied Zack. "I'm not real fond of finding out how steep before one rolls over, so if you don't mind, we'll skip that one, OK?"

"Just checking", said Henry. "This is the first time out for your people, right?"

"We've fought several practice fires, one out-of-control demonstration fire, and a few of the guys even have experience in fighting a refinery fire", answered Zack. "In fact, you may have rubbed elbows with some of our guys last season. We loaned most of them out to CDF during fire season last year, so you might spot a few friendly faces in the ranks".

"That's where I'd heard the name before!", exclaimed Henry. "It's been bothering me ever since Abner introduced you guys. I did work with one company of firejumpers on the ground last season over by, where was it .... yeah over by Ukiah".

"Yep, they were there. Probably under Jack Bazranian, our current Ground Boss".

"I remember Jack. He seemed competent enough. I got the feeling he had fought forest fires a couple of times before".

"Several. He and I worked mostly in the Big Bear area. I'm surprised our paths haven't crossed before now, Henry".

"Oh, it's not really that surprising. I used to work for a logging company, running their fire department". His eyes seemed to look off into the distance as he remembered the past. "That was where Abner and I met. He was going around to the fire departments in our area as a kind of CDF liaison. He liked the way I ran the fire department at the mill and asked if I had ever thought about joining CDF. I told him I wasn't interested. Then, only about two years ago now, the mill went bankrupt and I was laid off. Abner vouched for me with CDF, and the rest, as they say, is history".

"So you've only been fighting forest fires for a couple of years? How did you get up so far in the hierarchy?"

"My big mouth!", said Henry with a laugh. "I used to contribute articles to a fire industry newsmagazine. I had looked into ways to innovate firefighting tactics. I guess a few of the Forestry folks took notice of it and tried me out as Ground Boss. My units were so successful that they moved me up the ladder to Fire Boss for this fire".

"So this is your first crack at a fire as Fire Boss? Well, I hope it works out. Nervous?"

"I'd be lying if I said I wasn't. This should be quite a show. A green Fire Boss and a green firefighting outfit!"

"Well, you know what they say. If it's green, it won't get burned quite as easy!", said Zack with a smile. "Don't count these boys out. The line commanders are all seasoned veterans and most of the crews are former military types. I doubt that many will spook when it gets hairy out there".

"Let's hope not. I think I'll let you guys fight as a cohesive unit after all. I'd thought of parceling your guys out among the veteran units in order to stiffen your lines a bit. From what you say, though, they might do OK on their own".

"It's probably a good idea to keep our units together. They've trained as cohesive units. Each group knows pretty much what the others can do. Split them apart now and you might undermine their confidence in themselves, especially if they found out the reason for your dispositions".

"My mind is made up then", said Henry as he got up. "Just make sure your confidence isn't misplaced. There's a turbulent air mass heading in. Once that mixes it up with this fire, there's no telling what can happen. You had better have your firejumpers on the ground soon. If the wind picks up they might sustain casualties on landing".

"Just tell me where you want them and I'll see to it. I think the transports are getting kind of tired of flying around in circles as it is. The aircrews are probably dizzy by now!"

"Can you superimpose a grid over this display", asked Henry. He pointed to the visual display. Zack punched a few buttons and a flowing grid appeared on the screen. "There, at grid ... 23. That would be an excellent spot. The fire's base for the right flank is just a half-mile from there and I don't think you'll have any problems with smoke distorting the view when your transports come in".

Zack toggled the radio transceiver and said, "Hawk One, this is Talon Fire Boss. Commence landing ops at grid zero-two-three, acknowledge".

High above them, the Hawkeye was making a graceful turn. The two attendant firebombers of the Tag-Team flew a racetrack pattern nearby. The senior controller acknowledged Zack's directions and began issuing orders to the distant transports. The 401st Heavy Lift Squadron (Alleycats) broke out of their orbit and began descending. Each plane in succession followed the lead transport down. Once they had all formed up, the 402nd Heavy Lift (Tomcats) also broke out of orbit and followed behind at 7000 yards distance.

The lead transport in each of these squadrons carried a team which would check the LZ/DZ ground for suitability. The first team would go down with the initial Cat Team drops. The second team would remain aboard the transport and await the arrival of the second wave, at which time they would bail out over the LZ/DZ selected for that wave.

"You sure they can't land this thing and let us drive off?", Jose asked one loadmaster in the third transport.

"Sorry, but it looks like you'll have to jump", said the loadmaster. Over in the corner, Manuel was giving their APC a last-minute parachute check. He looked over at a worried Jose and made a clucking sound like a chicken. Jose shot him an angry glance, then heard the loadmaster reply to something over his headset. The ramp began grinding downward and the rush of air could be heard outside. The rear blast deflectors were extended and full flaps applied. The cargo crew prepared to eject the APC.

As the transports approached their targets, Zack switched camera angles and directed Henry's attention to the fast-approaching transports. Both squadrons were now down to 3000 feet and flying in echelon formation. They slowed to drop-speed and suddenly drogue chutes emerged from the back of each, pulling pallets with vehicles strapped on from the rear of the first five planes. Each pallet was supported by seven or eight parachutes (extra chutes had been installed in case of streamers unbalancing the load).

"Is it my imagination, or are the headlights on those vehicles turned on?", asked Henry.

"Yeah, we have the crews turn them on before ejection so it gives the CAT Team crews an idea of where the ground is. It's hard enough getting them to jump at night. It would be harder still if they couldn't see where they were going!"

Once the pallets were out, several individuals also dropped out of each transport. As the last parachute opened, the lead squadron raised ramps and increased speed, quickly pulling away from the pursuing squadron.

"They can have that job!", said Henry under his breath. Zack looked at him out of the corner of his eye and smiled, then went back to watching the display. Zack checked the ID of the incoming squadron on the ATC display, then returned his attention to the camera view. Four-thirty in the morning, he thought. About time we get somebody on the ground.

Henry saw the other formation of transports coming in about a mile from the first squadron's Drop Zone. Once all planes were over open ground, they too ejected their cargoes, then sped away to the east. The parachutes quickly drifted to the ground and the meadow became alive with a flurry of activity.

"Man, I'm glad to be back on the ground, know what I mean?", said a smiling Jose.

"Forget about being on the ground and think about getting this thing off the pallet!", groused Manuel.

In a few minutes, diesel engines were coughing, then roaring to life. One by one, the APCs and bulldozers rumbled off their pallets. The crews then got out and attached tow lines to the pallets and towed them out of the way. The ground was examined by the advance team and pronounced fit for air-landings. The Chief Air Controller (CAC) was informed of this fact and the next three squadrons were given their orders. The lead transport squadron, 101st Lift Squadron (Ace Movers) broke out of their orbit pattern and began descending. As soon as the five planes in the squadron had formed up into a line, the other two squadrons carrying engine companies, 102nd and 103rd Lift (Roadrunners and Knights), began following them down.

Zack heard the orders from the ATC over the radio and saw the transports begin their runs in. "Now you're going to see quite a sight", said Zack with a look of satisfaction on his face.

"What is it?", asked Henry.

"Air-landing of our engine companies from those three lines of transports", replied Zack. "I must have seen this over a dozen times, but it still gives me a charge when these guys touch down. Watch".

The first line of five transports began to slow and distance themselves from each other using their SKE (station keeping equipment) radar to ensure proper spacing. The first transport skimmed across the early morning shadows as it passed the tree-line at the edge of the meadow. The green luminescence of the image added an eerie element to the picture. A group of white objects blossomed out the back of the transport as it skimmed low over the meadow. The drag chutes quickly filled with air and yanked the Zephyr out the back of the transport. Once the pumper was on the ground, it's driver proceeded towards the edge of the meadow, out of the path of the incoming transports. The pilot of its transport firewalled the throttles and rapidly climbed away as the next transport in line began his approach.

"That's a pretty slick delivery system you guys have there", said Henry admiringly. "I figured you were going to land the planes and then off-load your equipment at that time. This makes for a whole lot less delay, though".

"It can be a little rough on the equipment at times, but we've found it to be the most effective means of delivery to the fire", said Zack. "The trucks will now move to the edge of the drop zone and each turn on a pair of million-candlepower floodlights to illuminate the drop zone for the firejumpers. We get less casualties if they can see where they are supposed to land".

The remaining pumper transports each disgorged their cargoes, then formed up by squadrons. After checking with CAC, they headed back to San Bernardino to pick up the remaining companies. Each engine crew was busy bundling up the parachutes when the ATC gave orders for the firejumper transports to commence their approaches.

The lead transport of the 104th Lift Squadron (Roadhogs) began reducing altitude to 3000 feet and headed due north, closely followed by the remaining planes in the squadron. Next came the 105th Lift Squadron (Long Haulers) tagging along behind the 104th. The 104th was now seven minutes out. The jumpmasters began their litany as the red jump lights came on in the cargo holds.

This time, all the firejumpers would be able to eject during the first pass, since the meadow was over a mile-and-a-half long.

"I see another group of transports coming in on the ATC display", said Henry as he stared intently at the down-linked radar plot. "Are these more engine companies?"

"Nope, these are our firejumpers", replied Zack. "We only brought two companies along. The other three squadrons have probably already headed back for the second wave. Let's see, yeah. See the three groups of planes heading south? Those are the three squadrons which just off-loaded the engine companies. They should be back with the rest of the companies in a few hours".

"Better tell them to make it snappy", said Henry. "Like I said, there's an unstable airmass crossing the coast now. It will probably be here in another three or four hours. If you plan to do any more airdrops, it might get a little tricky with turbulent air".

"I'm glad you mentioned that", said Zack. "I'd better relay that to them now, before they move out of CAC's range". He toggled a few switches on the communications panel, then relayed this information to the Hawkeye. The departing squadrons were given the word and all of the transports accelerated to maximum speed, which would get them to San Bernardino nearly twice as fast as the trip north, since they didn't have to slow down for the firebombers on this return leg.

"OK, that should get them there by a little before six", said Zack. Given two hours to reload and lift off, and a little over an hour for the return trip to here, they should be on station by about 9:30 A.M."

"That's going to be cutting it a little close timewise", said Henry. "Let me go check with our weather station people and see what they've heard about that front. Be back in a minute".

Zack watched the two companies of firejumpers descend on the meadow, then reminded CAC to inform the other two departing squadrons about the incoming front. With that done, he decided it was a good time for a leisurely cup of coffee.

The ATC directed the Cat Team transports to land at Sacramento Metropolitan Airport. All except for 'Thunderbolt', which was attached to the Long Haulers for the return trip to San Bernardino. There, the crew would transfer to the mechanics' specially-outfitted transport and bring it north with the second wave. In the meantime, the other Cat Team transports were to refuel and park until such time as the Cat Teams were ready to be embarked for the homeward journey.

"Well Henry, what's the weather report", asked Abner. He had come over to Zack's CCC van to discuss strategy when Henry returned from the CDF Meteorological station.

"That front is moving a little slower, but it's still going to be nip and tuck as to whether your people can be on the ground ahead of it", replied Henry. He handed the report around to Zack and his staff.

"How soon are those transports due back in?", one of Abner's assistants asked Abner.

"About 9:30, right Zack?", Abner asked. "My instructions to the crew at the tower was to let us know when the planes land and when they take-off again. They were given your phone number here, Henry. I trust someone is monitoring the phones at all times?"

"You betcha", said Henry. "Sometimes that's the only way I get reports on fires. Not everybody who lives up here has a radio, you know".

"Will someone come and get us if a call does come in, or will they simply post it on the board?", asked Zack.

"I can tell them to notify you if you want", said Henry.

"It would be a big help if you could", said Abner. "Otherwise, we're going to have to check the board every five minutes".

"Consider it done", said Henry, who started to leave.

"Wait a minute!", shouted Zack. "What about the crews we have on the ground now. Where do you want them?"

"There are a few Cats and pumpers working the left flank now", replied Henry. "They're trying to keep the fire away from Brownsville and pinch it in at the same time. If you can pinch the right flank with your existing crews, that should be enough. Until you're up to full strength, let's just carry out a parallel attack along the right flank. When the rest of your guys arrive, then we can consider a combined attack on the right flank and the right side of the head.

"Have your tankers lay a chemical line starting a few miles ahead of the right side of the head and proceeding down the flank, while your Cats and hand crews form a line from the base up the right flank. I'd say your remaining personnel should arrive just before you finish the line, then we can think about a direct attack to smash the head".

"OK Henry, we'll get them right on it", said Zack. "Ready Abner?"

"I think I'm clear on the plan, yeah. I'll go start my staff on a plan of attack for the firebombers. You going to start moving your people up?"

"I guess so", said Zack. "You know, it might be better if we keep the CCC vans here. We're closer to the CDF planning staff. I don't think we could do much up at the fire anyway".

"Except maybe get in the way", chortled Abner. "I left my back-seat driver's license at home, I'm afraid. We get a better overall picture from the Hawkeye anyway. I vote for staying here".

"That's settled then!", said Zack. "Enough of this chit-chat. Let's get on with the operation".

Zack radioed Jack Bazranian and informed him of Henry's instructions. Jack filled the unit commanders in once he got off the radio. Soon, the firefighters and equipment were winding their way into the trees in the direction of the fire.

At the same time, Abner informed the ATCs on Hawk One what he wanted the firebombers to do. The ATCs began directing firebombers onto their targets. Pieter's squadron was tapped by CAC first.

"Pathfinder leader, you are to proceed to grid zero-zero-three and execute an east-to-west drop pattern fifty yards south of the projected fire edge", the ATC intoned. "Wind is from two-seven-zero degrees at three-point-five knots, please acknowledge".

"It's about time we get something to do!", Pieter groused. He acknowledged the orders, then turned to Ralph. "That business of flying in circles was getting pretty old".

"Yeah, and this fire isn't getting any smaller while we circle around picking our noses, either", replied Ralph. "Looks like it's advanced another two or three miles into the Sierra foothills since we arrived. I was getting worried we were going to run out of fuel before we even dropped our first load".

"Dial up those coordinates and let's see where we're going", said Pieter. Ralph punched a few buttons and the display changed to show the grid overlay and relative positions of the planes.

Pieter stabbed his finger at the appropriate coordinates and said, "There it is! Looks like we'll be bombing ahead of the right flank".

"Let's do it!", said Ralph. Pieter turned away to the west and began lining up on the target area, still fifteen miles distant. One by one, the remaining planes in his squadron followed him down. For the moment, the other squadrons maintained their orbits. Since this was their first actual fire, Abner had decided it would be better to use a single squadron at a time and gauge results individually. Once they were sure that each squadron was performing satisfactorily, groups of squadrons could be ganged together.

"I wish that sun would hurry up and get over the horizon", said Ralph. "It's hard to see clearly with all these shadows. Lucky we've got the low-light TV built into the TRIDINT gear, huh?"

"It does make a difference", answered Pieter. "Imagine what this sort of operation would have been like without the TRIDINT equipment to see with!"

"I think I see why you guys didn't like bombing at night", replied Ralph. "OK, I see the target area. Range is four point seven miles. Do you want a linked salvo?"

"Sounds good", agreed Pieter. "With twenty-five firebombers, I don't think we need to be stingy with our drops today. Besides, this fire has a forest canopy to hide under. All's we've fought so far is grass fires with nothing protecting the fires from our drops. Now, we've got to get this stuff through the trees. I'll pass the word on to the rest of the squadron".

Ralph punched in the coordinates and pressed the 'Master Link' and 'salvo' buttons while Pieter informed the other planes of the game plan. As soon as they had dropped their loads, Pieter banked left and brought 'North Star' around for a look at their workmanship.

"Looks like it penetrated", said Pieter. "But like I said, it's hard to tell with all of these shadows".

"Yeah, I can't tell for sure either", said Ralph. "Let's hope that does the job. Time to reload?"

"I do believe it is at that", said Pieter. He banked the plane back slightly right and headed for the closest water source, Bullards Bar Reservoir.

Hawk One began issuing instructions for the remaining firebomber squadrons to begin extending the line Pieter's squadron had laid down. Soon, an unbroken line of retardant stretched several hundred yards down the right flank.

Jack was leading the ground crews along the flank, slowly climbing the side of a hill alongside an area already burned by the fire.

"Make sure those spots where the snags are have been completely extinguished", Jack called to the unit commanders. "Get your people in there and trench along the edge of the burn just to be sure".

Crews from the firejumper units began fanning out along the line and used their handtools to dig around the ashes. Jack saw one over-eager firejumper start moving out into the burned area next to a suspicious-looking pile of ash.

"Hold it!", Jack yelled. "Art, pull that idiot back. There's a pit there!"

The line commander quickly pulled the firejumper back, then carefully advanced on the spot where he was heading.

"See this fluffy ash, son", Art said. "This here was where a big stump was. Give me your Pulaski". Art pushed gently against the ash and it caved in to reveal a red-hot firepit where the remainder of the stump had burned out. "You could have fallen into that if Jack hadn't stopped you. You'll have to be more careful next time".

Art walked on down the line and the firejumper looked at the pit, then back at Jack's fire engine as it slowly drove away from him. This wasn't quite the picnic he had expected it to be .

The companies began deploying along the fire line an hour after they had moved out from the LZ. The Cat Teams had been sent up ahead with orders to begin a Cat line at a point three miles above the base of the fire, then work east into the hills as far as they could, allowing for terrain.

"I don't think we'll be able to use the ball-and-chain with all of these trees", said George Ostermann. "We'll just have to go around for now".

"It was pretty easy going for the first mile with just grass to clear", remarked the other Team Panther Cat driver.

"Yeah, but it looks like we'll have to make a slight detour around that knoll up there", George replied. "I don't think there's any kind of fire road up here, so we'll just have to make one of our own".

"What good is a Cat line going to do in these trees?", asked the other Cat driver.

"Not much if we get a crown fire up there in the tops", replied George. "But I don't see any areas right around here where it's just grass. We'll have to hope the wind doesn't shift much until the firejumpers can clear-cut this area. Let's get started".

Once the Cat Teams broke out of the trees the four bulldozers were grinding their way up the hill, followed by the six APCS. A firebreak four blades wide was being constructed along the edge of the fire and it soon ranged far ahead of the other ground units.

"We just received word that the first transports have landed at Talon Aerospace", Jerry told Joe. Jerry had stepped into the Fire Center where Henry and his staff were conducting operations when the phone call had come in.

"Figuring a turn-around time of one hour and a transit time of over an hour, we should see them up here within about two-plus hours, I guess", replied Joe. The initial excitement of the operation was beginning to fade now and he was getting sleepy, despite the six or seven cups of coffee he had drunk since arriving. It was, after all, over 24 hours since he had slept last.

"I assume the first Hawkeye is going to be relieved soon" , stated Jerry. "At which time I would recommend that you also take a rest. You appear to be extremely tired".

"I am a little tuckered at that", said Joe. "But I'll only leave if you promise to wake me if anything important happens".

"You can be sure that I will."

"OK, I'll take off, then." Joe walked to the doorway, then turned. "Remember, you promised to call me".

"Have a pleasant rest, Joe", said Jerry.

Joe walked over to the dorms where he found an unoccupied bunk. He was asleep a moment after his head hit the pillow.

Jerry had already snatched a little sleep at Joe's suggestion, so he felt he was good until Joe relieved him. He scrutinized the two displays to see what progress the firefighters had made. Precious little, by the looks of things, he thought. The ground crews were not up to strength yet anyway. Once they had achieved full mobilization, they should be able to contain this fire. He noticed that the Talon firebombers were concentrating on the right-hand side of the fire. Presumably, the ground crews were there also. Two hours before the remaining units arrived. How long after that first transport arrived would the last one arrive? And how long after the last crews were on the ground until they reached the actual fire? So many questions to answer. And of course the fire was not standing still waiting for them either. The firebombers were following an obvious pattern, dropping loads from just past the leading edge of the fire down the right side. Jerry decided to tune in on the command frequencies and follow along with the battle. That would give him something to do until he awakened Joe.

"Is there a Patrick O'Toole around here somewhere?", a pilot in a Firebombers flightsuit shouted as he walked into the transport hanger at Talon Aerospace. Patrick came hustling out of the back of a transport and advanced towards the pilot.

"Ah, you're here for us at last", said Patrick. "And who might you be, lad?"

"Steve Guzman", replied the pilot. "I was given orders to deliver you and your repair bird up north. Are you ready?"

"Aye, that we are!", said Patrick. He turned and yelled back at the transport. "Arne, finish strapping down that scissors lift. They're here for us!" Patrick turned back to the pilot and smiled, then said, "We found out we'd almost forgotten tah take our scissors-lift along. We just moved the beastie intah the plane when you lads arrived. It won't take but a moment to finish securin' it. If you lads will excuse me, I'll be about helpin' Arne wit' the business at hand".

"We'll begin the pre-flight while you finish securing the gear, if that's all right with you", said Steve.

"Fine, fine, you lads do what you have to", said Patrick as he hurried back to the transport.

Once he had gone back into the cargo bay, Steve turned to his co-pilot, Glenn Washington, and said, "Now there's a busy youngster".

Glenn shook his head and with a crooked smile said, "Somehow I get the feeling we're not going to have a quiet trip going north".

The Roadrunners finished loading as Steve's crew entered the flight deck and strapped in. The ground crew moved the C-130 out onto the tarmac. Steve and Glenn finished their pre-flight check and started the engines. They rolled over to the fueling pad as the first flight of transports (Ace Movers) was lifting off, followed shortly by the second squadron (Roadrunners). Both squadrons were carrying the two remaining engine companies (504th and 505th) north. The third transport squadron (Knights) was in the process of being outfitted with inserts for the firejumpers. The Knights had just finished this job when the fueling crew topped off the tanks on Steve's new charge. The two remaining squadrons of transports, 104th and 105th Lift (Roadhogs and Long Haulers) were already loaded with firejumpers and on the taxiways preparing to depart when Steve moved into position behind the last plane in the Knights squadron.

One of Henry's aides went rushing past the CCC van Jerry was in. Jerry decided to step outside to see what was going on. He stopped the courier on his way back to the office and found out that the first group of transports had just departed San Bernardino. That gave him another hour, maybe an hour-and-a-half before he would have to call Joe. After the aide left, Jerry decided to go visit Zack in the Fire Boss CCC van.

"What news?", Jerry asked as he stepped inside.

"Not much", replied Zack. "The Cat Team has broken out of the trees and found a good open area to clear. They should be able to stay in the open for the rest of the time. We need to fell a few trees to complete an adequate firebreak".

"Do you have any chainsaws along to clear a path?", asked Jerry.

"Yeah, the APCs and some of the firejumpers are carrying chainsaws. The trees extend along our Cat line for about a half mile. Once the rest of the fire companies link up with the Cat line, I think I'll detail a group to go clear-cut that patch of trees".

"How much farther do they have to go?"

"Less than a mile. I just got word that our second wave is on the way. We should be up to full strength within another two hours. Then we can do some serious firefighting".

"The chemical line appears to be finished, sir", said one of Zack's assistants. "Abner will probably want to start operations on the head".

"Call over and tell him to do so when the flank is done", said Zack. "Have them start at the beginning of the flanking line and work northeast".

The Black Widows had just made their last drop, finishing the chemical firebreak, when the call came in from the ATC to reload and return to their holding area. Pieter's squadron had already loaded up and was awaiting further instructions.

"Nice to see the sun up finally", said Ralph. "Now we can see what we're flying into for a change".

"Yeah, I'm still not 100% sold on this TRIDINT gear", said Pieter. "I like being able to *see* what's ahead of me. That HUD equipment they showed us over at Talon Aerospace was pretty neat, though. I told you about that simulator, didn't I".

"At least a half-dozen times", Ralph replied blandly.

Pieter gave him a disarming smile and said, "Want to hear about it again?"

"Is this a trick question? You know, one of those types that's tied to promotions and raises?"

"You mean brown-nosing?", Pieter asked innocently.

"Yeah, that's it!"

"Could be", said Pieter, who was still smiling.

"In that case I'd be delighted to hear about it again!", gushed Ralph. "Oh *please* tell me all about that fantastic, incredible, absolutely marvelous HUD you saw!"

"Now *that's* what I call a positive attitude!", said Pieter. They both broke up laughing. Their reverie was interrupted by a call from the ATC directing them to begin attacking the fire's head.

"It's a good thing we dropped the beginning of that flank ahead of the leading edge", said Pieter. "The fire's only swept a little ways past it now. We can angle up slightly and catch the fire before it goes too far. Thank God for slow-moving fires!"

"I just hope it stays slow-moving", said Ralph.

Pieter brought his plane around on a north-easterly heading and reduced altitude. Soon, a line of chemical retardant was spread from the flank to a point over two miles from the right side.

"I see a line of red stuff up in the trees over on the other side of that little gully", George Ostermann called over the radio. Zack had just called over to tell George that he should be getting close to the chemical firebreak dropped by the firebombers. "I think we should link up in about half-an-hour at this rate of speed. The brush has gotten pretty thick along here and it's too uneven to use the ball and chain, so we'll have to rely on our blades to clear this stuff away".

"Understood", replied Zack. "Once you've linked up, I want you guys to head back down the hill and clear-cut that patch of trees you left behind. When that's done, the flanking line will be in place and we can start moving into the heart of this thing".

"OK, we'll finish up here and should be back at that grove in, oh, two hours tops", replied George.

"Sounds good. Check back with me when you start down", said Zack.

Back in the Fire Boss van, Zack's aides plotted the progress so far on a map, then transferred the data to the computer up-link to the Hawkeye. That way, everyone, including the crew on the Hawkeye, knew where the gaps in the fire line were. Those gaps would have to be plugged before the flank could be considered contained. When the Cat Teams finished their line, the only remaining gaps on the right flank would be the grove of trees and the area remaining for Jack's crews to clear, about a mile of brush and grass. The wind began to shift direction at this time, however, and a small finger of flame started moving towards the grove of trees left behind by the Cat Teams.

"What's our distance to Redding?", asked Steve Guzman.

The navigator checked his chart and said, "About 143 miles, sir".

"That puts us about twenty-five minutes out", said Glenn. "Want me to whistle up the ATC and get directions?"

"Yes", replied Steve. "Looks like you were wrong, Glenn. Our passengers have been pretty quiet back there".

"Probably busy talking shop", replied Glenn as he dialed in the ATC frequency. A few moments later Steve altered course slightly from the remaining transports and began lining up on Redding.

"CAC, we're starting to get low on both fuel and retardant up here, how about a refill?", Pieter called over the radio.

"Roger that request, 'North Star'", replied CAC. "We are scrambling the refueling squadron now. ATC will get back to you with intercept instructions directly".

CAC contacted the refueling squadron at Sacramento Metropolitan. The tower gave the squadron permission to depart twenty minutes later and the planes lifted off behind a Southwest Airlines jetliner.

The ATCs were also tracking the incoming transport flights. After conferring with Abner and Zack, CAC directed the transports to unload over the original LZ. The LZ inspection crew originally inserted into that location indicated that the meadow was still fit for air-landing operations. The two leading squadrons in the long line of transports began reducing altitude. The three squadrons with firejumpers on board were put into holding orbits by CAC until the engine companies were down, then they also reduced altitude and deposited their passengers on the ground. The entire operation took less than an hour to accomplish and the transports were soon winging their way towards Sacramento Metropolitan.

Steve Guzman landed the maintenance transport at Redding and taxied over to park by the other Firebombers transports. There were now over 1600 personnel on the ground and the fight would soon begin in earnest - more earnest than those coordinating it realized.

Chapter 28

Joe could almost reach their hands. Just a little farther, he thought, just a few inches more. He reached out to Martha and Desiree, but the instant he drew close enough, they suddenly were pulled away from him and drifted back towards the flames. "No!", Joe cried out in anguish. "Stay out of there! Not again!"

"Sir, are you all right?", Joe heard someone say. He slowly opened his eyes and saw a Red Cross nurse shaking him.

"It's just a nightmare, sir", she was saying. "Wake up!"

Joe looked around. He was lying on the bunk in the dorm at Redding. His face was covered with sweat and the nurse stood over him with an anxious look on her face. "Are you all right, sir?", she asked.

"Yeah, just a bad dream", said Joe. "I'm OK now, thanks".

She looked at him with concern for a moment, then nodded and walked away. It had been a long time since Joe had had that dream. He ran his hands through his hair and tried to blink the tears and sweat out of his eyes. He rose slowly and walked back towards the washroom. After he had splashed some water on his face and cleaned up a bit, he grabbed a styrofoam cup of coffee (which tasted more like lacquer after being reheated all night) and walked slowly out to the CCC vans. He found Dave slumped over the command console in his van, snoring loudly. He walked over to Zack's van and found Jerry watching the displays intently. Several parachutes could be plainly seen descending on the meadow miles away from the circling Hawkeye, the image captured on its cameras.

"I see the second wave has arrived", said Joe as he sidled into the crowded van. There were no spare seats left, so he stood and sipped his coffee.

"I was just about to come and get you, Joe", said Jerry. "Did you have a pleasant nap?"

"Fine", Joe lied. "I take it that new weather front hasn't arrived yet".

"Doesn't look like it", said Zack. "Henry's last report on it put it about fifty miles west of here, just creeping along. We may have our perimeter completed before it arrives. The head is almost completely surrounded. We have the right flank virtually sown up. The Cat Teams are heading down from the junction between the chemical line and their firebreak to clear-cut a patch of trees. Once that's done, we'll be able to start moving the troops into the fire itself. We plan to have these newly-arrived companies push up from the base towards the present location of the other companies. The whole group can then angle across from the base towards the left flank, extinguishing the fire as they go".

"What about the Cat Teams?", asked Joe.

"I think they'll probably be busy for awhile with that clear-cutting", said Zack. "The fire was heading away from that spot until a little while ago. It's started moving to the southeast now. At the present rate of speed, the Cat Teams will easily be able to clear a path. If that new front stirs things up, though, we could be in trouble".

"How are the guys over on the left flank doing?", Joe asked.

"From what we've heard, they've kept the fire out of Brownsville", answered Zack. "Their air-tankers are building a line towards ours along the head of the fire. We expect to link up in a short while".

"There, I see the tanker ahead!", said Ralph. "Range is about ... two-and-a-half miles".

"Yeah, I see him", said Pieter. "Adjust your course to intercept".

The boom operator saw the approaching squadron and informed the tanker pilot, who proceeded due north at 120 knots. The pursuing firebombers quickly ate the distance up, then slowed down as they neared the extended booms.

"Easy does it", said Pieter. Ralph was driving this time. He had wanted to attempt a refueling himself and Pieter had consented to let him try it this time. "Remember, you've got two probes to hook up: one for the fuel and one for the retardant. Even though they're joined together, you've got to align them carefully in order to make good contact".

Ralph eased the plane up to the refueling drogue and inserted his probe in it. Then he eased over slightly to the other side to connect with the retardant drogue. When they had both been accepted, the boom operator indicated that he was beginning transfer. Ralph watched excitedly as both tanks refilled.

"That wasn't nearly as hard as I thought it was going to be!", he exclaimed.

"It takes a little getting used to", said Pieter, "but once you've got the hang of it, it's no problem at all".

"Looks like everybody else is hooking up OK", said Ralph as he swept his gaze across the squadron. All around him planes were refueling from the KC-130s. The boom operator interrupted their conversation when the tanks were both full. The drogues were disconnected and 'North Star' dropped away from the tanker. Ralph accelerated and banked right, followed at intervals by the remainder of the squadron. Since the tankers were up there, CAC had decided to refuel and reload all of the firebombers, so the Ridgerunners slid in behind the Pathfinders after they detached and began fueling themselves.

"Well boss, how'd I do?", Ralph asked Pieter.

"Not bad for your first try, Junior", said Pieter. "Now why don't you go get us a load of water and we'll see what we can do to that fire down there".

Ralph banked the plane back to the south and reduced altitude. Soon, the Pathfinders were skimming over the reservoir, refilling their tanks.

"Feels like it's getting a little choppy on the surface", said Pieter. "Or is that just you?"

"No, it feels a little choppy to me too", replied Ralph. "That weather front may have finally arrived".

"I think I'll check in with Abner and see what we can expect out of this front", said Pieter. As he did so, Ralph headed back towards their holding grid. A moment later Pieter had Abner on the radio.

"From what we've been told by the meteorologists here, there could be thirty mile-an-hour gusts out of this thing, so be careful", warned Abner. "I was just about ready to put out a high-wind warning to the squadrons. You guys beat me to the punch".

"How long is this front supposed to be with us?", asked Pieter.

"Unknown", answered Abner. "It's already changed direction and speed a couple of times since it crossed the coast. We had expected it to be here sooner. In fact, we were afraid it might interfere with our second wave".

"So we had better make our drops from a little higher altitude from now on", said Pieter.

"Probably not a bad idea", agreed Abner. "I hate to lose the extra cohesion in the loads, but I think it would be a whole lot safer if you guys could operate with an extra thirty or forty feet of altitude".

"Yeah, I don't think anybody wants to get up close and personal with any trees today", replied Pieter. "As you say, though, we're going to lose some effectiveness in penetrating the canopy with a longer load transposition time. The fire is also likely to pick up speed if we start getting gusts. How are the ground pounders doing on finishing that line?"

"We estimate 95% completion within the hour", replied Abner. "There's one little grove that the Cat Teams have to whack down, but the firejumper companies have pretty well roped off the rest of the flank".

"We're about half-way done with the head ourselves", said Pieter. "Give us another ninety minutes and we should have it sewed up. Sooner if the Forestry tankers keep making drops from the other end".

"You don't suppose we could put this one to bed by sundown, do you?", asked Abner hopefully.

"Too early to tell from what I can see", replied Pieter. "From my vantage point, I'd say we've got the left and right flanks contained, but the head and the base still need more work. The wild card is going to be that wind. We'll see".

"Always want to hedge your bets, don't you Pieter?", asked Abner.

"Whenever possible, yes", answered Pieter. "We'll keep up the pressure here, you just make sure those boys on the ground hold up their end of the bargain".

Ralph had returned their plane to the orbital grid assigned by the ATC. The remainder of the squadron formed up behind him. They watched as the other firebombers skimmed across Bullards Bar Reservoir. By the time the Black Widows were beginning to reload, the ATC directed the Pathfinders onto the next portion of their firebreak. Ralph began his descent and the routine was repeated again. The wind was beginning to pick up, now. Fifteen mile-an-hour winds were whipping up the water on the surface of the reservoir.

At the southern end of the fire, the Cat Teams had just reached the grove of trees they were supposed to fell. The bulldozers waited their turns as the APC crews got out and used chain-saws to cut deep into the trunks. Once they were sufficiently weakened, the bulldozers would finish the job with a strong push.

Far away, the plotting crews for CDF and Zack's staff noticed the sudden change in speed and direction of the fire. Zack had just received word that the Cat Teams were clearing out the first trees in the grove and that two squads of firejumpers had been sent up to begin clear-cutting the grove from the other end. The engine companies had started their push into the fire-scarred landscape to mop-up the spot fires remaining there. They planned to close on the leading edge of the fire from behind. They were in no danger from this sudden wind change, but the Cat Teams were.

"CAC, get the Tag-Team over that grove ASAP!", Abner called. "Have them drop a trailing load ahead of the fire to slow it down".

"Copy that Air Boss", CAC replied over the radio The location of the grove was determined by the ATC and he switched his set to the Tag-Team's frequency.

"Tag-Team leader, commence bombing op at grid zero-three-five", the ATC called over the radio. "Wind bearing three-one-five degrees at fifteen knots, gusting to twenty-five knots, acknowledge".

"Got it, Hawk Two", replied Jimmy. "Proceedin' to target now, out".

"Our turn?", asked Tim.

"'Bout time, too", said Jimmy. "Ah was gettin' kinda sleepy just circling around up here".

"So I wonder what this is all about anyway?", asked Tim. His question was answered a moment later.

"Tag-Team leader, this is CAC", said the voice over the radio. "The wind has shifted and pushed the fire towards a breach in the right flank. All the other squadrons are closing off the head of the fire and are unavailable. The Cat Teams are clearing timber down there and will be overrun by the fire at its present speed. You are to slow it up with dispersed drops. Do not, repeat, do not make any salvo drops. You must cover the entire gap on your first run, so use trailing drops only, understood?"

"Understood, CAC", replied Jimmy. "How far to target, Tim?"

Tim punched in the coordinates and checked the display. "About twenty miles", he replied. "The fire looks like it's approaching the breach already. We'll have to hurry".

"Ah needs to get aligned with the existin' line, too", said Jimmy. "Feels like we's picking up a little turbulence".

"Just what we need right now", said Tim.

"Panther leader, are you receiving me, over", Zack called over the radio. His first message to Team Panther had not been acknowledged.

George was in the process of pushing over a tree when Zack's first message came in. When the tree finally fell, he replied, "Go ahead, Fire Boss".

"The fire is moving towards your location at around fifteen miles per hour", said Zack. "You are to withdraw your team to the west of the fire and begin constructing a new Cat line along the right flank of this protrusion. Do you understand?"

"It would be quicker to move uphill away from the fire, Fire Boss", George answered. "We're just into the grove here and it's another half-mile before the grove thins out, over".

"Negative! Negative!", Zack replied angrily. "You know better than that George. Fire runs quicker uphill than you can move, especially with this kind of wind behind it. Besides, you're at the base of an arroyo. That place is going to act like a chimney going uphill. Move to the west of the grove and begin your firebreak there, understood?"

"Understood", replied a chastened George. "Is there going to be any help along to assist us, or are we on our own, over?"

"We've detailed the Tag-Team to assist you for now", answered Zack. "It's not much, but the other squadrons are busy trying to lock in the head of the fire. The fire companies are already too far into the base to be of much help out there. We'll send more help over as it becomes available, out".

"Wonderful", muttered George. He stepped out of his Cat's enclosure and tried without success to make himself heard. He ran over to Jose's APC and made a quick search, locating what he was after in only a few seconds. He punched one of the buttons on Jose's makeshift control panel and a deafening 'Ah-oogah' sounded from the hidden PA speaker. Chain-saws quickly fell silent by the time George had sounded off a second time and a crowd gathered around the APC.

"I'm glad to see that you put this illegal contraption back in your APC Jose", chided George. Manuel shot Jose an angry glance, while Jose tried to find a convenient hole to climb into.

"We've been ordered out of this grove. The fire is heading this way and this wind has whipped it up enough that we won't be able to drop enough trees before it gets here. The boss wants us out of here pronto. Mount up and let's get moving. We'll assemble once we're west of this grove".

Several drivers began to protest, but smoke began blowing into the trees as they spoke. The fire was indeed getting close. George didn't wait around to bandy words with them. He climbed aboard his Cat and fired up the engine. Reluctantly, the crews gathered their tools and moved back to their vehicles.

"TRIDINT shows that the Cat Teams haven't moved out of the grove yet, Jimmy", Tim warned the pilot. "We're going to have to be careful with our drop. We don't want to dump on them".

"Ah know", said Jimmy. "With that wind we's goin' to spread south rait over them boys. Ah'll adjust th' course a little north of the line. Ready?"

"Just a sec", said Tim as he punched in the new coordinates. "Ready". Tim punched the 'split' and 'Master Link' buttons and received a blinking 'Ready' light as confirmation.

"Bob, you fellers ready?", Jimmy called to his wingman.

"All set, Jimmy", Bob replied.

"Here's hopin' that wind don't gust when we drop", said Jimmy. The two planes flew higher than usual over the tree tops, buffeted slightly by the thermals from the fire and the occasional gusts from the wind. The range came down quickly. One thousand yards ... seven-fifty ... five-hundred... two-fifty ...

"Here come the planes!", said Manuel as he hurried to get inside the APC. The sunlight was abruptly tinged with a red haze as the retardant showered down onto the tree-tops. Some small amount drifted onto the departing Cat Teams, but the bulk of it landed just ahead of the fire.

"Bullseye!", yelled Abner as he looked at the Hawkeye pictures. "CAC, pass along a 'well done' to the Tag-Team. Have them reload and return, out".

"Now we have to get down to the business of how to stop this thing", Zack said after watching the Tag-Team bombing run. "All of our firebombers are occupied with the head, which is getting really unpredictable up there. It may be threatening that town up there, uh, Challenge. I'll bet the CDF Air Boss is going to have his hands full for awhile keeping the fire out of there, so we'll be left with completing the line.

"And in the meantime, this protrusion could expand into one nasty little front of it's own. Where are the first wave companies now?", Zack asked one assistant. The assistant pointed to two sets of marks on the screen. "Nope, too far away. We can't insert any more firejumpers with these gusts either. It's probably going to have to be a bomber solution. Tell that detachment of firejumpers with chainsaws to return to their units and have the Cat Teams continue their firebreak down the west flank of the breach.

"There's a town in the general direction of the breakout, which one is that?", Zack asked as he looked over the map. "Dobbins, that's the one. We've got to keep it out of there. I'd better talk this over with Henry". Zack sent one of his aides to get Henry, then stepped outside to stretch. Joe and Jerry were out there already, talking quietly among themselves.

"Problems?", Joe asked Zack.

"Yeah, the fire has breached our line and is heading towards a town", Zack replied. "We've only got the Tag-Team to throw at it. They're having problems up at the left corner of the fire, so our bombers are needed there right now. If we had some more planes to make drops, we could probably stop it, but nothing is available. In fact, Forestry has requested some tankers from CDF for a fire they're fighting up in Tahoe National Forest. Seems our little thunderstorm was busy over there, too".

"Has Henry said they're going to withdraw the other air-tankers for that fire?", asked Joe.

"Not as of yet", answered Zack. "That's why I sent my assistant to find him. We need some answers, fast!"

Henry returned with Zack's aide a few moments later. He had a worried expression on his face which unsettled Joe.

"I'm afraid I have some bad news my friends", said Henry. "I'm going to have to pull all my tanker support out of the fight for the town of Challenge and ship it east. The Feds are having one devil of a fight with a fire over around Calpine. They may lose it if we don't send them all we can. That may include some of your firebombers as well".

"You're going to need our help just to finish the line in front of Challenge, aren't you?", asked Zack.

"For the moment", said Henry. "But as soon as that's done, I'll have to ship your squadrons east".

"What about the threat to Dobbins?", asked Joe. "If you pull all of our firebombers east, we won't have anything to stop the fire from gutting the town!"

"Don't you think I know that?", said Henry anxiously. And every minute we stand here debating, the fire is moving closer to both Dobbins and Calpine. If only we had more air-tankers!"

"There are none available?", asked Zack. "How about Oregon or Nevada?"

"I'm sure they'd let us borrow some if there were any left to send", replied Henry. "But we've depleted every source within eight hundred miles. No, we need a local solution".

Henry stood there and thought for a moment. He looked at the sky off in the distance and saw a hawk circling above the trees at the edge of the airstrip. As he watched, the hawk evidently spotted a mouse or rabbit on the ground and plummeted towards the earth. Henry's gaze followed the hawk down until his view was blocked by one of the Firebombers transports. His eyes rested on the C-130 for a moment, then they suddenly sprang open wide. "That's it!", he shouted.

"What's it?", asked Zack excitedly.

Henry turned towards Joe and asked, "How many of these C-130s do you have over at Sacramento Metropolitan?"

"Uh, I don't know exactly", Joe answered in confusion. "I think most of the planes we have are over there now. That would be about forty, I suppose. Five of those are refueling tankers. Why?"

"I may have a solution to our problems!", Henry shouted over his shoulder as he ran back towards the Fire Center. Joe and his friends began running along behind.

"Jennie, get me the warehouse on the horn", Henry shouted.

"Yes sir, right away", the CDF operator answered.

"Find out how many of those MAFFS pallets we got in".

"What is a MAFFS pallet? asked Zack.

"Something developed by FMC back in the early '70's", replied Henry. "The initials stand for 'Modular Airborne Fire Fighting System'. It's a pallet that's designed to fit into the back of a C-130. We just got a shipment in to divvy up amongst the C-130s we use on contract, mostly Air National Guard and Air Force Reserve planes. The units installed in those planes were getting pretty old, so we were going to rotate them out this summer. The pallet carries 3000 gallons of long-term retardant, which can be discharged in about 10 seconds over a fire. *That* might take some of the fight out of this fire!"

"We have ten MAFFS pallets stored here", said the Jennie. "Do you want me to have them pull them out of the packing crates?"

"Yes indeed", said Henry gleefully. "Zack, I need you to get another seven C-130s over here right away. I'd recommend you tap your best pilots, since they won't have any training on these things other than the quick intro we can give them in twenty minutes, or so. We'll load up the three you've got here with MAFFS now and indoctrinate those crews first".

"I'll go tell Abner to scramble his best transports over at Sacramento Metropolitan", said Zack.

Henry rounded up a crew of forklift drivers to move the pallets from the storeroom into the back of each of the three transports already on hand. Suzie West and her flight crew rushed out to pre-flight 'Double Trouble' for the new mission. Once they fired up the engines, she taxied over by the warehouse so that the forklift could load the MAFFS pallet. Patrick and the Talon ground crews hustled over to help in securing the pallets. After the three planes were loaded up, the aircrews were called into Ops for a quick course on how to use the MAFFS equipment. Twenty minutes later, the other transport squadrons were beginning to lift off from Sacramento Metropolitan and head north.

"Have the ground crews ready to withdraw the paratrooper inserts from the planes equipped that way as soon as the planes park", said Abner

"I don't think we'll have enough personnel to secure the units in that many planes all at once", said Henry. "And it takes almost two hours to load and secure one of these things, by the book".

"I think our ground crews can show you some shortcuts in that department", said Zack confidently. "We've been faced with the need for quick turn-around time of inserts since day-one. Our ground crews have contrived some pretty nifty techniques to speed up the process. I just wish we'd been able to bring them all along with us".

"Just be glad the mechanics commandeered that transport for maintenance purposes", Abner pointed out. "If they hadn't, we would have been hard-pressed just getting a few transports converted to bombers. As it is, we've got enough ground personnel along to give us a healthy chance of knocking this bugger down before it torches the whole valley".

"Yep, you're right there", agreed Zack.

The first transports began landing as they finished talking. The ground crews motioned them over to the fence by the warehouse and began loading the pallets into the cargo bays. The aircrews trooped over to Ops and were indoctrinated on how to use the MAFFS. By this time, Suzie West and her cohorts in lst Composite Squadron were fully briefed on what to do. They sprinted back out to their planes and were soon taxiing over to the retardant tanks at the Air Attack Base to fill up. The MAFFS units were quickly charged and the planes taxied onto the end of the runway in preparation for takeoff.

A short while later, the first transports arrived over the head of the rapidly advancing fire.

"I hope this works as easy as that Forestry guy said it would", Suzie said to Ken as they lined up on the fire. "All of this smoke is going to make it difficult to see anything".

"I wish we had TRIDINT gear like the firebombers have", said Ken. "Low-light TV by itself just doesn't cut it".

"I can't see a blessed thing in here!" said Suzie. "CAC, you'll have to give us the cue when to drop".

"Will do, 'Double Trouble'", answered the senior controller on board Hawk Two. "Continue on present course for another few seconds. I'll let you know when to drop. Just a little farther. Hold her steady. Ready... *drop!*"

Two streams of retardant sprang out the back of the C-130, coating the canopy of the trees with a red stain. In ten seconds time, it was over. Suzie applied full military power and pulled up. Each transport in turn made its run with CAC's direction, producing a continuous, if not quite uniform, line of chemical across the path of the oncoming fire. The planes from lst Composite Squadron returned to Redding Air Attack Base, taxied over to the retardant tanks behind an S-2, and awaited their turn to recharge.

The other transport crews finished their briefings sometime later and raced out to help with the final securing of the MAFFS gear in their planes. Less than an hour later the scratch force of transports comprising the lead planes of each squadron tanked up and lifted out of Redding, shaping their course towards the Sierras. The planes of 1st Composite Squadron rolled up to the retardant tanks again and began tanking up shortly after the other transports had left.

Zack and Abner had moved out onto the flight line to watch the activity. "Looks like we might have a chance licking this thing after all!", said an ebullient Zack.

"Don't get your hopes up too high", warned Abner. "This bugger isn't dead yet and these aren't firebombers doing the runs. There's going to probably be holes in the firebreaks that the Tag-Team will have to plug. This fire still has a lot of life left in it and the weather isn't helping matters any".

"We'll have to hope for the best then, won't we?", said Zack. They walked back to the CCC vans where Abner passed the plan of action along to CAC, then sat back and watched the plotting crew marking the progress of both the fire and the line of retardant. So far, the fire was winning.

"Keep checking those ash piles!", Jack shouted at the advancing line of firefighters. He had just heard about the line breach and looked south to see the ever-increasing trail of smoke rising into the air. He knew they were too far away to be of any help, and Zack had told him of the narrow escape of the Cat Teams from the oncoming flames. He already had three firejumpers injured, all relatively minor. The company medics had dealt with them effectively, but they were out of the fire line for the duration of this operation. He glanced over at one of his smokechaser teams as they uncovered another fire-pit and eliminated it.

"How's your retardant holding out?", he called over to the three man team.

"We're down to less than half a tank, sir", the team leader called back.

"I don't see any water sources for another two or three miles", said Jack. "Try using your tools more and less retardant to snuff them".

"Will do", affirmed the team leader. They moved off to the left of the engine company they had been following and began trenching around a section of thick, smoking brush. Jack's engine companies were using their water sparingly, knowing from the same maps Jack had studied that there was no water for a ways yet. Overhead, Jack could see groups of planes returning from the breach. He stared at them for a moment, then rubbed his eyes and looked again. Those were transports returning from the fire!

"Looks like we're closing fast with the head", said one of Jack's assistants. "Another few miles and we should reach the chemical line".

"I hope our water lasts that long", said Jack. If only we had a means of air-lifting water in, he thought. Something to consider for the future. Jack's attention was drawn to a series of shouts from over to the right. A burning log came rolling out of the flames above some firefighters, heading straight for them. They ran to get out of the way, but an engine couldn't move quickly enough. The log collided with the pumper, knocking the bumper off and wrecking the water intake.

"Looks like we've got some loose stuff up above us", said the aide. "Too bad we don't have our maintenance crews along to fix that intake".

"Yeah, that crew isn't going to be able to refill even if we do find water soon", agreed Jack. "I wonder what other good news we have in store. Did you see those transports heading over just a minute ago?"

"I wasn't really paying attention", said the aide. "What were they doing over here, I wonder. Dropping somebody else's smokejumpers in front of that breach?"

"I don't know", said Jack in puzzlement. "I'll have to ask Zack about it".

"While you're at it, maybe you could ask for some water", said the aide jokingly. "Are we still in contact with the CDF people over on the left side of the line?"

"Last I heard", replied Jack. "I don't think they're having an easy time of it with this fire, either. I haven't been able to spot them since we dropped below that ridge. Last I saw, they were keeping up with our line, though".

"The last thing we need now is to get separated from the rest of the guys working this line", said the aide. "The way this wind is whipping around, we might get in a heap of trouble if that happens".

"As long as the fire has burned the fuel this thoroughly, I don't think we have anything to worry about", said Jack. At least he hoped not.

Back at Redding, Henry was checking the placement of the new chemical line being dropped by the transports. Almost all of the first wave had finished dropping their loads now. The head of the fire was completely enclosed.

"The head of our little renegade is held, gentlemen", Henry told his staff. "Now we can go to work on the flanks. How many aircraft do we have left en route?"

"Our Air Ops reports two Firebombers air-tankers are presently dropping on the left flank", replied the CDF Air Boss. "The remaining MAFFS-equipped birds are just about to land here".

"If we can get the left flank of the breach under control, we can keep this thing from threatening the town of Dobbins", Henry said after staring at the map. "Hal, go tell the Firebombers Air Boss to seal off the left flank completely before he tackles the right flank".

The aide hurried out to relay the message to Abner, who immediately informed CAC of the plan. Abner then called over to Zack.

"Zack, how are your Cat Teams holding up?", Abner asked.

"OK so far", Zack replied. "They're a couple of miles from the head of that breach fire, though, and falling behind every minute. That sucker is really moving!"

"The next series of drops will be made over on the left flank", remarked Abner.

"So I see. When are you guys going to begin dropping on the right flank of the breach?"

"Not for awhile yet. It's going to take some time for the transports to sew the left flank up".

"OK, just give me some warning before you turn them loose on the right flank. That will give me time to get the Cat Teams out of the way. I don't want any casualties due to poor drops".

"I don't see why you're so concerned anyway", protested Abner. "They're fully protected in those tanks of theirs".

"No need to take chances, is there?", replied Zack testily.

"All right, I'll let you know when we start getting close", said Abner wearily.

"Thanks Abner. I'll pass the word along to my crews, then", said Zack. He toggled the controls on the radio and spoke into the mike. "Come in, Panther leader. George, are you there?"

Many miles away, Team Panther and Team Tiger were grinding along the edge of the breach. "I read you, Fire Boss", George replied. "I've seen a bunch of transports off in the distance. Are you inserting firejumpers ahead of the fire?"

"Negative. We're dropping retardant from the transports. That's why we need that Cat line completed. We can contain the head and the left flank, but we don't have enough planes to plug the right flank for now. Continue your Cat line and I'll call you before they start dropping retardant in your vicinity. Understood?"

"I've got the idea", replied George. He quickly filled in the other Cat Team personnel.

"How's the fire look?", asked Henry as he stepped into Zack's van.

Zack pointed to the displays. Several transports were dropping on the fire as they watched. "That is, assuming the wind doesn't drive the fire out of our enclosure", said Zack.

"Could the fire get past the chemical line?", asked one of Zack's aides.

"With enough wind, sure", replied Zack. "We'll just have to hope we don't get that much wind. What does the weather report show Henry?"

"This front is just about spent", Henry answered. "It should move out any time now, and there's stable air behind it. If we can finish that left flank and the fire doesn't jump the line within another, say, half hour, we might be in the clear. I think your people have sewed up the line outside of Challenge, haven't they?"

"Just putting the finishing touches on it now", replied Zack. "Do you want our firebombers diverted to help Forestry when the line's complete?"

"I don't think they'll need all of them", Henry answered. "Maybe send them three squadrons and let two take a breather".

"They have been at it awhile. OK, we'll pull down the 204th and 205th for a breather and send the other three east under our CAG's supervision".

Henry got a puzzled look on his face and asked, "Your what's supervision?"

"CAG. Commander Air Group. The guy who leads the firebombers out at the fire. You may know him, Pieter Van Vrees? He was one of the first guys to be hired on by Joe Talon".

"No, I don't think I know him. OK, I'll agree to your plan. As soon as we're sure that Challenge is safe, divert your squadrons".

"I'll pass the word on to Abner, so he knows what we've decided", said Zack. The wind was already starting to die down when Zack and Abner had finished their radio conversation. Henry had headed back into the Fire Center in the meantime and was directing the CDF firefighters closing in behind the now-quiescent fire. The line before Challenge was completed shortly thereafter and the firebombers parceled out as planned. Jack's companies had neared the head of the fire in their sector by the time the transports returning from Redding were finishing the chemical line along the right flank of the breach. The only portion of the line incomplete was rapidly being sealed off by the two Cat Teams.

"Nearly five o'clock and we're not done yet", groused Abner. He didn't like the idea of loaning out his aircraft to Forestry without having any control over them himself. Hawk Two was still able to keep track of them, but Forestry was directing their drops. "Those guys probably don't even know what our planes are capable of".

"Cheer up Abner", one of Abner's aides said. "We have this fire almost contained, so we don't really need them".

"I guess not", said Abner. "It's just that I like to have more help than I need available. We already got a taste of what it's like not having enough planes this afternoon. If Henry hadn't come up with that brainstorm about using our transports, we would really have a disaster on our hands now".

"The Cat Teams seem to have pretty well roped off the last part of the line on the breach", said the aide. The plotting crew had up-linked the latest progress reports, which showed only a few hundred yards of open ground remaining.

"Air Boss, this is CAC", the radio crackled. "All transports have completed drops. Do you want them to reload and return for another run, over?"

"CAC, this is Air Boss", replied Abner. "No, have them cease operations and return to Redding. Pass along our thanks, over".

"That's a roj, Air Boss. CAC out".

"I think I'll go over and see what Zack's people are doing", said Abner. "Keep an eye on the store while I'm gone".

"Will do", replied the aide.

Abner stretched luxuriantly once he had stepped out of the CCC van. He had been under a lot of pressure today and was happy to finally get a chance to relax. He stepped around Zack's CCC van and popped through the door. Joe and Jerry were already there, making it a rather crowded place.

"How soon do you project containment?", asked Joe.

"By six, I'd say", replied Zack. "Jack is going to have to hoof it over from the east end of the main fire in order to finish off this finger, but the Cat Teams have the firebreak nearly completed. Technically, we won't have it contained until that line is finished, but actually, it's contained now. The Forestry line has reached the maximum excursion point, just outside of Challenge. They're declaring their part of the fire contained, if not controlled".

"We just got word from CAC that the last of the MAFFS drops are done", said Abner from the doorway. "I've given orders for the transports to touch down here. Three squadrons of firebombers are still up at Calpine, the rest of the firebomber crews are stretching their legs over at Sacramento".

"They all deserve a break", said Joe. "They've been up since almost dawn yesterday. I'll bet Pieter nods off before his head hits the pillow tonight!"

"With luck, we'll be celebrating tonight", said Zack. "Once Jack's crews get over to that finger and finish mopping it up, we're done here".

"How long will that take?", asked Joe.

"If the wind doesn't pick up, and it doesn't look like it will, I'd say they'll be done by just a little after sunset", replied Zack. "That fire was fast, so I'll bet it didn't do much to the undergrowth below the trees. They should be able to move through there fairly quickly".

"Hadn't we better lay plans to transport them back down to civilization then?", asked Joe.

"Yeah, I keep forgetting we don't get them there by bus", said Zack. "We'll have to see if the CDF guys can loan us some of their transport for awhile. I'll go talk to Henry about it. Abner, you want to come along? He may need the persuasion of a friend before he's willing to send his busses out into the boonies".

"OK, but it's going to cost you!", said Abner, with a twinkle in his eye.

"You're as bad as Pieter!", grumbled Zack. "Must be a common feature of pilots, or something".

"I do believe you're catching on!", said Abner merrily. "Shall we?"

"It's a relief to see them more relaxed now", Joe told Jerry after Abner and Zack had left. "When they're worried, I'm worried".

"Generally a good philosophy to adhere to", replied Jerry. "I have found that they know more than they generally say. Perhaps they do not wish to alarm the uninitiated, such as ourselves".

"You're probably right", agreed Joe. "What do you say we take a hike ourselves. I'd like to see what's going on with that other fire over by Calpine".

"Very well", replied Jerry. The two friends exited the CCC van and walked over to the Fire Center. The three transports comprising 1st Composite Squadron were just taxiing up to the Air Attack Base as Joe and Jerry went inside the Fire Center. There was a large gathering around the map table inside, including Zack and Abner. Henry had just finished speaking when Joe and Jerry walked up.

"What's the good word, Henry?", asked Joe.

"The fire over near Calpine is about 75% contained", replied Henry. "We expect them to have it completely surrounded by 10 P.M. tonight. At that time, your squadrons will probably be released by Forestry".

"Good", said Joe. "Those pilots are going to be some mighty tired folks".

"Yeah, but from what I've seen here and from what my friends at Forestry have said, they've earned some high praise from everybody", said Henry. "I was more than just a little concerned about your outfit when we first met. So were the Feds when we offered to loan your firebombers to them. I think it's safe to say that those doubts proved groundless. Speaking for both CDF and Forestry, we'd like to commend you guys for a first-class job of firefighting. Not only did your people keep their heads during a crisis, but they doused these fires faster than any of us have ever seen before!"

"Does this mean you may call on us in the future?", asked Joe expectantly.

"No, it doesn't mean that we *may* call on you in the future", replied Henry with a smirk. "It means that we absolutely *will* call on you in the future!"

"That's what I was hoping you meant", said Joe. His face immediately broke into a big grin and he shook hands with Henry.

"Fire Boss, this is Panther leader. We've just linked up with the chemical line", George called over the radio. "The right flank of the finger is contained".

"Sorry Panther leader, the boss is out right now, but I'll certainly relay the message to him", the aide answered.

"This looks to have been exclusively a crown fire", Jack told the commander of 501st Engine Company. They had just reached the base of the breach. "Not a very wide breach, at least not here at the base".

"It appears to spread out farther along the ridge, though", replied the company commander. "There's almost no undergrowth through here and not too many gullies, from what I can see. I'd say we can move through this stuff in no time. Let me take my engine companies in first, then the firejumpers can follow us and the smokechasers behind that. We'll fan out as we go".

"Reasonable plan", said Jack. "Carry on, then".

The five engine companies swept into the woods and were soon deep into the finger. The fire was practically out on the ground, having done very little damage there. The treetops had been almost totally destroyed, however. The engine companies, their water tanks running near empty, managed to put out most of the remaining fires they encountered. The firejumpers moved in behind the engine companies, mopping up what few spot fires were still smoldering.

"We've got 100% containment, Joe", Zack called from the CCC van less than three hours later. "Jack's going to need a few more hours to mop up. Then he'll pull out towards Dobbins. The CDF busses will pick them up there".

"Are they going to cart them all the way over to Sacramento?", asked Joe.

"No, CDF has set up some bunks at Grass Valley Air Attack Base, which is where they want to bivouac them", replied Zack.

"Better have Abner send the transports over there to get them, then", said Joe. "I'd like to get them down south as soon as possible".

"I'd advise against it", said Zack. "That fire is out now, but we may have missed a spot. It could rekindle. Better to take them out tomorrow morning after we're sure it's dead"

"OK, you know best, Zack", said Joe. "Is it time for that celebration you were talking about?"

"Yeah, I think it is", said a smiling Zack. "Assuming anybody can stay awake long enough!"

"I don't imagine the ground troops are going to feel much like celebrating", said one of Zack's assistants. "Their idea of a wild time will probably be a hot meal and a soft bunk in a dark corner".

"The pilots will be coming in later, I expect", said Joe. That's probably *their* idea of a good time tonight, too! Call up the aircrews over at Sacramento and tell them to take the night off", Joe called over to Abner. "Make sure they don't celebrate too much. I plan to be heading out first thing in the morning".

"I'm sure they'll be ready by then", said Abner. "I'll go check with Henry to see if our firebombers are coming back soon".

The fire at Calpine was contained shortly after 9 P.M. that evening, at which time the firebombers were released. They headed back to Redding, weary but victorious. The firejumpers would be bussed down to Grass Valley by shortly after midnight. CDF had also loaned Zack some tractor transports to move his Cat Teams' equipment down the hill (George had offered to drive the Caterpillars and APCs down the road from Dobbins, but it was decided their treads would do too much damage to the road).

Zack's celebration consisted of some beers passed around a barbecue at Redding (Joe and Pieter settled for soft drinks). Aside from the CDF and Firebombers command staffs, there were few people attending. As Zack pointed out before turning in, he didn't see how anyone would be able to sleep with the volume of snoring in the dorms. Joe figured they would manage somehow and he was right.

Chapter 29

Joe was up by nine the next morning. A CDF spotter had been sent out, as had Hawk One. No fires were spotted outside of the containment areas, even with IR scans, so Henry released the Firebombers personnel and turned the remainder of the mopping up over to CDF crews. The fire over at Calpine was also in the mopping up stages by the time Joe was up. It was decided that they had more than enough help over there with the local air-tankers.

After pulling the MAFFS units out of the transports at Redding and reinserting the paratroop inserts in three squadrons, the transports were sent down to Grass Valley Air Attack Base to collect the Talon firefighters. Hawk One coordinated the air traffic. The constant stream of aircraft into and out of Grass Valley Airport (which the Air Attack Base was part of) drew a sizable crowd, not only of base personnel, but also of people from the surrounding communities. There was insufficient space for all of the C-130s to land at once, so Hawk One kept them cycling through. As one squadron left, another landed.

Since the Grass Valley Airport runway was fairly short, Abner directed the transports to use their JATOs to get aloft. The transports of the first wave carried out three firejumper companies (701st through 703rd) and two engine companies (501st and 502nd). A contingent of residents from the communities which had been threatened by the fire erected a large banner expressing their thanks by the side of the flight line and waved enthusiastically as each plane rocketed off the runway. The flight south was boisterous, as flight crews swapped stories of their exploits with their passengers.

The crew from 'Thunderbolt' flew the maintenance plane down directly from Redding. Patrick was feeling his age that morning, and all of the ground crew members who had flown north were tired after their exertions swapping inserts the previous day and before departure that morning. As the transports arrived at San Bernardino with the first wave, the ground crews pulled the paratrooper inserts out of the planes of the 101st squadron and replaced the JATOs which each transport had spent getting the first wave off the ground with fresh ones. Abner had called ahead to San Bernardino and ordered the ground crews to load up 'Thunderbolt' with enough JATOs to equip the Heavy Lift squadron transports coming south in the second wave. 'Thunderbolt' came north with the returning transports, carrying fresh ground crew to install these JATOs. The second wave aircraft were soon winging their way south with the remainder of the Firebombers personnel.

Joe had only just entered his office when he received a phone call from Allen Sims asking to talk to Joe. Allen walked into Joe's office a few minutes later with his attaché case and Horace Kemel in tow.

"Hello, Joe", greeted Allen. "Successful expedition?"

"Splendid expedition!", beamed Joe. "So, what have you gentlemen got for me today?"

"First on my list is a subpoena from our friends at L.A. County", answered Allen. "They have changed the trial date to November 30th. It appears that the judge designated for the August trial required emergency heart surgery and was therefore unable to preside over our trial".

"Can't they find someone else to replace him?", asked Joe.

"Apparently, his caseload has been divided among the remaining courtrooms on a priority basis", Allen replied. "Ours was deemed to be of a lower priority and was therefore given a later trial date. Personally, I am pleased to see it. This will not only give my staff more time to prepare the case, but it will also give your organization time to garner laurels for its performance, one of the key points on which I plan to base our defense. If you can persuade influential people to vouch for both your character and the organization's effectiveness, we may have a chance of clearing your name and that of the corporation".

"We'll do our best to garner some of those laurels", said Joe. "Have you heard any news about our elusive Mr. Holmstead?"

"Our arsonist is no longer elusive", announced Allen. "My people caught up with him in Hamburg, Germany approximately twelve hours ago".

"And ... ?", Joe leaned forward over his desk.

"And I daresay we uncovered more than even you suspected", replied Allen. "It appears your hunch about those witnesses who so conveniently disappeared was right. The arsonist was employed to engineer their disappearances".

"I thought so!", said Joe triumphantly. "What else? Was he involved in the fire at Mathias Flick's place?"

"Yes, he was", said Allen. "And, as you might have suspected, our friend Mr. Davis was the man pulling the strings" .

"Things are beginning to fall into place rather nicely", said Joe. He leaned back in his desk chair. "Any sign of our Mr. Davis stateside?"

"We have not checked for the past week", answered Allen. "He was missing before that time, though. I would imagine he will remain out of the country, especially if he has received word that his arsonist was apprehended".

"Do you think he knows?", asked Joe.

"Certainly he knows we were pursuing his agent", Allen replied. "Holmstead told us that himself. Sodium pentothol derivatives are wonderful things for loosening the tongue".

"I don't know that I agree with your method of information extraction Allen", said Joe quietly.

Allen became more pensive after Joe's statement. "Odd, you were never squeamish about such things in the past. We felt it was the most expedient means available".

"I've changed my stance on a number of practices we used to consider 'acceptable'", said Joe. "I would recommend that you clear such activities with me before proceeding in the future".

"I see", said Allen uneasily. "I believe the German Federal Police were most pleased by the information we gathered, though I doubt they can use it in court".

"You've handed him over to the German authorities?"

"Yes, it seems he was wanted for questioning regarding several suspicious deaths in Germany as well. They were quite pleased to get him".

Joe looked at Allen for a moment and saw something which bothered him. "You're not telling me everything, are you?"

Allen's eyes darted around the room for a moment. He's obviously uncomfortable about something, thought Joe. Allen looked at Horace, then motioned him out of the room. Once the door was closed, he turned back towards Joe. "This will not be easy for you to hear, I'm afraid", he said after a moment. "While under the influence of the drug, Mr. Holmstead revealed that he had had other dealings with Ethan Davis in the recent past, dealings of a most foul nature".

"What sort of dealings?", asked Joe. Inexplicably, he felt a chill begin to creep up his spine.

"Dealings in setting a certain forest fire", said Allen. "A forest fire which occurred in the vicinity of Kingfisher Creek".

Joe suddenly felt numb all over. "The fire in which...." He couldn't finish the sentence.

Allen nodded his head slowly. "Yes, old friend. The fire in which Martha and Desiree were killed. It seems that Mr. Davis wanted primarily to kill you, but our Mr. Holmstead was delayed in his arrival at the cabin. He did not realize that you had left already. Seeing the car still there, he assumed you were there also.

"It was not until after the fire, when he heard the news that the arsonist realized his mistake. Mr. Davis instructed him to lay low for awhile after that. Evidently, Davis thought it would be prudent to eliminate Mathias Flick in the meantime. Perhaps he thought someone would begin to suspect him if another attempt on your life was made. Who knows what goes through the mind of such a man".

Joe struggled with his emotions for a few minutes. Finally, he managed to say, "We've... you've got to find Davis. If he has gone this far, there's no telling what he might do next".

"I agree", said Allen. "I would recommend you keep Horace with you on a full-time basis from now on. It seems obvious that Mr. Davis is far more dangerous than we had believed at first".

Joe seemed not to hear Allen's statement. He stared down at his desk. "They were deliberately killed", said Joe despondently. "It was no accident, no simple forest fire. It was my own stupidity in antagonizing Davis. All of this, all that I've built has been for nothing. Firebombers Incorporated is meaningless. It's my fault they're both dead. Better if I had died in the fire with them. That's what I deserved!"

Allen was silent for a few moments, then said, "It was not all for nothing. I have read the reports of how your organization fought the fires in Sunland and Signal Hill, and I have heard the news reports of how they stopped the fire from reaching that community up north - Dobbins was the name I believe. If your organization did not exist, there might have been greater damage and loss of life at that refinery fire. And the town in the Sierras would probably be a smoking ruin now. You have already made a great difference in the short time since this new company was founded. Had you died in the fire, Ethan Davis would have won and those other people would have lost their homes and, in some cases, their lives".

"You really think so?", Joe asked weakly.

"I am certain of it!", replied Allen forcefully. "In addition, most of the Firebombers personnel would be unemployed".

Joe looked up at Allen. His resolve slowly began to return. "You're right", Joe said finally. "We have made a difference. And I intend that we should continue to make a difference. I appreciate the job you and your people did with Holmstead. I would like you to begin work on finding Ethan Davis. Spare no expense. Leave no leads unexplored. Hereagain, nothing illegal, just good solid surveillance and sleuthing. Find him for me, Allen. I have a score to settle with the gentleman".·

"Consider it done", Allen asserted. "Actually, I took the liberty of doing some advance work in this regard already. I had anticipated some interest on your part in the matter".

Joe smiled and said, "That's probably why we've worked so well together over the years. We understand each other".

"Most of the time. I believe that is all I have for the moment. Nothing yet on license to manufacture Firebombers equipment here, I'm afraid".

"That's all right. Catching up with our slippery friend was quite an accomplishment in and of itself. Now, let's see if you can repeat your performance with Ethan Davis".

"Rest assured we will find him. If there is nothing else, I shall go convey your wishes to my staff".

"Good hunting!", Joe called after him. Joe's thoughts turned to his family briefly, then he forced the memories out of his mind. He returned to his work with a vengeance.

The command staff debriefed everyone involved in the Sierras operation. Joe called a staff meeting a few days later in order to discuss their findings.

"One of the critical items which was lacking in the ground campaign was up-to-date information for the Ground Boss", said Zack. "When will that fourth CCC van be delivered?"

"Approximately two weeks from tomorrow", replied Jerry. "The plant manager asked me to relay a message to you about the damaged truck. It seems that the vehicle will require more extensive repairs than first believed. It appears that the shock of the log hitting the vehicle did some widespread systems damage. Although the damage is not catastrophic, it has impacted several systems. Since they already have the vehicle, they would like to take· this opportunity to make repairs. He estimated a delay of an additional week to complete their repairs and testing. Would this be acceptable?"

"I don't suppose we have much choice, really", grumbled Zack. "Yeah, let them keep it. We should be receiving our next pair shortly anyway".

"By next Monday, from what he said", Jerry mentioned. "I shall relay your decision to him, then".

"In the meantime, why don't you use my CCC van for Jack", said Joe. "He certainly needs it more than I do".

"I'm sure he'll appreciate the loan", said Zack. "Another critical item is the need for an ambulance evacuation vehicle. We had several casualties at this fire, but no way to get them out. I don't want to withdraw a pumper from the line to carry them down to the aid-station. Could those APCs move along with the engine companies for this purpose?"

"I would prefer to keep the Cat Teams intact for now", said Joe. "The APCs are meant as a rescue vehicle for people trapped by fire. We have no other means of filling that need".

"Could we buy some more M-113s and simply use them for ambulances?", asked Zack. "They wouldn't have to be fireproofed like the ones in the Cat Teams".

"I'll take it under advisement", said Joe noncommittally. "You realize that in order to get these additional APCs to the fire we would also have to buy more transports. I'm already purchasing an additional twenty-five C-130s so that we don't have to play this game of 'who goes in first' every time there's a fire".

"Yeah, I know", said Zack sourly. "Money doesn't grow on trees".

"That's for sure", snorted Joe. "Don't worry, Zack. I didn't say no, I just said wait. If the money starts coming in from sales of our firefighting products, we may be able to afford some extra APCS. Have patience".

"Is there any way we could airlift water to the fire line?", asked Zack. "We almost ran out, even with 1500 gallon capacity on each engine. Could the transports drop containers of water on pallets or something? If it hadn't been for those guys in Ryder trucks hauling it up to the line, we would have run dry before the fire was out."

"I know the Army runs fuel up to the front with what they call bladders", said Pieter. "But I think they generally use helicopters to transport it. I don't know whether the bladders would survive an air-drop, even from low altitudes".

"I've seen firefighting helos bring buckets of water up to the line units at a few fires", said Zack. "Could you look into it for me, Pieter?"

"I'll see what I can find out", replied Pieter.

"We also have a problem retrieving our crews once they're on the fire line", said Zack. "We had to sweet-talk the folks from CDF into loaning us their busses to cart the firejumpers out from the Sierras after this fire. Is there any way we could transport busses to the fire?"

"Hereagain, that's going to require extra planes to get them there", cautioned Joe. "How about if we simply make arrangements with a local transportation company near the fire. They could contract several busses out to us for a fraction of the cost of buying busses and transports. We wouldn't have to maintain them, either. Besides that, CDF or the local Forestry outfits usually have trucks and busses at the fires for their personnel. We could work out a deal where they hauled our guys and gals back to civilization for a price".

"If they don't mind stranding their guys out there in the woods", said Zack skeptically. "I just hope we don't get into a fire really far out in the boonies. There might not be any bus companies around there to rent to us".

"An option in that case would be to airlift the busses from wherever they were available and land them at some local airstrip", said Abner. "They could be driven from there to wherever your firejumpers were located".

"I'll buy that", said Zack more cheerfully. "That sounds workable. It's not as good as having busses of our own, but it's the next best thing".

"I'm glad that's settled", said Joe. "Pieter, what suggestions do you have?"

"I think we should only have four squadrons of firebombers airborne at one time", replied Pieter.

"Crew fatigue?", asked Joe.

"Yeah. The guys were getting pretty sloppy by the time we finished fighting that fire at Calpine", said Pieter. "If we rotate the firebomber crews the same way we did with the Hawkeyes, I think we would be able to get better results. The temptation to keep the firebombers up there too long is pretty strong. We've equipped the planes to remain airborne indefinitely, but we forget about the pilots, who wear out after a few hours of intense operations".

"Do you think having only one squadron down at a time would be enough?", asked Joe. "What about resting two at a time. That would give you even more flexibility wouldn't it?"

"They don't need eight hours of sleep", replied Pieter. "Even just a couple of hours off would do them good. Besides, we're there to fight fires. If I have too many planes on the ground, it means we aren't hitting the fires hard enough. No, I think one squadron on the ground at a time would be plenty" .

"I think we should also retain one company of firejumpers, sort of as a strategic reserve", added Zack. "We got caught short by that breach up by Dobbins. We could have used an extra company building a fireline in front of the town".

"I'll OK both of those suggestions, then", said Joe. "Anything else?"

"I was wondering when the additional transports were slated to arrive?", asked Pieter.

"Jerry, what's the schedule on those?", asked Joe.

"Projected delivery date is in early September, I believe", replied Jerry.

"Suits me fine", said Pieter. "We'll need some time to hire and train the new aircrews anyway. They should be ready by the time the planes arrive. Dave, I still haven't heard anything about the low-level avoidance gear. What's the story on that?"

"They're working day and night on that over at Talon Electronics", Dave replied. "They've run into several bugs with the system".

"How soon do they plan to begin field testing of the system?", asked Pieter.

"Unknown", Dave answered. "Until the first one works on the bench, they won't be doing any field tests. I doubt you'll see it available before the first of next year. Sorry" .

"I guess we'll just have to avoid power lines until then", Pieter grumbled. "I think we should also consider adding an additional transport to the 1st Composite. That C-130 the maintenance crews outfitted came in handy up at Redding. If we hadn't had those guys along it would have taken longer to convert the transports for firefighting. I suggest we rearrange our transports to accommodate more of our ground crews as well. Just something to think about for the future. Lastly, I think we should consider outfitting our transports with TRIDINT equipment in case we need to fly them through heavy smoke again". He turned to Joe and said, "That's about all I've got to report".

"Thank you, Pieter", said Joe. "One thing which was pointed out shortly before we left was equipping the ground troops with some kind of night-vision gear. Dave, what can we get from off-the-shelf sources to fit that need?"

"My recommendation would be to adapt the low-level TV systems we already incorporate in the firebombers to the Cat Team equipment", Dave answered. "We could also provide some night-vision goggles for some of the firejumpers. That would probably take care of just about any situation we're likely to encounter".

"I was wondering why you guys don't get some helicopters for shuttling casualties back from the line", said Abner. "Then you could also move supplies and water back up to the line crews, like Zack was talking about".

"Before you joined the organization, we had considered that problem at some length", said Joe. "The problem is, helicopters are too slow to keep up with our other planes and they also have insufficient range. We really need something which is fast, but can operate vertically when needed, like a helicopter".

"There is a plane which might be of some use for that job", said Abner. "An Osprey".

"That's it!", shouted Pieter. "I'd been trying to remember the name of that thing. The Air Force calls that a V-22, don't they?"

"I don't know whether the Air Force has really been involved with it", replied Abner. "I think the Marines were the ones really interested in it. It would provide them with a great transport for their ground troops".

"Yeah, that's right", agreed Pieter. "It's been a few years since I'd heard the name, but I think you're right, that might just fill the bill for what we're looking for".

"What's an Osprey?", Joe asked.

"A tilt-rotor aircraft which was being developed a few years ago", replied Abner. "That was when the military boom went bust. I don't even know if production ever began. It seems to me that they would serve the purpose of not only keeping up with your planes, but filling the roles of ambulance and supply ferry".

"I think you fellows have something to do a little research on", said Joe. "OK, anything else?" He scanned the room, but no one spoke up. "No? Very well, meeting adjourned".

Jerry came up to Joe outside the conference room. "You look tired, Joe", said Jerry. "Have you been sleeping at night?"

"Not as well as I would like to be", said Joe. "Those nightmares about Martha and Desiree keep recurring, not every night, but often enough".

"Have you talked to someone about them?", asked Jerry.

"Not lately. I figure they'll go away with time", Joe answered evasively. "It's been a long time since they really bothered me this much. I don't know why they've come back. That information Allen's operatives got out of the arsonist must have unsettled me more than I thought".

"I can see why it would", said Jerry sympathetically. "But you can't let it dominate your life. Remember what happened the last time it did?"

"Don't remind me. That was something I don't ever want to relive".

"All the more reason for you to seek out help", Jerry persisted. "It would be best to nip this problem in the bud rather than allowing it to continue to fester inside you".

"I can handle it, OK?", snapped Joe. "I just need some time, that's all!"

"As you wish", replied Jerry softly. "I hope you find your answer soon".

As Jerry walked away, Joe realized that he had been unreasonable with his friend. What was wrong with him? What did he need? He shook his head and slowly walked back to his office.

That night, he took out Martha's Bible and began reading from it. He had been reading out of it on an intermittent basis and found the words, especially those of Jesus in the New Testament, comforting. As he read, he felt the anguish in his heart begin to abate. That night, he slept much more soundly than he had in weeks.

Chapter 30

Over the rest of the summer and early fall, Firebombers Incorporated earned the reputation of a mobile, hard-hitting firefighting organization, just as Joe had wanted. Through the course of many fires in California and the West, the name became widely known. Both Federal and the various State firefighting outfits called on FI frequently.

By the time the official fire season came to an end in the middle of autumn, the firejumpers had been outfitted with their own transports. Five new squadrons of C-130s were added to the ranks, 106th through 110th Lift Squadrons (Parahaulers, Nightriders, Jumpstarters, Cargomasters, and Cannonballers, respectively). The fourth CCC van and its transport became operational, and the maintenance transport was also added, bringing 1st Composite Squadron up to its full complement of nine planes and allowing Joe and his staff to have one CCC van to themselves again.

Dave had finally made good on his promise to provide a low-level wire-avoidance radar system on the planes. The system, dubbed High-Wire was a resounding success and in tests had detected wires across the path of low-flying aircraft from several hundred yards away, allowing the crews to pull up before colliding with power lines, especially at night.

Joe had managed to make it to most of the fires his organization engaged. Those he missed, due to company business, he kept on top of by radio. Sales of firefighting products were growing exponentially. The operation was still not self-sufficient, but Joe considered the initial investment to be worthwhile for the promise of the future.

Joe and his staff planned to tour the western United States in late Fall for the purpose of demonstrating their organization's firefighting prowess. By the time the middle of November arrived, Firebombers Incorporated was putting on a show just outside of Tucson, Arizona.

Far away, in the foothills of the San Gabriel Mountains northeast of Los Angeles, a brushfire was beginning. Firefighters from all over the area were converging on the blaze, but Santa Ana winds were quickly spreading the fire across the foothills out of control.

"Joe there's a phone call for you", Zack called from the Fire Boss CCC van. Joe was annoyed at the interruption. The engine companies were just being air-landed and Joe always enjoyed seeing that operation.

"Hello, this is Joe Talon", he said sharply. It was Henry Luce.

"Joe, what are you doing over there?", shouted Henry. "Don't you know there's a fire here in L.A.?"

"Sure, I know there's a fire there", Joe replied testily. "But I've been told to keep my people out of L.A. County until further notice by the officials there".

Henry was dumbfounded. "What idiot ordered that?", he asked.

Joe explained the story to Henry, after which Henry seemed to get very angry. "We're pulling in fire companies from as far away as the Canadian border on this one!", he shouted. "Let me talk to those 'gentlemen'. I'll get back to you on this. And get your gear packed, you're to be here as soon as I get it approved, OK?"

"I think I'll wait to see what develops first", Joe replied noncommittally. "I've dealt with these guys before. I don't even think an emergency will change their minds".

"We'll see about that!", shouted Henry. Joe heard the phone slam down at the other end, then went back to watching the show. He wondered what kind of hornet's nest Henry could stir up. He was not optimistic, but there was some small possibility Henry's gentle persuasion might just work.

An hour later, the demonstration was finished. Joe walked over to Abner and Zack. Pieter and the firebombers were just landing behind them.

"Abner, I want the planes fueled up and the equipment loaded up immediately", said Joe. "Zack, I want your people to stow their gear aboard the transports and have everything ready to move out on a moment's notice".

"The fire in L.A.?", asked Abner.

"Yep. I received a call from Henry Luce about an hour ago", replied Joe. "Seems he was a little ticked about our exclusion from the party. I don't think I would want to be in the Supervisors' shoes when he comes calling".

"We'd better get some food shipped over here quick, then", said Zack. "Jack, can you find out if there's a catering service available? It would be quicker than sending two thousand guys out to restaurants!"

"Besides that, we'd know where they were", agreed Abner. "No late-comers, no auto accidents on the way out or back".

Pieter walked up a few minutes later. "What's going on?", he asked.

"We might be getting a new lease on life in L.A.", replied Joe. "Henry called up and wants us at that foothill fire".

"What about that restriction from the county?", asked Pieter.

"Henry is evidently going to bat for us on that", Joe answered. "I've told the guys to get everything in order for a hasty departure, just in case. Go get your guys refueled, Pieter. And tell them to stick around. We've got meals on wheels ordered".

"Will do!", said Pieter. He trotted back to the firebombers.

Abner and Zack put out a message over the radio instructing the crews of the new orders. After a small amount of protest, the crews turned to their tasks. Jack was able to find a catering service to bring in lunch and everyone was already chowing down when another call came in for Joe.

"I had to do a little head-bashing over at city hall and the county building, but I finally got them to rescind the order", said an obviously ecstatic Henry. "So, when can you guys be here?"

"Well, it just so happens that the guys are finishing up lunch now", said Joe. "We figured to move out as soon as they're briefed, say, about an hour from now?"

"None too soon for my needs", said Henry. "At least you should have a tail wind with those Santa Anas behind you!"

"I don't know. I think we'll have headwinds for the first part of the trip. It's been kicking up a little over here from that same high-pressure area. We almost had to cancel the firejumper demonstration because of the gusts".

"Whatever", said Henry. "Just hurry up will ya? We've got a fire from Heninger Flats in Altadena clear across practically to Azusa. We need all the help we can get! I need to talk to your command staff to decide on a point of attack."

"You got it", said Joe. "I'll give you Zack next. We'll see you when we see you!"

Joe handed off the phone to Zack and went to announce the news to the troops. Despite missing a night of relaxation, most of them were excited about the prospect of some action close to home. Zack had already returned to his van by the time Joe was done talking. As the crews finished their lunch, Joe walked over to the Fire Boss CCC van.

"What did you guys finally come up with for a plan of attack?", Joe asked as he stepped inside.

"We've come up with two, actually", said Zack. "If the winds are minimal, we'll airdrop the firejumpers into the area we've been allotted above Monrovia. If winds are too high, we'll land at San Bernardino and bus them over to the fire, along with the Cat Team vehicles on our truck transports. There's no other airport that we'd want to land at except Ontario. If we're already clear out at Ontario, we might just as well put down at home. The difference in time to the fire will probably be about fifteen or twenty minutes. If we land them to the west of the fire, we'll have to fight rush-hour traffic to get them there. That pretty well eliminates the other airports big enough to handle us".

"What about the engine companies?", asked Joe.

"We'll land them at Talon Aerospace as well. The whole outfit can make their way to the fire as a unit, allowing them to go into action together."

"I'd like to suggest an alternative to your plan", said Joe. "Instead of putting the engine companies down at Talon Aerospace, I want to do an air-landing at a light-plane airport, like Cable or Brackett".

"Why? The amount of time we'd gain by being closer to the fire would be minimal and the danger of damage to personnel and equipment, especially in this much wind, would be pretty high. What possible reason could you have for running this high a risk?"

"Publicity", said Joe firmly. "We took a beating from the press after that little debacle at City Hall. I want everyone to know that we've been called back to bail the city out. I want the press on hand when we land and I want them along with us every step of the way when we go up to the fireline".

"Much as I'd like to rub the city fathers' collective noses in this, I don't much like the idea of risking our people's necks to salvage our reputation", replied Zack. "If we do this, it's over my objections".

"I understand", said Joe. "But you've also got to understand this. Those fires we fought this year barely paid for the gas to get us there. The brunt of the cost has fallen on Talon Industries in general and on me in particular. If we don't make a major splash with this fire, projections are that sales of our firefighting products are going to start tapering off. Without that to bolster our finances, I'll probably be forced to disband the organization.

"Also, consider the fact that *all* our transport pilots are former military pilots. They've trained to fly through and land in all types of weather. That, coupled with their experience from doing air landings in practice and at fires gives them an edge over any pilots you've ever seen. I'd put these folks up against the best transport pilots in the world any day of the week".

Zack stared at Joe for a moment, carefully weighing the risks in the light of his statements. Finally, he sighed heavily, shook his head. "OK. Abner, let's air-land them at Brackett Field".

Abner looked from Zack to Joe and said, "You guys are serious about this? Like Zack said, we are going to be running a pretty high risk with these Santa Anas blowing".

"I'm confident we can do it", Joe stated. "Are you?"

"Sure, we can get the equipment in if we use our JATOs to get out again", replied Abner. "I wouldn't want to actually land C-130s there, although we might manage to get off again. Airstrip's too short for that. Assuming the gusts are minimal, it should be fine for touch-and-gos".

"Good thing the transports didn't use their JATOs today", said Pieter. "I don't suppose you would have wanted to stop by the base to pick any new ones up, would you Joe?"

"Nope. I want us to get to the fire as fast as possible", Joe replied. "So we're all agreed on the plan? Then get your people briefed. I'll have Jerry call up a charter service so those busses are ready and waiting at Talon Aerospace, in case the winds are too bad to air-drop the firejumpers".

Less than an hour later, the crews were briefed, transportation arranged for, and the personnel loaded. The airport tower gave Hawk One clearance a few minutes later. As it lumbered down the runway, close to 100 planes were lined up on taxiways awaiting their turn to depart. First Composite Squadron led the air wing out. The refueling tankers followed and behind them came the slower-moving firebombers. Finally, the Lift and Heavy Lift squadrons piled out.

Joe was looking at the visual display of the Firebombers planes a short while after they had formed up and climbed to altitude. Dave had designed a system for providing aircraft power and a data-link to the Hawkeyes for each CCC van during transit. This allowed the staff to keep in touch just in case there was a change in status at a fire while they were still enroute.

Joe was looking at the view from Hawk Two's aft-looking cameras and it was breathtaking. He could see all of the planes from lst Composite Squadron and the refueling squadron distinctly, followed by the massed squadrons of firebombers and transports flying in neat 'V' formations. The aircraft became less distinct farther back and finally appeared as mere dots back at the end of the line.

Despite the fact that they had filed flight plans, radar operators from three states were alarmed to see the armada of aircraft entering their sectors over the next hour. Henry Luce had called ahead to the local airports around Southern California advising them of the incoming aircraft. The skies were already cluttered with air-tankers, helicopters, and spotter aircraft grappling with the brushfires in the hills above L.A.

Although the Santa Anas had decreased, winds were still too gusty when the air wing approached San Bernardino, so the firejumper and Cat Team transports set down at Talon Aerospace and the firejumpers hurried out to the waiting charter busses. The tractor transports were loaded up as quickly as possible with the Caterpillars and APCs.

CAC had radioed Brackett Field in La Verne to alert them to the incoming traffic. The controllers began diverting the light planes normally frequenting the airport so that the C-130s could insert the engine companies and CCC vans. The press had been alerted and the California Highway Patrol had also been advised of the incoming fire equipment by the Forestry officials. They had agreed to provide an escort to the fire just in case rush-hour traffic (or gawkers) became a problem.

The long line of royal-blue transports came in low across Pomona on their approach to Brackett Field. The transports carrying the CCC vans were up first.

"Well Ken, here we go again", said Suzie as she lined up 'Double Trouble' on the distant airstrip. "Think they could have found us a shorter strip?"

"Cheer up!", said Ken. "It could be worse. It could be an aircraft carrier!".

"Now wouldn't that be fun to try?", said Suzie. "Gear coming down. Ramp down!", she yelled into the intercom. The loading ramp began to descend and the loadmasters disconnected aircraft power and the communications cables from the CCC van as Suzie chopped power close to landing speed. The range was still coming down rapidly, even at this slow speed.

"Brackett Tower, this is Hunter leader", Suzie spoke over the radio. "Are we cleared for LAPES op?"

"Hunter leader, this is Brackett Tower, the field's all yours", replied the controller. "Wind bearing zero-four-five degrees at fifteen knots, gusts to twenty knots".

"Copy that, tower", replied Suzie. "I don't like all these bumps, Ken!"

"You and me both!", replied Ken. The gusts of wind were buffeting the transport as it approached the landing strip, requiring the pilot and co-pilot to work together to keep the plane properly aligned.

In the CCC van, Joe noticed the buffeting as well. It had been choppy ever since they had departed Tucson two hours before. Dave was looking a little green at the moment. Joe began wondering about the wisdom of adding air-sickness bags to the van. Zack's already had them.

"Are you all right Dave?", asked Jerry. He had noticed Dave's coloring as well.

"I will be once we get on the ground", Dave answered weakly.

"That should be any second now", said Joe encouragingly. "Hang in there".

'Double Trouble' crossed the end of the airstrip as a slight downdraft occurred. The plane dipped closer to the ground, too close for Suzie's liking.

"Let's get rid of this thing!", she shouted to Ken. "Drop load!", she called over the intercom. The drogue chutes deployed out the back of the transport and the CCC van slid out of the cargo bay.

"Load clear!", shouted the loadmaster.

"Full power! Engage JATOs! Raise ramp! Gear up!", Suzie commanded. The JATO packs flared to life back on the fuselage. The big transport shuddered with the sudden increase in power and lift. It rapidly sped away from the landing strip, heading west over Puddingstone Reservoir. A powerful downdraft dropped it thirty feet with a sudden lurch seconds later. Overhead, the Tag-Team orbited protectively, scanning for fires in the unlikely event the JATOs had started any.

"Now comes the really fun part", said Suzie. "Clearing those hills up ahead!"

"With no load, we should be able to do that with no problem, don't you think?", asked Ken nervously.

"Just as long as we don't get any more of those downdrafts", she replied.

The van bumped onto the ground at which time the driver quickly maneuvered the vehicle over to the side of the landing strip, away from the incoming transports.

"Thank God, we're back on solid earth!", said Dave.

"Remind me never to come along if there's turbulence again, will you Jerry?", asked Joe.

"I shall try to remember that", replied Jerry as he unstrapped himself.

The Anderson family was heading home on the 210 freeway after a pleasant day visiting friends in Diamond Bar. Ahead of them, the sky had a dirty brownish tinge due to the brushfire to the west. The three kids in the back of the station wagon were all exhausted from playing and their parents were enjoying the peace and quiet for a change.

Their car had just passed Via Verde offramp and begun heading downhill going north when a large royal blue aircraft suddenly shot across the freeway, seemingly just above their car. The sound of the powerful turboprops at full output, along with the spectacle of the flaming rockets near the rear caused Mr. Anderson to swerve his car inadvertently, thinking they were going to collide. The youngest child was dozing with her face turned towards the west when she was startled by the sudden noise up ahead. She opened her eyes and saw the plane rocket across the freeway above the car and her eyes grew as big as saucers. Her brother and sister were quickly awake as well and pressed their faces up against the window to watch the transport slowly move out of view amongst the hills to the west.

The youngest turned towards her parents in the front seat, who had recovered their composure by now, and gleefully shouted, "Do it again, Daddy! Do it again!"

Zack radioed Henry once their CCC van was on the ground. As they talked, transport after transport came soaring in, deposited their cargoes and rocketed skyward. Soon, all five engine companies and the four CCC vans were on the ground.

"I see you have the CHP here to meet us", Zack told Henry.

"They were happy to oblige", said Henry. "We need you guys at the fire yesterday and they know it. I just hope your fancy fire trucks can keep up with them. Oh, and did the press corps make it?"

"Yep, they're snapping pictures for all they're worth", said Zack. "Joe's already invited several to ride with him to the fire. We'll let you know when we reach Monrovia".

The convoy was soon streaming out of the airport, CHP cruisers interspersed with the fire trucks and CCC vans, their emergency lights flashing and sirens wailing. A trio of CHP motorcyclists led the way and took turns peeling off to block cross-traffic at intersections ahead of the convoy to speed them along. A few minutes later, motorists on the 210 freeway heading north were surprised to see the convoy racing up the Covina Blvd. onramp. Even though the average speed of the traffic was over the 65 mph speed limit, the long convoy quickly pulled away from them, heading towards the burning hills beyond.

"CAC, what's the status on our firejumpers and Cat Teams?", asked Zack.

"They're inbound with CHP escort now, sir", replied CAC. "Just passing through Ontario. ETA is twenty-two minutes at present speed. The maintenance bird and the tankers set down at Talon Aerospace a few minutes ago".

"Very well", replied Zack. He turned to one of his aides and said, "Let's just hope they can maintain present speed".

"Look at the fire!", said Dave. He was looking over the Hawkeye's TRIDINT display in Joe's CCC van. "It must spread for miles!"

"Almost twenty miles, according to the scale", said Jerry quietly. "How much help do we have available to fight it?"

"Lots", replied Joe. "At last count, there were over sixty engine companies on the line. Add to that the ground pounders from out of state and our people and we've got four thousand firefighters".

"Plus all the air-tankers", added Dave. "Look at all the radar blips out there!"

"I'm glad we've got both Hawkeyes along", said Joe. "I don't know if one could track all of this traffic".

Over in Gold Hill Estates, the flames were plainly visible on the nearby hills. Thus far, the fire had confined itself to the upper elevations of the hills there. The wind kept shifting, though, and both the homeowners and the local fire officials were concerned about the fire reaching the homes in this northernmost development. Many families had already packed their most prized possessions and left. A few hardy souls, fearing looters more than the fire and not wanting to give up their homes without a fight, stayed there and kept an eye on the as-yet distant fire.

"TRIDINT's off-line again Jimmy!", said Tim in exasperation.

"Ah knew we should have checked that thing agin 'afore we left", grumbled Jimmy. The TRIDINT display had been acting up ever since they had departed San Bernardino for their show at Tucson. "See what yew kin do with the thing, Tim".

"I think we've got a bad processor board", said Tim. "There's not much I can do without a new board".

"Give it a whang. Sometimes that's th' only way to git the thing's attention!"

"That did it! I just hope it stays fixed until we can get it back to the shop for servicing".

"Ah wouldn't count on it if'n ah was you". Jimmy looked out the window at the groups of circling firebombers. "Looks like CAC's got ever'body lined up fer business".

"Yeah, and I can see why. We've got a lot of business to be doing. I wonder where we start?"

"At th' beginnin', of course!"

"Abner, what's the status of your firebombers?", Henry called over the radio as the Air Boss CCC van raced along the freeway heading north.

"They're loaded for bear. They refueled on the fly and just finished loading up from Morris Dam. Where do you want them? Monrovia?"

"Not just yet", answered Henry. "Let's hit the fires out in Duarte. They're getting out of hand with the wind change. I'm afraid they're going to get into some of those developments close to the hills. Bradbury Estates is being threatened now and the hand line is in danger of being breached. If you could augment it with a chemical line, they might be able to hold".

"Understood, Fire Boss", Abner replied. "I had planned to hold back one squadron, but it looks like we're going to need all five. I'll get them redirected now. He dialed up the Hawkeye and gave CAC instructions regarding the firebombers.

"Pathfinder leader, proceed to grid one-five-three and commence bombing op", the ATC called over the radio a few minutes later. "This will be a west-to-east vector in support of the companies engaged there. Wind is twenty knots bearing zero-four-five degrees with gusts up to thirty knots, acknowledge".

"Acknowledged, Hawk One", replied Pieter. "First run of the day, Ralph my boy!"

"I'm glad we're coming in out of the west", said Ralph. "That will keep the sun out of our eyes".

"And out of the TRIDINT's eyes, too. This wind is what worries me the most, though. We're going to have to drop high. No telling what kind of scatter we're going to get on the drops. If those fire crews are too close, they may get a bath".

"Better that than having those houses torched, I suppose. She seems to be bucking an awful lot with these gusts. I hope this wind lets up after dark".

"It's the first time I've had to fight these Santa Anas", said Pieter. "I don't know if they go away after dark or not. I seem to recall that they stick around even after the sun goes down, so they've nicknamed them 'sundowners'".

"Won't that be a fun combination. Smoke, darkness, and downdrafts. Mixes like that make for some fairly spectacular crashes, I'll bet".

"Let's hope not tonight", said Pieter. He now broke out of his orbital grid and led the squadron down towards the line of smoke above Bradbury. "I'd say those fellows have their hands full", he said as the plane lined up on the leading edge of the brushfire.

Below them, 250 CDF firefighters supported by over a dozen engines fought a losing battle to stem the relentless march of the fire. They had already fallen back twice and the line was now drawn up before the doorsteps of the first row of houses on the hilltop. Ordinarily they would not have tried to stop the fire until it had reached the top of the ridge. This time, however, the top of the ridge was lined with million-dollar homes.

There had been several casualties on the retreat up the ridge and one small group had been cut off when the fire had swept over their position on its march up the hillside. They had had enough sense to uproot all the brush and grass they could and to extinguish the few remaining clumps which caught fire. There wasn't time for the next step, which was to deploy the one-man emergency shelters each man carried. They all suffered some burns, but the fire soon passed them by and they retreated down the hill.

"Hose down that candle over there!", shouted the battalion chief as a tree went up in flames. Air support had been promised, but he didn't think it would get there in time. They would lose these homes in another five minutes if help didn't get here by then.

"Hawk One, this is Pathfinder leader", Pieter spoke into the radio. "We are beginning our attack run now".

"Understood, Pathfinder leader", replied the ATC. "Be advised there are firefighters trapped below the ridge. You have only a narrow margin for your load, so choose your spot carefully".

"Roger that", answered Pieter. He toggled the transmitter off. "Just what we need. More complications!"

"I get the feeling that's going to be the byword for this operation", said Ralph. "You want to go for a linked operation with all of this wind?"

"Yeah. With only five planes dropping at a time we should be able to get away with it", Pieter replied. His knuckles were beginning to turn white from the strain of keeping the plane steady on the approach. Suddenly, an alarm horn went off and a flashing line appeared on the TRIDINT display.

"Power line dead ahead!", Ralph shouted.

"Coming up! Pathfinder flight, pull up about 100 feet to clear power lines ahead, acknowledge!"

"Whew, that was close".

"Yeah. Remind me to give Dave a big kiss when we get back home".

"I didn't think you were one of those kinds of guys, Pieter".

"I'm not, but it will probably shock the heck out of Dave, which makes it all worthwhile", Pieter replied with a chuckle.

"OK, we're set", said Ralph a moment later. "One linked salvo on the way".

The first shake roof started to smoke as the flames closed on the top of the ridge. The heat was becoming too great for the firefighters to tolerate. The chief was just about ready to give the order to fall back when he heard aircraft engines off to the west. He couldn't see anything because of the smoke, but the sound was getting louder. Suddenly, a royal-blue bomber charged out of the swirling smoke less than a hundred feet in front of his line. The lead plane was followed by four more in quick succession, all flying at treetop level. As the line of planes drew exactly opposite of the chief's position, red retardant streamed out the bottoms of each plane simultaneously, smothering the advancing flames.

"That's knocked it back some!", shouted a company commander off to his left. "One more like that and we should be able to start heading down the hill again!"

The tired firefighters paused for a moment as the last wisps of retardant landed in front of them. Almost the moment the retardant settled, another squadron of firebombers, the Ridgerunners, raced in and dropped a load of retardant behind the first one. As the crews watched from the hilltop, three more squadrons dumped their loads at various places along the leading edge of the fire, effectively stopping its forward progress.

"Advance the line back down the hill!", called the relieved battalion chief. The firefighters extinguished the isolated patches of burning brush on the hilltop and began working their way back downhill. To the east of them, the Pathfinders were already reloading at Morris Dam in preparation for their next assignment.

"Where are our firejumpers now?", Joe asked Zack as he stepped out of the Fire Boss van to stretch. Several hours strapped into his seat while in the air (due to turbulence) and another half hour on the road left a good deal to be desired, even with padded seats. The reporters were recording every word said. Joe's voice was already beginning to get husky from talking and the pervasive smoke wisps. Ash fell all around them like fluffy snowflakes. The acrid smell of smoke was overwhelming.

"They're just coming around the bend of the 210 over in Glendora", replied Zack. "They should be here in about fifteen minutes".

Joe looked up at the hills above Monrovia and shook his head. Years of slow growth by the Pacific sage and mesquite bushes was going up in smoke right before his eyes. It would take decades to replace the foliage on those hillsides. He turned away and looked over at Abner, who was just emerging from his van. "What news?"

"Our bombers just creamed a portion of the fire over in Bradbury", replied Abner. "The line was just about to cave in there. We got a big 'thank you' from the battalion chief. The tankers have just completed refueling at Talon Aerospace and are waiting for CAC to give them the word to take off".

"How soon are you going to start working over the fire up here?", Dave asked.

"The firebombers are reloading right now", answered Abner. "They should be ready for their next drop in a few minutes. I think Henry wants us to lend air support to the guys over in Duarte before our ground personnel get here".

Joe was surprised by that. "What about the fires above Monrovia? I thought those were a priority target?"

"The wind has shifted. The fire has retreated farther up the hills away from the housing. He wants to take advantage of the lull here to shore up the line over in Duarte".

"I hope he knows what he's doing", replied Joe skeptically. "With the speed this wind is blowing the fire at, the brush isn't being completely burned up. The fire could sweep right back over a previously burned area and be in our laps before we could react".

"Our engine companies have redeployed along the Monrovia-Duarte border, now", one of Zack's assistants called out of the Fire Boss van. "Do you want them to move out or wait for the firejumpers?"

"Where are the firejumpers now?", asked Zack.

"Nearing the 605 interchange, about four miles out", replied the aide.

"Tell Jack to hold on. We might as well get some additional ground support with those engines."

"The fire is pretty active in that region right now", Zack told Joe. "Henry wants us to concentrate on the area just to the west of Bradbury Estates, then pivot from there towards Monrovia once the fire has been driven back from those houses".

"Who else do we have on the flanks?", asked Joe.

"Duarte and Monrovia Fire Departments have sent every unit they have up to the left flank. They've been fighting this thing since it started and are due to be spelled. CDF has an entire battalion over on the right flank. With our guys moving in, the DFD and MFD units will pull back to rest and the CDF will pull some of their guys out for a breather too. We'll plug the gap and start spreading out from the middle. Our anchor points will be Bradbury Estates on the right and the area around Norumbega Street on the left".

"Zack, Henry needs to talk to you!", an aide called out from the Fire Boss van.

Zack walked back into the Fire Boss van and put on the headset. "What's up Henry?"

"We have a crisis developing in northern Arcadia", Henry replied over the radio. "We need you to commit your two Cat Teams up there. You can truck them up to the grounds of Foothill High School. Do you see that on your map?"

"Affirmative. Where do you want the Cat line?"

"They are to move east and begin a Cat line just past the property line of the school, understood?"

"Clearly understood", replied Zack. "We'll switch them over to your command frequency so you can direct them. Out. Patch me into the Cat Team truck transports", Zack shouted over to his assistant.

"Hey, look at that!", said a young boy to his friend in his back yard. They could see the line of truck transports rolling past their house.

"Looks like a tractor or something on the back", replied the friend.

"They're heading for the school grounds!", shouted the first boy. "Let's go see!" They both hurried out the gate and arrived up at the school grounds as the first vehicle rolled off the transport. Men were running all over the grounds starting up their vehicles.

The two boys came running up to Jose as he was dropping the ramps from the truck holding his M-113. George was just preparing to drive his bulldozer off another truck.

"Hey mister, what's going on?", asked the older of the two boys.

"We're going over there to clear all that brush away so the fire doesn't come down and burn up your houses", replied Jose. Manuel shot him a nasty look and motioned for him to stop talking. Jose pointedly ignored the message.

"Can we ride along?", asked the younger boy hopefully.

"Sorry, kid. No riders today. You wouldn't happen to have an older sister who might like to ride along, would you?"

"Not me", answered the younger boy.

"I do, but she's not home right now", said the older one.

"Maybe I could stop by later when we get done here and take her for a ride then."

Manuel finished removing the restraints from the trailer at this point and came around to the side of the APC. He grabbed Jose roughly by the collar and began dragging him away from the startled boys.

"I'll be back later!", yelled Jose as he was taken away. "Tell her to meet me here at eleven tonight, OK?"

"You ain't gonna be here at eleven tonight, Romeo", snarled Manuel. "You're gonna be up there driving this hunk of junk around, understand?"

"Hey man, we're not in the Army anymore", protested Jose. "You can't tell me what to do after hours, so get off my case!"

"Get in there and drive!", shouted Manuel as he forced Jose through the rear door of the APC. The boys watched as the two Cat Teams formed up, then moved off east, plowing through the chain-link fence (no one could find a gate on that side big enough for the equipment to go through) and into the hills beyond.

The boys looked at the churned up field and the ruined fence. "What a mess", the older boy said as they walked away. "Do you think they're going to come back and clean this stuff up?"

"I don't know", said his companion. "I don't think we should tell anybody about this, though".

"Why not?"

"Because they might try to blame us for the mess!"

"Yeah, you're right", the older boy said with disgust. "Nobody ever believes us anyway".

"Our firejumpers have arrived and are moving into position, sir", one of Zack's assistants told him. Joe had come over to see what the Fire Boss was up to. Abner was still directing the firebombers to attack the fire above Bradbury. The fire there had been driven back almost half a mile, but still showed no signs of diminishing.

"I wish we could attack this thing from the base instead of from the head", Zack complained. "I definitely don't like seeing people going downhill against the head. That combination makes for more casualties than you can shake a stick at".

Joe stepped out of the van and looked west. The sun was slowly slipping below the horizon. The smell of smoke was overpowering. The sky was almost completely filled with smoke, coloring the setting sun a deep red. It was gone a short while later and twilight settled over the surrounding communities. Joe watched the light from the now-hidden sun creep up along the higher mountainsides. Soon, they were completely bereft of sunlight. He hoped the wind would die with the onset of night, but Henry's meteorologist said it didn't look likely. It would be a long night, Joe decided.

"Forestry tankers just flattened the center of the fire below Mt. Wilson!", Zack exulted an hour later. "They threw over twenty tankers and choppers at the sucker in one massive series of drops. Tore the heart right out of it. They have the line split now. CDF is going to handle everything from Arcadia east and Forestry will start rolling up the flank from Arcadia west".

"That's pretty risky using their air-tankers this late in the day, isn't it?", asked Joe.

"They used their own spotters to lead the tankers in", said Zack. "All's the tankers had to do was drop when the spotters told them to. Worked like a champ!"

"How are we doing out here?", asked Joe.

"So far, so good", answered Zack. "The two Cat Teams are clearing a two-hundred yard wide swath above Arcadia right now. That should reduce the chance of any kind of fire penetration over there. Our own fire companies have been pushed back by the fire over above Duarte. They haven't been able to push any farther north, let alone pivot and head west. Looks like Monrovia will have to wait".

"Is the fire still staying up in the hills there?", asked Joe.

"Looks like it. Abner is keeping the Tag-Team over that area just in case it starts moving down out of the mountains again".

"Our firebombers are making another drop above Bradbury", said one of Zack's aides. "That should complete the chemical line there".

"Good, good", said Zack with a smile. "If that wind doesn't start whipping up any more, CDF can flank the fire we're having trouble with. Add in the full weight of the bombers and I'd say we may just about have this one on the run".

Joe wandered back over to his CCC van. Jerry and Dave were intently watching a portable TV Dave had installed in the van.

"Well, what's the news?", asked Joe as he stepped inside and sat down.

"Looks like we're beginning to get the upper hand", said Dave. "The portion of the fire around Pasadena-Altadena is 50% contained now. They expect full containment by morning".

"They have said nothing about our part of the fire, however", added Jerry. "Did Zack have any forecasts on that one?"

"He's optimistic", said Joe. "But our line is still being pushed back and the portion above Monrovia is almost completely unprotected".

"I wouldn't worry too much", said Dave reassuringly. "These guys know what they're doing".

"I just hope you're right", said Joe quietly.

"That ball-and-chain is really clearing out this stuff", George told Zack over the radio. "If we had to do this with just our blades, we would have been here for days!".

"Glad to hear it", replied Zack. "How are you guys doing on fuel?"

"Still more than three-quarters full", said George. "We should be done here in another forty minutes, an hour tops. Where do you want us after that?"

"Unless Henry says otherwise, proceed east and start clearing brush above Monrovia", answered Zack.

"Understood. Oh, by the way. About the fence at that school..."

"Don't worry, we have that covered. We're going to be making regular monthly deductions from your paycheck to make up the cost".

"Gee, thanks boss. You're all heart. No Christmas card for you this year!"

"So what's new? I didn't get one from you last year!"

"Can I help it if you didn't give me the right address?"

"Complain, complain, complain. All's I hear all day long is complaints!", said Zack with a laugh. "Never mind about the fence. We'll take care of it. Fire Boss out".

George finished the last row of his portion of the firebreak and pulled over to the side. He climbed out of the cab and looked over the scene around him. Far above him, the mountain was being consumed by flames. Below him, the rest of the bulldozers were completing their task as the APC crews used hand tools to clear patches missed by the Cats. He looked over to the east and noticed that the fire seemed to be lower on the mountains there than it had been twenty minutes before.

"CAC, we're getting a little low on both fuel and retardant", Pieter called over the radio, "Suppose you could send some liquid refreshment our way?"

"Already taken care of, Pathfinder leader", replied the senior controller. "The tankers were scrambled twenty minutes ago. Turn right to new course zero-niner-zero and climb to 3000 feet. I will detail the tankers to rendezvous with you there, acknowledge".

"Acknowledged. Pathfinder leader out. Care to try your hand at some night refueling kiddo?"

"Sure, why not", replied Ralph. "Is the insurance paid up on this thing?"

"Ha! If you ram that tanker, you won't be around to collect any insurance".

"Now there's an encouraging thought", Ralph observed glumly.

"I just calls them as I sees them", Pieter replied wistfully. Far ahead of them, the refueling squadron was orbiting over La Verne. CAC relayed instructions to the tanker leader after which the squadron executed a slow turn and began running east at minimum speed. Within minutes, the Pathfinders were being refueled as the remaining squadrons continued to fight the fire above Duarte.

Once the first squadron had been refueled, they broke away and returned to Morris Dam to reload. CAC ordered the tankers to proceed west in order to meet up with the next firebomber squadron needing refueling, the Night Hawks. The tankers turned east over La Verne and repeated the refueling operation with the new squadron. This scenario was repeated until every firebomber squadron was tanked up and ready to go, at which time the tankers returned to San Bernardino for their own turn at refueling.

"Henry, what's the word on the westside fire?", Abner called over the radio.

"They're making splendid progress over in Pasadena", replied Henry. "Not quite so good in Altadena, though. It looks like they won't be able to contain this thing by midnight like they had hoped. All in all, it's going pretty well, though. How are your pilots holding up?"

"The firebombers just reloaded and should be starting the next series of runs over this Duarte fire", answered Abner. "The fire over in Bradbury looks to be in the mopping-up stages now, so I've diverted the bombers away from there".

"That jives with my information, too. If your line crews can hold the fire above those homes, I can swing the whole line across onto the flank and start rolling the fire up".

"You'll have to talk to Jack Bazranian about that. I think he's had some problems keeping ahead of that fire with no air support".

"That will change real soon, it sounds like", observed Henry. "Keep an eye on the hills above Monrovia. It looks like the wind is starting to push the fire back down the hill. That brush has been there for years and is thick as all get out. If the fire gets in there, we'll have a real fight on our hands".

"Don't worry, my guys' drops can even penetrate that stuff".

"I'll call up Jack and see how he's doing. Keep those drops coming, Abner".

Jack Bazranian was getting mighty tired of backing up. His units had already given up several hundred yards of ground trying to hold off the fire. With no air support, he had to rely almost exclusively on his pumpers, and there were too few of them to maintain the four-mile-long frontage he had been assigned. His firejumpers were doing their best, but the lack of hoses simply couldn't be compensated for by hand tools, especially when the smoke and heat was being blown into the firefighters' faces.

"Pressure from the hydrants is starting to drop, Jack!", yelled one of the company commanders.

"Keep hosing it down anyway!", Jack yelled back. At least we *have* hydrants to work with this time, he thought. There had been a half-dozen fires this past summer when he would have killed to have hydrants available.

"Ground Boss, this is CAC", a voice crackled over the radio. "We have two firebomber squadrons standing by. Where do you want it?"

"CAC, put it over on our right flank", Jack spoke into the radio. "Tell your guys to watch it, though. My people are right up at the fire's edge!"

"Copy that, Ground Boss. CAC out".

Jack called up his engine companies and told them to pass the word: incoming air strike on the right flank.

"Pathfinder leader, this is Hawk One. Commence bomb-run at grid coordinates one-five-two. Wind bearing zero-five-zero degrees at twenty knots, gusts to thirty knots. Watch for personnel in the area, do you copy?"

"That's a roj, Hawk One", said Pieter. "Turning to two-seven-three and commencing bomb-run, out".

Ralph peered into the TRIDINT display. "I see a bunch of people down right by the fire. We're going to have to play 'thread the needle' again".

"So what else is new? Reducing altitude. Set us up for a linked salvo. Pathfinder flight, this is Pathfinder leader. Rig for linked salvos and follow me. And be careful! We've still got plenty of downdrafts".

The other planes acknowledged Pieter's message and began following him down.

On the ground below, the firefighters could barely hear the approaching aircraft over the roar of the fire. When they realized what was coming, they sprinted back fifty yards from the fire and waited for the inevitable. Seconds later, they saw the firebombers rush over, their blue bellies glowing eerily in the firelight. As the fourth plane in the line crossed in front of the firefighters, the planes' bombays opened and retardant came streaming out. Steam hissed out of the dying flames as the retardant cascaded down on the fire's edge.

"Good thing we pulled back", said one firejumper commander. "Those guys were bang on target, even with the wind!"

"Yeah, maybe we've got a chance now", said his companion. A second wave of firebombers could be heard off in the distance, so the firefighters took a breather while the firebombers did their work. Another line of aircraft rushed past and another section of the fire down the line was extinguished seconds later. When the firefighters could hear no more planes, they moved back up to the fire and began trenching again.

"Pathfinder leader and Night Hawk leader, those were two perfect bullseyes", CAC remarked over the radio. "Well done. Reload and return, out".

"Why don't you take the wheel for awhile", Pieter said to Ralph. "My hands are getting sore from bucking all this wind".

"Will do, boss. "Back to Morris Dam?".

"Yep, that's what the man said. I think that last drop took a little pressure off of the guys on the fireline. A few more drops like that and they should be able to start chasing this fire back into the hills".

"It's just about ten now", observed Ralph. "Think we'll have this section contained by midnight?"

"Not if that wind keeps whipping it around", Pieter answered. As if to substantiate his statement, a downdraft dropped the plane several feet. "See what I mean?"

"I just hope it doesn't do one of those when I'm over the fire. I don't feel like auguring in just yet".

"Me either", agreed Pieter. While the Pathfinders and Night Hawks were heading for Morris Dam, the other three firebomber squadrons kept the pressure up on the fire above Duarte. Soon, the line of firefighters was advancing towards the hills.

In the meantime, the fires in Altadena were being roped in. The head of the fire was stalled just above housing developments and the few air-tankers able to fly at night were sealing off the left flank. The fire was now contained on three sides. Once the remaining air-tankers finished the line around the base of the fire, the Forestry and city personnel would move into the heart of it and finish it off.

"Fire Boss, we've completed the firebreak above Arcadia and we're awaiting further orders, over", George Ostermann called over the radio.

"Panther leader, this is Fire Boss", Zack replied. "I want you to leap-frog with Team Tiger over towards eastern Monrovia. Try to clear as wide a break as you can with two Cats. The fire above Monrovia could move downhill any time now, so watch your left flank".

"Understood, Zack. Team Panther will move one mile east of the Monrovia-Arcadia border and Team Tiger will begin extending the firebreak from this location, out".

George passed word onto the members of the two Cat Teams, then he and the other Team Panther Cat driver raised their blades and reeled in the ball-and-chains. Team Panther followed an overgrown fire road along the hills, while Team Tiger began clearing the brush behind them. When Team Panther had traveled one mile, George and his companion Cat driver dropped their blades, ran out their ball-and-chains, and started clearing a firebreak. Unknown to them, above and behind Team Panther, the fire began rapidly moving down the slopes and was soon crossing the gap between the two Cat Teams.

"Zack, you'd better look at this", one of the Fire Boss assistants called from the CCC van. Zack had stepped outside for a breath of air after the Duarte fire was pounded by the firebombers. He and Joe stepped back into the van and looked at the TRIDINT picture. On the screen, the red and white blotches marking the fire above Monrovia had marched down to less than a mile from the first line of homes.

A look of concern crossed Zack's face and he nodded. "It's moved down the hill, hasn't it? I was afraid of that. And we've got almost nobody to stand in it's way. Where are the Cat Teams?"

"Team Tiger is about a mile due west of the breach", replied the aide. "And Team Panther is almost half a mile to the east".

"I'd better call Henry and let him know about this", said Zack.

To the south of the fire, families in Gold Hills Estates watched the rapid onrush of the flames as they headed directly for the homes. Some people raced outside and began hosing down the roofs of their homes. Children watched in fascination as the fire continued to approach. Above one of the two roads out of the development, Alta Vista Avenue, a pine tree was wrenched loose from the ground by the wind and began to lean precariously towards the road below. Falling rock and earth soon cluttered the road, making it impassable to vehicles. Henry received Zack's call and directed the resting Monrovia and Duarte Fire Department companies to get up to Gold Hill Estates pronto.

"Zack, this is Henry", the CDF Fire Boss called over the radio. "I've sent a couple of companies to fight it, but they may not be there soon enough to stop it. Most of my air-tankers are grounded by darkness. Can your firebombers slow it down till the companies get there?"

"I'll check with Abner and see. I'll get back to you when I find out". Zack changed channels on the radio. "Abner, who do you have available for a quick drop in Monrovia?"

"The Tag-Team is orbiting over there right now", replied Abner. "The other squadrons are just finishing a drop on the fire over in Duarte. They should all be reloaded in another twenty-five minutes".

"Understood. Finish your drops, then get them over there as soon as you can".

"It looks like there's people on those housetops!", said Tim as he looked at the TRIDINT display a few minutes later. "Jimmy, you'd better tell CAC there's still civilians with those houses. That fire is going to be on top of them in a couple of minutes!"

"What do you mean there's still people there?", Zack asked CAC incredulously a moment later. "CDF told us that area had been evacuated hours ago!" Zack thought rapidly what to do, then replied. "OK, have your Tag-Team bombers try to delay the fire from reaching the houses on the hilltop. I'll tell Abner to get some additional squadrons over there to help".

"What was the problem?", asked Joe. He hadn't been paying attention to Zack until he shouted orders into the radio.

"Crazy homeowners", grumbled Zack. "Some people decided to stay home and watch the fire instead of leaving like they were told to. We've got almost nobody to stand in the way of the fire and it's headed straight for them!"

Joe felt the hair on the back of his neck begin to stand up. "You mean those families could get caught in the middle of that fire?", he asked.

"If they don't get out of there now, yeah", replied Zack with concern. He pointed to the TRIDINT display and explained. "The fire has already moved past our Cat line on the left side of the hill. It's moving into the homes down below this hill now. MFD and DFD have sent units up to handle it, but they won't be able to stop it until it's in among those houses. The fire is also moving fast on the right side of that hill, torching a newer development here. If those people don't leave now, they may not be able to make it out in time. I'd estimate that the fire will reach the hilltop in another five minutes, tops".

Just like my family, thought Joe. Not again! "You've got to get them out of there *now* Zack!", Joe shouted anxiously.

"I've got nothing to get them out with!", replied Zack in anguish. "The Cat Team can't be there for another ten minutes, minimum. We've only got two firebombers to throw at the fire, which means they have to use trailing drops, not salvoes if they're to cover enough frontage".

"How long will a trailing drop hold the fire?", Joe asked quickly.

"Not long enough. But I guess it's the only choice we have". He turned back to the microphone. "CAC, have the Tag-Team drop a trailing pattern in front of those homes. We've got to buy some time for the Cat Team to reach the civilians trapped up there. Detail

Team Panther to proceed to the hilltop immediately!". Behind Zack, Joe settled into a chair and began to pray, unseen by the command staff, who were busy with their tasks.

The radio in George Ostermann's Cat crackled to life a moment later. "Panther leader, this is CAC. You are to break off from present assignment and move post-haste to hilltop at grid coordinates one-five-five for civilian pickup, acknowledge".

"Acknowledged, CAC", replied George. He looked out at the nearby hilltop and saw the fire beginning to climb the hill. He switched to the team frequency and passed directions onto his teammates. The blades on the two Caterpillars were raised and the entire group pivoted hard right, then churned southwest at full-speed.

"Ah wish we could git a break from this wind fer just a coupla' minutes!", complained Jimmy. They had received their instructions and situation report from CAC seconds before. Jimmy had led the two Tag-Team planes east briefly before turning and reducing altitude to begin the attack run. "That TRIDINT display looks mighty shaky, Tim".

"I don't even want to breath on it as long as we're getting something", Tim stated pensively.

"There it goes agin!", shouted Jimmy. The TRIDINT picture had blanked out. "See what yew kin do with that thing!"

Tim started beating on the enclosure, but to no effect. "It's gone!", he shouted. "Pull up before you plow into a hill, Jimmy!"

"Nope. Ah got a good look at what was ahead afore that thing went out", Jimmy replied resolutely. "We ain't gonna git a second chance at this, so jes' hang on!"

"Jimmy hasn't linked us for a trailing drop", Dick Morrison said to Bob Mitchell as they followed Jimmy down. "Jimmy, do you copy?"

"Yep, but ah'm a little busy right now. Talk to Tim".

"Tim, what's going on up there?", asked Dick. "We don't get any acknowledgement for a linked drop".

"Our TRIDINT gear is out! Jimmy is going to try eyeballing the drop".

"That's crazy!", protested Bob. "Let us get in front, then you guys can drop off of our location".

"There ain't enough time for that!", Jimmy shouted back. "Ah knows what ah'm doin'. Them folks on the hill ain't got a chance les'n we drop now!"

"I don't like it", said Bob. "But I guess we don't have any choice. Dick, you're going to have to do a manual drop. Let it fly when you see Jimmy's load drop".

"OK", replied Dick. He reset the drop controls and fixed his gaze on the lead plane. The range was coming down quickly. Below them, Dick could see the flames licking up towards the top of the hill, the people still hosing down their roofs. "We had better inform CAC".

"Wonderful!", the senior controller replied when Dick told him the news. "Like the man said, we don't get a second chance at this, so make this one count!"

"That's the truth", affirmed Bob. "Here goes nothing!"

Over on the Alta Vista side of Gold Hill, firecrews were trying to clear away the debris blocking the road. The wind was whipping up again and suddenly, more rocks started to fall as the pine tree on the hilltop wrenched loose and tumbled to the street below. One firefighter was pinned under a limb of the fallen tree. His friends began pulling the tree off of him. He had suffered a broken rib and had to be evacuated by ambulance. The road was now well and truly blocked. The fire crews began trying to dislodge the tree when a house off to the left side of the road burst into flames. Soon, the sparks had reached the brush on either side of the road and the tree itself was beginning to steam and smoke from the heat. The engine crew began hosing down the brush and tree, but they couldn't get through.

One older couple who had stayed with their home on top of Gold Hill realized they couldn't save it now. They got into their car and started down the Alta Vista side. Finding it blocked, they doubled back and started down the North Street side. Pieces of burning brush blowing across the road started getting caught under the car and the gas tank began heating up. The driver glanced through the side-view mirror and saw smoke coming from underneath his car. He quickly stopped the car in the middle of the road near the base of the hill and the couple ran the rest of the way down the hill. No sooner had they reached the base of the hill than the gas tank exploded, showering cars parked along the side of the road with burning gasoline.

By the time Monrovia Fire Department vehicles reached the road, it was effectively blocked by several burning cars. The firefighters looked on as yet another car exploded, showering the surrounding property with red-hot metal and flaming gasoline. The North Street entrance to Gold Hill was now sealed off to emergency vehicles. The Cat Team was the only hope left. Team Panther was just topping the rise when the two firebombers raced over them heading for the hill.

"Ah see the edge of the fire", said Jimmy calmly. He knew he had to compose himself if he was to make a good drop. Next to him, Tim was poised to release the load over the fire. The flames had begun to light trees on the top of Gold Hill.

"Just about there, Tim. Ready .... *drop!*"

The families on the hilltop were startled by the sudden appearance of the planes out of the darkness. Blinded by the smoke and deafened by the roar of the fire before them, they hadn't noted the approach of aircraft. The two firebombers shot across seemingly only a few feet away from the houses, red liquid streaming out of their bellies. The gust of wind produced by their passage caused a vortex which forced people close to the fire back a few feet and scattered embers on the adjacent houses. People quickly watered the embers down before they could start any new fires.

"Bullseye!", shouted the normally passive CAC. "That was an incredible drop 'Wind Dancer'! Well done!"

"So what are we, chopped liver?", sniffed Dick.

"That's what you get for just following their lead", replied Bob with a grin.

The fire had been denied the top of the hill for the moment, but fire was still closing in from the flanks. One of the families had already tried to drive down North Street only to find the way blocked by the burning debris. They had returned to inform the others. A eucalyptus tree had fallen across the east end of the street, blocking anyone from leaving the hilltop. The homeowners knew it was only a matter of time before the flames would circle around behind them and engulf the hilltop.

"That's slowed it down some!", said Zack. "Now if the Cat Team can just get there in time".

"How long before they reach them?", asked Joe apprehensively.

"At least five minutes. I've given CAC instructions to assemble all the firebombers in order to plaster that ridge, but it will be seven or eight minutes before they've reloaded. I'm afraid of bombing the hilltop anyway for fear of injuring civilians".

The trapped families clustered in the front yard of one home on the hilltop. Smoke was everywhere and they all were having trouble breathing. The fire was beginning to move up the street from both sides. House after house went up in flames as the fire crept closer. Burning embers showered down around them and they realized that their situation was grim.

East of the hilltop Team Panther had intercepted a dead-end road leading from the brush into the development. George could see the fire beginning to engulf the hilltop ahead.

"God help us", he muttered under his breath, forgetting he had the transmitter on.

"What was that boss?", called Manuel over the radio.

"Nothing. Hurry up, that's all", replied George in embarrassment.

"You heard the man", Manuel said to Jose. "Andale!"

"Man, I'm glad I'm not out in that", said Jose. "Looks like the only thing not burnin' is the street!"

"Take a look at the street behind the Cats, buddy", said Manuel.

"Madre de Dios!", whispered Jose. The asphalt was beginning to smolder and smoke on the edges of the street and the Cat tracks were digging deep into the melting pavement as they drove over it. Smoke restricted visibility to only a few feet in all directions. Homes were bursting into flames on both sides of the street and that foliage which was not already burning was beginning to smoke. The air conditioners on the team's vehicles were working at full output and were just able to keep the temperature inside the vehicles tolerable.

"Ow! I hate it when the vents seal!", Jose complained. "It always makes my ears pop!"

"Want me to open the hatch so you can get a breath of fresh air?", offered Manuel.

"On second thought, it don't hurt that much".

"CAC, we're in position now", called the pilot of 'Windjammer'.

"Copy that, Black Widow leader", replied CAC. "You are to orbit until we receive confirmation that the Cat Team has removed the civilians, acknowledge".

Pieter heard the acknowledgement over the radio. "That wind had better slack off before we have to drop", he said to Ralph. "We've never tried a five squadron linked drop in this much wind before".

"We'll just have to hope for the best", replied Ralph. He was watching the activity down below, as MFD units tried to fight their way through the wreckage and fire on North Street while the Cat Team neared the road to the hilltop. Seconds later, the big Caterpillar downshifted to start up the steep section of road ahead. Behind it, the second Cat followed with the three APCs in tow.

The smoke on the hilltop had increased in the past few minutes. Some quick-thinking people had soaked old T-shirts and rags in water, placing them over their noses and passing more to their neighbors to keep the smoke out of their lungs. One man still kept a hose handy to water down bushes along the side of his house. Several people on the hill could begin to hear the approaching equipment now that the lead Cat had downshifted. They followed the sound to the east end of the street. The smoke obscured the families' view of everything but the flaming tree at the east end of the street. The sound of the diesel engines kept getting closer. Suddenly, the flaming tree exploded in a shower of sparks as it was thrust aside by the blade on the advancing Caterpillar. The line of vehicles rapidly drew up alongside the group of stunned people.

George flung open the cab door on his Cat and yelled out, "Did somebody here call for a taxi?"

The shocked looks on the faces of the people quickly changed to one of excitement and relief. A ragged cheer went up from the families. The rear ramps went down on the APCs and their crews hustled out to help the people into the back. Once everyone was loaded, George pivoted his Cat and led Team Panther back down the hill.

"Fire Boss, this is Panther leader", George called over the radio. "We've got them all. No apparent casualties, repeat, no apparent casualties. Do you read me, over?"

Joe let out a sigh of relief at the news. "Roger that, Panther leader", Zack replied. "Well done. Proceed down North Street and hand off your passengers to Monrovia Fire Department personnel there, then return to your firebreak, acknowledge".

"Acknowledged, Panther leader out", came the reply.

"Not again", Joe muttered to himself under his breath. "Never again".

Zack turned to look at Joe, who looked exhausted and said, "They got them, Joe. All of them".

Joe slowly nodded, then looked up grimly at Zack and said, "Now blow the sucker away!"

Zack turned back to the radio and dialed up the Hawkeye. "CAC, plaster that ridge!"

"Pathfinder leader, this is CAC", said the voice on the radio. "Commence bomb run, acknowledge".

"'Bout time, CAC", replied Pieter. "We're coming down now". And let's hope those winds don't pick up before we get there, he thought. Pieter's squadron broke out of its orbit and began to descend. Behind the Pathfinders, the other four squadrons acknowledged the command and began following them down.

"What happened here?", George asked no one in particular. He had just reached the wrecked cars at the base of Gold Hill. Monrovia Fire Department had managed to douse most of the fires by now. George lowered his blade until it was just above the road and easily cleared a path through the roadblock. He was just delivering his passengers to MFD when the line of firebombers thundered over a ridge to the east behind him. The wind began to ease off as the weary families filed out of the APCs and over towards the waiting emergency vehicles. They turned towards the sound of the incoming firebomber squadrons and watched them race towards their homes.

"Keep your fingers crossed, Junior", said Pieter. "Here we go!" Pieter's plane came opposite to the end of the east-west ridgeline the fire was advancing up and all five squadrons of firebombers dropped salvoes simultaneously on the flames below.

Joe and Zack sat hunched over the TRIDINT display from Hawk One in the Fire Boss CCC van, staring intently at the image. As they watched, the irregular line of blips representing the firebombers reached the computer-determined drop-point. When the pattern of the planes matched the shape of the forward edge of the fire beneath them, the blips flashed for a few seconds, indicating that they were dropping their retardant. Abruptly, the red and white blotches constituting the edge of the fire dimmed and flickered out.

"That's got it!", shouted Zack. He called over the radio and said, "CAC, pass along a hearty 'well done' to Pieter and the rest of the squadrons. That was a picture-perfect drop" .

"Copy that Fire Boss", replied CAC.

"I think that tore the heart out of the fire", said Zack. He turned to Joe, who looked like he was about ready to keel over. "You OK, Joe? You look like you could use some rest".

"Probably so", replied Joe. "I think I'll be able to sleep tonight, for a change". The nightmares were gone, he knew, never to return.

Chapter 31

The winds which had begun to die down the night before picked up from time to time the rest of the night. By dawn the next morning, they had died away completely, allowing the fire to be brought under control. Two more days of hard work passed before the fire was completely contained, allowing the weary firefighters to finally head home.

Joe was sitting in his office at Talon Industries a few days later when Nancy informed him that he had a phone call from a Miss Thaxter. Joe didn't remember hearing the name before, but took the call anyway.

"Hello, Mr. Talon?", said the voice. "My name is Phyllis Thaxter. I represent the Los Angeles County Supervisors".

"Oh", said Joe in surprise. And this had been shaping up to be such a pleasant morning, he thought ruefully. "Yes, Miss Thaxter, what can I do for you?"

"I just called to pass along our thanks for the way your organization handled itself in the recent brushfire and to let you know that, after deliberation, the Supervisors have decided to drop the lawsuit against you. There was no evidence that you had been paying Hans Zwickau before the demonstration in Sunland. In light of the service you have rendered to the community in both the recent fire and the Signal Hill refinery fire last Spring, they have unanimously approved a dismissal of the charges against you and your affiliates in this matter".

"That's most gratifying, Miss Thaxter", said Joe in astonishment. "Pass along my thanks to the Supervisors. Hopefully we can do business again in the near future".

"I'm sure they feel the same way, Mr. Talon. Preferably under better circumstances".

"Yes, let's hope so".

After he had hung up, he called the executive staff into his office to give them the good news. Later, he passed a memo around to all of the divisions for general distribution highlighting this favorable turn of events.

There was a party on the weekend sponsored by Joe at his mansion, open to everyone from the company who could attend. His place was mobbed and both food and drink had to be replenished twice before the last guests left.

The following Sunday, Joe called up Jerry to see if he could go to church with Jerry and Diane. After the service, Joe greeted the pastor on the front steps of the church.

"Hello again, Mr. Talon", said Pastor Walters. "I haven't seen you in a while. How have you been?"

"It's been a rough time, Pastor Walters", said Joe. "I think I'm through the worst of it now, though. I was wondering if you had some time this afternoon. I'd like to talk to you about some things".

"Why certainly, Mr. Talon", replied the pastor. "Just name a time and I'll be there".

"How about after you've finished here?", said Joe. "My driver is waiting to take us wherever you'd like to go for lunch"

"This sounds fairly important to you, Mr. Talon".

"Let's just say it's a matter I should have attended to a long time ago", said Joe. "It fulfills a promise I made during the San Gabriel's wildfire a few days ago. I want to accept Christ into my life".

Jerry's jaw nearly hit his feet. Diane poked him in the ribs when he continued to gawk. Joe ignored him.

"Yes, that is an important decision", agreed Pastor Walters. "Very well, we can leave in just a few minutes".

Joe talked with Jerry and Diane until the pastor was ready, then bid them farewell. He didn't arrive home until shortly before dinnertime that night. Pieter called and asked if he could stop by. Joe asked him over for dinner.

After dinner, as was their custom, Pieter and Joe sauntered into the study.

"You seem different tonight Joe, more at peace with yourself. What gives?"

"I made a fairly important decision today, Pieter. One which gives me a great sense of peace. I choose to continue down a road, one which I had started on in the midst of the fire in the foothills".

"What road is that?"

"I became a Christian today", Joe answered quietly. "And my whole outlook changed. Before, I thought I would never see my family again, but now I know I will, sometime in the not-so-distant future. Before, I had no firm grasp of what was right and what was wrong, something which had cost me a great deal at times. Now I have a Guide to show me the way. Before, I had vast worldly wealth, but little spiritual wealth, and didn't realize how bankrupt I really was".

"Those are pretty radical changes, Joe. What brought all this
bout?"

"The realization during the fire that, despite all my wealth,
espite all my earthly power and prestige, I couldn't be sure that the
refighters could reach those people trapped on that hilltop in time.
'hat in spite of the fact I was considered by many to be a powerful
nan, I could not influence events in my favor. After I had done all I
ould, I realized that it took someone greater than me to save the
ituation. That's when I prayed to Jesus that He would help me to
ave those people and promised Him to do all I could to help save
thers if He would just show me the way. There are, after all, worse
nings than dying in a brushfire. Things like losing your soul for all
ternity".

Pieter looked at Joe for a moment, then said, "Yes, there are
vorse things than dying physically. I think we both know only too
vell that there can be hell on earth even before the body dies. So
ell me, is there room for more than one on this road you've started
own?"

"There's room for everyone, Pieter. All that's involved is
naking the choice to follow the Leader".

They talked for a while longer until Joe started staring over at
ne curtainless windows.

Pieter noticed his gaze and began to worry. "What are you
ninking, Joe", he asked cautiously.

"Oh, nothing much. I was just thinking about redecorating,
nat's all".

"You're finally going to hang some curtains, huh?"

"Yeah, I think so", replied Joe wistfully. "How do green
urtains strike you?"

"I thought you didn't like green".

"People change, Pieter", Joe answered quietly. "People
hange".